TALL HOUSES IN WINTER

By the author of
THE GENTLE INSURRECTION

Doris Betts

TALL HOUSES IN WINTER

G. P. PUTNAM'S SONS

New York

All names, characters, and events in this book are fictional, and any resemblance to real persons which may seem to exist is purely coincidental.

Library of Congress Catalog
Card Number: 56-10222

MANUFACTURED IN THE UNITED STATES OF AMERICA

In Memory of Julia Anne Wallin

AUTHOR'S NOTE

Most people are surprised to learn that they have inadvertently (perhaps even unwillingly) had a share in other people's projects. A book is such an encroaching thing that all people and all experiences shape and influence it whether they will or not.

This is an attempt to acknowledge my appreciation to some of those people who have had major influences on this one, although I know in advance most of them will be surprised and some—in terms of the product . . . downright horrified. But they are not individually responsible; the contributions which they made were mostly unconscious and unknowing, not only through things they have said and done but in the people they themselves are, or in something particular they were at a certain point in space and time.

To these, then, my appreciation:

To Lowry.

To two men dead, my grandfather, John Guy Freeze, who would never have read it because he had no time to read books; and to Howard W. Odum, whom I never knew.

And to: Hugh Holman, Jessie Rehder, Rupert Vance, U. N. C.; Louis Graves and Phillips Russell, Chapel Hill, N. C.; Richard Bardolph, James Painter, Elizabeth Duffy, Marc Friedlander, A. A. Wilkinson, Woman's College, Greensboro, N. C.; Robie Macauley, Alexandria, Va.; Peter Taylor, Kenyon, Gambier, Ohio; Frances Gray Patton, Durham, N. C.; Meyer Isenburg, University of Chicago; The Rev. H. Louis Patrick, St. Louis, Mo.; Diarmuid Russell, Russell & Volkening, New York City; Mrs. Earle G. White, teacher; and my parents, William and Mary Ellen Waugh, Statesville, N. C.; Louise Hardeman Abbot, Louisville, Ga.; and Philip C. Schinhan, Chapel Hill.

Contents

APOLOGY

It was proper for them, awaking in ordered houses,
Among russet walls where fruit grew ripe to the hand,
Walking on lawns where fountains arched in the summer,
To praise through their gentle days the dwelling virtues
And architect epics to honor the good and the brave.
And easy perhaps for the desert-maddened preacher
With his withered loins and the dirt hard in his pores,
To lash with his locust-tongue the uncertainly happy
And call on the townsmen to shrive and to shrivel for God.
But we who have climbed to the top
of TALL HOUSES IN WINTER
And heard in the gathering silence the limp of the clock,
Who dunned by our need through the days are unfailingly traitors
In Sad and Undignified Ways to each circle of friends,
How shall we praise in our poems the simplified heroes
Or urge to the truth we have never been true to ourselves?
O love that forgives because needing forgiveness also
Forgive us that we have not lived through *A Virtuous Day,*
That we asked to be judged *In the End by* our own *Compassion*
Thief calling to thief from his cross with no Christ in between.

BY ANTHONY CRONIN
New World Writing
4th Mentor Selection

Part One

IN SAD AND UNDIGNIFIED WAYS

1.

He had always said the only way he would ever come back to Stoneville would be in a pine box, one of the plain rough-hewn frontiers kind, so that people seeing it unloaded at the train station might just once, just briefly, wonder if there were other more vigorous lives being lived in other places than this one.

The prospect had always made a very pleasant picture to his eye: the sight of old Mr. Sando with his railroad hat on backwards coming out of the strange dark runs of the station agent's building to stare; spare children edging up wide-eyed to see the box handed down by the grunting men (the dead are always heavy); and fellow passengers gaping, looking away, shrugging their shoulders. Perhaps it would have shaken them for a second; perhaps for the length of a minute some of them would waver and look back.

"Who is it?" They would sidle, whisper.

"I'm not sure. Somebody used to live here, I guess."

That was the way Ryan Godwin had always said he would come home and yet here he was, putting his watch to his ear impatiently, wishing for the hundredth time he had at least come by that very train instead of by bus, and glimpsing vaguely the squares of field and green lawn that caught and held and passed in the small bus window. These flicked in and out of his consciousness like scenes in a stereo viewer: that man transfixed—sun-yellow—at his plow, two thin children waiting till the bus had passed to cross the road, a peeling filling station and a silver bridge.

It's not quite the pine box, he thought wryly, but then it's not far from it, either. It's a matter of whether death contains or whether it is contained. And he winced and told himself: *I must not think of that,* and shifted and crossed his legs. *Jim said I must not think of that.*

The tall man in the seat next to him had been trying to start a conversation for more than twenty miles; he tried again now, making use of one of the Great Universals.

"Hot enough for you?"

Ryan nodded his head slightly and smiled to show he was not above conversation, although he did not really feel like it. He had recently begun to understand why the aging millionaire turned with a feverish haste to philanthropism; the Near-to-Dying could ill afford to alienate, he thought. And when he remembered this thing (it was always just beneath the crust of thought, like a partially opened package waiting to be taken up again) Ryan touched his own throat almost reverently. He felt like a Gila monster with a hidden sacred gland of poison.

But Jim had said he must not think of that. He said aloud, "Perhaps we'll get rain. Rain would cool things off."

The man beside him screwed up a ruddy face until it looked like eroded farmland, and Ryan was not sure if the expression was one for delight or ferocity. But when the man spoke, he saw it was not delight.

"Haven't had a decent rain all season," said the man bitterly. He now took form in Ryan's mind as some sort of small-time farmer, and probably not too successful at it. "Just little dribbles now and then, enough to burn the juice out of things. Sucks it right up."

The man had extended his great right hand in front of him and was watching it open and clench fiercely; it gave Ryan a little-boy notion of God-in-the-Rainclouds, squeezing out sponges. Until now he had almost forgotten how people around Stoneville felt about the rain: their tribal anxiety, the prayer services in which grizzled old farmers might petition on behalf of parched crops, that anticipation with which they watched the sky for "a little cloud out of the sea, Elijah, like a man's hand . . ."

Then Ryan was ashamed. It was their whole livelihood, how the elements behaved. I won't go back to Stoneville a snob, he thought; that's a luxury for the young. Besides I want to see . . . this time I want to see. . . . But what was it he wanted to see? Jim had asked him that. "There isn't time," Jim had said, half angrily, "and besides, pilgrimages are out of date."

"Only a little while," Ryan had pleaded. "I want to see . . . I want to find . . ." But he had not been able to say it to Jim either. Perhaps he did not know himself.

The bus was hot and full of motion, and the conversation had reminded him that the air was dry and the ground dusty for miles. He turned to the man next to him now and said aloud sincerely, "I'm sorry about the rain."

At this the farmer looked quite bewildered and began to fumble about for some reply, as if he were riffling through a set of well-thumbed cards for something that would suit. At last he gave a nod that was meant to be reassuring and said firmly, "That's all right. It isn't your fault."

Ryan could not help but smile as he turned to watch three windowfuls of pines go by. *That's* something anyway, he thought.

"You're not from around here?"

Ryan nodded, still facing the glass. "From Stoneville, originally," he said. "I've not been back for years." Not since she died. He pushed that thought away. "Almost ten years," he finished, carefully. And now he was forty-eight and Jessica was dead.

But the farmer nodded as if this were something he could well understand and Ryan turned to look at him closely.

He was a huge man, very strong. He looked like a woods animal which takes up the camouflage of the world around it—his hair was straw, his skin burned red-brown like the soil, his clothes dark and inconspicuous as tree trunks. There was no guile in him. Shrewd he might be and businesslike, and aware of dangers and incomprehensibles; but he still had eyes like a squirrel or a bird. He might run from dogs but not from other squirrels or other birds. These might be quarrelsome or selfish or ugly, but this man would feel there was no genuine harm in them. He believed with all the surety of leaves and sky that one was at home with his own species.

He looked at Ryan now with all that surety (was it trust? Almost.) and smiled. "You going back to visit now?" he said. "I 'spect you'll find things somewhat changed." He smiled, apologizing for progress.

Almost involuntarily Ryan ran an index finger up the edge of his windpipe, touching it with respect. "I'm not sure how long I'll stay.

This time may be for good." He did not comment on the possibility of change. That he did not believe; a mountain falling across Stoneville might change it, or an inrush of sea, but nothing less than these.

The man accepted him; Ryan had known he would. "No place like home," he confided. "It's as good a county as most. Most seasons we get more rain than this. Soil's good. Lots of good people live in this county."

Ryan said he was sure they did.

"Me, I've lived here all my life," said the farmer, almost expanding from his seat. His eyes were blue and sunwashed, and wrinkles radiated out from them. "And all my folks have lived here before me, and most of *their* folks." He put a big hand timidly onto Ryan's knee and when there was no objection gave it a man-to-man pat, one that would not be misunderstood. "My people always believed in living in shouting distance of each other, so one generation goes to a hill and hollers down to the next." He grinned at this proudly; it was a saying of his family.

Ryan had turned now to look at him again, curiously. All this man's life, and his kin beyond and after him, thought Ryan; and tried to see what difference it made, if it gave the man a kind of mental inbreeding that was visible on his face.

But he could make out nothing of the sort. The farmer was tall—taller than he—red-faced and stocky, and his face was somewhat pitted, as if he had caught chicken pox late in life from one of his many children.

On an impulse Ryan said, "Do you have a big family yourself?"

The man nodded. "Six," he said. "And five of them boys, which is some help. All of them are black-headed like my wife except the oldest. I always said once he got born with all that red hair I was never too sure somebody else ain't had his finger in the pie."

He laughed at this and so did Ryan, letting out a breath so explosive that he wondered how long and how tensely he had been holding it. Perhaps it had been cramped up in his chest all the time since he had left Massachusetts.

"I'm Ryan Godwin," he said, putting his hand out almost fearfully. But he need not have worried; the big one clasped it considerately, giving just enough pressure not to insult him, but—mindful he was a city man—not too much, either.

"Hobbley, Tom Hobbley. Pleased to meet you, Mr. Godwin."

They both smiled broadly.

"You're some of Miss Asa's kin," said Hobbley, and Ryan nodded.

"Her brother," he said shortly. "Do you know Asa well?"

The farmer shook his head. "Don't care to tangle with her, though, if you'll pardon my free speaking. A sharp woman, Miss Asa is. She drives a hard bargain. I expect you have to be that way, selling land and all."

She *did* drive a hard bargain, all departments. "I wouldn't care to tangle with her myself," said Ryan, almost grimly. But he *had* tangled with her, after that funeral was finally over; and he had gone away and said he would not be back until they carried him in feet first.

"You're a professional man, seems like."

"Teacher." Ryan said it almost meekly, feeling self-conscious before this Great Outdoorsman, feeling as though he were one of life's luxuries that could be dispensed with.

"That so? Funny I don't remember you. Maybe you was too old for me to have remembered you as Miss Asa's brother from Stoneville."

"I expect that's it."

"Did you go to Stoneville High School?"

"Yes." It seemed a very long time ago.

"I used to play basketball for the Mount Hall school. That's out in the county."

Ryan said he remembered it. He was suddenly tired; the reminder of the differences between this ruddy younger man and himself had drained the strength from him, lowered the level at which he had kept it for some weeks. He sat stiffly in the uncomfortable bus seat, growing quite old, tired, very hot, very thirsty—all in the space of a second or so. There was only time for one hot cotton field to pass whitely in the glass. He sucked on his tongue and made a dry attempt at swallowing; then he wondered how long it would be before his palate and tongue became conscious of that obstruction, living there so secretly, so that perhaps he would not be able to swallow at all. It would be like having a hand back there, like having a fist balled up in his throat. He felt quite shaken by this thought, and put his head against the plush seat and closed his eyes and became gradually aware of the drone of the motor. He had not heard it before, while they were talking. In the silence it was very loud;

it swallowed him up; he became some fragment whirled about in sound as in eddies and storms.

He had, in fact, quite forgotten he was not alone until Hobbley touched his sleeve and said anxiously, "Course a man's only as old as he feels."

He thinks he's offended me, Ryan thought quickly, and he opened his eyes and made himself smile without any reservations, in spite of how tired he was.

"That's right," said Ryan warmly. He was not that tired. He wanted to reassure this man: *it is only the dogs and the guns we must fear, and not each other.*

After a while he closed his eyes again and listened to how the world went by outside the bus. Over the drone of the engine he could catch the whish of a bridge they crossed, the roar of a car passing them, the closed-in sound which came when there was forest or high banks on each side. Hobbley had also closed his eyes, as if from courtesy.

In a few more miles they came to the last stop before Stoneville, a smaller town called Monbury, eighteen miles west. The driver called out a ten-minute rest stop as he pulled into the station. All up and down the rows of seats papers and pocketbooks and rumpled skirts brushed back and forth in readiness. There were many old women on board, one blind boy, six silent Negroes in the back who seemed to be making a conscious effort not to talk or laugh or shift their feet too loudly.

"I think I'll get a sandwich," Hobbley said when the bus had stopped. "You coming in?" When Ryan shook his head he added, "Can I bring you something?"

"Pack of cigarettes," said Ryan, fishing in his pockets for some change. "Chesterfields." He thought (but not with much interest), Jim says I shouldn't smoke.

The farmer nodded, joined the others filing from the bus and going into the Traveler's Café. A thin old dog sat at the door of the café and watched them pass without any interest. Once someone spoke to him and he lifted a limp tail and let it fall back to the ground. It had the appearance of an Indian rope trick that had failed and Ryan smiled at it briefly.

The driver put his head back in the door of the bus and looked at Ryan reproachfully. Everyone else had already gone outside. "Rest stop," he called again, a little louder.

But Ryan shook his head and settled himself more comfortably in the seat until the driver went away, looking as though he were aware of great ingratitudes.

Left alone, Ryan looked up at the light above the seat, ran his tongue experimentally as far back as it would go until he made himself faintly sick. There was a buzzing at his head; he looked up and saw three flies on the other side of the glass trying hungrily to find him. This cheered him up somehow; he thought (part to himself and partly to the flies) *Not Yet*. They made a small procession up and down the glass.

He could see his own reflection in the very place they were, and he looked at his face curiously. It was very ordinary. The hair was sandy, showing a little gray. The eyes brown, but not very brown; the nose straight and a bit too long in his face. The brows were too thick; once he had grown a mustache but under the brows it had made him feel too full of bristles; his whole personality had gone fierce until he took it off again. An ordinary face, he thought again, and not very old. He thought with a small satisfaction, There is no malice in it.

And to the flies he said silently: *Not old enough.*

He shifted on the seat, looking for softness, and tried to think. It was hot and airless in the bus. "There is no thinking in some climates," he muttered angrily.

But he could not, whatever the weather, have said just what he was doing here at all, why he was coming back to Stoneville without the dignity of the pine box he had promised, and without the strength of superiority. He thought, I'm making recantations after all these years.

If Jessica had been there, that would have been entirely another thing. Then he would have, of course, gone home; he would have put his head against her hair; he would have said, "Now I am sick and you must help me."

But she was dead, and somewhere underground perhaps that very hair had grown long and long, and lay over her in that box like a soft covering; and the rest of it—the eyes and the mouth and the flesh—whatever they had become was under all the hair and could not be seen, not ever.

He opened his eyes, thinking angrily, I have not remembered Jessica this much in years. It was foolish to come back. Jim was right.

A movement caught his eye; the old dog waiting at the café door rose with an effort, turned, flopped into place again with his head facing the other way out of the sun. Now that the others had left, the bus had gotten very still and the motor was quiet; Ryan could hear only a faint *blunkety-blunk* and realized with surprise that it was his own heart, going about its business as if nothing were out of the way.

He turned his back to the window (and to the flies, and to the limp dog) and moved his legs awkwardly. The kneecaps were stiff; he bent and unbent and changed the angle.

I don't know why I'm going back, he admitted half angrily, in spite of how I feel about Asa, and even though Jessica has lain ten years on Methodist Hill under a chaste white stone. There's nothing to find in Stoneville, nothing to take hold of now. Jim was right. I should have stayed in Massachusetts and gotten this other thing done. It's no good putting things off, especially this. And he touched his throat, cautiously.

Then he sighed; perhaps that was really why. Maybe he had some urge to mingle his dust now with hers, after these years, or perhaps it was because of the boy (he would be—how old? Twelve? Thirteen?) or maybe it was none of these. Maybe it was just the old sick elephant and the valley of elephant bones.

Hobbley startled him when he dropped the cigarettes into his lap.

"Nothing else?" he asked. Hobbley was drawing energetically on a straw that was stuck in a bottle of root beer. Between swallows he sighed from heat and effort.

"That's all," said Ryan. "Thanks." Outside, the dog was sound asleep. The flies were gone; perhaps they were on the dog and he could not be bothered noticing.

He lit a cigarette, inhaled deeply. He wondered if they were making any preparations for his arrival in the big old house on Walnut Street where he had been born, if Asa had gotten out the good china so as not to be disgraced, if the boy was curious, what they had told him about his uncle, what they had told him about Jessica.

"How come you decided to come back to Stoneville?" Hobbley said, sinking into his seat again. He had just gone to a window and thrown the bottle out; the clank had scared the wits out of the old hound who was on his feet now, in the sun, and who looked as though life would never be the same again.

Ryan said easily, "I was wondering myself, while you were inside. Like elephants, I guess."

"That's right," said the other, nodding his head, looking serious. "They never forget, do they?"

And Ryan smiled. Yes, he wondered if they were making ready for him in Stoneville and what they would say when he came.

2.

IT SEEMED to Fen they had all been up since dawn, crying out messages and directions to one another, clattering up and down the stairs to the attic, getting ready for his Atheist Uncle. Here the whole functioning of his mind paused curiously and went back and chewed through those two words again—Atheist Uncle—imparting a kind of holiness.

Fen had never met an atheist before, but he had heard of them for years and years from Reverend Barnes and from Aunt Asa. He knew that they came in two types—the cold type (these looked like British butlers, and beneath that cold exterior they were miserable and very lonely) and the Wild Sailor type, made up of disillusioned men who had been driven from God in moments of terrible sorrow and crisis.

The first group were mostly scientists (such men had built the atom bomb, the tank, the burglar-proof bank vault, flame throwers); or they were teachers in state universities where books of Darwin lay on every bedtable.

The second group was composed of warmer men who had only made the mistake of concentrating too much on the Things of This World so that death or war or avalanche had shaken their faith to nothing. They were thoughtful men, Reverend Barnes admitted, but they had no courage. They lacked tenacity. They would get entangled in the question of undeserved pain (over warm beer in smoky places they would ask each other: *If there was God, would He make a Hell?*) and other things which were not—at base—the real questions. They were not grounded. They were not buildèd on a rock.

Fen believed that even though he was a teacher in Massachusetts, his Uncle Ryan belonged to this second group. He was probably the kind of man who had once believed quite deeply and who had been shaken by catastrophe until he had taken to drink and living with harbor women.

Fen also had some notion that his uncle's face would reveal his fall from grace. It would be blotched and lined from what Aunt Asa said was Dissipation and down one cheek there might run a still half-parted scar, left from a knifing in some low saloon.

Fen stood now in the doorway and watched Aunt Asa and Miss Clara plumping the pillows—where, this very night, a scarred face would lie—and tugging at quilts. They were going to put Uncle Ryan in the left-over bedroom, the one with no shape to it except corners and angles. That was appropriate, perhaps—to put him in the crooked room.

He scratched at his nose absently as he watched the two women; excitement always made him tingle. His arms and legs would be like phone wires across which messages were forever pouring and tumbling, and he would scratch at the singing in his limbs without stopping to think about it.

He scrubbed at his neck, and in the bedroom Miss Clara flapped out a blanket like a tent and let it settle. Asa was tucking in the sides.

"Don't gape." Suddenly Asa threw the vague reprimand over her shoulder like something discarded. "Make yourself useful, boy."

"What shall I do?" He dug his fingers into all the tickles hidden on his ribs.

Miss Clara, who was very deaf, had turned from the bed in time to see him scratch and now she lifted her hands like white pads of paper and flapped them in the air. "He's coming down with something!" she chattered rapidly. Then she said it again twice more (almost mechanically) and took her hands back down to tuck the spread around the pillows. Miss Clara nearly always spoke in rapid triplets, as if since she was deaf herself the rest of the world must be dangerously close to it and needed things made clear.

"Don't catch anything, boy," said Aunt Asa sternly, turning to give him a reproving glance. "None of us has the time for such."

But she appeared, as always, to be looking slightly to the left or right of him. It seemed to Fen he could never remember a time when Aunt Asa had once looked into his face as though the cast of it (or whatever lay behind) were real and of importance. Sometimes he dodged this way and that, as though to step into her sight, but it was never focused on him.

He bobbed his head once now, seeking to find her gaze. "I'm not sick," he protested. "I'm just scratchy. When's Uncle Ryan coming? When will he get here, do you think?"

Asa corrected him. "When do you think he will come? You must watch your English. It's important. I think the bed looks all right." Then she began to answer his question, first shrugging her shoulders so that all over her, sharp little bones seemed to unfold and settle back again. "As to when he's coming, goodness knows," she said. "The whole letter was very unsatisfactory. Nothing about how long, and most of all nothing about why he's coming back. I can't think what he'd want here. He said he'd never come." She paused, frowned, and stared at one of the rosebushes with which the wall was pinkly spattered.

Fen glanced at it, too, out of curiosity but it was just like a thousand others and he looked back to Asa's face. She had started again on the bedcovers, giving a deft tuck and turn here that took the last wrinkles away. "I can't think why he'd come back," she said more crisply, "unless he's in trouble of some sort. That's it, I'm sure. I hope he doesn't think he can borrow any money."

Miss Clara had caught the last word and her eyebrows flew wildly into her hair for she thought a great deal of that subject. Perhaps that was because she had no money of her own and had lived with her cousin Asa for nearly eleven years.

"What's that about money?" she cried in triplicate. Asa, for once, looked quite put out with her.

"Fools! Soon parted!" shouted Asa impatiently, and Miss Clara subsided at this like a heap of clothes ceasing to flap in a wind.

Miss Clara was an enormous woman, tall and stout, and beside her Asa looked like a not quite full-grown rat. Asa was thin and gray —even her face was bluish gray. She looked like a little rag doll stuffed with crackly chips and sticks. Fen could not remember a time when she had been larger or whiter or plumper.

"Why hasn't Uncle Ryan been here before?" asked Fen, whenever the shouting was over between the two women. "Why is it I don't remember him? Did I ever see him?"

Aunt Asa put on an expression of Biblical sternness which she did well from long practice. "I cast him out," she said firmly; and when Miss Clara clucked in bewilderment, "Mouth? Mouth? Mouth?" Asa turned on Fen in anger.

"Now see what you've done!" she said irritably. "And now I've got to scream it all to Clara. Do be off somewhere, boy, and ask me all these things some other time!"

Fen felt somewhat chastened although he was still curious and his forearms continued to tingle from excitement. He walked out of the bedroom and down the hall, hearing Asa's bellow ring out behind him. "I SAID RYAN. CAST RYAN OUT, I SAID."

"What for?" asked Miss Clara without great interest.

"DISRESPECTFUL," Asa shrieked.

Miss Clara grunted deep in her chest at this. She said Ryan had once tried to play cards with her.

"The quality of card playing is no test of character," said Asa crisply. She said it so crisply that it had to be done over again at top volume. "At any rate, Clara, you've no business playing cards all the time. Not at your age. It isn't seemly."

"What was that?"

"I said you SHOULDN'T PLAY CARDS."

"Can't hear you," Miss Clara said in a tone that was faintly self-satisfied.

By that time Fen had stepped out of earshot. He had heard all this a thousand times before and it was not worth eavesdropping.

He started down the carpeted stairs, stopping as always at the fourth one from the top which he sometimes called The Prophet. This one step had in its tread a monstrous creak, but if one stepped exactly on a certain spot with a certain pressure, it remained silent and one could pass safely. It was important that Fen set his foot exactly upon that spot each time he went up or came down those stairs.

If he found the silence on first attempt that was an excellent omen—good luck awaited him—but if it took a while, or if he tramped all over it and never won, he shivered at all the evil which the day must hold.

When Fen had been much smaller he had believed a little god lived within that stair—something green and venomous and oblong—and whenever a foot crossed His roof, He blessed and cursed according to His mood.

Now Fen no longer believed in that, of course, but he was careful.

It never hurt to be careful—Aunt Asa insisted on that in everything.

Now, pausing, he considered the step gravely, and then he placed his foot on the back far right, wincing at the small *sqrrk* that sounded underneath his toes. He moved his foot a barest fraction forward and everything was still. It would be a pretty fair day then—Atheist Uncle and all—and he went down the steps like a soldier.

He found Lady Malveena in the dining room, counting out silverware and real Irish linen for the dinner table that night. She was grumbling under her breath to the Good Lord, who always seemed to be conveniently at her elbow, listening with sympathy to her running commentary. Lady Malveena called him Mister, out of politeness.

But Fen imagined the Good Lord, Mister or no, as plump and puffing, always rushing after Lady Malveena so he would not lose the thread of her complaint.

"And Mister Lord, there's some things a good woman don't have to tol-er-ate beyond her strong spirit. There's just a time when the bucket runs over and you might as well buy a new, and Miss Asa's done about tramped on my toes the last sweet time. . . ." Lady Malveena went on mumbling angrily and incoherently, clinking the knives and spoons together as if it would please her to scratch their surfaces and dim the table's glory.

"Hello, Lady Malveena," Fen said softly, coming in the door; and she jerked her head up as if by a hidden string and looked at him suspiciously.

"More pussy-footing in this house than honest faces," she said darkly, making a bang of knife against china and then looking down hopefully to see if she had chipped anything. "High falutin' notions goes before a deep valley and a devil's snare," she said in disgust; and looked out over the splendid table which was gleaming and elegant and—so far as she could see—unmarred.

The table *was* beautiful. It looked, Fen thought, like the Lord's Supper laid out in a bigger finer church than he had ever seen, and when he thought of his Atheist Uncle eating and drinking the Lord's Supper, he giggled.

Lady Malveena frowned at him for this, so he said generously, "Everything looks very nice." She made a snort high up in her nostrils.

"Yes, I suspect it do," she said grimly. "Being as how some hands haven't bent themselves to do no helping and poor Lady Malveena been put upon past the endurance of the spirit, as Mister Lord can see."

She was about to be off on her grumbling again, so Fen slipped on past her and into the kitchen where he edged a knife down the banana pudding and gouged out a bite. When he put the meringue back over it, it hardly showed at all.

"What you doing in here?" Lady Malveena's voice from the door was threatening, but fond.

"Looking," Fen said, swallowing fast.

She peered at his busy throat. "Take care you don't choke on your eyesight," she said.

Fen loved Lady Malveena. There was nothing particular in his twelve and one-half years he could take hold of to say why this was so, but when he thought of Lady Malveena his memory was one dark goodness. It was made up of so many kindnesses across so many days and nights that he could remember none of them separately. But she was brusque; she talked mostly to her appendage-God and to herself, and her smile was very rare. When it came, it opened her face out like a dark flower.

"Are you sorry Uncle Ryan's coming, too?"

"Naw. He'll be all right." There was a certain pride in Lady Malveena's voice he had not heard before.

"What's he like?"

She was stirring a pot on the stove; now she turned the spoon in the liquid slowly. "He's good," she said.

That was all, but to Fen it was molten shock. He could never remember her having said that of anybody. And what of the scar and the harbor women after that?

"He used to be here lots," said Lady Malveena, half dreaming. "When you was one and two years old, he'd have you on his back. You look some like him."

Fen was stunned at that possibility and a little horrified.

"Was that when my mother lived here?"

Lady Malveena put a lid onto the pot with a great clang. "Yes it were. And a long time past and gone, those days," she snapped. Then she looked at Fen oddly and yet warmly, too. "Your mama and your Uncle Ryan, they was . . . they was good friends." Her voice had grown businesslike at the end. "Few enough friends there be, and nothing to belittle. And you just mind that now."

So Fen stepped back with a feeling he had been lectured about something he knew nothing of; and he went on out the back screen door and down the steps into the yard. Her mumbling followed him faintly, like a swarm of bees.

Outside he stopped just in the yard and took one thorough look around, the way he always did, to see things whole. It gave him a good feeling to pick out some detail that was different from yesterday—a bucket moved, the gate closed, ajar, open, and the two big cats which sometimes dozed in the tall tan grass and sometimes roamed abroad.

There was a rusty wire fence about the main back yard (bent down so far that even dogs walked up and jumped across) and a warped old gate which never quite fitted into the space that had been left for it.

Here, too, stood the old carriage house grown up in ivy and six rosebushes Aunt Asa had once ordered all the way from Atlanta. They were neglected and dry and leaned against the carriage house like things grown tired. Sometimes they managed an occasional bloom as if from sheer stubbornness; and once each season Miss Clara would come out to see them, and would stand absently plucking at their leaves as if she were grooming them for something.

Beyond the leaning fence was a field of matted grass which always went quickly from an early green to its nearly neutral hue. Here grew two rows of fruit trees and a grape arbor. The rest had once been gardened and had given—or so Aunt Asa said—the sweetest melons and real golden squash and tart red radishes. That was before Fen's time, but it was what Aunt Asa said and she was never wrong.

The matted grass ahead of him where the orchard stood was almost like a sea; brown mottled rats rose from it like flying fish and were pursued by the two cats. These darted in that sea as swift as sharks.

Of course Fen had never really seen the sea, and yet he knew so well how it must look and sound, and how the wet salt taste would feel upon his lips, and what the sand was like and the shells. When he had been younger he had played with rafts upon this orchard sea, but secretly, so Asa would not laugh.

Not that Asa laughed very much. She was too busy for that.

Fen walked now out of the yard and sucked himself in small to slide through the rusted gate without dirtying his fingers. No one seemed to know when his uncle would get here, he thought, and no one seemed too pleased about it either. Aunt Asa was dashing here and yonder with things to put in and take out of Ryan's bedroom, while Miss Clara made small outcries at every small detail and Lady Malveena grumbled at the extra work. Perhaps even Mister Lord looked with ill favor on whatever was bringing Uncle Ryan home after all these years. But what had Lady Malveena meant when she said, "He's good"? He was frowning as he detoured past the tree that was full of caterpillars and walked to the lower part of the orchard.

Here he sat on the grass and began absently to munch the bitter wrinkled peaches which lay underneath the tree. It was August; the good ones were long gone. Sometimes Fen only took the dry tasteless pulp away and broke the peach seed between two bricks and ate the brown kernel which lay secretly inside.

I ate a whole peach tree, he would think proudly, remembering how Lady Malveena had fooled him when he was a little boy by saying all seeds sprouted in the stomach.

"Swallow a hair and pass a snake," she always finished grimly, until he would lie awake in fear at night, hearing beneath his ribs the stealth of reptiles and the brush of leaves.

Lady Malveena had worked for Aunt Asa as long as Fen could remember, way before he was born probably. Aunt Asa said she had been given her double name because her mammy had a sense of humor, and she thought how great a joke it was that all the white folks should have to call her Lady. Aunt Asa never smiled when she said it, so she must not think it was much of a joke. As for Fen, he liked the name. It seemed to suit her.

Now Fen lay back in the grass and let loose all the fibers of his mind so that it ranged, lazily; he thought about how Lady Malveena was browner than peach kernels, and how Uncle Ryan had been cast out of the house so many years ago, and whether God might strike him dead on the premises because he was an atheist. Yes, he thought that might be interesting. He had a vision of Walnut Street going up in flame like Sodom or Gomorrah.

And then some bird began to chirp drowsily in the orchard and he lost everything else in listening to it.

It was strange the way he sat up straighter, almost in anticipation, as the houses flicked in and out of the window oftener and Ryan knew the bus was almost into Stoneville. He leaned forward in his seat and looked curiously out the window—unfamiliar machine shops, a neon-girded restaurant and (invasion of the modern world!) a drive-in movie theater. Did Stoneville youngsters go to such things now in their parents' cars? It did not seem believable.

This was where one noticed the changes in a town, he thought, in the outskirts, seeing the queer new tentacles which the organism has sprouted: its one or two self-consciously "modern" houses; the landscaped area of what was to become (said the sign) the Rest-haven Resting Grounds with its small distinctive markers (such a change from Methodist Hill, he thought, where Jessica and Avery were buried); a small hosiery mill that was so built that neither light nor air should contaminate its workers—all these unfamiliar "young" things which had sprung up on the edge of town.

Gradually, however, there began to be a few landmarks that he remembered—an ancient brick house where some long-ago governor had once spent a night, the reservoir (could it be possible that it was so much smaller than he remembered?), the Tea and China Shoppe which Amy and Laura Hodges had started back when they were girls, that treacherous curve that opened on a bridge and an intersection—how boasting an alarming battery of lights and signs and arrows—and after these the small business district which was the heart of town, looking almost the same despite the coats of paint which must have come and gone since he had seen it last.

Seeing Stoneville now so much like he remembered, Ryan half expected everything else to fall in line, to see Jessica walking down the street in that slow preoccupied way of hers, to pass again the sign that said in 1890's lettering ASA GODWIN, *Realtor*—almost to see himself as he had been ten years before when Jessica lay in the hospital hardly breathing, or even twenty years or twenty-five, when everything might have been different.

He knew from one of Asa's letters that the Godwin realty office had been moved upstairs in some building, and that Asa had taken in a partner whom she did not like. But that was all he knew. Except for that change it might all have been the same; and in another moment he would see Jessica walking in the streets with a white scarf through her hair.

Unexpectedly the bus driver droned, "This is Stoneville. Change here for Columbia and Greenville. The bus will be here five minutes taking on passengers."

Ryan straightened in his seat and began to wonder if his luggage had arrived on the same bus. Usually it did not; it would have gotten on some totally foreign bus and gone to Norfolk or Raleigh or Savannah. How this was done (it was beyond the realm of accident) he had never understood. He placed such things in the category of How-Laundries-Get-All-the-Buttons-off-my-Shirts.

As he rode down Main Street on that bus, across the square and by the hotel and the post office, he began to miss young Hobbley, the farmer who had gotten off some miles outside of town. It would have been good to have Hobbley as an ally when he first stepped down in Stoneville, stepped down like the Pilgrim Fathers onto a pagan land.

At this Ryan grinned. Me a pilgrim father! How angry Asa would be at such comparisons!

The bus pulled into the station and groaned and stopped, scattering before it a dozen hungry sparrows off a heap of popcorn.

"Stoneville," said the driver in a bored and automatic voice.

The passengers stirred. "Is this Lancaster?"

"No."

"Didn't he say Lancaster?"

"He said Stoneville, whatever that is. I'm from Tampa, myself."

"You know, I've got an aunt lives in Tampa . . ."

Ryan got up and took his brief case off the rack. He was the only passenger getting off except for one lipsticked young miss who was changing for Columbia where, she had told them all, her soldier was at Fort Jackson and would be a corporal next week. It made him feel conspicuous to get off with the hippy youngster; he covered his embarrassment by nodding brusquely to the driver and taking his brief case from one hand and shifting it, carefully, to the other. He said he would come back for his bags.

The driver could not have been less interested. "They'll be here," he said. Ryan resisted a desire to tell him that he doubted it profoundly.

But by that time he was outside the bus and could look around. Quickly he smiled; until now he had half forgotten that the bus station was only several doors down from the dead-end street which spread into Stoneville's unimpressive railway terminal. From where he stood now, he could just make out old Mr. Sando, standing in the door to the station agent's building and squinting jealously to see what passenger had dared to come by bus.

Mr. Sando would, no doubt, be frowning. He would be muttering to himself that it was no wonder they couldn't get more than a spur into Stoneville and two trains a day when people wouldn't use the service. Mr. Sando felt that everyone who came into Stoneville any way except by train deprived him of a raise in salary and a building which was warmer and would not leak.

All of that made Ryan feel he was really home. He waved his hand toward the terminal and Mr. Sando, baffled, took a step forward so he could see better. Ryan turned his back to tantalize him; he would know soon enough the way news traveled in Stoneville.

It was after five o'clock, a supper recess in town, so that at first the cab driver hunched down into his seat and tried not to see the wave of Ryan's hand. The cabstand was near the bus station less out of enterprise than laziness. The mountains came to Mohammed, once an hour.

Ryan waved his hand again, with the brief case in it this time so he would look more prosperous. At this the driver gave up and made a great flourish out of starting and turning the car, throwing up gravel, drawing up to Ryan with the door half open in one synchronized motion and drawling without much interest, "Where to?" Ryan moved his toe forward half an inch and touched the calculated position of the rear right tire.

"309 Walnut," he said, getting in and sitting down, reaching for the door which was already closing from some practiced flick of the driver's hand.

"Right," said the driver. They left the station in a roar.

As they rode (back along Main Street again to the square and then south, across Wynberry to Walnut) Ryan looked out the window curiously.

He had forgotten, for one thing, how many old trees there were in Stoneville—great giants of oak and elm whose roots had lifted and cracked sidewalks so that pedestrians moved always in an up or down-hill slant. When they turned onto Walnut Street, passing some new brick building and then the Damrosch house on the corner, Ryan sat forward in spite of himself. He had always liked Walnut with its shaded prim old houses looking rather like starched matrons who doubtless concealed hearts of gold. He remembered as in the old days that there was not, after all, a single walnut tree on the street, although perhaps there had been once in the days when Stoneville was young.

Then (it was a short trip; Stoneville seemed smaller, seemed contracted) the cab was stopping before the house, stopping, in fact, so near the curb that one could scarcely have run a pencil in between; and Ryan handed the man a dollar, got back forty cents. He grinned—that much had changed at least—the old thirty-five-cent taxi had passed off into history.

The man thanked him and gave him a card with his cab number on it.

"Call me again," he said.

"I will," said Ryan, automatically. The car was gone amidst noise and exhaust.

Ryan stood on the sidewalk a minute after it had gone, looking up at the old curliqued house. It was exactly the same. It stood three-storied and tall, and knobs and carvings hung from all the eaves and the roof of the porch. The house was white and gave the feeling of being somewhat thin, as though it needed more mass from left to right instead of spreading, as it did, down the back of the lot. Because it was so slim it would have seemed even taller had it not been for the massive oaks in the front yard, and these grew up past its chimneys and were full of thick summer leaves and sun.

Just for one minute the sight of the house wrung at his heart (he could not say why) and he thought of himself running in this house as a boy; he saw himself coming home from college; or sitting on this very front porch with Jessica the night he decided to break it off once and for all; he remembered the long long day he had sat miserable in the kitchen, without rights and privileges, and waited for Fen to be born. He thought of his father at work forever with his sums in his dusty little study, and of Lady Malveena eternally sweeping the hall, and Miss Clara huddled over a million radio programs with the volume up as high as it would go. He thought of Asa going up and down those stairs with her back like a ramrod and her eyes, as always, straight ahead and unwavering. He was suddenly sad because, after all, none of it (and none of *them*) had come to more.

Then he saw the front curtains shiver violently, heard Miss Clara cry, "He's here! He's here! He's here!" He could imagine her going up the steps like an express train, lumbering down the hall with her great arms askew.

He heard the iron in Asa's voice. "Call the boy. Where has he gone?"

"I'm coming," someone said.

At that Ryan took a half step forward. For a moment that voice had sounded . . . for one moment he had thought . . .

He pushed it away. He looked up at the old oaks and told himself sternly, as a practical man ought, *It's turning cool for August. Trees will be bare early this year.*

The house was very quiet then, waiting.

3.

HE KNEW that everything was going to be chilly at first when no one even opened the door to him.

Although Ryan knew they were all now informed of his coming, they waited silently within the house. There was no outward move to greet him or to call him in, and this irritated him by its foolishness. After the one cry from Miss Clara and Asa's response, the house had fallen quite still and Ryan saw that the amenities must be observed; he must walk up and use the brass knocker (which had always reminded him of a tongue, so that he felt he was putting his hand in a dead man's mouth) and after a decent interval there would come faintly the sounds of unhurried movement in the house, as though the occupants were half surprised to learn that anyone was there.

Ryan came up the steps, and taking up the unpleasant knocker dropped it hurriedly into place. It clanked dully, like a breadbox closing.

He did not bother to knock again, and after a few minutes he heard to his amusement the subdued tones of his sister's voice as she called like a regular gentlewoman bothered on a busy afternoon — "Lady Malveena, will you see who's at the door, please?"

Ryan leaned against the wall, weak with unlaughed amusement at the sweet propriety within. This was completely unreal; and then there flashed into his mind the thought: *I'm dead already and this is what Heaven is—the ability to laugh at all the foolishness in our lives without bitterness.*

But in another second the door had swung wide and there stood Lady Malveena, gaunt and brown and very real (not like Heaven at all), with eyes that almost twinkled through her look of disapproval. The disapproval was like a veil she had put on too hastily and could not quite stop smiling behind.

For a second Ryan knew a small sharp pleasure. I think she's glad to see me, he reflected in surprise.

In another moment he was sure of it, for Lady Malveena said gruffly, "Took you long enough. Ten years since I closed the door behind you and you just got around to knocking on it again."

At this, if Ryan had been a boy again, he would have caught her at the waist with joy. Even now he put out an impulsive hand and said warmly, "I'm very glad to see you, Lady Malveena." He had not dreamed there was anything left in Stoneville that could move him still.

But Lady Malveena was staring down at his outstretched hand with indignation.

"Plain to see you been up North too long," she said insolently, closing the door behind him. "None of this touch and touch of the elements. As Mister Lord says, the next step down is plain old forn-i-ca-tion," and Ryan smiled and took his handshake down. Even Mister Lord was still with them, he thought, and not a day older by the sound of Him.

Nor did Lady Malveena seem any older. She had always been thin. She had a mouth that was full and yet seemed to be slightly pursed with pride and aristocracy. The eyes were as before—very still and very deep.

That made him remember a day when he had come home on vacation from the State University, freshman year, his skull absolutely bloated from knowledge. And suddenly he had *seen* Lady Malveena, had really seen her as a person; and he had been struck by something in her eyes that was wise and timeless. He had blurted, "Sometimes I think you know more than the whole world."

And she, pleased and flattered, had smiled and said, "Well, I'm getting older. I disremember some of it these days."

She said to him now, taking his hat and coat, "Hold up your shoulders. You got a rubber band for a backbone? What you think people say about slumpers?"

Involuntarily he straightened in the old way.

Then, as if some invisible stage director had prompted her on cue, Asa came in from the parlor, nodded to him unsmilingly, and turned up a cool gray cheek. Ryan kissed it politely, thinking how like it was to flint or flakes of granite. When this was done and Lady Malveena had slipped away, Miss Clara barged in from behind her, propelling a thin young boy who was all eyes and lashes, and who kept scratching at his wrist.

"Ryan, Ryan, Ryan," said Miss Clara in pleased diminuendo, and took a hand between two large ones of her own. She smiled at him with her customary vacancy, unable to hear any of the conversation; and after a while looked down and saw she still held his hand and dropped it hastily, as if she had committed an indiscretion.

Asa said, putting a hand onto the boy's shoulder, "And this is Fenwick. Fenwick, this is your Uncle Ryan. He hasn't seen you since . . . since you were two years old."

The boy took a step forward, half shy, half curious, and the sharp familiarity of that movement jolted somewhere back in Ryan's mind. He said with a smile, "Hello, Fen," and put out his right hand.

The boy took it in his own and shook it four times, all the while staring at it as if he had expected this to be different from other hands, and stealing a look upwards as if something in Ryan's face were missing, as if he had neglected, for instance, to wear his nose that day.

When Fen looked up at him like that, the cast of his features was too familiar, younger and vaguer, but not unknown. It was a face he had always remembered. The eyes he knew well and the shape of the young mouth, and a way the boy held his head, as though it might be fragile. And there was something else, too; he was trying to place it when Asa pointed it out to him.

"I didn't remember Fenwick looked so much like you, Ryan," she said.

It was true. But he said only, "You remind *me* very much of your mother, Fen." He hoped it did not sound trite and ordinary, like all the tedious things relatives are always saying.

Fen said quickly, "Lady Malveena says you and my mother were very good friends," and Asa cleared her throat like a motor starting and began to change the subject.

But Ryan said, "Yes, we were."

"Well," said Asa with some disapproval, "well, let's sit down and catch up on things. We're all a little in the dark about this unex-

And then he looked across the room at Asa (who was watching him; trying—perhaps—to see inside his skull?) and at Miss Clara (who was looking at her hands so closely that she might be counting up the fingers) and at Fen. Fen was watching him too, but in a thunderstruck way. It was as though he saw his Uncle Ryan as a horse or a giant toad or a garden tractor—or some other incongruous object there in Asa's parlor.

"I'd like to wash up and get some unpacking done before dinner, if that's agreeable," Ryan said into the silence. Asa inclined her head. Miss Clara had not heard him; she turned her hands over and possibly read her future in the palms.

"You will stay to dinner, I hope?" said Miss Clara suddenly, looking up at him, seeing him on his feet.

Ryan nodded to her politely; it was easier than answering.

"Good," said Miss Clara, "I'm hungry." She smiled at Asa as if to say: Was that all right?

Asa, he was glad to see, had asked Fenwick to help him carry the bags, although the two heavy ones were at the station still, and take him to his room. He carried the brief case and Fen the small Gladstone, and they went silently upstairs.

There was one moment on those steps, near the top, when Fen stopped and seemed quite worried. (Is he going back downstairs? Is he afraid of me?) And then he made a great off-balance step and skipped one stair tread entirely, looking very much relieved. Ryan glanced back over his shoulder but that step did not appear to differ from the rest, and he frowned. I'd forgotten how at a certain age the world is alive with spirits, Ryan thought, and turned again to follow down the hall and to his door.

It appeared that Asa had given him the same old room because she knew he had always detested it. Airless and sunless, it was of a queer shape; it had been thrust in as an afterthought amongst buttresses and unexpected chimneys, so that the walls went in and out at queer angles. He could remember the times he had risen in the night, only to bump over and over into this or that projection. When he was younger he had thought this was like Poe's room, forever contracting about him to a tomb.

Now he put a hand out to the wall and to all the roses, and an incredible sadness came over him. He could not have said why, whether it was the room, or the time of day, or frozen Asa—whether it was because he had remembered much or forgotten much. It was impossible to say. He sat on the bed like an old man and he looked at his hands as closely as Miss Clara had studied hers.

I was mad to come back, he thought sharply, I was altogether mad.

Fen saw him sink down, moved toward the door and said shyly, "I'll see you later then, sir." He stood with his hand at the knob, ridiculously thin and awkward with those absurd eyelashes which were so dark in his face. He was a handsome boy, or would be when he filled out a bit and got some confidence.

Ryan got up from the bed and opened his bag to show he was not, after all, very tired. "Don't go unless you must, Fen," he said. "Stay and talk to me while I unpack."

"All right," said Fen. He came into the room and stood there scratching himself on the elbow, looking very ill-at-ease. He looks like me, thought Ryan again, and then stopped thinking it. There was no way of knowing now, and perhaps it did not matter.

"How old are you now?"

"Twelve," he said. "I'll be thirteen in February."

"Yes, I remember. You go to school, I guess."

"Yessir."

What a wasted conversation this was, no more and no less than the way the generations have always pretended to communicate, Ryan was thinking. No more than the way my own bumbling uncles talked when I was young. And how I hated them!

"Do you have . . ." and then he stopped in horror. My God! he thought, I was going to ask him if he had a girl! He shook his head over and over, and had to concentrate to finish the sentence in some acceptable way.

"Do you have a picture of your mother?" he asked instead.

The boy's face brightened. "A small one," he said proudly. "A small one in a round frame."

"I have one too; I'll give it to you."

Ryan was immediately aghast at what he had said; why in the world should he have ever offered to part with Jessica's photograph? But then he saw Fen's look of anticipation and could not take it back. After all, he thought, why not? He was so little when his mother died, while I remember all.

He said abruptly, "Do you suppose we'll have cauliflower for dinner? Creamed yellow cauliflower like Asa always used to serve?"

The boy took a step backwards. "Why, I don't know," he said, surprised.

"I hate cauliflower."

Ryan glanced at the boy surreptitiously as he reached into the bag, took out a sock or two, all with exaggerated slowness. He moved quietly and cautiously, like one not wishing to frighten a small animal one is attempting to befriend. Fen, he could see, had begun to smile.

In another minute he had given up the scratching and crossed the room and come to sit on the edge of the bed. Ryan, not seeming to notice, stepped to the dresser drawer and slid a shirt inside.

"I do, too," said Fen.

"Hmmm?" He examined the drawer closely, fingering the elaborate brass, still keeping his back turned.

"I can't stand cauliflower."

"Oh." Ryan smiled broadly as if they were sharers of something remarkable, took another shirt from the bag, slipped it into the drawer.

"It tastes like cats," the boy confided.

Ryan considered this new idea, nodded gravely. "In melted soap," he agreed thoughtfully, and then added—after the way of a conspirator—"We used to have it all the time when I lived here before."

"We still have it enough." The boy leaned forward and peered with frank curiosity at the clothes remaining in the open bag. "You're not like I thought," he said after a moment, looking up. "I thought you'd be cut."

This was a startling thought. Ryan turned it in his head and could make nothing of it.

"No, I'm not cut," he said finally. "What made you think so?"

"Oh, you know," said Fen, flipping his hand at the wrist in a gesture of dismissal. "I thought you might be tattooed, too."

Ryan smiled, tried to imagine what on earth Asa might have told the boy. He put out a hand and ran it over one of the wall's angles, as if he were testing some bony rump. "What in the world makes a room come out like this?"

Fen smiled. "It didn't have any place else to go," he said. "There was something else on every side of it."

Like a tooth, thought Ryan, which has to come in crooked when it's pushed.

"It's like a lopsided hexagon," Fen was saying.

Ryan paused between case and dresser to look at him. "Where did you learn about hexagons?"

"Oh, books and things."

He saw that the boy had flushed slightly, as though he was embarrassed at letting something slip out of his fingers, something he had been meaning to hold for himself. So it had been with Ryan, too, in this house . . . a long time ago.

"Your grandfather was a mathematician, of sorts," Ryan said, and then changed the subject. "Is the orchard dead? And the grape arbor?"

"No, just a tree or two. The grapes are good every year, and Lady Malveena sometimes makes a little wine."

Ryan smiled at this. More often than Miss Asa knew, he thought, remembering the dusty crocks that had been hidden in nearly all the nooks and crannies of the house, under the back steps, back behind her own bed in the Second House, where Lady Malveena lived. The Second House had been built up next to the back porch and was connected by a short dark passage.

"The bitterest peaches," said Ryan nostalgically now, returning to the thought of the orchard, and here again he saw something respond in the boy's face. I don't know exactly what I'm up to, he thought grimly, whether I really like this boy or if I just want to make a division in Asa's household.

Suddenly Fen grew quite tense and leaning forward, fixed him with dark eyes. "Uncle Ryan," he began, giving him another penetrating look from under the thick lashes, "Uncle Ryan, don't you really believe in God?"

Ryan was startled but he did not let it show. He said, as honestly as he could, "Sometimes," turning to look at Fen and noting that flash of something that went like light across his face—relief? disappointment?—probably Fen did not know himself.

The boy nodded his head, almost as though he had surmised this much already since his uncle was not cut and did not have tattoos. "What kind of God?" he said. "When you do, I mean."

Ryan continued to watch him, considering the question with the seriousness it deserved. "Personal," he admitted finally. "A God of love."

He almost smiled, so much aware was he that he would not have used those well-worn words except before a child.

"And Mother. She believed in him, too, didn't she? Asa said she always went to church."

To this Ryan nodded, not knowing what to say. There ought to be an answer as honest as the boy's question, but if there was he could not think of it. And he was no gadfly to small boys. Besides,

Jessica had believed quite deeply, although she had seldom prayed. She had said sometimes she never prayed because she could feel the love of God around her like a cup. "So what could I ask for but that?" she would say.

And Ryan would say, "I don't know because I don't know how that feels."

Remembering, Ryan stood there and nodded his head to Fen; and after a minute he went back to the contents of the bag and continued putting things evenly inside the dresser drawers.

In a few minutes he said, "Asa doesn't talk about your mother much, does she?"

"Not much," said Fen. "She talks about my father more. Miss Clara says my mother was pretty but that she whispered. Miss Clara thinks the whole world whispers. Is it true they had the wreck because of something Mother said? Asa thinks they might have been quarreling and my father was upset."

This much Ryan was sure about. "Your father was never upset," he said firmly. He did not intend it as a compliment.

"He *was* even-tempered, wasn't he?" said Fen proudly. "That's what Aunt Asa says."

"Your father was as even-tempered as a stone," said Ryan grimly. In another minute he added, "It was just an accident. It really was just an unavoidable accident that no one could have foreseen or prevented." This was a lesson he had taught himself over and over in the last ten years.

"Except God," said Fen automatically.

"Well, possibly Him," said Ryan. Fen handed him a pair of socks and he dropped them in with the others.

"Clara has two cats and they go after rats out back."

"Do they?" He felt a little tired from the attempt to match the leaps and hurdles of the boy's mind; he crossed the room to the window and stood looking out into great oak limbs and coarse leaves.

"I had forgotten the house was so tall," he said absently. "It's out of fashion to build three stories any more."

"The attic's full of junk," said Fen.

"It always was."

Behind him the boy stirred on the bed and finally stood up as though he, too, might walk across the room just to look out into the tree.

"In the wintertime," said Ryan, mostly to himself, "that tree looks like a tall black man with many arms. I remember that from before."

It was Lady Malveena who answered with a piercing call from below.

"Them as don't make the table on time are to be satisfied with small leavings!" she screeched from the foot of the stairs in a high loud voice. In another minute the last echo rose from the eaves of the house and faded away, and everything was still again. An old clock on the mantelpiece in Ryan's crooked room moved time around in clicks and clocks above his head and Ryan thought: *Nothing changes.*

The two of them smiled self-consciously and started out of the room and down the hall to the stairs. They could see Asa and Miss Clara near the curtains which hung before the dining room as they started down the stairs.

Once Fen reached up and caught his arm fiercely and shook it up and down. "Don't step on that one," he whispered urgently, shaking the sleeve and pointing to a certain step. "Step high over that one."

And Ryan obligingly smiled and skipped it just as Asa turned her head and nodded at him. "What's the matter?" she said, seeing him with his foot raised. "You have a bad leg?"

He lowered it from the extra high step he had taken. "Old age," he said.

This time Ryan smiled and the boy smiled back at him gratefully; and he was nearly staggered from that smile. Out of somewhere deep in him there welled up a hundred old tender things and it seemed that the rib cage tightened on his heart.

But he looked away quickly from Fen's face and from the eyes that were like other brown eyes under lashes that had been just that thick. I'm just hungry, he told himself fiercely. It's nothing but that.

4.

EARLY the next morning Ryan woke and lay under the light coverlet and watched a thin wedge of sunlight that had worked in by way of the small window, watched it lengthen as morning came more swiftly until it was halfway into the room.

When it comes all the way across and up the bed to my face, I'll get up, he thought languidly. It will be like the day itself touching me.

He lay motionless for a while, not quite permitting himself to think, letting the day happen to him. Sounds filtered into his consciousness—somebody went by the door on light feet, a second door closed somewhere; outside the window leaves stirred and settled as though birds were going by.

After a while Ryan got up, stretched, began to dress. Thoughts came into his mind like turned-on faucets, and to his hurt amazement he began suddenly to retch, hacking and tugging at his empty stomach until he turned his face into the roses on the queer-shaped wall and stood there with his hands trembling. He was very cold and his face was wet. Oh God, he thought.

Through it all he heard faintly from outside the sound of Lady Malveena's voice, sending someone to market, sending the boy probably. He had a picture of Lady Malveena standing in the front door of the house with shadowy Mister Lord peering perhaps across her shoulder, and of Fen going hurriedly down the street, going away from the tall house to stand at some vegetable bin, scratching his nose.

Then he was very sick again and his stomach tossed and heaved until he let the wall hold him. It'll be over in a minute, he thought. And he swallowed and swallowed at whatever it was that wouldn't come up and wouldn't go down.

He crossed to the bed and lay back down again, putting a hand across his eyes.

This was what Jim had warned him in Wellman he must watch out for, this early unnecessary sickness that might come from his mind rather than from his body.

"It can panic you if you don't expect it," Jim had warned, turning his spectacles in an embarrassed way in his fingers. "You'll get to thinking things are further along than they are."

"What makes you sick? Does everybody get sick?"

"Just the ones who feel things strongest. It's the very thought of cancer. We've a national complex on this particular disease, though Lord knows there are worse ones."

"I wish it could be somewhere else besides the throat."

"And you'll go on thinking about that and feeling it down there like something alive until one day the thought itself will make you nauseated. I wish you'd stay here and get on with this thing. We could save you so much more than time. We could save you some of this thinking, and all of this worrying." Jim had frowned with real concern; they were old friends.

"Who's worrying?"

Now Ryan rubbed his own forehead, wishing he could slip his hands inside his head and softly knead that brain until he had soothed it down. The brain, he thought, has its own tricky digestion. Give it a disagreeable thought like death and it wants to regurgitate and throw it out again.

He lay there a minute longer until the contortions at his middle quieted down, and then he wiped a chill wetness off his face and neck and went on dressing.

He was almost better, he thought; his objectivity was beginning to function again. There was always a second Ryan on the periphery of events who watched and commented, and never became involved. Now this second man had begun to lecture him on emotional self-control. He could hear the dialogue going on in his head; he could hear the little man making his points quietly but insistently. There was never any raising of that voice.

So I'm getting back to normal, he thought. For me, anyway.

But when he walked downstairs he had a ridiculous desire to skip Fen's step, except that he could not remember which one it had been. He tramped heavily on all of them as an adult should, feeling a little foolish.

In the hall, Lady Malveena was thrusting a feather duster in a warlike manner at the hatstand.

"A sloth and a sluggard are sad for the eye of man," she threw at him effortlessly over her shoulder. "Consider the ways of the ant and cease to be an insect."

This bit of advice Ryan turned in his mind with confused pleasure.

"Is it late? Is it too late for breakfast?"

"You mean normal or actual?"

"Both," he said.

"Normal it is; the others eat and gone already," she said decisively. "Actual I can find you something." She was already tucking the duster underneath her arm.

"I'll be obliged." He followed her meekly to the kitchen. Walking behind her, he thought again how tall and straight she was and had always been, and how she walked on the balls of her feet with beauty and dignity.

She set out the chipped blue-flowered plates and began to beat two eggs with milk and salt and pepper, trying to look disagreeable about it, trying to look as if she were not pleased to have him to herself a bit. The coffee was still hot on the stove; he poured a cup and sat down to watch her.

"Where's Asa?"

Lady Malveena snorted. "Not a trusting bone in that one's flesh," she said. "Gone as usual down to the comp'ny, not willing to leave it in them other hands. She's none but a bother to them now, but who'd have the starch to tell her?"

"Who really runs it now?"

"A fancy man from up North with a fancy name. Mr. Gaskill the lawyer is just a name on the door. And Miss Asa, of course. She's not a help except the name of Godwin has a sound for people buying land in this town."

Ryan nodded. Flambert Godwin had been the first successful realtor in Stoneville, and the only one for years.

"And Fen, where's he?"

"I sent him off to market for dried apples. Good ones, I directed him, but he'll likely pick them puny and poor tasting."

"Fried apple pies?" said Ryan hopefully.

She nodded, dropped the egg mixture noisily into a hot pan, stood glaring down at it as if she defied it to burn or to cook in any other fashion but perfection.

"Lady Malveena, you're how old?"

Her back stiffened. She went on examining the eggs closely. "In December I am sixty-seven," she said shortly.

He knew suddenly how much aware she was of growing older, and he was sorry he had asked her. He wanted to let her know he understood exactly how it was; he felt the same way himself for his own reasons, but he said nothing about it. What could people say to one another about such things?

She slid a heaped-up plate before him and a bone-handled fork he had used in other years, and set out lukewarm biscuits and a bowl of jam.

"Time passes like crows flying," she said, snapping her lips shut on her words to close the whole subject. She refilled his coffee cup silently. In another minute she had said without any apparent relevance, "Fen is a good boy."

Ryan nodded, took a cautious bite of the food and discovered to his relief that he was starved.

Lady Malveena was standing by the stove watching him hopefully. "This is no good house for a boy like Fen to be," she said. "And three peculiar old women for his only company." It was as if she were waiting for him to make some answer and when he did not she added almost pleadingly, "He's like you was, Mr. Ryan, at that age. Or like his mama." This last she added only after a careful pause.

"I'll be home a while," said Ryan hastily, hoping to placate her. "I want to get to know him well. This is mighty good food, Lady Malveena."

She gave him an accusing stare and carried the frying pan onto the porch to scrape off into the trash, grumbling to herself. She hated indirection, and to have it fail was gall and wormwood, salt in wounds, insult on injury.

Left alone, Ryan ate hurriedly. He felt guilty, but what could he do—offer to take the boy away somewhere? Not that Asa would let him even if . . . even if it weren't automatically out of the question.

When breakfast was over, he walked uptown to get his bags.

Summer had made things green although it was August green, past its first lushness. Ryan walked slowly and with real pleasure. This seemed everywhere the Stoneville he remembered, and the better part of it—quiet, great-treed, having its own schedule of club meetings and church revivals and local observances, issuing its gossipy semiweekly *Stoneville Beacon*, eternally busy in small quick ways—like Martha in the old story.

The houses on Walnut Street were old and dignified, set about with ivy and wisteria and well-clipped shrubs. Colored men came to do the lawns regularly. They kept all the bushes carefully clipped, and to Ryan none of them seemed more than an inch or so taller than when he had seen them last, ten years before.

At one house two ladies leaned from their porch rockers halfway on the banister to see him pass, and then fell to speculating as to who he was and where his business lay. He nodded, though he did not remember who they were.

He stepped with caution past a chalked-in hopscotch game on the walk, nodded to an elderly gentleman watering his lawn against the summer heat, dodged from the path of two bony-kneed girls who went by making feverish work of skip rope. He heard their singsong:

I like coffee, I like tea
I like the boys and the
Boys like me.
Yes no maybe so . . .
Yes, no, maybe so
Yesnomaybeso. . . .

Everything about the atmosphere lulled him. It seemed as if the world began and ended at the start and end of this one shaded street, and as if here lived all the sane and sensible people who inhabited the earth. It was possible for a few minutes to forget completely that anything lay outside this (wars, prison, syphilis, welfare workers, lunatics, nuclear physics). For a little while, too, he put out of his mind any possibility that even Stoneville might possess its undercurrents, that here and there a black man stood against a white, the young developed dementia praecox, and men and women moved in worlds of sex and anger.

All of this might be true (he even thought objectively it *must* be true; for the little man was always on duty in his mind), but at this moment he did not believe it. Actually he believed only the trees and the ladies on the porch and an old gentleman worrying because his grass might die from all the August sun. He walked on, lazy.

A woman went by him, dragging by the hand a reluctant little boy. The child, unable to contain his venom any longer, turned back and made a fearsome face as Ryan passed. Even this made him smile; it seemed so tiny and insignificant an imitation of evil.

Then he was turning left into Wynberry Street, past the clinic and the empty corner where he had once played touch football and baseball. Here he stopped in amazement—a sleek building housing optometrists and beauty operators and insurance agents stood smugly in the place where there had once been much brown grass and hidden stones which had bruised them all. He passed it, frowning.

After he got the other two bags and had them sent home by taxi (he could tell that the driver was amazed at this expense when no one was going to *ride* anywhere) Ryan stood outside the bus station on Main, undecided as to what he would do next. It was strange not to have the whole day compartmentalized ahead of him, not to be meeting and dismissing classes or clearing one's throat over the usual text and the usual lecture.

His throat. That knowledge was never very far away.

"Isn't that Ryan Godwin?" said an old man at his elbow so sharply and wheezily that he jumped and whirled around. He stood staring down at the man, who was grasshopper-folded, racking his brain for the name that went with the red and crinkled newborn-looking face, that black cane, the shirttail always hanging out. An elder, he thought desperately. He's an elder at the church.

"Yes, I am," he said aloud, putting out his hand and sparring for time while he probed for the proper name. "It's been years since I saw you. How've you been?"

"Tollable," muttered the old man, taking the hand in a stringy claw of his own. "You've aged somewhat," he added gloomily.

That sounded strange, coming so blithely out of that shrunken skull.

"Yes, I suspect we all have."

Ryan remembered him now—he was that aged elder who had always sat in church holding a magnifying glass above his hymnal in a quaking hand, making a quavery noise whenever he located the place for a minute, then rushing along again, trying to find where they were singing now. "You're looking well, Mr. McBane," he said, feeling pleased for having remembered him.

Amos McBane nodded his head heavily and Ryan winced from a sudden fear that the cords in his neck might snap and the head go bouncing to the street. The man seemed so tightly strung.

"When'd you get in?"

"Just yesterday. Town doesn't seem to have changed much."

"Never changes. That's its strength." Mr. McBane swayed to the left and spat a long yellow stream into the gutter. "What ails the world," he said direly. "Change."

Ryan, unable to think of a suitable answer to this, gave a self-conscious smile. He remembered now that there had been a Mrs. McBane somewhere, a round dark peach seed of a woman with long black hairs showing in the nostrils. He started to ask about her and then thought better; perhaps by now she had died. Had there been children? He could not recall.

"You remember Tony? My son Tony?"

He would not have to fumble after all. "I certainly do," he said heartily. "How is Tony doing these days?"

"Dead," said Amos McBane. "Korean War."

Ryan cleared his throat and wiped off the smile at the same time. "I'm sorry to hear that."

"Lord's will, I suppose," said Mr. McBane. There may have been a small secret doubt in his voice, but he was fighting it. "John Anderson. You recall him. He was in your class in school."

"Yes, I remember him." This time Ryan did not yet smile; he would not be caught off guard a second time.

"Working in the bank."

He let the smile show. "That's good."

"Got three children. You never did get married, did you?"

"No, I never did."

"I always thought you and that library lady would hit it off."

The library lady was Cornelia Satterfield, an old schoolmate to whom people had been trying to marry Ryan for years. He said nothing.

"You going to work in the real estate business now?"

"No, I'm just here for a short visit."

"They could use you. That Travis man lives on the inside of a bottle."

"But Asa says he can sell real estate."

"Matter of no import," snapped McBane. "Wait a minute. I got something for you."

He began to fish in and out of his many pockets, sometimes catching his fingers in the holes. (Mrs. McBane must surely be dead; she would have kept them sewed.) At last he found it, a crumpled and dirty bit of paper which he laid out in one tremulous palm and smoothed down with the other hand.

"Never hurts to be reminded," he chortled, glancing up at Ryan, fixing the paper to his satisfaction, finally holding it out with a toothless gape that was meant for a smile of charity. I'm glad I won't get to be that old, thought Ryan sharply. He gave a polite nod and took the paper from him. "Good salesmen don't counteract bad drinkers," said Mr. McBane, going back to the talk about Mr. Travis.

Seven Steps to Salvation, the little folder said. Mr. McBane stood on the concrete, wheezing, eyes wrinkled against the sun, watching Ryan's face as if for a sudden sign. Ryan nodded to the old man in what he hoped was an encouraging fashion. Seven days; seven deadly sins; The Seven Against Thebes. He shushed the periphery Ryan and concentrated on the pamphlet.

The paper contained seven Bible verses, leading all the way from a conviction of sin and its punishment to acceptance and conversion. "The wages of sin is death," said the first step in menacing capitals.

(Seven angels holding seven vials.)

Ryan nodded to Mr. McBane again, mostly because he could not think of anything to say. "Thank you," he said finally. "Thank you very much."

"You got to shake off the infection of the world," McBane persisted, catching onto his sleeve.

"That's right," said Ryan uncomfortably. "I'll do that."

He remembered the many times he had heard Amos McBane "testify" at spring revival meetings and the way people had glanced patiently at one another whenever he got up to recount again the story of his conversion, quite as enthusiastically as if it had just occurred. McBane would always stand there throbbing and sighing, and behind him his fat little wife would repeat in a bored monotone, "Amen, Lord. I say Amen," until he was finished. People were rather proud of them as if they were organists or evangelistic singers, as if they were trained performers.

"No man can serve two masters," McBane cried now to no one in particular. He had begun to edge away, still talking aloud until it was doubtful if he remembered Ryan was there at all. "Confess with thy mouth," he muttered darkly. "Except a man be born again . . ."

He had shuffled off in an instant into the crowd, still reciting the verses, and at his side the black cane dragged unnoticed, making a scraping noise. Ryan put the piece of paper into his pocket. Seven steps, the seventh day, the seventh commandment. That would be adultery. He stopped the line of thought firmly.

When he walked on toward the center of town, he remembered Lady Malveena had told him Asa had come uptown to the realty office. He thought he might find her now and ride home in the ancient Buick automobile whenever she was going. He had not been in the real estate office since it had changed locations.

He was not sure where it was, so he checked it in a telephone book. *Gaskill, Godwin, and Travis, Real-Estate,* the book said.

Palmer Building. This made him smile. The Palmer Building was an ancient structure with a drugstore on the first floor and a few cramped offices upstairs. It was dim and the halls were always full of people with toothaches. The address looked quite regal in print somehow. It sounded much newer, much more elegant.

When he stood before it, however, it was as he remembered—only a seedy brick building (that peculiar wine-red brick of older buildings, painted perhaps?), and the great black lettering of DRUGS which had been installed the year he left was shabby. Half the G was gone.

He went up the dark stairs and each one gave, groaning, to the pressure of his foot. They were old and wooden, and in the center of each a valley had been worn.

Upstairs he found the same dark halls with the swinging light-bulbs making things dim and flickered-yellow, the old-fashioned office doors along the hall with the gold and black lettering which was stuck on from the inside and sometimes peeled off if a careless job were done. The doors said: NICHOLS, DENTIST. They said: PRIVATE. They said: JOHN MOLTIN, PHOTOGRAPHER. Finally one of them said GASKILL, GODWIN, AND TRAVIS, and that one he opened.

It was a cranny of a waiting room with a cracked green leather chair and a two-year-old issue of *Life* magazine dated December, 1952, and one ashtray on a stand. On the wall hung a map of Stone County drawn with seventeenth century flourishes by a local artist. There wasn't much room for anything else. A door stood open into an inner room and in it a short dark man glanced up from behind a desk without much interest. He looked at Ryan over the rim of a paper cup, and a bottle of familiar shape and flatness stood on the desk at his elbow where he had just put it down. In the small waiting room which was very hot Ryan could smell it strongly.

"I'm mostly the janitor, but I'll do as well as anybody," said the man behind the desk. He kept the paper cup to his face like a shield, although he did not seem to be drinking. "What do you want to do, sell high or buy cheap?"

Ryan took a doubtful step toward the inner office. He had seldom heard a man talk so rapidly; when the stream began again he stopped just on the threshold not at all sure if he should go inside. Asa was obviously not here, he thought. She would have put an end to all this chatter.

"Or are you selling something yourself? Calendars? Pocket testaments? You look a little like the type. Full of intensity." The man took another swallow from his cup (still not having taken it down from his face) and squinted past it. "Well!" he cried. "Are you going to come in or aren't you?" He drained the cup and put it onto the desk with a little click, giving a last sad look inside. "Let's talk about cholera in Asia," he finished in an unhappy voice. "Or the germ propensities of houseflies. Or do you talk at all? You'll never sell anything that way."

Ryan went on into the office, but not very comfortably. This is my morning, he thought, for characters. He edged into the other chair in the small room and then looked up to see the man full face for the first time. There was something of a shock involved in that. He had never seen an uglier man than the queer hunched hoptoad grumbling behind the desk. His hair was thin, not adequate for the head, and his nose was long. He looked as if he would have been more at home running a Greek hashhouse in an army town, or a pawnshop, or a watch repair place at the end of a dark alley.

The man said, "Can I, after all, sell you something? Nice shoebox-size house in a development? Piece of land with no frontage? Swamp? Lovely eroded hillside site?"

"I'm Ryan Godwin. . . ."

"Not another one," sighed the hoptoad man, and he shuddered, pouring some raw whiskey into the cup and downing it with a wince and a frown. "As you can see," he said confidingly, "I am now trying to forget the visit of the first Godwin who was just in, that veritable Gorgon. You aren't her husband, are you? Maybe been locked in the attic for twenty years?" He shook his head wisely, like a man containing secrets. "No, that one wouldn't have a husband. But my God, Godwin . . ." (at this he stopped in delighted surprise). "Did you hear that? My God, Godwin! That's pretty good, isn't it? I'm a genius under the influence."

"Asa's gone, then?" Ryan was making a desperate effort to keep the conversation under some sort of control. And the little man in his skull was asking: *Why does this fellow talk so much so fast?*

"Out the window on a broomstick, I suppose," said the other. "I don't suppose you'd care to join me in a toast to her memory or some other convenient excuse?"

"If it wasn't so early in the day . . ." said Ryan half apologetically.

The ugly man sat up very straight. "You mean you Godwins

drink at all? Startling thought. First thing you know you'll destroy the legend, have me believing you go to the bathroom, too. Eliminate just like ordinary beings." He subsided into bitterness. "That would be a hell of a note," he confided to the bottle on his desk.

"I've just had breakfast," Ryan said again. He always felt embarrassed when he was the only sober one in a room—any room.

"Don't you pay any attention to those W.C.T.U. rumors." The hoptoad man leaned, or rather spread out loosely, in a confiding way across the desk. "The first thing to do is to drink alone so you won't talk too much or get in any fights. The second thing is to drink first thing in the morning so the day is halfway bearable."

I ought to give him Amos McBane's pamphlet, Ryan thought with a grin. But I don't believe at this point he could manage Seven Steps to anywhere.

The other man had barely paused in his talking. "I think I know who started those old saws about drinking alone and before noon anyway," he said angrily. "I tell you who it was, it was the dirty Communists, and I'm all for fighting an ideology like that. Irreparable harm." He took up the bottle fondly and held it like a torch. Then he grinned. "Did that pretty well, didn't I?" he said. "Think I'll run for the Senate. I oughta be great on TV."

"You're Mr. Travis, aren't you?"

The ugly man shook his head, which was a bad idea because he had a hard time getting it still again. Ryan had spread out a little in his chair, matched the other's friendly look. The thought of Asa having to cope with such a man filled him with dark pleasure.

"Somebody's been telling those ugly stories that Travis drinks again. No, I'm not, but I knew the boy, that Travis," the man was saying, "knew him well in the days before evil living got him. Shadow of his former self. Gone to pot. Gone to the dogs. Gone to hell and back to cool his burning feet." He added in a friendly manner, "It's not very good liquor, but it's all I could get last week."

This made Ryan remember that Stoneville and Stone County were very dry, so that a man bought what he could from bootleggers and cab drivers when they made the rounds on Thursday.

The man said vaguely, "This fellow Travis, he meant well, you understand. Had a good mind once. Used to keep it honed like an expensive tool." He shifted attention abruptly. "What in hell would any man come back to Stoneville for? You're Asa's brother, and why would you come back to this putrid town?

"I don't know myself," said Ryan honestly. "I take it you don't like Stoneville much."

"Putrid," said the man. "Putrid town." He patted the bottle gently, as if it might have been a well-loved dog. "Hot as hell," he whispered, presumably to the bottle. "Must be over ninety-five in here today."

"Why do you stay here if you dislike it so much?"

Travis looked a little startled; glanced at Ryan as if he had just now noticed he was there. "What was that?"

"I said if you don't like it, why do you stay here?"

The man frowned, looked glumly at the desk. "Foolish question," he muttered. "No place else to go."

"What a crazy idea!" To his own amazement, Ryan had grown angry, even though he felt no good could come of arguing. It seemed doubly important to refute this point of view, because it was so closely akin to something someone else had said, a long time ago.

The man on the other side of the desk looked at him intently. "I am very ugly," he said.

At this Ryan felt both furious and helpless. He scolded about like a chicken, like a schoolmarm, making motions with his hands. "That's crazy. That's an excuse. It's not even a good excuse."

"It's an external fact."

"But not all facts have equal importance. And that one isn't of very much importance."

Now the other man was angry. "Spoken like a man who doesn't have the problem. How tall are you, six feet? A little over? How fat? How old?" He lifted his bottle as though he might—pushed far enough—throw the damn thing.

His last question Ryan answered. "Forty-eight," he said. But the periphery Ryan probed at the problem of ugliness and whether Travis was lying.

"And all that hair yours? How long's your nose?" Then Travis shrugged and lowered his voice. "You're the reasonable type," he said with less anger. "I hate reasonable men myself." He put the bottle down again and taking his own hand like a gavel, pounded halfheartedly on the desk's surface. "Untrue to the spirit of the age, that's what you are. Don't you know this is a day in which we coddle all our weaknesses, lay them out on dimpled leather couches, give them the pretty old Greek names?"

"The purpose of psychiatry," said Ryan, "is not to coddle but to help us understand."

Travis laughed. "I can see we're in for some red-hot arguments on that score. I know your type—you'll argue from first principles; I'll argue from present practice. If you were leftist you'd talk about Engles and Marx and Lenin; but I'd keep yelling about the Soviet State."

Now Ryan laughed too. "That *is* a fault of mine," he admitted. "Everybody says so. Everybody says I do that." He and Jim had shared some strong arguments because of that.

"Hell, you're the teacher, aren't you? Don't you teach some place?"

"Used to. Maybe I will again. Occupational hazard, you mean?"

"Sometimes. You know that fellow Travis we were talking about? That sharp boy gone downhill? Did you know he used to teach?"

"I've never met him."

"Needn't bother. He's a husk. He's a widower, too—did you know that?"

"No, I haven't . . ."

"Won't get him to tell you. Reticent. The man has his secrets. Fancies himself an eighteenth-century wit, or did at one time. Always used to tell the clever anecdotes at parties. Knew a lot of amazing facts and biographies. Turned out none of it was much value to him in the end, but all the couch-sitters and glass-holders in that town—they remember him, I guess."

"I think . . ."

"His ghost hangs in a thousand living rooms. His breath—just faintly alcoholic, he didn't overdrink in those days—whispers all manner of interesting junk. He used to talk a lot about man and society. Do you have any opinions on man and society?"

"Well, I sometimes . . ."

Travis dismissed these with a snort. "This boy could also talk about Velikovsky's stuff and Lecomte de Nouy ad infinitum. All that stuff goes great with the chaise-longue thinkers, you know. The coffee-spoon intellects."

"That's T. S. Eliot." Ryan threw the words desperately. He felt he had to get into the monologue somehow.

At this the fellow roared with such laughter that he seemed about to weep. "I caught you there!" he crowed. "I see you know the parlor game yourself. The game is to see how many books and names and theories you *recognize*. The game is to quote bits of poetry. The game is to tell intimate stories about James Joyce and the Marquis de Sade and Arnold Toynbee. Don't bother reading them. Just know the edges, the fringes. The embroidery. People will ask you to parties. They'll say: Mr. so-and-so is *such* an interesting man." He grew sad. His ugly face crumbled. "I ask you, friend—I ask you, why do we have so many automobile accidents? Do you know how many people are killed that way? Have you heard about that? Does it bother you?"

Ryan had given up trying to talk. He leaned back in his chair and watched and listened. A widower. How long? he wondered. Something special there?

"I sit in this office and I look down on this little town, on Main Street in Stoneville five and one half days out of every week. I look down like God out of Heaven, except hotter. (This is the worst August I've ever seen.) And I tell you, Mr. Godwin, if I could answer six or seven questions I would be able to understand the world in 1954. All of the world in this particular year. And that's one of the questions. Why are we all dying so much and nobody paying any attention?"

Ryan had followed the other's gaze to the window and the open Venetian blind. He saw the sun hot on the Beacon Building across the square and he didn't feel like God looking from Heaven. He felt a little sleepy.

The man behind the desk looked offended. "You listening to me? You want to hear the other questions?"

Ryan said he certainly did.

The man half stood, frowned, and sat again gingerly in the chair. He recited:

"If Billy Graham and Joe McCarthy and Herman Talmadge died tomorrow, would anything change? I'll answer that one—not really. There are always more of them. Can we take Darwin and Einstein and Freud and the death of God in stride and still affirm that life has value and beauty? That isn't original, that's Gide. Is it conceivable that war can be stopped by some silly simple way, such as if women withheld sex as in the old play, or if everywhere all the little people in the world say they are too busy growing wheat and having babies to be bothered fighting each other? Is it possible that there is only one comfort in the world—the comfort of continuity—which means no more than that I will die and someone else will be born?

Why are love and honesty so difficult?" He paused, grinned. "That's quite a feat, reciting all of that, considering I was sober when I memorized it. Six questions. The Mastery of Life—like the Rosicrucians—for this point in time anyway. You want to answer any of them?"

"Not today," said Ryan. "But I think sometime I'd like to hear . . ."

"Me do the answering? That's beyond my function, sir. The Day of the Specialist. I only pose the problems. Typical professor. You ought to know that. Used to teach yourself, didn't you?"

Ryan thought of part of one of the questions and of another Fen had asked him. "Is God dead then?" he said.

"Not here," said the man. He almost exploded it. "You know how when you bury the dead, sometimes the hair goes on growing long after life is gone and gone. That's the way Stoneville is. Stoneville and lots of other little towns like it—Stoneville is the hair on God's head."

That was too much to comment on.

In another minute the man said, "I'll not remember that tomorrow. That's pretty good. I wish you'd tell me that tomorrow."

"If I see you," Ryan said. "Do you think Asa will be back any time today?"

"My God, I hope not! That negation of woman! Did she hatch from an egg? What time is it?"

"No. Eleven. Little past."

"I think you're the only good Godwin I've met. Good Godwin—I've done it again. What a marvel of speech! Good Godwin—it may sweep the world of profanity. That would be a timeless contribution to make to the progress of man."

Ryan was grinning; he stood up. "I'm going now."

"That's good. You've made me tired. I hurt in the vocal chords."

So do I, thought Ryan; but he did not dwell on it. That was another subject.

The man was squinting to read the print on the whiskey label. "You know what this says? This label?"

Ryan considered. It maybe said Life. Power. Money. It maybe said Forgetfulness. He took the periphery man and shoved him out of sight, under the thalamus.

"What?" he asked.

"Hell, that's the seventh question! I wish you'd go home. You tax my conversation."

"Impossible. Good-by," said Ryan.

Ryan went out through the tiny waiting room and into the hall with some relief. A colored man was sweeping greasy dust and empty cigarette packs in the hallway; he bobbed his head respectfully. Behind him Ryan thought he heard the first of Mr. Travis' snores. The man slept soundly, like someone who has been up and down mountains.

Whew! Ryan thought, hearing it. I'm pretty damn tired myself. Where did they latch onto that one? He must be too much for Asa.

The steps were dark but the heat rose toward him tangibly, and outside he could see the fierce sunlight on the street. It was a hot day to be drunk, he thought.

And he had walked halfway home, wondering about the ugly man and where he had come from and why before he thought of his throat at all. That was the longest lapse of time he had spent without thinking of it, one way or another, since Jim had first given him the news.

At this Ryan felt proud of himself, like a fingernail biter who has spent the morning in abstinence.

But it proved nothing, no more than Travis' drunken questions had proved anything. Travis was talking his way through something; Ryan was thinking his way through something else.

People keep their heads above water in different ways, he thought.

5.

No ONE was home when Ryan returned to the house. Asa was still uptown somewhere and Fen was out back. Ryan thought about walking down to the orchard to talk with Fen but then he felt he had no business going yet, that he would wait until he was invited. He could still remember times when the interest of adults had seemed to him a perpetual invasion, made without honor.

He stood at the kitchen window and watched the boy in the orchard, watched him climb one tree and come back down again, sit in the grass, walk in this direction and that, all without any apparent plan to it.

"What's he doing?"

Lady Malveena shrugged. "I'm too old to remember," she said.

He stood at the window a little longer, trying to remember what he had done when he was twelve, what thoughts had passed through his mind on such a day as this. Finally he gave it up and turned, shrugging, toward the little library which opened off the hall.

It was the very thought of himself as once awkward and skinny and twelve years old that sent him curiously into the library, that musty old room that nobody used now, even Asa. The mere opening of the door seemed to shatter dust all ways into the room and he put his arm against his eyes.

Sharply then, with the dark against his eyes and the feel of the door jamb and the remembered smell of the small room, he remembered that first time—when he and Jessica had blundered together in the darkness in this room, so that all his good intent had gone for nothing, and they had kissed each other for the first time among the dust and the books.

Those thoughts he pushed away. He reached again for the small-boy days he had been thinking off; and when he took his arm away and could really see the room it was easier. Only in this room did Ryan have any real memory of his father. He had almost always seen him there, in the evenings, working.

And now as he pushed the door back and stepped inside he half expected to see his father rise from the chair (a leather chair that had always smelled terribly of tobacco and sweat and dogs just in from rain) in the old way, and peer at him pettishly—also in the old way—through the gloom.

"Yes? Yes, what is it?" His father would have been chirping at him impatiently (he always did), looking as though he had been disturbed in the most important of all tasks and if things should now go wrong he would know exactly who to blame for it. His father had been large of head and very bald; he had looked like the Mad Scientist in later comic strips.

Ryan came on into the room and put a hand on the back of the chair where, in years past, Flambert Godwin had so often leaned that bare pink head, his eyes closed, finger tips resting together, as he added long columns of figures in silence. He had done mental arithmetic all his life and to it he attributed his success; it was a form of exercise for using all his thinking muscles. His father had thought of the brain more or less as a larger and grayer bicep, needing only regular contracting and releasing to make it stronger.

Of Flambert Godwin's children, only Asa resembled him—inside and out.

Asa would have been bald herself had she been a man, and even now her hair, gray and sensible, was thin and seemed to be pasted carelessly onto the scalp. Their father had always been suspicious of men who kept their hair to any age. They were likely to be imbeciles, he had always said, with all that growth to sap their mental strength. He liked the look of flesh on the head, unimpeded by decoration and covering with bare practicality the pulsing and tensing which went on underneath.

In his later days he had been fond of saying, "Hair is vestigial, like the third eye," and pursing his lips and raising his brows while he dared anyone to disagree.

Ryan was fairer than Asa and his father; he was very much taller; and Avery had also been fair but inclined to pudginess.

Ryan started slightly when he realized that Lady Malveena was standing behind him, had been standing there for some time.

"The invention of the cleared throat was for courtesy purposes," said Ryan drily.

Lady Malveena put one long brown finger on his forehead briefly. "Don't get skotchy," she said. "I couldn't hear nothing but the wheels going round and the gears running together." She made a face into the old library. "What a mess."

"This room stay closed up all the time now?"

She nodded. Her eyes were going from object to object with the certainty of dustcloths. When she glanced toward the ceiling he saw her give an angry mental swish at all the cobwebs.

"Why don't you clean it up?"

"*Hah!*" said Lady Malveena. "Why don't I sell houses and sleep in the front bedroom! 'Cause I'm me and not her, that's why!" She could not bear it; one hand went out almost involuntarily to test the dust on the woodwork by the door. She spat on her dirty fingers and wiped them angrily onto her apron—on the underside. "You think she'd have a plain broom come in here? A plain old ninety-five-cent broom?"

"I suppose not."

"What you looking for in here, anyway?"

"Nothing. Just looking *at*," he said. "These books are still good. Somebody ought to make use of them."

"Fen gets a book to read now and then." Lady Malveena gave him a sly look. "Fen's a smart boy for his age."

Ryan said nothing to that.

"Oh well." Lady Malveena was good-humored. She grinned at him. "You'll see," she said. If it was a threat, there was fondness in it. She turned and went through the dining room toward the kitchen, humming. It was completely tuneless; she sounded like a buzzsaw with good intentions.

Ryan went on inside the small library which had been his father's and closed the door behind him.

The books were arranged in the little room as in the same patterns: worn Greek grammars (another kind of exercise but not so successful; the Greeks told too many silly stories) and finance magazines and banking journals (his father had longed for Wall Street as some men seek Paradise); books on interest and tax and one whole shelf of biographies. Ryan glanced at them now and they were the ones he remembered, the ones he had been made to read: Theodore Roosevelt, Jefferson Davis, Plutarch's *Lives*, Oliver Cromwell. There were also an unread Shakespeare and a leather-bound Bible, placed respectfully together because they came in the category of books that everyone should have. His father had read the Bible but not Shakespeare. Nearby, too, were a dictionary, an exposé of the flaws in astrology and phrenology, one odd volume of Herbert Spencer's works, and a copy of *Tom Jones* which Ryan felt certain his father had never opened.

Ryan himself had used this room many times since Flambert Godwin's death but it had kept the stamp of his father's personality always upon it. Asa maintained it like a shrine, dusty but revered. She would not throw anything away. When Ryan had used it for study on college vacations, Asa had gone up and down the hall outside the door, worrying.

In the days when Flambert Godwin was newly dead, Asa would come to sit in the smelly leather chair herself (looking quite strange, looking very out-of-place) and bask in the atmosphere of strength and practicality she believed was there, and contagious. But later the room came to embarrass her slightly because she was not a man and it was not the same, so it had grown darker and dustier with years. If it was a shrine, it was surely an unwilling one.

His father, thought Ryan now, had made them what they were—but not directly. How neatly he had planned their lives for them: Asa to be a mid-Victorian sampler worker, reading aloud light poetry in the afternoon as she aged delicately, and turning out all her days the most exquisite forget-me-nots in dainty linen corners. And he, Ryan, to grow stubbornly into the shrewd businessman who would make and break large fortunes without a flicker, a perpetual Frank Norris money-man, perpetually cornering the market. He would have sent many telegrams and moved in worlds of men and orders and deadlines, and no one would have been able to cheat the son of Flambert Godwin.

Why, thought Ryan now in some surprise, Why, how I hated him!

When Asa opened the door and spoke to him, he started guiltily.

"It's dark in here," she said.

"I didn't know you were back from town," he said. "It's dirty. You ought to let Lady Malveena clear this junk away."

This she ignored. Asa never answered remarks on which she felt her position to be already clear.

"You'll go to services tonight, Ryan," she stated matter-of-factly, and added, "if only for the boy's sake."

Services? Then Ryan remembered it was Wednesday—Prayer Meeting night in Stoneville ever since he could remember—and he had not been to prayer meeting since his college days.

He said quickly, "Not tonight, Asa." He knew now she had walked into the room with an argument waiting on her tongue.

As a matter of fact, Asa had already turned and was walking away into the hall, so sure she was. When Ryan spoke she halted, and if a backbone could have registered sheer indignation, Asa's did so now. She came back and frowned at him. Her words were poised and ready but she had expected not to need them. She had thought he would simply nod his head; Asa expected everyone to nod his head. That was her vision of a suitable world.

"See here," she said now, "there are things I won't have you do while you're here, Ryan, and one is to influence the boy. I won't have you bothering his foundation. What you think is what you think—I've had no part in that for a long time. But I've put ten years in him and you can't undo it in one summer visit even if you try. But I don't want him upset. I won't have him bothered."

"What you must think of me!" said Ryan in real surprise. He was beginning to understand why Fen had looked for scars and tattoos. "But he's young, you know, Asa. Something will bother him sooner or later."

"Only temptation, and he's braced for that." Asa's lips clicked shut decisively so that she reminded him for all the world of a snapping turtle. A small one, but sharp of tooth.

"Am I temptation?" He asked it teasingly.

"It's hard to say. You might be." Asa was not at all embarrassed by saying this; in fact, now that it was said she looked as though her duty was altogether done. She stepped back into the library and looked around her, putting the first subject aside.

"Whatever are you doing in here, anyway? I've never seen so much dust." She lifted one hand and waved it ineffectually in the air like a small flag.

"Looking around. When you came in, as a matter of fact, I had been wondering about what Father was really like."

Asa said firmly that Ryan ought to know *that,* at least. She turned to the bookshelves, ran her finger lightly along the old dark bindings. "He used to sit in here till past midnight," she said, half to herself. "A smart man," she added.

Ordinarily Ryan might have quarreled with that but he knew by now there was no need getting involved with Asa defining terms.

It was, however, as if she had read his mind. "Oh, I know you never thought so." She gave him an angry look. "Anybody could have told that. You were the scholar of the family; you never let us forget it after you went away to college!" (Her voice was bitter; he wondered, Was I that bad?) "But Father had qualities you've always lacked. And since you lacked them, you've never given them much value." She began to enumerate, still touching rather gently the row of dusty books. "He was practical. Progressive. He took some interest in this community instead of just criticizing it, like you always have. He was a churchman and a leader. You never thought he was smart because he'd rather add up expenses than read philosophy, but I say he was smarter than you are. He knew his limitations and was content to live within them."

Inside himself Ryan said to Ryan: I know my limitations! And I keep learning more about them! But to Asa he said nothing.

She said, "Father was a remarkable man."

Ryan nodded. He was embarrassed, seeing Asa's loyalty to her father against the background of the knowledge that Flambert Godwin had not really cared for her much. She had made him ill at ease because she had his own temperament. He was a businessman; it was not thinkable that a woman—especially his own daughter—should also be a businessman. That was to be Ryan's vocation.

But here they were, years later, each gone his own way. Ryan watched his sister, feeling the same sadness that had touched him when he first came up the walk and to the house. Why were things thus? Had he been so insufferable and snobbish with Asa? And she, at what point had she stopped not only being feminine but even being flexible?

She met his gaze head on. She always had. "You never understood Father as I did," she said, "but he was a fine man and a credit to everything he did."

The periphery Ryan was perched in one temple, analyzing them both; he could not be angry. "Father and I were different. It doesn't mean that one of us was all right and the other was all wrong," he said very carefully.

Asa looked proud and fierce. "At least I've done what he wanted, been what he wanted. You couldn't even do that much for him."

She actually believed that. "It was no secret I disappointed him," said Ryan.

"That's right, it wasn't."

"I did what I had to with my life. People do, you know, Asa. Most people." He added gently, "So will Fen."

But Asa's chin went up like a bird beak. "Fenwick seems to have made his decision. We think he has The Call."

"The call?" It made him think vaguely of a rush trip to the bathroom.

"The ministry. Edward Barnes has been a big influence on his life." That made her veer back to their original discussion. "And I won't have you spoiling it either, Ryan Godwin, just because there's things and people you can't understand about."

Ryan was disgusted. He had disliked Edward Barnes with consistency for years. "Is Barnes still here?"

Asa's expression showed that she plainly despaired of him. He had not appreciated their father's virtue. What could he know of a man like the Reverend Barnes?

"I tell you this, Ryan," she said, "if trouble ever comes in your life, you'll learn to appreciate a man like Edward Barnes! He has things to stand on, strength to sustain him, values you've never dreamed about!" And because Asa was partial to Barnes, had always felt they were as nearly soul mates as she could reach, she stood there with her anger gone to pinpoints in her eyes.

If trouble ever came in his life! That was a fine thing to say to him now! Ryan was getting angry in spite of himself.

He said irritably that if she meant Barnes could escape from feeling life too deeply or letting it bother him too much, that was right, of course. "Barnes can always project everything out into the ether and let God and the Devil explain it away. The type of religion Barnes has takes all the burden off man, but it takes all the responsibility off him, too." In his mind the vision of Barnes, with his belly like a summertime robin, rose and hung—disagreeably.

"Oh, Ryan." Asa was angry with him, but it was from a vast distance; it was down from the towers of the elect. "Let's don't discuss it. All I really care about is that you won't upset the boy." She turned, started out the door again.

But his annoyance was too far gone. "This Call," he said, "this wonderful Call—it's a fine example of ventriloquism, you know."

Asa closed the door sharply and the dust puffed out in all directions.

Left alone, Ryan half expected to hear from the depths of the cracked chair a dry remark from Flambert Godwin: "You and your sister, always quarreling. Here, calm yourself. Find me the cube root of three thousand seven."

Oh, damn the cube root, thought Ryan petulantly to the empty room.

He went back out to the kitchen where Lady Malveena was cooking dried apples for the apple pies. She stirred carefully into the pot as though she had not heard him enter, as though—in fact—she seldom heard anything.

"Don't be coy," snapped Ryan. "You know you caught every word of that."

She was unconcerned. "Never said I didn't. Quarreling before meals makes a sour stomach at bedtime. Never say I didn't warn you." She turned and shook a dripping spoon and then replaced it hastily when she saw it was spotting the floor. "No point you two fussing anyhow," she said over her shoulder. "Not since you was both little. There's never any end to it—just a stopping till the next time. You never meet, you and Miss Asa. Some roads don't, you know."

Ryan shrugged. He said after a while, "I haven't seen Miss Clara all day."

"She went upstairs. She's got a earache."

"A what?"

"Earache, she says."

He remembered then that Miss Clara had no social disease such as the convenient headache or allergy but had—in her own logical fashion—surmised that her weakest point was the ears, and that no one would question any ailment connected with them. Thereafter she developed some form of ear trouble whenever she wished to be left alone, either to nap or to play at full shriek a small radio propped up against her head or cheat her way through solitaire, which she played very badly. Once Ryan had thought of teaching her a game she might play in company with someone else; they had tried gin rummy. But Miss Clara had been insulated against the world too long; the thought of exchanging anything with it, whether love or hatred or responsibility, was not understandable to her. He wondered now if she had ever been young or slender or involved in anything—if she might perhaps have wept nights over some mustachioed young man she could not have and whose voice she would never even hear.

But he could not imagine it. He could imagine her days stretching back and back, never any different from these.

He said absent-mindedly, "What time is lunch?"

Lady Malveena took offense. "Soon as it's ready, I suspect," she said, cutting her eyes around at him. "Was you aiming to fix it yourself if you got hungry before then?"

It's not my day, he thought.

"Is Fen still down there in the orchard?" He squinted through the kitchen window but was not able to see him.

"He was a minute past," said Lady Malveena shortly.

"I don't see him."

"Likely he's down in the grasses."

"Oh."

He stood there another minute and thought that, after all, he might go outside and look around. It had been a long time. Lady Malveena was telling Mister Lord that it was a shame when a man had to have his life sitting on the mantelpiece, with all the minutes marked. She said hurrying brought the grave nigh to hand if that was what you were after. She said as far as she was concerned that last six foot was a long step down.

Ryan went out the door and down the back steps and stood in the yard, stood in that hard packed earth that was lined by Lady Malveena's broom, and saw that everything was just as he remembered except more seedy, and a little smaller.

Off the back porch led the hallway to the Second House, where

Lady Malveena lived; and in the main back yard nothing grew from much walking, except at the edges where the tall brown grass began. It was like a fringe of hair circling an enormous baldness.

The fence at the back had warped and rusted and leaned down. Ryan could remember when his father had first ordered it put in; it had seemed handsome to him then, shiny and painted black, and it had been taller than he was. Now it was bent almost down and in another year or two it would settle and the grass would grow up between the rails and hide it.

The carriage house (how many afternoons had they played there —Avery and he and Asa) was leaning slightly off-center and seemed to be supported only by the matting of ivy which grew on it in all directions and held it down like tent ropes in a wind. He remembered the balls they had thrown across that roof to each other. He remembered hide-and-seek and home base late in the evening among the lightning bugs. He frowned. Had there not been roses? Somewhere in all that mass of ivy?

After another minute he walked over and pushed open the door to the carriage house and blinked in the gloom. It was empty now except for dust and iron hoops hung up on nails and in one corner a heap of all manner of junk, including an old belt, two rusted buckets, screws and dirty jam jars, and the remnant of a Chinese screen he could not remember having ever seen before.

Ryan went back outside and tried the back gate, which flaked off in dark red rust against his palms and did not move. He bent it back until he could step over, and walked out into the field where the grass was already August-dry and came up to his knees.

A perfect place for snakes, he thought, watching his feet.

At the far end of the field the grape arbor grew, looking weedy now, rundown, unproductive. Fen said at least that Lady Malveena still made wine. Ryan could remember her slipping down on long-ago nights, gathering the fruit under the moon, talking to herself. She said the moonlight helped make that wine smooth and evil, and from that brewing Mister Lord was always excluded.

"There was Cana and the wedding feast," she'd say, "and us Christians ain't going to quibble about that." Then she might add, enviously, "*Hah!* He even made it out of water!"

Once Asa had tried to grow a garden on this land. The finest in the neighborhood, she always said, but actually it had been only passable and the corn was always spindly. Asa had none of the patience of a farmer. Whenever seeds failed to sprout into perfect plants, her attitude was one of accusation. Well, she seemed to say angrily, there was rain and soil and sunshine—what more did they want?

Ryan stopped near the first tree in the orchard. It had caterpillars now; that seemed to him especially horrible and he did not want to look at it. He called aloud.

"Fen? Fen, are you here?"

The boy's dark head bobbed like a cork to the surface of the grass. "Here I am. Over here."

Who'd want to lie in these weeds with maybe a dozen snakes around? thought Ryan, heading that way. But he had never once thought of snakes when he had come and sat in these same places.

The boy sat up and watched him curiously. "Hello," he said.

Ryan came near and—glancing down apprehensively—sat in the grass beside him. "Hello. It's hot down here."

"It's hot everywhere." Fen's voice was always very careful, very polite. It was the voice of all boys who have been brought up exclusively by women, Ryan thought.

Then it occurred to him that boys such as Fen had retreats such as these just so they could get away and not have to make foolish conversation with adults about the weather. He said now, hastily, "I only wanted to see how things looked down here. I won't stay long."

But Fen smiled so that crinkles appeared at his eyes and a dip came in his cheek and Ryan thought: *How much like her he is!* And he began to doubt the very existence of snakes, watching Fen smile.

Fen said, "I don't want you to go. I've been wondering where you were all morning."

Ryan lay back in the grass and put his arms beneath his head and closed his eyes. Fen's face was too familiar. It was a hurt to his eye.

"I used to come here myself sometimes," he said dreamily. "I've been uptown. Had a terrible morning, in fact. I seem to be quarreling with everyone, even strangers."

Fen nodded, soberly.

"Well, not with you at any rate, I hope," said Ryan.

"Oh, *no* sir."

The orchard was quiet, restful. There were no sounds louder than crickets and the click of grass blades springing back up by his head. Ryan felt as though he were being actually rejuvenated by the stillness and the sun, as if self were flowing back into self so that somewhere an inner dialogue was taking place:

Where have you been so long?
Oh, here and there. Running about the world.
A *little tired?*
Quite right, a little tired.

He had to smile at this fancy of such an impeccable welcome, like the reunion of two European aristocrats, for he was not like that at all—whole or in halves. Even the little man at the periphery was not like that.

Fen said abruptly in a stage whisper, "Have you gone to sleep, Uncle Ryan?"

He opened his eyes and squinted in the sun again. "No, but I'm likely to. It's so quiet here." He thought a minute and then added seriously, "If there was one thing I could pick up and carry away from Stoneville, it would be this—this orchard and sun and a day like this one feels. I'd like to keep a thing like that handy."

Fen said, probing, "Asa says life is miserable in a big city." He leaned forward so that his face came suddenly under tree shadow and grew dappled, like a fawn.

"No more than anywhere," said Ryan lazily. "People are happy in cities, too."

"Were you?"

He lay quite still, thinking about it. "Most of the time," he said finally.

Fen took up a grass blade, put it between his two upper teeth and began to move it back and forth in the small space there.

"And were you happy here? In Stoneville?"

"Sometimes." He looked at the boy closely. "Are you?"

"Oh, yes. I guess so," said Fen. In a few more minutes he added, "School isn't much."

"It gets better as you go along," Ryan said.

"I hope so."

"College isn't bad."

"You say that because you're a *teacher*. I might like any kind of school if I was a teacher."

Ryan grinned. "Good point."

"Aunt Asa said you might do some writing while you were here. What kind of writing?"

"I don't know." He was annoyed. "Asa always takes a sentence like that too literally."

"Are you going to write a book?"

Was he, really? He had often thought about trying that. Time—always there was time to remember and reckon with. Starting a book might be a promise of some kind, a superstition which would bring him good luck. But under such peaceful August sun, he did not want to think of that. "I might," he said.

Through half-closed eyes he looked across at Fen's face and saw that the boy was thinking deeply, creasing up his brow. My God, he's working at making conversation with me, Ryan thought, and it ought to be the other way around.

He said, gaining momentum as he went along, "I've missed out on a lot of your years, Fen. I wish you'd tell me about yourself. That's a silly way to ask it because it embarrasses you to start. But I wish you would. What do you remember from when you were little, for instance?"

Her face? he wondered. The hair? That small tired mouth? Do you recall Miss Clara in the parlor smelling flowers warped about in wreaths?

"I don't remember you," said Fen apologetically. "I don't remember much before first grade."

Ryan was relieved.

"I remember you've always sent me presents. Real nice things. I remember the real baseball with the autographs on it, and the chemistry set."

Now all of them seemed to Ryan a shabby lot and he was ashamed.

"I especially liked the chemistry set."

"That's good."

"And I remember Aunt Asa said you would never come back because you had an argument with her. About the funeral."

"I had lots of arguments about it." He felt grim all over again; he felt cold from inside deep. "It was like a carnival in reverse. Deliver me from some of our fine old Southern customs."

Fen was frowning. "She said you wouldn't come by and look at them in the coffins." He had blurted this last, sounding a little angry, sounding as though all his heredity had made him insulted and he had—by proxy—been angry for ten years.

Ryan said as steadily as he could (why had he ever gotten started on this?), "Fen, they were already dead. Everything important was gone. What was there to see?"

At this the boy's face turned a dark red and his jaw congealed in a shape that Ryan had thought he would never see again. "My mother was there!" Fen said angrily. His small fists were tight on the ends of his arms; he looked as though he might leap up and bang his uncle atop the head.

Suddenly Ryan was angry too. He rolled onto his stomach in the grass and he caught the boy's leg cruelly. "Listen," he said (too loudly), "listen, I loved your mother!"

"Did you?" said Fen. The fibers in him let up a little bit.

It was all right; love was still a sexless word—nothing had slipped. Ryan said, still angry, still squeezing the leg, "Yes," and released him and rolled onto his back again and closed his eyes. What a silly business *that* was! he said to himself.

When he spoke again he made his voice as flat as he could.

"For some people, like your Aunt Asa, a funeral is a way of expressing love. Love and loss. But as far as I was concerned, it made everything ugly. It was staged for the benefit of other people—people who hadn't known." And who hadn't loved, and who hadn't lost—he added silently. Inside of him all the old angry seas were moving. How could he say to Fen how it had been? That he could not have looked down into satin at a soap-white brow knowing that when it was warm and pulsing it had lain against his neck. And that he could not see that mouth again (they would have wired it closed and painted it on with care) and remember that his tongue that been on those teeth and round that tongue how many times? And the little breasts gone rigid in death and the thighs stiff and the hair on the belly cold and never to come up and forward again.

And when Ryan thought of all this the floodgates dropped and the sea washed up hot and undiminished as though it were only Tuesday she had died and he were new bereft. Suddenly the August sunshine seared him and the blades of grass were sharp.

And he looked across at Fen and thought to himself, *This is what remains.*

He said, as he had said before except that now his voice was very gentle, "I loved your mother."

"And my daddy?"

"Not the same way and not as much." That, at least, was an honest answer. He lay back and closed his eyes again.

"Why don't you come and live with us? Do you have to go back?"

"I don't know. Perhaps I will." He lay burning in the sun and there was no breeze. In the grass somewhere a cricket cried aloud. "What will you do, Fen? Are you going to stay in Stoneville all your life?"

"I don't know," he said. "I guess so."

"What do you want to do when you finish growing up? Name somebody that you'd like to be."

Fen shifted and flushed, shot him a covert glance. Then he said, "Oh, I don't know. I don't know anybody." He looked terribly embarrassed.

Ryan thought of Asa and he almost ground his teeth. But he said —not changing his tone—"How about Mr. Barnes? Would you like to grow up to be like Mr. Barnes?"

"He's okay, I guess."

Ryan went searching back in his memory for what that kind of answer meant when one was twelve years old. It seemed to him it was a device which sometimes hid too strong a hero worship and sometimes hid a great dislike—but he could not be sure which one this was.

He thought how good it was not to be twelve years old.

"Where did you teach when you lived up North" The tone of Fen's voice made it sound distant and strange and full of arctic weather.

"I taught at a girls' college in Massachusetts. Taught literature." It sounded small when he said it, as if he had mended plumbing or bottled pop.

"Did you like that?"

Ryan felt a slight surprise to realize how much. Jobs were like wives, perhaps; one has to be reminded that the initial stimulus was love. "I liked it very much," he said. "I like telling people what I think about things. It looks as though that's one of my bad qualities you might get too well acquainted with while I'm here."

"Oh, but I like to hear you!" Fen was all protest; he had started up as though he might be called upon to hold his uncle physically from leaving. "I don't get to talk to people much. Aunt Asa's always busy. And I've *told* Lady Malveena everything."

"And Miss Clara's deaf." Ryan said it musingly, to himself.

"Yes sir."

"Do you think you might like to teach someday? Or sell real estate uptown? Or maybe preach like Mr. Barnes?"

There was a silence and one of the peach trees creaked like a tiny door opening.

Then Fen said in a small choked voice, "I'd like to go away. The other doesn't matter much."

Now Ryan was ashamed that he had made the boy say this. At first he reached out a hand to touch him but then he thought better of it. He sat up and felt noisily in his pockets for cigarettes and finally lit one with many unnecessary motions.

"Then you do it, Fen," he said earnestly, making a great rattling with the cellophane. "You do what you want to do." He consulted the grass carefully to make certain the match was out.

Fen stood up and stretched and scuffed one of his feet. He looked into the sky and at the peach tree under it, but not at Ryan's face. And Ryan took the cigarette out of his mouth and frowned at the end of it as though he were daring it not to burn.

"Well," said Fen vaguely, "I don't know."

You don't know what you really owe to Asa, Ryan said silently, and I don't know either.

Fen said, as though one thought had led to the other, "This is Prayer Meeting night."

"Asa told me."

"Are you going?"

Suddenly Ryan was angry in an enveloping fashion that took in everything, even Fen. He sucked on the cigarette as though he might draw the whole thing into his lungs and he thought, Are we going to fight that old war on this small battlefield?

And he did not want to answer Fen's question.

"Will you go?" said Fen again. He sounded as though whatever Ryan said would tip a balance in some direction.

It's just a visit, Ryan thought. And I'm going to cut it short. I'll not stay long enough here for it to matter to this boy what I am, or what I'm not.

So he said shortly, "No, I probably won't go."

And at this Fen looked—how did he look? Shocked, like a firm young Christian ought to look? Relieved and inwardly rebellious himself? Ryan looked at him closely but all he saw was the hair that was like *her* hair and the chin that turned at the same angle *hers* had turned, and the eyes that were—well—that were rather like Ryan's own.

He thought, frowning, And I'll not stay long enough for this boy to matter to me, either!

But he felt like a general breaking his tent to flee with the enemy already scattered through the camp.

6.

As IT TURNED OUT, none of them went to prayer services that night because it rained, a regular cloudburst. It banged into the side of the house and washed in rivers down the gutter pipes from the porch.

Asa complained that the weatherman had said nothing about rain that morning. She blamed him not only for the lack of warning but for the rain itself. And she was suspicious of Ryan, as though she thought he might have conjured it up in some conspiracy.

"Not that I'm a Fair Weather Christian," she grumbled, frowning at the dining-room window.

"Sit yourself and eat," ordered Lady Malveena and then added, "why don't you?" so it wouldn't sound too disrespectful.

Miss Clara was already seated and looked as though any minute she might bang her knife against the tableware for service.

"Oh me," sighed Asa. She came and sat down with a long-suffering look upon her face. She detested rain, always had. She claimed it made her ache all over and stopped her head up so that she felt smothered from inside. During the rainy seasons of the year she grew too irritable to live with and everyone in the house tiptoed and avoided talking to her. She had no conversation at such times except the rain, how hard it was, how wet it was, how endless.

Now she said gloomily, "And soon we'll have September. Equinox."

"Happens every year," said Ryan without much interest.

She eyed him as if she suspected him of harboring a secret glee. "Will you have white or dark meat?" she said, and she asked it as though his answer might be some very special shibboleth.

"White," he said—and almost added, *for Purity.*

It was a particularly hard rain, causing Lady Malveena to remark on one of her trips from the kitchen that it must be "thumping on tops of graves tonight," which made all of them stop in their eating to stare at her, all except Miss Clara. Miss Clara said Wasn't that nice. For the rest of them it conjured up a rather unpleasant picture of legions of dead, all snug in their coffins, listening sedately to the rain above them.

They ate for a while in silence and the rain whipped up at the dining-room windows as if it intended to come inside.

"This is very good chicken," Fen said when Lady Malveena passed by, and she put a hand briefly on his back.

"Thass good," she said. And she looked at Ryan sharply as if to say: *You see what a nice boy this one is?*

His mood deepened and widened and he made himself frown thoughtfully at the chicken as if he himself could hardly believe the taste of it. She swept off to the kitchen, sniffing.

"I'm sorry I couldn't be home your first day here," said Asa after a while. She looked brave, ignoring the rain the way a Southern lady at Gettysburg might have ignored the sound of guns. "I had some things to attend to at the office. And Clara and I went shopping."

"It's delicious," said Miss Clara to nobody.

"I stopped by the office looking for you," Ryan said. "Met Mr. Travis, I think."

"Was he drunk?"

"Well . . ."

"If he was drunk, it was Ian Travis."

"Why do you keep him then?"

Asa shrugged. "It's Lawyer Gaskill's doing. When he offered to buy out most of the company he said he had a man in mind to run it. Who was to guess he'd be so rude? He's not stupid, mind you." She sighed, glanced at the wavery window and averted her eyes. "I almost wish he was a stupid man. Then I could fire him in good conscience."

"I don't think he likes it here."

"Hates it. Only stays to plague me."

Ryan said, unable to curb his sarcasm, "Never goes to church, I expect."

On Asa it was lost. "I should say not. Positively rude to everyone who calls on him."

"I should think that would be enough to undermine any value he might be to you in Stoneville. Unless he's an exceptional salesman."

She gave a grudging nod. "Oddly enough he is, for no reason that I can see. It's as if everyone thinks Mr. Travis couldn't be trying to cheat anybody while he was that disagreeable."

Miss Clara leaned forward abruptly so that it looked for an instant as if she might fall prone across the table and said in a great voice, "BREAD PLEASE!"

Ryan passed it to her hastily.

Miss Clara was resplendent this evening in a scarlet dressing gown which had faded all over in streaks of pink and orange and peach. It made her seem much larger, like a gaping wound.

Across the table Fen sat very quietly and moved food off his plate and into his mouth without talking. The routine was so precise that it must have been practiced; and after watching him for a while, Ryan could see the pattern. Fen counted through the meal. He chewed thirty-two times and picked up a morsel of food on the count of ten and every sixth swallow of food he took a tiny sip of water.

The care and precision took Ryan back to a few times in his life when he had lived just that way—one bite, one swallow, one careful step at a time. To concentrate on this doorknob and that pencil and this coin, and to mark the passing of minutes and the number of toothpicks in a table holder: these were ways an adult used to keep from going mad.

He caught Fen's eye and smiled and Fen smiled; but he did not lose the rhythm.

Miss Clara leaned forward again now and two dangling garnets wobbled from her pierced ears. Ryan had not noticed them before.

"Hello, Fenwick," she called for the first time.

"Hello, Miss Clara."

"What was that? What? What?"

"I said, HELLO, MISS CLARA!" Fen was red with effort and the rhythm of his eating lost.

"How's your earache?" shouted Ryan, who had taken pity on him.

Miss Clara turned and widened her eyes in shock and he could not imagine what she thought he had said. He touched his own ear hopefully.

"Ear! Earache! Ear!"

She nodded and smiled and probed for the garnets with a fat finger. "Yes, they are, aren't they? Really lovely. Lovely, Asa."

Asa nodded briefly and went on eating. Once in a while she sniffed and rubbed her forehead with one hand and then sent a long-suffering look around the table. It was plain to see, the look said, how little they knew what she went through. They and their garnet earrings!

Ryan saw Fen pause like a soldier waiting to get back into step, and then the meal resumed with the same monotony. He felt a little dizzy, watching it.

"I saw Amos McBane uptown, too," said Ryan, after another silence.

"Getting on in years," said Asa. "Must be eighty-five or eighty-six."

"Is Mrs. McBane still living?"

She looked a little surprised and disapproving that he had not kept up better with the McBane household all the time he had been away.

"Goodness no," she said. "Adelia must be dead fifteen years. She dropped dead on the street one day of a stroke, right in front of the bus. So distressing. There was a big funeral."

"That's good," said Ryan feebly.

"You know their son was killed in Korea."

"I didn't until today."

Fen made one of his rare attempts at conversation. "Mr. McBane is the man with the magnifying thing, isn't he?"

Asa frowned at him. "Don't poke fun, Fenwick."

He looked unhappy. "I wasn't, Aunt Asa. Really I wasn't. I was just asking."

"You'll be old some day," said Asa.

"Yes ma'am," said Fen.

"Mr. McBane gave me a pamphlet," said Ryan hastily. "The Seven Steps to Salvation."

Asa gave him her best look of sisterly concern well savored with reproach. "Well, you could do worse than to read it. A man at your age ought to be thinking of such things if he hasn't already."

"You'll be old some day," said Fen soberly, but his eyes were twinkling. Ryan started, stared at him. Asa turned.

"Fenwick?"

"Yes ma'am."

"Was that remark delivered . . . how was that remark delivered?"

Fen said, all innocence, "I don't understand." And Lady Malveena swept in like an army to the rescue, straightening up quickly from the position she must have held on the stool in the butler's pantry, and wanted to know if she couldn't get them more coffee. Asa said she could.

"I'm serious, Ryan," Asa added when Lady Malveena had gone. "You ought to restudy all the things you turned aside when you were younger. People change. Needs change."

There was no question about that. The food suddenly stuck in Ryan's throat and he took a careful drink of water. Lady Malveena came in and poured the coffee cups so he did not have to reply.

"Ain't no dessert," said Lady Malveena. She shot an accusing glance at Fen and Ryan because they had eaten all the applejacks at lunch.

"That's all right," said Asa. Why should there be luxury amidst rain?

They drank their coffee in silence and Ryan lit a cigarette although he knew Asa did not like it and Lady Malveena hated ashes in the chinaware. And Jim had said, of course, that he shouldn't smoke.

Asa frowned at the window glass where water flowed down. "I feel as if I were at the bottom of the sea," she said.

"It's very still at the bottom of the sea," protested Fen.

The wind banged the back screen door. "Well, I should hope so," said Asa irritably. She sniffled and rubbed her head again.

There was another silence broken only by the clink of china and the roar outside, and once by Fen who took too big a swallow and made a loud gulp getting it down. He looked terribly embarrassed and shot a quick look out to see who had noticed.

Ryan blew the smoke up and watched it hang and shift at the ceiling and break up. He saw that the striped paper on the walls had faded and now hung down in little shreds about the windows. On the sideboard, as always, sat the silver service and a cut-glass bowl, and in the dark glassed-in china cabinet was the rest of his mother's crystal. His mother had died of smallpox when Ryan was but a year old. He could remember how Lady Malveena had always said it was a mercy, too; she was a pretty thing and small and fair, and as it was she never knew how the pox had ruined her face.

(At this Ryan had a sudden picture of his father visiting her in her bedroom, saying how nice she looked, saying how lucky it was that she would have no scars. But that was his imagination. He did not believe Flambert Godwin had ever cared that much for anyone.)

"Are you ready to have the table cleared?" said Lady Malveena. She was anxious to get the dishes done and be off to her own room. What did she do there now? In the old days there had been the grape wine, and stories for children hidden out of beds, and an old photograph album full of stout colored ladies and toothless colored gentlemen. And sometimes her husband—her second husband—had played on the guitar.

When she asked them now about clearing the table, almost all of them jumped a little in their chairs. They had been thinking all kinds of inner things not mindful of the others. Now they got up self-consciously from the table, Miss Clara last, after she noticed the others.

They went into the parlor and Asa asked if they didn't think a fire would help dispel the dampness.

"It's much too hot," said Ryan.

She looked at him once, brave and martyred.

Fen said, "I'll get you a sweater if you're cold, Aunt Asa."

"I'm not *cold*."

They sat down, looking for something to touch, looking for things to take up in their hands.

Ryan settled for a magazine he found, a Christmas issue three years back. He could not imagine who had been extravagant enough to buy it. He read the second chapter of Luke soberly, as if he were seeing it for the first time. Miss Clara had produced a deck of cards, seemingly from midair, and began to flip them down onto a marble-topped table, wearing a grim face. For a minute, because of her expression and the faded dressing gown, she looked rather like a broken-down prostitute, fresh come from a bottle of gin.

Fen sank to the floor and began to tie and untie his shoelaces. And as for Asa, she stood with her back to the rest of them and stared into the empty hearth (reproachfully?) and held one hand out toward it.

Ryan turned a page, read without much interest complete directions on how to make Santa Clauses out of red paper and wisps of cotton, followed by a nostalgic iambic-pentameter poem about the good old days when one had strung real popcorn for the tree.

Asa turned and came to sit beside him on the sofa. "Don't do that," she said absently to Fen and he abandoned his shoelaces and began to scratch his ankle very carefully. Asa said, "Have you heard about the college, Ryan?"

He frowned. For years "the college" had meant to him Wellman Women's College in Wellman, Massachusetts. For years that had been so large a part of his life and now it all seemed to have happened to some other man, a long time ago.

"What college?" he said.

"Some talk of putting up a college here, outside of town. Some rich man wants to endow it if they'll name it for him."

Ryan put down the magazine in genuine amazement. "A college? Here in Stoneville?"

"It's just a rumor," said Asa. She was pleased at having made a stir. "Don't do that," she said to Fen. He moved his hand from his ankle and held it carefully in the other palm, as if he could not think of any place else to put the thing down.

"Where did you hear about it?"

"Real estate people *would*," said Asa. "There's been talk in the air for some time. Most of the townspeople aren't too pleased about the prospect, I can tell you. The businessmen like it, of course. They say it would bring in revenue."

He had never looked at a college particularly as a source of revenue. "I suppose it would," he said.

"Mr. Barnes was telling me about it, and he thinks some good might come of it. He says the Lord can use knowledge." She smiled proudly. "Of course Mr. Barnes is something of a liberal man."

Hell, yes, thought Ryan in disgust. But there was no need going into that. Asa had been half in love with Edward Barnes for years, as much as Asa could be in love. Besides, Barnes was no longer typical. Every time Ryan became annoyed with rank fundamentalism he reminded himself that for every Edward Barnes there was a Paul Tillich, there was a Reinhold Niebuhr.

"What kind of college would it be? Agriculture? Home economics?" He could not quite keep the sarcasm out of his voice. Edward Barnes a liberal man indeed!

Asa pursed her lips in irritation. "Liberal Arts, I believe," she said crisply. "With emphasis on what Mr. Barnes calls the Humanities."

"The Humanities, oh yes," said Ryan sourly. "I've heard of them."

"Evidently the man is very rich, the one who wants to endow

it. I understand he was born around here and now he wants to do something for his birthplace."

"That would be doing something for it all right!" Ryan warmed a little. "Why not build it at the North Pole? Or in the middle of the Sahara? Or deep in the Himalayas with only a footpath for access?"

"What's access?" said Fen. Behind them all there was the flap flap flapping of Miss Clara's cards against the table, like waves upon a shore.

Asa ignored his sarcasm. "What's the matter with agriculture and home economics?"

"Nothing, if you think an education is to prepare you to make a living. To give you certain skills with which you can barter."

"I know about barter," said Fen to nobody. "That's to trade. That's in my geography book. Mesopotamia."

"Don't interrupt," said Asa.

"But if you're concerned with the enrichment of the individual . . ."

Asa actually laughed. "I wish you wouldn't talk like you were sixteen. Do you think I have anything against the enrichment of the individual? Or Edward Barnes?"

"Not within certain limitations," said Ryan.

"And don't you believe in limitations?"

"Some," he admitted.

"But all of them self-imposed. Isn't that the difference?"

He shook his head. "I have to accept certain physical limitations. Certain environmental limitations, too."

"But never the Law of God."

He said, deciding to smile, deciding he would not argue, "I always thought the apple in Eden was a dirty trick, myself."

"Why are you so defiant?"

"I'm not, usually. People accept each other more where I live. But here I always feel pulled about. The ruler is always up on the town and everybody being measured against it. Every action so many centimeters high against the standard."

"Sometimes," she said, "you sound to me just like you did when you came home freshman year from the University."

Ryan smiled in spite of himself. "I know I do. That's what comes of being on the defensive."

"I actually do think a college might disrupt some of the Stoneville way of life. You just said people accepted each other in that college town you live in. Is that a good thing? Ought we not to be concerned for each other?" And Asa looked at Fen, possessively.

In that moment she looked very much like their father. "Not to the point of ownership," Ryan said. "What do you mean when you say the Stoneville Way of Life?"

"Not what you mean," she said. "But things would change."

"Change how?"

"Oh, you know." She waved her hand. "Crowded. Students drinking. Lots of noise. Things like that."

"Oh yes," said Ryan. "I'd forgotten."

"It would have to be properly supervised."

"Properly," he repeated.

Fen said abruptly, "How old do you have to be to go to college?"

"You have to be through with high school," Asa said.

"There are lots of colleges," said Ryan to Fen. He was pleased at Asa's frown.

"*Aha,*" cried Miss Clara, finding the ace of hearts. Everyone jerked convulsively they were so surprised to remember she was there. "I've won now," she added gleefully to no one in particular. She began to peek under all the bottom cards to plan her strategy.

"Was your college very big?" said Fen. "The one you taught at?"

"Medium, as colleges go."

"Did you teach the" (he stuttered slightly) "the humanities?"

"That's right. I was in the English Department."

"And are they better than" (he hesitated) "than the others?"

"I wouldn't say that. But I'd say a man studying the sciences needs some balance and perspective from the humanities."

A low grumbling arose from Miss Clara who could find no way to uncover the card she wanted. She began to drum her fingers on the marble surface of the table where they made a dull sound like the passing of distant horses.

"I wish you'd stop that!" Asa yelled. "MY HEADACHE."

"Oh," said Miss Clara. She stopped it.

"Mr. Barnes says we must be open-minded about the college until we know more about it," said Asa in her normal tone of voice.

Ryan said caustically that this was an admirable virtue. "And is he expecting some Heavenly visitation to give him the final decision?"

Asa primped the papery mouth. "Don't blaspheme," she said.

It was silly to be so angry. On top of that his own attitude at this moment was every bit as extreme, as fanatic, and as unfairly reached as Asa's might be. It surprised Ryan to catch himself repaying one prejudice, one narrow-mindedness, with another; and he thought, That's not like me, is it? Am I not usually fairer than this?

He lifted the old magazine before his face like a mask so he could think about it. It was hard to say whether it was only a natural reaction due to the state of his health (euphemisms, he thought wryly, always in euphemisms) or whether it might actually be the influence of Stoneville itself. Which was he fighting, and to what purpose?

Perhaps, after all, it was the combination of these two things. Each of them reinforced the other. And that made him wonder if he ought to stay in Stoneville any time at all or if he ought not to get up and go first thing in the morning, before Fen was awake.

For Ryan felt that here the individual slipped down into the mass of the community and was so utterly swallowed up that (for instance) the problem of death had to be translated into a familiar religious problem before one could think about it at all.

I want to come at it in my own terms, he thought stubbornly. But what those terms would be he did not know. And he almost envied Jessica and the quickness of her going. She had been granted only a few hours in which to take what material she had (that God of hers, with his hand cupped round her warm) and small Fen and —yes, perhaps he himself, Ryan Godwin—and build a hasty structure that would serve. In that short time she had added it up, balanced the books and had (this he believed) decided it was all to the good. Being alive at all had been worth everything.

But Ryan was not able to go at it in Jessica's way. To do that he would have had to own all of the years and experiences which had made her up—he would have to have been Jessica herself.

No two of us are alike, not even in love, he thought—and that, as always, cheered him.

Into the well of silence Asa said unexpectedly, "Have you done any writing yet?"

"What? What was that?"

"I said, have you done any writing yet?" She wore a look of satisfaction, like an adult about to catch him in a clumsy lie.

"Of course not," he said, somewhat impatiently. He was sorry to be bothered in those other thoughts. "I just got here."

Asa gave a triumphant glance toward Miss Clara as if to say: *See? I told you so!* But Miss Clara, who had lost at solitaire, was laying the cards out once more, a determined set to her chin. She did not care about Asa or Ryan or Fen. She cared about fifty-two slips of colored paper and about getting them laid out in the same pattern she had laid them in yesterday.

"What is it you were thinking of writing?"

Actually Ryan had not thought of it at all, but he did not intend to say so. "I was thinking of making a book out of some of my class notes and lectures. All professors try that. Dostoevsky, perhaps. I taught that course a while."

"In other words, you hadn't quite decided."

"Not definitely."

He turned the pages of the magazine and read with obvious concentration a recipe for old-fashioned plum pudding.

"What would you write about him, this man you mentioned?" Asa was not to be put off. Businesswoman that she was, she sensed contracts, sales, lectures, commissions, and royalties. Asa liked to think of herself as some auxiliary motor to many projects. All people needed to be pushed, she often said. She was leaning forward in her chair now, watching him, looking as though any minute she might cross over and put a pencil into his fingers and wait—expectant.

Ryan frowned. "Oh, something about his significance for modern fiction. His parallels with the existentialists." (Asa raised her eyebrows at this but asked no question.) "His interest in crime and propitiation. A portrait of Ivan as the man of our time."

"Who's Ivan?" interrupted Fen, big-eyed.

"He . . ." (Ryan paused, feeling inadequate to answer.) "He's partly a man in a book," he said finally.

Fen looked a little disappointed, as if he were not convinced men in books were—after all—of much importance.

"This book of yours," said Asa, looking thoughtful, "would it sell well?" He saw the mental tumblers going around in sums, and he thought of Flambert Godwin tabulating in his head. In spite of himself, he laughed aloud; but whether at Asa's undaunted practicality or at the prospect of some *True Confessions* fan engrossed in Dostoevsky, he could not have said. For one happy moment he saw them, hanging from their subway straps, devouring *The Brothers K.*

"I think not," he admitted, still amused. "It would be nonfiction. Not even one of these biographies that sometimes sells. Very limited audience, actually."

But Asa was not to be dissuaded from her original course. "Seriously, Ryan, why don't you write a novel? You could certainly turn out a better one than some I hear about. They sell so much better than something like that. You can't tell me every writer doesn't want to be read. And with all the English literature you've taught, you must know how it's done."

He laughed again at the cool confidence of this, but then he sobered. "No," he said. "No, I'm afraid I don't." And he thought of vanished youth, in which he had known all there was to know about writing novels, having babies, growing up, making love, attaining bravery. Dying well.

Fen said, "Is it hard to write a novel?"

"Harder for some than others," Ryan said. "Very hard to write a good, even a passable novel. Hard, steady work it is—and only once in a while exciting. And to write a great one . . ." He paused. "I don't know what that's like. Maybe the great writers span the gap with something more than work." Whatever that was, he thought. Wherever that Daemon came from, and of whatever rare stuff it was made.

Seeing that none of this was going to plan, Asa had another suggestion. "Maybe if you stay in Stoneville long enough, they'll build this college and you can teach in it. You could write at night." She had never approved of his teaching before; he fancied she saw some social advantage in it now. With a college, so to speak, on the doorstep, teaching would become a local (hence respected) profession. It would be as good as having a brother Principal of Stoneville High.

But Ryan shook his head.

"In the first place, they'll never get such a college." At least not in time, he thought. Not nearly enough in time. "And in the second place, even if they should, I wouldn't like it here. I never did."

"The character of the town might change," said Asa. "Might alter the level of what you've always considered our mass stupidity."

"I never thought you capable of satire," said Ryan, grinning.

To this she made a snorting noise, which saved her from having to give any further comment.

"Why don't you stay?" asked Fen. He looked unreasonably distressed. "Why don't you?"

No ties, thought Ryan. I mustn't make any ties here. But he said gently, "I didn't mean to sound so definite about leaving. I can't tell what I'll do at this point."

One of the windows rattled sharply and Asa clapped a hand to her head as though she were holding it on by force.

"This is a real belly washer," Fen said in a grown-up way.

"Gully washer," Asa snapped.

Miss Clara, across the room, drummed her fingers dully on the tabletop and concentrated deeply. That barely perceptible chudding appeared to be all Asa could take.

"Well, I may as well go on to bed," she said. "Get an early start, since I'm sure I won't sleep. Such a horrible rain. You'd better come along too, Fen." She stood up, expanded her shoulder blades slightly; that was as close to an uninhibited public stretch as she would ever come.

Fen stood up too. "Yes ma'am."

She nodded briskly, and Fen shot back a longing glance and followed her toward the stairs. "You'll be here tomorrow," he said.

"Oh yes. Good night, Fen."

Until that time Miss Clara had not heard them go and when she looked up and saw that only Ryan remained, she grew quite flustered and began to gather up the cards with great swooping movements, spilling them onto the floor in every direction. Ryan helped her pick them up and smiled to her cries of leave-taking. He saw her go hurriedly out of the parlor and up the stairs, looking always like a bird too large for its cage, always banging and flapping into corners and edges.

When they had all gone, Ryan sat down again a while longer, but not to any purpose. He felt tired, not physically, but in the realm of *feeling*, as though all day he had gone about with his heart turned up one notch too high. He felt the love in him, weary and sagging, and he said to himself, He's only a little boy. He was all right before I came.

He got up and walked back to the kitchen and told Lady Malveena he was going to bed, too, and did she want him to lock any doors or anything?

"I'll do it," Lady Malveena said. She had been scrubbing the kitchen floor; it was damp and shiny.

"Quite a rain we're having." For some reason he was oddly reluctant to go upstairs alone.

Lady Malveena nodded and they stood without speaking for a minute, sharing the sound of the storm outside.

"We need it," she said. "Everything's drying up." And while she said it she watched him. He thought she was waiting for something and it made him angry.

"What are you looking at?" he snapped.

One corner of her mouth quirked up at that, ever so slightly, but she only said in a dry voice, "I wouldn't be scared of a little boy."

He could have shaken her for dragging everything out in the open this way. He wanted to say *I'm sick, goddammit, why don't you leave me alone?* But he said, "What in the world are you talking about?"

She gave him a level look. "Her and you," she said.

He crossed over and sat down at the kitchen table, weary beyond words.

"Nothing ever finishes," said Lady Malveena. "Changes, but never breaks off."

And he said dully (to himself, really, but aloud), "There is no line in the universe. Just color. One color leaving off where another one starts."

She was frankly smiling. "You talk too fancy, but there's good stuff in you."

"You're impudent," said Ryan, without caring.

"Listen," she said sharply, "I use to wipe your bottom when it was a bird pucker! I use to pick you up and set you down and put food in you. I use to wash your elbows. I use to . . ."

"Oh, shut up," he said fondly. "I know you did."

"You go to bed. You think. There's time."

"Not . . ." He stopped. "Not as much as there once was."

She said, "You hear me out—I know you've got some secret brung along. You put it on that bus and you carried it right down here with you and I know you got it. But *I* don't want to hear what it is. You'll fix it. You always did." Her voice was confident and proud and her eyes had gone soft with remembering things he did not remember, about a little boy in this house whom she had fed and watched and maybe taught to walk.

And he thought, So it comes to this, the people you can count on one handful of fingers. There was Jim at Wellman, an old old friend; there had been Jessica; there was Lady Malveena. Was there Fen? He would think about that tomorrow.

"Good night," he said.

She nodded. The mood was leaving her. "Sleep good, Mr. Ryan," she said almost automatically.

"You, too."

He went upstairs (which was that step, the magic one?) and into his own room, feeling his way along the wall with grunts and bruises until he came to the small window. It was too dark to see the oak tree which rose up by the house outside. He had only an impression of motion and wild wet thrashing.

In a few more minutes he undressed in the dark and went to bed.

7.

FOR SOME REASON, Ryan woke quite early the next morning, thinking of his brother, Avery.

And this he did not want to do; it was too close to that other thing. There were days and nights with her so intense that he did not want to come over them again, not even in thought.

It was still dark gray outside his room; it was Thursday; the rain had stopped not long before. Outside the small window he could make out the occasional brightness of wet leaves against a leaden sky. Sometimes they caught on the surface what little light there was and turned, for an instant, silver and beautiful.

His feet were cold under the one coverlet; he curled them up beneath him and remembered that tomorrow was the first of September and it would likely be an early winter. All about him the house was very still. When a drop of rain went from a tree to the ground he heard the splat of it all the way upstairs—or thought he did.

And he thought that it must be a day like this that had brought Avery back to mind—that dull, quiet, stodgy brother. That overgrown Boy Scout.

But there was no true dislike in him for that brother, because he—Ryan—had done him an unadmitted wrong and he could feel no anger because of that. How many times in those old days he had thought he might find himself holding onto Avery's lapels, saying in a loud voice, "I LOVE YOUR WIFE!"

What would Avery have said to that? His imagination floundered; it went no further than the look of slow bewilderment.

Beyond the weather, Ryan could not imagine what had set him to thinking of Avery at all (he almost never did), unless perhaps sometime during the night he had dreamed of him. By now he had the habit of considering Asa and himself as Flambert Godwin's only children; he always had to be prodded before he remembered Avery at all. And he knew that this was partly because Jessica and he had acted as if there were no Avery. They had not spoken his name to each other when they could help it. They had been like superstitious children: if they did not acknowledge him, perhaps he would vanish and everything be solved.

But it had not worked that way, of course. She was Avery's wife. Even when Avery died, he did not do it alone. In life he had owned all the official claims on her—on her time, her activity, her daily living.

But not, after a while, her thinking. Ryan had owned that part of her. And he would not have traded that one for the other.

He wiped those thoughts off his mind as off a slate and made himself hear again the water falling and the tree stirring just outside the house.

He turned onto his back in bed and followed with his eyes a long, irregular crack in the ceiling. Avery seemed to him very dead, absolutely Put-An-End-To in his dying. Of Avery, the memories had to be dredged up from the bottom, sought after. The little boy Avery had to be built again (and not in accuracy) out of the vague shadow he recalled. Avery had been on the edge, the fringe, of any event Ryan could now remember. There was somewhere a ball game, green grass and shouting and excitement; and somewhere watching it was The Brother of Me, whose face was indistinct and unremembered. There was a room in a tall house, and another boy across it in another bed, always sleeping, always with his back turned. School: and the other boy in the hall or walking the street, looking how? Looking no-way. Looking like shoes and trousers and a cap and nothing more.

And now when he was dead all of those things were blurred a little more.

Nor could he remember how the voice had sounded, and not one phrase or word that had come from that mouth was with him any more, except the mottoes. As an adult, Avery had loved mottoes.

And when he thought all of these things, Ryan did not believe that Fen was Avery's son.

He's *my* son. I always knew.

And he wanted to get up out of bed and go down the hall and find Fen's room and put a hand on him as he lay there, sleeping.

A creaking and grumbling arose now in the house from some of the outdated plumbing and Ryan wondered if Asa were still awake after the rainy night, if the aches and the stopped-up head had kept her from sleeping as she said. She would (he fancied) be a little disappointed if they had not. He pictured her bent at a lavatory, washing a puffy face, angry before the day had started.

Avery was Asa's brother, he said now to himself, but without much sense of reality to it. And mine, he added after a time. But nothing mattered yet; it was all just words said in semidarkness by a wakeful man. There was not much emotion.

Then he said to himself, *Avery was Jessica's husband;* and something stirred deep in him; something protested after all these years and after all their pretending Avery had not been real.

He could not remember much of Avery from early childhood except that he had been quite fat. He was fat and he was the middle child, and he bit his nails until there were only tiny portions left imbedded in the chubby finger ends. There remained no real memory of Avery's face; but he recalled the way the stomach had folded down below the belt, and the way he used to sit solemnly in Sunday school, stroking the insides of his thighs with chubby bitten fingers.

From the first Avery had been almost inarticulate. He had talked quite late and when he did—finally—it was in the polite expected language of the adults about him. All of his life Avery had been full of "How are you?" and "Isn't it hot today?" and he had bypassed all the stages where he might have invented words or mixed their meanings or said any of a child's foolish wonderful explanations. Later he had been bewildered by poetry, and to hear a wind called green had thrown him into bewilderment and consternation.

Grownups liked him ("Such a little man!") but other children never did. To them he seemed a Pretender. Any minute now he would be revealed, growing a genuine beard on his face or having real lipstick and permanent curls like all the other Pretenders they knew. He had no spontaneity. He was not excited, or enraged, or ever silly with giggling. The grownups called it self-control, but the children knew there was nothing to control—he did not experience, as they did, the great hot rushes of pure feeling. He was a finished product very early in his life—he had no place else to go.

He ate a great deal. He smiled politely as he did so and said "Yes thank you," so that grownups were not aware he overate. Children his own age he regarded with bewilderment. What was the matter with them anyway? Why were they so often red of face and flashing of eye? What did it matter if one did or did not take a stick and hit some ball across a fence? Who cared about frogs or dogs, about running and fighting?

In his early years, Avery had excelled in almost nothing except sheer weight. Sometimes he would fight for one gang or another, having been chosen for the sole purpose of sitting heavily on opponents; it was the only reason they would accept him. But Avery did not care; he was not grateful, or hurt, or loyal; he would lumber about sitting upon this boy and that without any great discrimination. If they did not ask him to play he went aside undisturbed and sat alone somewhere. "Did you ever see such a child?" The visitors and aunts would watch his sober countenance. He shook hands with his uncles very gravely.

"Very different from Ryan."

Ryan had, indeed, been different. He had shrieked and climbed and pelted, wept bitter tears, fought terrible battles. He had loved intensely a little girl who later moved away. He had bosom friends among the neighborhood boys and sworn enemies. He also played alone, up and down the bank of the Katsewa River (a long walk away) and dangerously upon the railway trestle. (*Now the train would come; he would hang down into space to save himself; it might cut off the fingers of one hand but still he would hang until it was safe to climb up again. Nothing would kill him, ever!*)

And Ryan had played alone along the cotton warehouses near the track. He had picked the seeds from fallen cotton, working the lint off cleaner and cleaner and smoother and smoother. He had read the wonderful names on the boxcars (even on a railway spur there were wonderful faraway boxcars) and—breathless with terror—had crept under a parked one and to the other side to prove to himself that he could.

In the afternoons he had come home from school by a million shortcuts, through people's yards and over difficult fences. He had nibbled black locust and spat the seeds at friends. At one place they always walked a sewer tunnel which took the ditch under Wynberry Street, and he had hated that. The tunnel was dirty and smelly and full of damp moss and toadstools on the walls and ceilings, sickly and faintly green. But it was important to know what you could and could not do. Someday there might be kidnapers who would torture him terribly for secrets. One had to steel oneself, find where the breaking points were in all directions, and then extend them farther out.

Not so, Asa.

Always Asa had eyed their father with the awe Ryan gave to a thousand other things. Trestles and sewer tunnels—what were they to her? The strongest and hardest and bravest thing in the world was to make a living. Look at the hundreds doing it day after day, and being tired out and often killed with the force of it!

Their father was thus a warrior, infinitely brave. When she saw him uptown he seemed to her greatly changed from the way he was at home, more compact and concentrated. In the evenings it seemed to Asa he came in weary off enormous battlefields.

Asa had excelled in her studies as her brothers had not, because she believed she would someday use everything she learned to help her father. To tell the truth, Flambert Godwin was oddly disgruntled that she might even be brighter than his two sons. When report cards came he would lecture both Avery and Ryan in anger and give them sums to do. He did not care for Asa's achievement except in comparison; she had surpassed the males.

But Asa—blind and deaf to this—said always, "He loves me most, because I get better marks than you."

Avery was fated to move always in the shadow of one of the other two. He came to grade school when Asa was still there; he remained until after Ryan came and then moved on to junior high school, which Asa had not finished yet. Teachers and students alike never remembered him. He was Asa's younger brother, Ryan's older. He was the Middle Godwin, the fat one.

When Avery graduated they wrote under his picture in the annual: A Modest Man. He was still quite fat when the picture was made and had acquired eyes like an owl; he seemed to be peering out of the page into some sharp illumination, great-eyed and altogether blinded by the light. He looked faintly rebellious, as if he had done the best he could and it ought to come to more.

The Last Will and Testament, printed in that same annual, said:

I, Avery Godwin, leave my unobtrusiveness to be more equally divided among all comers.

Ryan could not remember what wiseacre had penned that line.

It was significant (thought Ryan now, easing the pillow out from beneath his head and lying flat) that his father had not made clear-cut plans for Avery, as he had for the other two. He had asked his middle son over and over, "What is it you yourself would like to do?" as though that were a challenge, as though the boy might surprise them all and become something altogether startling, like a man who cleaned hog's entrails.

But he had not, of course. Avery had looked about him, decided that certain things were expected of all human beings in the world and then had set out to attain just those (no more) like a man filling a grocery list he never wrote himself. So-many small bags of success, but not an oversupply to spoil, a carton of family, a small box of outside interests, a pound of virtue, two pounds of good manners.

Lying in bed now, thinking of Avery for the first time in many years, Ryan asked himself seriously if his brother had been perhaps slow-witted? Had there been something lacking in the cerebral make-up that had never developed, or had grown in some inverted way?

But he honestly did not think this was true. He thought there had been less a lack in mentality than in personality, not reason, but feeling. Avery had found himself in a world where he had nothing particular to say or contribute and he was not of a nature to criticize or rebel. Indeed, he was never aware there might be anything to rebel against. It did not occur to him things might have, or ought to have, happened any other way.

Human beings, Avery had always believed, were born, were expected to learn to eat in a civilized way and not to soil themselves; later they were to be sober and industrious and godly, marry women, have healthy children, decorate annual Christmas trees, join lodges, buy an automobile, save money, take out life insurance, die without spasms or indecency, be buried in a prepaid plot. This was the way he understood things to be and it seemed to him quite sensible and sane.

In the summer after Asa graduated from high school, Flambert Godwin died.

Ryan had been left with an uncomfortable feeling that, although she loved him, Asa had coolly willed her father's death. She was out of school; he had refused indignantly her offer that she might work in the office.

"You'll manage the house, of course."

"But Lady Malveena does that very capably."

"There'll be none of that silly talk from you, Asa. Real estate is a man's job. There are certainly duties here adequate enough to occupy your time."

Flambert Godwin had been inflexible on the subject; indeed (Ryan suspected) he had been a little horrified.

"All right," Asa had answered him, looking dutiful—but she was very bitter and all of them knew. She loved her father, but she was like the Elder Son—if she had to slay him to achieve her own position in the tribe, she would do so.

So that Ryan had half believed once she was home and out of school she had concentrated some great mental force until her father, bewildered at his own inclination, wore away and died.

Certainly there had been a slow draining of his strength—first the lung infection with a cough that wore away stubbornly at his characteristic vitality, and after that a siege of influenza and some vague stomach ailment. Then in the end his heart had simply stopped, as if it would not put up with any more of this nonsense.

Lady Malveena had found him one suppertime in his study, still almost bolt upright in the leather chair, his fingers marking a page in some unfinished (now never-to-be-finished) book. He had looked quite startled about it all, as if he had heard Death whisper at him and had refused him in no uncertain terms, and had then been carted off against his will.

Ryan had been eleven at the time and Avery fifteen. Lady Malveena had run the house and the three of them as long as they could remember. They had believed vaguely that she always would—being, they thought, both irreplaceable and indestructible.

But she had been replaced in authority almost immediately, and by the same girl whose nose she had often wiped and whose mousy hair she had braided.

It seemed remarkable to Ryan now—the way Asa had taken over everything so quickly, managed the funeral and her father's business affairs as if she had done it all her life. He could still recall how shocked he had been when they came home from the cemetery on that day and Asa, taking off her hat and veil, had said matter-of-factly, "Well, that's that." She said it after the manner of someone who has gotten through some unpleasant task and now intends to put it out of his mind and eat a whopping big sandwich.

Yet Asa had loved her father. Had she loved him more when he was dead and she less cramped? Who was to say about that?

On the day after Flambert Godwin's funeral, the Stoneville newspaper carried the announcement that Godwin Realty would be continued as usual and that Miss Asa Godwin, daughter of the late Flambert Godwin, would take over the management of the company. Miss Godwin, it added, was a graduate of the Stoneville schools and had been fully versed in the real estate business by her late father.

(This, Asa said later, was not true at the time; but it made for good business.)

Two years after their father died, Avery quit high school. He was seventeen. It was, perhaps, the only thing he did in his life that had not been carefully ordered on his mental list.

This strange thing happened right after the war had ended, and everything seemed to be slightly off stride, like a runner just hitting an even pace who decides suddenly to slow to a walk. Stoneville had not really been very much interested in the war. A few of the ladies had made bandages on Saturday afternoons and two boys from the Baptist church were killed.

And all of that was just over (that long-ago, almost little-boy war, so inoffensive did it now seem) when Avery quit school. It was (Ryan squinted and thought) in 1919—the year that Theodore Roosevelt died and Asa said wouldn't her father have hated that?

The announcement that Avery did not intend to complete his work at Stoneville High was worse than thunderbolts.

"What do you mean—quit school? What on earth would you do?" When she heard what he intended Asa went up in a flurry and ever after when she discussed it her limbs and her clothes would appear to be blowing in a great wind.

(Not that she had any great respect for education as such, even then; but it had its advantages; it was one of the things one did—people like Avery and she—as they wore stockings and were thrifty. One could be, for instance, trained for some good profession.)

And when Asa asked him in such great agitation what he would do if he quit school, Avery said without any prelude and without much emotion that he would like to go to sea, thank you.

The other two were stunned. A river running backwards could not have been less believable.

"Go to sea?" said Ryan. His voice was changing and the croak was, at the moment, extremely appropriate.

"Go to sea, Avery? Go to *sea?*" Asa had sunk into a chair with a series of small gasps. "Whatever for? What would you want to do such a thing for?"

"It's what I'd want to do," said Avery, too loud. He looked scared and desperate. This was not, he knew, an Expected Thing; it did not come on the lists.

"You can't even swim!" Ryan sneered. He was fourteen and he thought Avery was an awful sissy.

"Hush up," said Asa. "This is the wildest thing I ever heard."

Avery made no particular defense or plea. He sat in a chair before them both, not even looking up. He wore on his face that frightened look, and also one of strange surprise, as if he had never expected to dare such a thing. It was as though he had looked into a mirror that day and had seen a strange little man peeping out his eyes, some little alien who lived in a secret cave behind his nose. And now that man was running things, clicking the switches and pulling all the strings.

"Well, I forbid it," Asa said firmly. "I absolutely forbid it."

It seemed to Ryan now it was funny neither of them questioned her right to forbid. It was always that way; she made her position clear on anything and they accepted it as docilely as doves. And Avery looked almost relieved.

The next term he returned to school without complaint, though Asa watched him carefully for months, as if she feared he might—without a reason—go berserk.

(Although, of course, he never did. If there was a little rebel living in Avery Godwin, he never showed again. He must have died shut up in there. He must have smothered to death.)

So in the spring of 1920 Avery graduated from Stoneville High School without any mishap, his owlish face preserved forever in the 1920 *Archives*. Ryan was in the eighth grade. He had then sandy hair and a few freckles and a terrible temper. He read a great many books but he did not want his friends to know about it for fear they would laugh. He thought he would join the F.B.I. or the diplomatic service when he was older.

After graduation Avery did nothing at all for a while. He slept late in the mornings and ate heartily of Lady Malveena's spoon bread and grew a little fatter. He went to church without enthusiasm or complaint and did not seem particularly interested except sometimes in the music. He liked the hymns the congregation sang and had a habit of keeping time against the book by thumping his forefinger. Like many fat men he had a powerful voice without much tune to it.

Avery was marking time. He was (perhaps) consulting his list and beginning to locate the next item. And the next item read (perhaps): *Religion;* then in parentheses (*also some inoffensive hobby*). Avery Godwin had the good fortune to be able to combine the two.

Gradually Asa and Ryan began to notice he was disappearing in the afternoons, and at this Asa's worry woke again.

"If you know what he's doing, you tell me," she said accusingly to Ryan. "You come on out and say it."

"I don't know, Asa. I never see Avery." And he didn't. Why should he bother? What had the two of them to say?

"Then you'd better find out."

And though he felt again, Why should I bother?—he obeyed her, of course. The discovery that he did not always have to obey Asa was still years away.

Finding out the secret was not hard, because Avery had no intention of making a secret out of it. The whole concept of secretiveness would have seemed strange to him. Were not his desires, above all else, like those of Everyman? What had any of us to hide from each other? Wherein lay the value of privacy?

So when Ryan wanted to know what Avery was doing with his time he had only to ask.

"Where do you go in the afternoons?"

"To church."

"*Church?*"

"That's right."

At the time Ryan and Avery had been finishing up a lunch which Lady Malveena had made for them. Asa usually took hers along to the company in a plain black satchel and ate when she had time. Now Ryan took a big swallow of water because he had almost choked at what his brother said.

"Nobody's at church that time of day!" He leaned across the table to look into Avery's face more closely. Was it possible Avery would lie to him? He did not think he ever had, but that might not prove anything. Whatever it was that had pushed him once to originality—might it do so again?

"That's right," said Avery again, placidly.

"Do you go there every day? I mean, what do you do there by yourself? Or are you . . ." (Here Ryan had cleared his throat because Asa had told him to find out if there was a girl involved.) "Are you by yourself?"

"The organ," Avery said. "I play the organ."

Ryan leaned back in his chair a little limply.

Nobody was left in the Baptist church any more who could play that organ since Miss Lucy Vandover had died the year before. There had been some talk of getting somebody to come in from the music school down in Atlanta, but it turned out that would mean a salary and no one would consent to that. Whoever heard (the congregation grumbled) of charging the Lord for employing talents in his service!

So nobody played the old organ in the church any more, but a thin aged gentleman who could read the right-hand notes picked out the hymn tunes on a rattly piano for everyone to sing by.

"But you can't play. You don't know how!" said Ryan after he had thought through this, after he had remembered the organ with its tall pipes and the foot pedals and all the things above the keys to pull out and push in.

"I'm learning," Avery replied. "I'm teaching myself."

"Teaching yourself how?"

"It's not so hard. I can pick out the music at the top. And the foot pedals are in the same order. You can take the lowest note on top and play it with your left foot at the bottom. And the rest of it I just fool around with."

"Fool around with." Ryan said it weakly, an echo.

"Some things you pull out make it loud, some soft. Some make it a little higher. One makes the music kind of wavery. And there's a pedal makes the music come way out and go back in."

"Out and in," said Ryan. What would Asa say?

"I like it," Avery said. He was not excited, but he was pleased.

For the first time in his life Ryan felt a certain amount of fondness for his brother. It embarrassed him terribly. He said, "That's good."

Later, telling Asa about it, Ryan was defensive. He was almost proud of Avery; he wanted none of it undone.

"So he likes it," Ryan finished. "And that's all there is."

Asa looked as thunderstruck as he had first felt. She said finally, "Avery hasn't any music in him. He sings like a frog."

"I know how he sings," said Ryan, sullen.

"Well, does he . . . does he think for one minute they'll ever let him *play* that organ in the church?"

"I don't know. I guess so." Then he said defiantly, "Why shouldn't they, if he gets to be good enough?"

"Why should he get to be good enough?" Asa could not believe it would come to anything.

It took over two years, but in time Avery did learn to play the church organ. He did not play well and never would (he had no feeling for music, but he had a certain sense of accuracy; and he leaned heavily on the key of C and simple triads and obvious combinations. During all this time nobody knew what he was doing except Ryan and Asa, and they did not take it too seriously.

"Does he still play that thing?" Asa might ask occasionally.

"I think he does."

At the end of those two years Avery walked to the manse one afternoon and announced to Preacher Kane that he could play the organ.

And that was how Avery became the organist at Trinity Baptist Church in Stoneville.

On that first Sunday morning, when everyone caught sight of plump Avery Godwin dwarfing the organ stool and wearing a long white robe that made him look rather like a pregnant lady in a nightshirt, there was a great fluttering and murmuring up and down the aisles and along all the benches. But after the opening prayer they sang with him (cautiously) "The Old Rugged Cross," and by the second verse they knew they had an organist, *sans* salary.

Everyone was very pleased about it—everyone, that is, but old Mr. Carter who had been playing the right hand on the piano for three years now and would not get to do it any more. Mr. Carter never forgave him. Mr. Carter took to walking about town like a man awaiting execution, and he would tell everyone he met that he might as well go to the County Home since there was no need for him now anywhere in the whole world.

Later he put up an American flag in front of his old house on

Walker Avenue and whenever the Godwins would ride by he would fly out in front of the flagpole and wave an old black umbrella at them.

Everybody clucked their tongues against their teeth and said they had never dreamed old Mr. Carter was a man so invested with self-love and vanity and pride. They would tell Avery he was not to mind it.

He didn't mind it. People always had to tell him who in the world Mr. Carter even was.

But that first Sunday at the organ in Trinity Baptist Church—that was the beginning for Avery of many things.

There was a great deal of talk in Mr. Kane's closing prayer about how the Lord made vessels of people and gave them certain gifts; and when that was over, Avery had been glorified. He was a personage on whom the hand of God had rested like a dove. People who had never noticed him at all before came up to speak to him now in praise. He stood there (pink, sweating, looking a little undercooked) and smiled vaguely into the faces, one hand resting on the organ cover, looking like Lazarus must have looked when he walked dazedly out of his own tomb.

Everything, so far as Avery was concerned, had come out all right. You followed the formula, mixed the recipe. You came out adult, accepted; you were a citizen of Stoneville and the other citizens liked you.

And Avery smiled warmly at Ryan and Asa that day where they sat watching (there was never any malice in him; he could not hold a grudge for lack of concentration) and began to reach out for people's hands. He began to talk a little, the proper polite things he had learned to say very early in life.

Ryan leaned forward on the bench a bit and squinted at his brother. It seemed to him Avery had grown a fraction taller; the paunch had receded an infinitesimal bit.

But that surprise was nothing to the next, when Asa rose from the bench and went forward with the others and kissed Avery lightly on the cheek.

"I always knew you'd do it," said Asa happily. "I always told you so, didn't I?"

Ryan was astounded. He could not believe his sister would tell so whopping a lie in the sanctuary.

And Avery said, "Thank you for all your encouragement, Asa."

It was too much. There is something these people know about living together which I don't know, thought Ryan as he left the church. They are ready to do things I can never do.

And when he got outside he saw that the summer was fading and the cycle of seasons would be around again, and in a sense of youthful high-flown tragedy he said in a whisper, "Ah, it will never end!"

And he meant summer and winter, and the delicate lying of his sister and his brother, and the people coming up these steps and down these steps and singing "The Old Rugged Cross"; and he thought (he was only seventeen), Life is very long.

That year Ryan was a senior at Stoneville High School.

He knew already what he wanted to do. First and foremost he wanted to get out of Stoneville and go to college; and once there, he wanted to learn as much as he could hold for the rest of his life. He thought of knowledge as having the same consistency as oil in the Psalms of David—he would fill his cup, it would run over.

He knew there would be trouble about it and he took a job at Smithson's Grocery, filling the bags and carrying them to cars for ladies; and most of his money he put carefully by. When the argument came with Asa, there would be only the minimum. If he wanted any leeway, he would have to make his own.

When the matter finally came up she was as firmly against it as she had been against Avery's going off to sea.

At first there was nothing but arguing; they could not even talk about it. Ryan would go down at night and drink cold wine in Lady Malveena's room and she would say, "Sometimes you just puts on a pot and step back and let it do its own simmering."

"She boils," said Ryan glumly.

"No no, she's coming. I feel her coming 'round."

"I don't feel anything."

"Drink some more wine," Lady Malveena would say gloomily, for she did not really feel anything either. "Go kiss some little girl."

But Lady Malveena was right and the objections cooled and simmered until they were able to discuss the matter.

"You know what Father always wanted. He wanted you to come into the business like he planned. I won't have you spending his money in ways he wouldn't like."

"But a share of his money is mine by inheritance." He had thought this through; it was practiced. Now was the time to keep his head. "I'm no good at business, Asa, you know that. I'd only make things difficult for you. You do so well at that kind of thing." He knew that deep down she wanted no interference.

"And I'll study with an end in mind; you won't have to support me afterward," he finished.

"What end?" She was not won.

"I think I might like to teach." He was not at all sure of this; teaching seemed to him very very dull. He had chosen it only because he thought it might impress her; he could not have discussed the ministry without choking, not even then.

"Would you come back to Stoneville and teach?"

About that he had to make his position clear from the start. "No. I don't ever want to come back to Stoneville except for visits."

She raised her eyebrows. "Already getting uppity from the education you haven't got yet! People always feel that way for a while about the places they grew up. What's wrong with Stoneville, Mr. Boy Genius?"

"I just don't like it."

In the end, surprisingly enough, he believed this was what really won her. She did not want him back there in the town where he would be discontent, where he might criticize, where he might endanger status or business success.

To his amazement she consulted their brother. "What do you think of it, Avery?"

"I think," (Avery was getting a little sanctimonious and the propriety of his conversation had begun to burn in Ryan's eardrums), "I think people must make their own decisions." He smiled magnanimously.

"That's what you think, is it?" Ryan said, sarcastic.

"We'll miss you, of course."

This was an unbelievable lie, but it was part of what Avery understood brothers were supposed to say to each other. Ryan groaned aloud and did not trust himself to speak.

"All right," said Asa, more crisply. "We'll give it a try and see what you do with it."

And in the fall of 1923, Ryan Godwin went away to the State University for his undergraduate education.

Among his possessions were two quart jars from Lady Malveena's stock. She had slipped them in, grumbling.

"You'll be getting wilder stuff than this, I guess," she said.

"Not as good."

"I've put Mister Lord on your trail."

"Well I don't know . . ."

"Oh, never mind." Lady Malveena grinned, affectionate, resisting the desire to touch him. "He ain't nosy."

He said (she was the only thing in the whole damn town he was sad to leave), "Have a good winter, Lady Malveena."

"Wear your socks." She was frowning, preoccupied.

"I'll see you Christmas."

She turned away with her brown jaw set as hard as stone. She said carefully, "I hope they learns you to hang your pants elsewhere than on a chair."

And he went away to college, thinking on the train that it would never be the same—and he was right, of course.

In retrospect, the year of 1923 seemed to him the year in which Ryan Godwin (whoever and whatever that was) had actually been born; not painlessly, of course, but out of a found necessity and into his own world at last.

To him it was the most exciting world he had ever thought about or wanted. Later he knew they were not all hungry to learn or eager to teach; but he did not know it then. Later he was to find that faculty people were often as narrow-minded and stupid as the Stoneville citizenry, and even more irritating; but his freshman year they seemed to him giants of intellect. He was just beginning to frown at the thought of God, but he saw no inconsistency in his attitude toward books and teachers and the University. He worshiped it, pure and simple.

He lived in a dormitory and had six friends—a Brooklyn Jew who was going into law; a boy from Cratham County who had been president of the National 4-H clubs; a dramatics major whom he did not earmark as a homo until his junior year; a poet who had been in the merchant marine and could outswear them all and outdrink anyone; a boy from Alabama who was nothing, absolutely nothing, but had a great deal of spending money; and a member of the college newspaper staff who planned to be a correspondent for the *Times* and have harrowing adventures abroad.

It was 1923, and *Ulysses* had been out a year and one whole edition had been burned by U.S. Customs. When the poet got hold of a copy and rented it two days for a dollar, all of them grew rich. And in later years when Ryan read it again he was surprised to find that it was not, after all, only a first-person narrative of a woman's life in bed.

The poet and the dramatics major and the newspaperman and Ryan talked all the time; they argued all the time; they fought bitterly. Every opinion was something to be defended to the death; yet they talked much about having a flexible mind.

Main Street and *Babbitt* were out, read, discussed. They sat in a café and shouldered the weight of American mediocrity. It was all true, they said. These were the people they knew.

"Gadgets," the poet would say, "and no soul."

Someone urged him to write that down but he shrugged. He had so many thoughts that he could afford to discard a pearl or so as he passed.

"Any of you ever heard of Stoneville?"

"Never."

"That's the way it is. More Babbitts in the street than phone poles."

"Mine too. What I don't understand is how in the hell it happens to people?"

And they felt quite depressed about it all as if, now that they knew the situation and the dangers, they were obligated to go hurrying home on vacations and in the summertimes to stir up great rebellious crusades.

Ryan could see himself on the square in Stoneville, holding the torch high. "Freedom of the spirit!" he would cry. And then, in spite of himself, he would grin at the idea.

But even though he knew not even *Main Street* was quite like the town he knew, Ryan was not concerned. There would be such a book, such a satire some day; and he, Ryan Godwin, would write it.

He would get even with the whole dullness of home—the snippy schoolteachers and the congregations and the local businessmen and the tea parties and the church socials and the silly girls who were trained to marry quickly and to know that no man wanted a woman as smart as he was.

In the café and the dormitory they said: Prohibition will never come.

And Ryan learned to drink with—he believed—dignity and taste and enjoyment.

They said: What America needs is an intellectual aristocracy.

They said: The Bolsheviks must have something. And look what provocation they had!

They said: Willa Cather is remarkable.

They said: Sinclair Lewis will prostitute his talent.

They said: God, how I hate to go home. What will I SAY to those people! We live in different worlds!

And it *was* very interesting, that first post-freshman summer Ryan was home. He talked too much, too confidently. He patronized everyone. They looked at him blankly at first, and after a while, irritably.

But he felt so very far grown away from Stoneville now. It was like disembarking on a barbaric island and feeling such hopelessness about whether or not the savages would *ever* be able to learn anything; they were so set in their ways.

And worst of anything he came home to in Stoneville was his brother Avery—still-plump, twenty-two-year-old, Organ-Playing Avery.

For Avery had truly found himself at last.

Heretofore Avery had merely played the game correctly, knowing all the words and the rules and the nods and the smiles; but now he had achieved some skill at it. He was like a tennis player who, though not a star by any means, has developed some flair on the court that is especially his. Avery had developed a flair and that flair was individuality. Not too much, not enough to be dangerous; but enough to be remembered, recalled, addressed, consulted.

And it had changed him. He was at ease. He liked himself and what he was; and he smiled at his brother Ryan as if from off great heights.

It was an enraptured smile that annoyed Ryan almost to screaming, and with it went a series of confident generalities and Biblical allusions which rang like rusty saw blades on his brother's ear.

Ryan would sit on the stair treads late at night and say aloud in the darkness to relieve his feelings:

"What goes up must NEVER come down."

"ALWAYS cry over spilt milk."

"No clouds have silver linings."

"Man DOES live by bread alone."

"A fool and his money are NEVER parted."

And after a while, changing his position and glaring down the hall toward a sleeping (oblivious) and invisible brother, he would add:

"No I do NOT think the weather is nice."

"To the contrary, I DESPISE college."

"I do NOT agree that wisdom is not all in books."

But it did not help him much. In the mornings there was always Avery, always smiling, to tell him, "Small towns are certainly friendlier than big ones."

And "Modern living is just too fast."

"Well, you must remember they haven't found the missing link."

One more day, Ryan would think desperately, and I hang myself in the parlor.

On top of these things, Avery was losing weight. He looked much better and the young matrons of the church simpered all the time about how such a nice young man ought to get married.

But worst of all, for Ryan, was that everyone else except himself assumed that Avery had always been this way; they had always thought he was wonderful; Asa had always believed in him; he had been musically talented as a child. This gave the summer a dreamlike quality, and the unreality was so strong that Ryan felt if one more person thumped Avery fondly on the back his face would fall in—leaving a fattish little boy who never talked very much and liked to eat.

At first he went around asking, "What's happened to Avery?"

And Asa said, "Happened? You mean his losing weight?"

And the boys who never chose Avery to play on their team said, "What do you mean, happened to him?"

And the ladies in the choir said, "I *do* like that suit he's wearing."

So he gave it up. And he thought: Fall will never come.

And always Avery was walking around the house saying, "There's no place like home," and worse.

Ryan never got over the strange feeling Avery gave him that summer, and for years afterward he thought he might lean forward suddenly and say to his brother, "You don't have to pretend with me, you know." Or that, even worse, sometime he might catch hold of this thinner bland young man and ask accusingly, "What have you done with my brother?"

For the first time, too, the religious atmosphere at 309 Walnut Street had grown thick enough to cut off in slices. It had not been that way before in all of Ryan's memory, though the roots of it were there. Flambert Godwin had been a churchman and stern, and rigid in his fundamentalism; but in practice he had behaved as though both he and God were too gentlemanly to intervene very much in each other's affairs.

And Lady Malveena had gone about the house with Mister Lord in tow as long as Ryan could recall, but that was not the same. Mister Lord was for companionship and solace; he was strictly a subordinate.

Now it was church everywhere, with lengthy blessings at mealtimes and a great deal of concern about liquor and the Faith of one's Fathers and the commercialization of Christmas. Avery gave the blessings. Once in a while now he prayed aloud in church meetings and his choir members said he did it beautifully.

Sometimes they would ask Ryan, "Have you ever heard Avery give a prayer?" He felt like saying he had never seen Avery do ballet or sing a solo or juggle china cups, either; but he said only that he never had, and all of them said he did it beautifully.

It was not long before Asa began to ask him why he was not more like Avery. And Avery asked him to sing in the choir while he was home. And Reverend Kane told him pointedly that Avery was a credit to his family.

So the freshman rebellion congealed into a war. The cockiness turned into superiority and took on contempt. There were arguments and scenes and Ryan said he would be damned if he would ever live in this priggish town and Asa said he shouldn't swear.

(But Avery said with a gentle smile that the only reason people swore was because they would not take the patience to develop a good vocabulary; and Ryan almost pushed his face in to see who was behind it.)

In the Second House, he and Lady Malveena sipped stealthily at wine.

"This wine never tasted so good," said Lady Malveena, "as it tastes this year. You want to know why?"

"The need is greater," said Ryan, deep in gloom.

"Naw, it's cause we got the flavor of sin in it these days. I always used to sneak about it but there wasn't much excitement. Now I know and you know Miss Asa would have a conniption if she was to come in. And don't it taste better?"

As a matter of fact, it did.

"I don't know what in the world got into Avery," said Ryan. Mentally he was saying to his brother: *I will look on the wine when it is red in the cup and I don't give a damn if it stings like asps and adders.*

Lady Malveena refilled her glass. "Preacher Kane say it was the Spirit." She said it cautiously, not looking at him.

"Do you think that?"

She spread her hands, shrugged. "All kinds of spirits."

"Well, I wish you'd have him conjured. I wish you'd get him back blank and dull like he used to be. At least he wasn't any trouble. Can't you overfeed him?"

She pursed her mouth, angry. "He say gluttony is as bad as drink. One of the seven sins or something. Here, let me fill you up again."

"I'll never get through the summer."

But he did, of course, and three more after that until he was through and a graduate assistant in English and then an M.A.

After that he was lucky enough to get an instructorship at Wellman Women's College in Massachusetts and it was as he had planned—Stoneville only for visits and not too often. There was nothing to draw him back, not at first.

By the time Ryan graduated from the University he had, as Asa would have phrased it, Lost His Faith—but without the agony supposed to accompany such an amputation. For Asa it verified all her belief that nonreligious colleges were, by definition, atheistic.

And she could never forgive him for his default. She seemed to think it was something he had done willfully to annoy her; and she clung even more to Avery. Even when Ryan had constructed back certain other kinds of faith, it was never anything she could understand, and the very fact that he kept exploring and reconsidering and changing his mind elated her.

"God is the only surety," she would write him.

So the two of them grew away farther and farther, and Avery pleased her more and more; and he never corresponded with Lady Malveena. When he went home he found her always as he remembered except saner, sounder, stronger. Apart from that, the visits were short; they were duties.

That was the way things stood among the Godwins until 1936, when Avery married a girl who had come from Greenway and who —properly enough—sang in his choir. There was his list again: a man must have a wife, reasonably attractive, rather quiet, womanly.

Ah, but Jessica had been—here Ryan grinned—she had been more than that. And he remembered once hearing her laugh in Lady Malveena's Second House; he remembered the sun on her face in the orchard; he remembered her hands, teasing . . .

Ryan swung his feet out of bed and stood up decisively in the crooked room. That was all of it for now. He would think about Jessica some other time; he would not do it now and on this day.

But in spite of his resolve he was depressed and he got out his shaving things with such ferocity that someone—looking in—would have thought him about to slash his wrists.

He had lain in bed later than he wanted to, half thinking, half drowsing, and now the sun was up and coming through the wet oak as through a filter. The leaves turned in a breeze and shone at the window.

He had a headache that swung from one temple to another like a great clock pendulum.

And frowning toward the window he thought savagely, *Into each life some rain must fall, eh Avery?*

And he remembered how he had once thought the greatest joke in the world would be to slip up to Avery on a dark night and whisper in his ear, "The husband is always the last to know." He and Jessica had laughed about that together.

Well, thought Ryan, getting a new razor blade, he who laughs last laughs best and the race is not always to the swift.

For in the end she had gone with Avery. The wife had died with the husband, which may have been proper. And Avery liked to have everything proper.

8.

It was very much later than Ryan had thought and the house was quiet.

Fen was standing at the foot of the stairs looking up anxiously, but when he saw Ryan he hurried between the curtains and into the dining room and stood there fiddling with the catch to the china closet as though it were the most interesting thing in the world.

He must have been up a long time, thought Ryan, smiling. He came up behind him and when he still did not turn, stepped boldly into view.

Fen did his best to look surprised and casual. "Why, hello. I didn't hear you come down."

"I was very quiet," Ryan admitted with another smile. "You must have been up for hours."

"Just about."

"Is it ten yet?"

"A little past," said Fen. "I think Lady Malveena saved you breakfast."

"Asa gone?"

"Yes sir."

The two of them walked into the kitchen. Lady Malveena was on the back porch and simply put her head in at the door to give a disapproving sniff.

"Good afternoon," said Lady Malveena pointedly. She gave another loud sniff but she was not really annoyed.

Ryan said, "Fen, have you ever noticed how virtuous early risers are?"

"No sir," said Fen.

"There's a whole group. The People Who Have Quit Smoking. The Non-Fingernail Biters. The Women Who Have Babies by Natural Childbirth."

Lady Malveena put her head in again to say that she didn't think baby-having was anything to talk about before twelve o'clock noon.

Ryan went over and shook the coffeepot hopefully, gauged it at two or three cups and put it over the heat. "Is there anything left for us sluggards? If not, I'll settle for a cup of coffee."

At this, Lady Malveena bustled into the kitchen happily, as if she had just been waiting to be asked.

"No reason there would be except kindheartedness," she said, pretending to be grumpy. Then she caught sight of Fen who was looking into one of the cabinets. "I hope you're not aiming to eat again."

"I thought I'd just watch," said Fen. "I wish I had a bicycle."

"Give him some coffee about half cream," said Lady Malveena to Ryan, handing out two cups and saucers from the shelf. "What would you do on a bicycle except test bones?" She got out a plate from the warming cabinet and put it with a fork at Ryan's place.

There were hotcakes on it, four hotcakes, already buttered with a creamy glaze. "Miss Asa wouldn't let you ride in the street."

"She might," said Fen. "How do you know?"

"Sun going to rise tomorrow—how do I know? That's the nature of it. You want more butter?"

"Nothing. Just time. Looks wonderful."

"Looks are nothing," said Lady Malveena. "Bite in. Bear down."

He bit in and bore down and they were good, light, fluffy.

"Here's your coffee," she said. Fen said thank you.

Ryan was pouring a thick red-brown stream of syrup over the cakes and thinking how rich and vivid were the colors of food—scarlet fruits and crisp green lettuce and sun-yellow ears of corn, brown-topped bread and rich cream and deep dark berry jam. It pleased him, as though someone had done it deliberately to tempt the appetite.

"They're good, too," said Fen, watching him smile into his plate. "I had some this morning." Fen sat almost hunched at the table, his feet propped on the chair rungs so that his knees came up like something on crooked froglegs. He had both his hands cupped around the coffee mug, Ryan noticed, the way we used to on chilly winter mornings. Asa and Avery and me, after Father had gone downtown. Asa would tell us to hurry up because she always hated to see people lingering at food.

"Hotcakes all right?" Lady Malveena sounded angry and suspicious since he had not declared himself.

"Wonderful," he said, taking a sizable bite for proof. "Asa uptown?"

"Um," said Lady Malveena. She looked like a woman making up her mind. In another minute she said casually, "They's going to be a carnival this week."

"A carnival? Where? When?" Fen had put down his cup.

"Oh well," said Lady Malveena. "Miss Asa won't take you. She don't hold much with 'em."

You sneaky old woman, thought Ryan, grinning.

"Couldn't you take me, Lady Malveena?"

"Who you think!" She positively snorted. "If you was a little baby that would be all right, but it's not seemly for you to go to a carnival with an old colored woman."

Ryan was sure that Lady Malveena had never in her life thought of herself as an "old colored woman."

"You can go with me if you like," he said. "I go to things like that with the other unrighteous." He grinned at both of them.

Lady Malveena said fiercely that for a minute there she thought that maybe the cat had gotten not only his tongue but likely his whole insides, heart and liver and all.

"You're a shameless old bitch," said Ryan.

"You do your bitching while you eat on somebody else's hot-cakes," said Lady Malveena, and looked as though she might take them up and slap them atop his head. These arguments were the things he had remembered from a long time back but they were—he could see—startlingly new to Fen, who was sitting with his jaw dropped down as if the hinges had broken.

"Don't you want to go to the carnival?" Lady Malveena demanded. "Where's your manners? You want to let on a Yankee fellow got more gumption?"

"I'm not a Yankee," Ryan protested.

"You got the disposition for it," she snapped.

"I'd like very much to go," Fen stammered, looking from one to the other of them as though they had changed radically before his eyes into two totally unknown people.

"All right," said Ryan. To Lady Malveena he added, "Satisfied?"

For all his joking he felt half trapped and she knew it.

"Don't go spoiling a sweet smell with a bad," she told him. "Trouble with you is you hate to be caught in a goodness. Was the same way when you was a little boy." She leaned forward. "I tell you—loving don't leave you naked."

"It could," said Ryan, grinning.

"You got a dirty mind," said Lady Malveena. "That's okay with me. I know you. I know you think joking gonna help. But it won't."

"What are you talking about?" said Fen.

"About you, what you think? Listen," said Lady Malveena, "this Ryan fellow here, he could buy you a bicycle. He wouldn't care what streets you rode in."

"What are you trying to do?" said Ryan, growing genuinely annoyed.

"If ever I throws the right switch, they gonna turn some juice into you," said Lady Malveena, looking bitter. "Listen, what they been doing to you up there in Massachusetts? They been hanging you out to dry like laundry? Used to be, you wasn't a bad boy."

"For that, I thank you," said Ryan, trying to tease but feeling a little stiff.

"Of course, you had good raising then," said Lady Malveena.

"And again, I thank . . ."

But she would not joke about it. "Listen," she said, almost lying the length of the table to get her face toward his. "Listen, how do you think Miss Jessica would take on to all this? She'd think they froze your insides, sure. Listen, where you get this idea you don't owe anybody anything?"

She had not lectured him so in years. He told himself sternly: I am forty-eight years old and I don't have to listen. . . .

"You know what it really is? You owe everybody everything! That's all. It don't fit good, but that's the way it is." She slammed a pot lid onto a pot on the stove. "You make me mad," she said bitterly. "You make me plenty mad. Let's not talk more on the thing, not this very morning. You listen to me, Fenwick Godwin, how would you like to have a bicycle? What color would it be?"

"It would be red," said Fen, but his voice was faint.

"That's good," she said darkly. "How many wheels?"

"Two wheels."

"Real tires with inner tubes?"

"Hold twenty-five pounds of air."

"That's good. How do you put on brakes?"

"You step the pedal down in the back."

"And what side of the street?"

"Right side, like cars."

"That's right," and she said angrily to Ryan, "Don't ever tell me I can't change no subject when I set my mind to it!" and walked out of the kitchen and onto the porch and sat down on the steps. Ryan was terrified for fear she might cry and he would not know what to do. He choked on the hotcakes.

"What's the matter with everybody?" said Fen.

"It's the rain last night," said Ryan vaguely.

"What are you fighting about?"

"Listen," said Ryan, picking up Lady Malveena's approach, "listen, I said I'd take you to the damn carnival, didn't I?"

Fen was completely bewildered. "What are you mad at me about?" he said.

Lady Malveena got up off the steps and came back into the kitchen looking tired. "Nobody's mad at you," she said.

"I'm not ever what people want!" cried Fen.

Ryan looked up at him, surprised at the outburst.

"What am I supposed to do about that!" Fen demanded, very close to tears.

"Everything's all right," said Lady Malveena. "You're just fine."

"If it isn't Aunt Asa, it's something else. Who do they want me to be?" And to the horror of them both he put his face down on the table and began to cry quietly. He did not sob; it was as though he had been through this too many times.

"Go back to Massachusetts," said Lady Malveena. She would not look at Ryan. She put her arm on Fen's shoulders and said over and over, "You're all right, Fenwick Godwin. You're just fine." And to Ryan she said, "Don't go stirring up hungers you don't aim to meet."

"I didn't!" Ryan protested. "It was you! I never meant . . ." And then he knew it did not matter who had started it and he came around the table and put his hand on Fen's shoulder and took up Lady Malveena's tune. "Everything's all right," he said. "You're just fine, Fen. You're fine with me just the way you are."

"Let me alone," said Fen; and he got up and went out of the kitchen and down to the orchard and out of sight in the grass.

Lady Malveena was disgusted. "Oh, you're a pretty one, you are," she said. She went to the door and stared down into the orchard where all the grass was motionless. After a while she said, still angry, but in a lower voice, "Whatever ails you, you don't have to take it out on a little boy, do you?"

Ryan said in a tired voice that he hadn't intended to take anything out on anybody.

Lady Malveena sat down. "But things happen, don't they? Half of nothing we never meant to start. You just gets carried on. You listen to me, Ryan Godwin, you think I meant to go loving that boy? I'm old. I've loved lots of people. I'm tired of all that business, getting the living sucked up out of you every time somebody hurts or cries or gets himself bothered someway. You got to be young to stand a thing like that."

"I'm sorry," said Ryan. "About everything."

"There was you when you was little, and there was Miss Jessica from a distance. And you ain't forgot I had a couple husbands long time ago. You was little then, too. But when this one come along, I meant to do for him proper but I never meant to step in that river one more time. I never meant to go under and downstream one more single time."

"Nobody ever does."

"Look," she said (half pleading), "he's a smart boy. He's nothing like his Daddy was. He's a little shy, maybe, but everything he starts to say gets chopped off 'fore he's through. You're no spring chicken any more. There's a time when you invest in the ones coming after. That is, unless you're pretty certain you got no need to. You got no need to, Ryan Godwin? You that well pleased with everything?"

"Lady Malveena, I know he's a nice boy. I like him myself. But what in the world would I do with him? Even if Asa would let him come, which she never would."

Lady Malveena put on her best shrewd look. She said, "Miss Asa's never adopted him. He's old enough now they'd take his wishes in account."

Ryan saw his whole life upset; he saw the apartment gone and some house rented near a grammer school; he saw the competent iron-faced housekeeper and oatmeal for breakfast. He said to Lady Malveena weakly (and he knew it was weak), "You sure have got a nerve." Besides, how could he plan for the future?

She looked at him a long minute. "Well *you* ain't, if that's any comfort to you. They could slice you up and I guess you'd never feel a thing. Well, that's handy to know, anyway." And she got up from the table and picked up the feather duster she had brought back earlier and shook it angrily over the garbage pail. "I just hope you sleeps good," she grunted. "I just hope you eats my cooking in satisfying ways. I just hope lightning don't reach down for you on the streets. That's all I hope."

And turning with a flick that was as contemptuous as a gauntlet she went out of the room and left him there with cold coffee, cold pancakes, congealed butter, ancient syrup.

Fen sat in the orchard and plaited grass very carefully so he would not cry or otherwise be silly.

He could have swallowed his tongue all the way backwards if that would have taken back the crying he had done in the kitchen in front of Lady Malveena and Uncle Ryan. He would have turned his nose so the hairs were growing outside, up and down between his eyes, before he would have done such a thing.

And he went on in this vein for some time, plaiting the grass very very carefully and throwing it away. Better that his ears had been dragged down to his ankles than that he should give himself away like that!

And he sat there and curled himself about the kernel that was ME and he said to himself, I have to be more careful.

For Fen knew how it was. He knew that you built the house you lived in brick by brick (he had been thinking about that for years, ever since the pigs and the wolf that had huffed and puffed and had never been able to come inside) and that you built it up about you in four walls on all sides. And the bricks were made of the Not-Things—the times you did *not* cry, the secrets you *never* told, the flicker of interest or enthusiasm you refused to give away. You made the house out of everything you kept for yourself away from everybody else, and after a while you were safe and warm in it, and NOBODY (not by the hair of my chinny-chin-chin) absolutely NOBODY, even strange uncles who were not at all tattooed, could come inside.

As for getting back outside yourself, who in the world would want to? Would one not have everything he needed, if he took care?

So now he sat in the grass in the orchard, plaiting and twisting, and every time he turned a blade of grass in his fingers he was mending a breach in the wall.

All that he understood about the quarrel between Lady Malveena and Uncle Ryan was that it was really over something a long time ago. She had told him that much. She had once said she could remember back before he was born (unbelievable, that was; and gradually he had learned that things had *happened* back in that mist. Not just the things in history books (although he doubted some of them) but things had happened to other people in these very places, back in the days when he was nothing. Now he knew that Uncle Ryan had once been no taller and had once been in this grass behind this house and that there were things coming out of that time he would never understand.

Being born was a mess, sometimes. It was very definite. There was a Before and an After for you from that time forward, and there was nothing you could do about it. If he had been born on the same day as Ryan they would go away together and he could let the wall ruin and wear down.

But then where would his mother be? And what would become of this little boy in the orchard now, who wanted a bicycle?

And he thought that there was no meddling with when you were born; that would gum up the works for sure.

Then he decided if you were the first man ever born, then you would have had a hand in everything. Nobody could remember past you. But then he remembered that the first man born was Cain, and that wouldn't be so good either; and probably Adam and Eve were always talking things he had not known about. The weight of time lay over him now full and enormous and heavy, like a fallen sky.

(He took his shoelace out and began to string it back with care.)

Aunt Asa said that the Lord made Cain a nigger (that was His Mark) but Fen hoped the Lord hadn't done that. He hoped the Lord had put that Mark so a man might hide it sometimes—cover it up or wrap it or comb his hair down over it, so no one could notice for a while. He thought Cain ought to have had that chance now and again to hide the thing.

And he saw Cain walking and walking on yellow hills, the only black man in the world; and he was so black that people saw him a long way off and would not come near. And maybe all his life Cain had never seen anybody except at a great distance, always going away. He had never touched anybody else, or put his hand on hair, or brushed his shoulder, passing, on their shoulders.

But the back of his mind said that Cain was supposed to have married somebody so maybe that wasn't so. Except if Cain was black, who would have married him? Aunt Asa said the Lord never meant for the black and the white to marry, like some people wanted.

And Fen said to himself, There was one girl somewhere, white and pink; and she didn't care.

But when he said that he looked around nervously. Nobody could have possibly heard what Fen said to Fen behind the brick wall, but it didn't hurt to be careful. He wouldn't want anybody to catch him saying that.

(All the time Fen was thinking these things the thought of Ryan and Lady Malveena and the carnival and the red bicycle were there, but they were dim; they were pushed down and back and over the edge.)

But if God had not turned black people black, he didn't know how they got to be that way at all, with their palms and feet still pink like something that had got left out. That had, as Lady Malveena said, missed the tarbrush.

There was an old old colored man in town (everybody called him Cheeper because when he talked he sounded like a cricket, very small, very lost; and he was so old that all his skin was spotted. It was as if the black paint on him had worn so thin it was finally peeling off, and now everybody would be able to see that he was white underneath and had been white all his life and none of them had known it.

Whenever he saw Cheeper anywhere uptown Fen would think that maybe when all colored people got old and died they turned back to white again, except he didn't see that would be much help to them unless it was in Heaven.

Then he had a clear picture of Heaven, very shiny, and crowded with people in white dresses; and having snowbanks and icicles. He and Aunt Asa would be walking down the street (there was snow but it was never cold, only beautiful) and everybody everywhere would be white all over and when you picked up the snow and held it in your hand it would glow warm on the skin.

(And he hated the thought that Uncle Ryan would not be there; and he plaited an angry weed and wondered if people didn't ever go to Heaven just for being *nice?*)

At any rate, they would be there (people who worked so hard at it as Asa did would go straightway—he was sure of that—and not have to wait for judgment) and when they walked down the streets between tall walls of snow, a woman would speak to them.

"Hello, Sister Asa. Hello, Brother Fen." She would smile mysteriously. She would be very tall and graceful and her fingers would be long and white and full of ruby rings.

"Hello," they would say, surprised.

Then she would tell them that she was Lady Malveena, and at first they could not believe it, it was all so strange.

But after a while they would know who it was for sure, because she would remember things to tell them—the orchard, and how the kitchen stove had smoked, and Miss Clara all the time playing solitaire. Fen was afraid Aunt Asa wouldn't like it much at first—everybody being alike—but being Heaven, what could she say?

And he turned on his back and smiled up at the sky as if he were pleased with it. That must be the way Heaven would be when it was, the same for all of them. And he saw that the clouds were as white as snowbanks passing over Stoneville.

The only trouble was Uncle Ryan and whether he would go or not. Fen thought he ought to pray about that (he had been told this was the thing to do) but it was so hard to pray in the daytime when the sun was out. He thought God got realer at night and during thunderstorms, and that maybe at such times it was because God had leaned down a little closer to the earth, knowing he would not be seen because of the dark and the rainclouds.

After a while Fen lay down on his stomach and turned one side of his face into the grass and thought about the bicycle and about going to a real carnival. There was a smell to grass that was different from any other smell—a sharp and tangy thing that hung at the back of the nose so that some days, even sitting in a schoolroom when summer was gone, you could remember how grass smelled, as if you held it in your hand.

He took a long breath of the grass and the orchard and put it way in the back of his nose and saved it toward some long day in the sixth grade.

Somewhere overhead bees passed, grumbling; and away way off (it was so far that he had heard it for a few seconds before he was aware of hearing it) a train whistled and went by taking things someplace.

Fen liked all of that. He liked smelling the things you did not try to smell, and hearing the things your ears were not set for—doing it all without thought or effort. It gave him the feeling that everything about him was in good working order, so that if the real Me should ever take a vacation away from the house, nothing would stop. The hands would reach and the tongue talk good English and the feet would carry him places, quite as if he were still inside.

Then Fen heard something else, something from underneath him, from deep in the earth—going *thump-bump, thump-bump, thump-bump;* until all up and down his body he could feel the deep persistent throb just under the layer of grass. It was strange; it sounded old and tireless. He grew tense from excitement and he pressed his whole body harder into the grass and pushed his ear down till the sand ground on it.

It's the heart of God! he thought excitedly. I hear the heart of God beating!

And he sucked in his breath so nothing should bother his ear from hearing the wonder of that great endless sound.

But in a few more minutes he discovered with sharp disappointment it was only his own heart after all, his own small heart thumping and pumping up and down in his body. He sat up quickly in the orchard grass with his shoulders motionless from shame; he felt he had blasphemed against eternity.

Then he thought to himself, Perhaps if God has a heart, it sounds very much like that. It sounds very much the way my own heart sounds.

He sat growing warm in the sun and feeling comforted.

9.

THE SEASON was passing and it was beginning to darken earlier.

Back in the summer (Ryan remembered) the end of day had dragged out long, and light would cling stubbornly to the sky even when one could no longer see the sun.

But now, when the sun went down of an evening, it seemed to do so with a great sucking motion so that all the light went out of the world with a rush like (he smiled at his unpoetic thought) like *the last water going down a bathtub.*

It was the day after the carnival. They had gone; they had seen the crazy mirrors, and the wild man from Borneo eat live chickens; they had ridden on the merry-go-round and Ferris wheel; they had gotten a teddy bear at the rifle range and some pink dishes from pitching pennies; and for the first time Ryan had heard Fen laugh aloud. He thought he would have gone to a hundred carnivals for that.

Now it was late the next afternoon and Ryan was on the way uptown. He thought he might go to a movie alone after he had eaten in some café. All that day he had gone through his notes on Dostoevsky and, to tell the truth, they had read like the thoughts of some other man. By late afternoon he had thought if he did not get outside that house he would climb up the draperies, gibbering.

On top of that, he had spent half an hour assuring Asa that the dishes and the teddy bear had been *purchased* at the carnival and not acquired in some low gambling game, and that he and Fen had behaved throughout in a perfectly acceptable manner. In fact, he had grown so annoyed that he had asked Asa why Fen could not have a bicycle and had been told that they were not only dangerous but expensive.

So by now Ryan was not in a good humor all the way around. He had, furthermore, put the end of a cigarette against a pair of good trousers and one of the things he would do if he got uptown in time was drop them off to be repaired.

He would take them (everyone in Stoneville did) to the shop on Main which belonged to the little Jew tailor and after that he would see what there was to do. And he thought, If I go back home the eyes of that boy will eat me. Why should a thing like an afternoon at a carnival seem to Fen and Lady Malveena the making of incorruptible covenants?

He had the trousers in a paper wrapping and suddenly they rattled in his arms like something live. And that made him think, angrily, that he should never have been smoking the cigarette that had turned on him and burned his pants. It was a good-sized hole; it would call for careful work. But that was all right, the little Jew was a good workman.

That made Ryan realize with some surprise that he did not know (none of them knew) the little Jew tailor's name. Perhaps years and years ago when the shop first opened up on Main Street (Number 10) it had been hung out on a sign, looking overconfident in its black and white newness for everyone to read. What had it said, that sign—a Berg? a Blum? a Stein?—he could not remember. It seemed to him now that none of them had ever read it really. They had all said, without undue concern, "If you need reweaving done or tailor work, there's a little Jew on Main that does his business well."

All kinds of unfairness, Ryan thought. There would never be a race riot in Stoneville. No colored boys would ever be lynched on any of these quiet streets. But the barriers were always up; and the people on both sides of them knew they were there.

So if ever a sign had hung it had grown, after a while, dim and peeling and flyspecked, and nobody had ever used the name at all or called him by it; until the little Jew tailor had finally taken it down.

At night! thought Ryan, sharply. The tailor had gone out one dark night when none of the good people of Stoneville could see and had taken down the shabby thing. It was as though he had offered something and had been refused. Thus they had taught him the pattern gently (oh so gently, for Stoneville was full of the well-bred); and the pattern said: *Everybody belongs in his place.*

The pattern said: *The truth is niggers are happier just the way they are.*

The pattern said: *Wouldn't have any trouble if it wasn't for the N.A.A.C.P. stirring things up.*

The pattern said: *All a Jew wants is money. Even the nice ones.*

And Ryan thought about the pattern and he looked about him thoughtfully as he walked, until it seemed to him nearly all of it was false, careful straight houses embroidered on fields of crisp green yarn.

All about him, up and down Walnut Street and the other streets, the houses were quiet and partially shuttered and dim lights showed from back rooms, from dining rooms and kitchens. It was suppertime. People in Stoneville were very punctual about suppertime; they ate soon after the businesses closed uptown. By now the children had all been called in and washed and soon the fathers would come in (false-looking fathers, like the ones in first-grade readers) and finish up their newspapers in the living rooms. At this time of day when some child was let play late outdoors because of some delay he would do so nervously, not very comfortable, knowing he could not start any lengthy soul-absorbing game. He was on borrowed time. He had an extra five minutes or ten, but when they finally called him everyone would be very cross and would blame him because his hands were not already clean. . . .

Ryan remembered how that was—the stolen extra time that was never wholly yours, and the first lightning bugs coming out and the shadows and the Hide-and-Seek that was oddly terrifying since it was getting dark and even your own front steps were growing unfamiliar.

He liked this time of day, always had. Twilights as such were something remarkable, out of time, something half-eerie; there hung a little holiness in this neutral ground that was neither night nor day and yet had elements of both.

Lonely times, twilights. A sense of suspension between dark and light that made one wonder *Who am I? Where is this place I am?*

Always they (poets and writers and such) said that dusk was gray or—in the fancier descriptions—silver; but that was not really how this was. How might one describe that last faint touch of yellow, that almost but not quite vanished light that haunted the eye everywhere, lingering not only in the sky but on grass and rooftops and between the leaves of trees? It was this which made the twilight seem so melancholy, Ryan thought, that bit of nearly invisible yellowness.

And at this he had a sudden sense of well-being, like a man who has suddenly crystalized and expressed the yearnings of generations. His own conceit amused him, and his irritation with home and with Lady Malveena's smugness faded.

Now there were no slamming doors (these were old houses; nobody ran in any of these hallways; and the old ladies had already left their porch rockers. The lawns were watered, darker green and shiny, waiting for night. Ryan turned into Wynberry, passed the new office building (it seemed cheap to him, cheap brick, crumbly concrete, too much chrome on the glass doors; and presently he was uptown.

Here, too, things were slowing down, getting quiet. Only a few cars passed and these were driven in a purposeful manner, bearing people who were going home, or running essential errands. The dress shops were already closed and it was the last hour for barbers and button-makers and watch repairmen. These stood in the doors of their small shops shading their eyes against the last bit of light, sometimes calling up and down to one another:

"Hot day!"

"What?"

"I said *hot day.*"

"Oh. Sure was."

The streets which had baked all day were cooling. At 6:15 the street sweeper would go up and down, spraying water and turning the brush that swirled and swirled and caught the papers in the gutter and took them on. Children who could would run out to watch it go by and the street-sweeper man would wave at them. He always moved slowly; if they ran they could keep alongside or get enough ahead to throw out leaves and watch the big brush spin them round and round. The man would frown at that as though one more leaf would be too much for his machine to carry.

And Ryan thought that Fen must watch the street-sweeper man go by when he could. Maybe he chewed the tar off telephone poles and tried to climb the prongs set in them for the linesmen. Maybe he took wide maple leaves and held them tense across his mouth and popped holes in them.

And he grumped up his shoulders like a dog ridding himself of rain and would not think of Fen any more.

He quickened his pace and came by the library where Cornelia Satterfield still worked, and would always work; and to the square and turned right onto Main. The Stoneville Hotel was on the square, five stories, the skyscraper of the whole town. He could remember when he had thought no building could be any higher, and had put the Woolworth Building down as some fairy tale.

It was an anticlimax to come to the dark entry to the little Jew tailor's shop and find it already closed and locked. Ryan stood outside on the sidewalk and the small man in his own skull was amused. What did you expect? Did you want to find the man inside, looking bitter and discriminated against? What would that have proved?

And he wrote on the outside of the package: *Cigarette burn, left leg. R. Godwin,* and dropped it through the large door opening which had been left for mail.

By that time it was six, and the street sweeper was early. Ryan could see it at the end of Main, coming slowly, leaving the street dark behind it and the gutter clean.

Two men went by and spoke to him vaguely and one said that the tailor's was already closed. Ryan nodded. In this town everybody spoke to everybody else; he was not used to that as he once had been. A woman passed, worrying too hard to see him, and he noticed the lint hanging in her hair like a cobweb. Up and down the street men were coming out of doors and climbing into the last waiting cars, and the man at the Buffalo Grill turned on his lights, including the neon one in the window that said BEER. That seemed a good idea, and Ryan went in and had one fast—to quench his thirst—and one slow, for enjoyment. He was working on the enjoyment when Travis came in and bought a bottle of ginger ale and sat down at another table and made himself a drink.

"You watch that," said the man behind the counter. Maybe his name was Buffalo. "If that cop comes in here again, you get that under the table."

Travis looked disgusted. "Have I ever failed to do that?"

The man shrugged. "One time you will," he said, "and I'm going

in here in the evenings. I have a room in a boardinghouse. I know all the other people in the boardinghouse but praise God they're no friends of mine."

"Don't you get lonesome?"

Travis screwed up his eyes and looked at him as if against a glare. "You mean women?"

"Well . . . that, too."

"There's a girl. She's . . . she's adequate. Are you asking because you're in the market or are you just asking?"

Ryan took a gulp of beer. "Just asking. Just curious."

"She runs a beauty shop. Out on the Greenwood road. Used to be married, husband drove a truck. One day he kept on driving. I go out there now and again."

Travis had himself another drink and Ryan started on the new beer. They were old friends.

"You heard about the college? The one they want to build here?"

"Asa mentioned it."

"I thought you might be interested, college man yourself and all."

"That's what she thought, too."

"Okay," said Travis shortly. "Pardon me."

"It's just that I don't believe any of it. Why would anyone build a college in a town like this? No business district, no rail facilities to speak of. Nothing to draw a college here. And was ever a town as close-minded as this one?"

"Probably," said Travis. "I've already said it's likely no worse than a hundred others."

"I don't believe it," Ryan said.

"Why don't we have supper together?" Travis proposed. "I'll get out of eating that boardinghouse crap and you won't have to look at your sister's arrowhead face all evening."

Ryan said he thought that was a fine idea but where in the world would they eat?

They settled on the hotel and finished beer and drinks and paid the man and left. It was dark outside. The streetlights were on but no one was walking under them and the ticket seller at the Monarch Theater was reading a comic book. She did not even glance up; one felt he would have to bang on the glass before she could be bothered to accept anybody's money.

They went into the hotel, had some more drinks, ate steaks, grew friendlier. They had an argument about society and individuals but Ryan was getting hazier by then and did not remember next day how it went. It was all interwoven with Stoneville—that he remembered—but whether they had argued about that part or if he had himself made that connection he did not know.

And Ryan, though he had never meant to, told Travis about the illness.

"You've not been back here, you say, for nine or ten years. So what are you really doing here now?"

"Don't know. Thinking. It won't be longer than a month or so. After that I have to go to Baltimore for . . . for some medical work."

"Something damned important," said Travis flatly.

"I guess so. If I decide to go at all. It's my decision."

"Always is," said Travis. He spread his hands. "If this medical work is *necessary*, of course, there's not much decision in it. Except for idiots."

"Necessary." Ryan considered the word soberly; or as soberly as he could consider anything by that time. "It is and it isn't, all at the same time."

Travis waited, expressionless.

It was then that Ryan realized how much he wanted to get it said, how much he had wanted to tell it for days and weeks. He remembered at first on the bus coming home he had thought he might tell it to some stranger he would never see again, just to get a hunk of the awareness taken out of him. So he said hurriedly (the way people do when they think it helps to be rapid about unpleasant things), "The chances are that it will only be a matter of prolongation."

Travis was looking into his own glass silently. And Ryan was angry at himself for having put the man in such an impossible situation. What in the world did I expect the man to say?

"Prolongation. That's a funny way to put it." Travis turned his glass. "I should think mothers might feel the same way when they keep their kids from falling on their heads out of high chairs. Let's prolong it by all means, that's the way I feel about such things. In fact . . ." (he looked at Ryan full face), "in fact, I don't care much for your attitude."

Why the son of a bitch! The smug uninvolved son of a bitch! Ryan got his mouth open to say as much in no uncertain terms.

"What's wrong with you, if you don't mind my asking?" Travis went on, unconcerned.

His anger went as quickly as it had come. It was the first time he had said it to anybody. "Carcinoma," he said—and then harshly, wanting to hear the thing at its ugliest, he corrected himself. "*Cancer* of the larynx. And then it isn't restricted any more. It seems to be into the sinuses, too."

Travis sat waiting calmly and Ryan plunged on. This isn't so bad, he thought in some surprise.

"Into the pyriform sinus," he amplified, quoting from Jim's words after the examination. "An extrinsic lesion—does that sound right? It's supposed to be a difficult piece of surgery."

Across the table Travis was filling their glasses again. "How about radiation?" Travis said, watching the ice and the glasses as though this ticklish job took all his concentration.

"It's pretty near the brain," said Ryan. "They may try roentgen rays. Jim tells me you've got two problems when you use irradiation to treat cancer—the local extent and character of the disease and what he calls contiguous cartilaginous infiltration. He told me what that meant too, but I've forgotten." He was a little surprised to find he remembered the words so exactly. It interested him, the way the brain stubbornly absorbed certain facts even when it did not understand them all, as though they might be essential to know later. Part of the survival business maybe, he thought.

"Who's Jim?" said Travis.

"Doctor. Friend of mine."

"Is he a good one?"

"I think so."

"In view of all this, I especially don't understand what you're doing here on an end-of-summer holiday," Travis was saying, "I'd think time was of the utmost importance."

"Time," repeated Ryan. How much? How long? He shrugged. "I was late finding out. They wanted me to go ahead, of course. With the surgery, I mean. But they weren't as optimistic as I had hoped." He swallowed. "There's a high mortality rate for the sinus business. The question boiled down to whether it would prolong or foreshorten . . . things. So I wanted a week or so to think about it. Or maybe longer." He had begun to feel defiant. "They can't *make* me have an operation, you know."

"That's right," said Travis, in the tone of voice one would use for an idiot or a child. "Asa said something about your doing a book."

"Asa would," snapped Ryan. He was annoyed by the other's tone.

"Fiction?"

"I only mentioned it to keep her quiet. I'd thought about some critical studies. Dostoevsky. Class notes and commentary."

"Will there be time?" This time Travis' voice was very matter-of-fact, as if he were talking about the lapse between now and the next train. Ryan was grateful for that.

"That's the big question. Suppose I stayed here without any treatment—there'd probably be time to get it done. The surgery, on the other hand, might mean no time at all; or it might mean time for two books or three after that."

"I see." He asked, as if he had just thought of it, "Is there pain?"

"Not yet."

"What would you call this book?"

This much at least he had thought about. "I think I would call it *The Lover of Souls*. It's a phrase in the Apocrypha."

"Meaning Dostoevsky loved souls? Or God?"

"Both. The apocryphal bit is about God as love. Makes a bridge between the Old and New Testaments."

Travis squinted at him. "Are we going to argue religion? Not now, I mean. I mean ever."

Ryan was surprised. "I don't know," he said. "Are we?"

Travis sighed. "Probably. Have another drink." The steaks were already gone. "Suppose . . ." said Travis, looking thoughtful, "suppose they built a college here and it was small but honest and open-minded. Suppose this operation of yours should be successful. Suppose—I'm feeling my way now—suppose this nephew of yours grew up a little more and needed a man in the house. Any chances?"

"I don't think so," Ryan said. "You know Fen?"

"He's a nice boy. Those women smother him."

Ryan rattled his ice.

Travis was looking at him in a measuring way. "I heard," he began, cautious, "I heard that you and Fen's mother . . ."

Ryan snapped in before he could finish. "There were never any rumors about Jessica and me."

Travis held up a peaceful hand. "There are always rumors," he corrected. "And I'm not judging anything. Couldn't be less concerned. But I would have thought you would have had more ties here because of that. And because of the boy."

"Is he an orphan? Is he homeless, crippled, being beaten or mistreated? What's the matter with everybody?"

Travis grinned. "Nothing. Who's needling you? Not Asa, not the deaf lady. Lady Wat's-her-Name, I guess."

He did not even answer him. After a while Travis shrugged and said if everybody was through he would go by the office and pick up another bottle and maybe they would go see Stella. Stella was the friend he had told Ryan about. Maybe Stella had a friend. Was he interested?

"Not tonight," Ryan said; but he did go across to the Palmer Building to pick up the bottle from the office. They sat up there for a while, drinking in the dark. Ryan's body had lightened like a man in a spaceship; he did not actively float, but he felt he touched ground less often.

They got somber. After a while they had a quarrel, in which Ryan said Travis presumed on too short acquaintance. Travis told him to go to hell. They started laughing and began to sing "The Wreck of Old 97," which neither of them knew. They could only remember the verse where he was found "scalded to death by the steam."

Later, much much later, Travis drove him home and let him out. At this point they hated to part. It was a friendship like none other in the vault of time. They shook hands like people on boat docks.

"Wish you'd come along," said Travis.

"Need the sleep. Don't want to rot away from the throat out."

"That's morbid. You better come along. You need it."

"Go to hell."

"That's okay, long as I don't have to travel that road by myself." And Travis drove off singing "You gotta walk that lonesome valley."

"Valley valley valley," echoed Ryan at the curb. And when he thought it might be time for it he threw in tenor, "You gotta go . . ." Travis was already out of sight. He wished he had gone to see Stella's friend.

He went toward the house and the cement walk had a conveyor-belt quality about it which did not confuse him. He knew it. He knew this house from a long time ago; he was not drunk.

He walked off in the yard to the oak tree just to give it a pat on the bark that was meant to be companionable. "You goddamn tall son-of-a-bitch," he said in a mellow voice, and he looked up and sighted along the trunk to the sky, where a star was hung. He put his face in the bark. I should have gone to Stella's. Nothing to lose. In people like Stella you don't make any investment. You leave money on the bureau or you bring candy the next time. Nothing gone, nothing shot, nothing wasted.

And he went sharply sad and stumbled up the steps with the thought in him like an ache: I ought to give that boy a bicycle.

10.

THE NEXT MORNING when Ryan woke in the crooked room, he wished he hadn't. He closed his eyes and groaned and considered the condition of his head. It was the point of a pyramid, an upside-down pyramid, resting dead center atop his skull. Or again it was a broom handle driven with great velocity and precision through his head from temple to temple. Or the emptiness impressed him; his whole head was empty and had been in the night refilled with Mexican jumping beans.

"I'll never do it again," he muttered as he had always muttered afterwards, not meaning it. He made the promise without thinking, more in the nature of upholding tradition than anything else.

And he thought that Travis was likely arising this morning undisturbed. The man must be pickled from the throat down, out of long practice.

Ryan closed his eyes and prayed: Let no door slam anywhere. If that should happen he believed the whole side of his face would cave in, like the last wall of a gutted building.

And on his head the pyramid pressed and the broom handle turned, and within it the Mexican beans jumped unceasingly.

He scrabbled mentally at time, decided it was Friday; all days were alike in this place; no need to get up. He took his head carefully between his fingers (he did not want the damn thing to shatter then and there) and sought a softer spot on the pillow. Then he went back to sleep for a little while.

When the banging came on the door he thought it was at least an army going by, heavy-booted against a long campaign.

Let them go, he thought drowsily. It's not my war. They can have Helen; they can have Alsace-Lorraine; they can overrun Jerusalem with Moslems.

But the door banged and banged until he could no longer maintain the fancy that it was something else.

He said in as discouraging a voice as he could manage, "Who's that and what do you want?"

Asa was not intimidated. "Get up, Ryan. We have to go soon."

"Good-by," he said. "Have fun." There was a pendulum hung in his head and it banged into the bone, now this side, now that. In a minute the skull would crack and what strange bird fly out? He put the pillow on top of his head to hold the noise out and the fledgling in.

"Ryan." He heard the door open. "You mustn't disappoint Fen. Even if you have foolish ideas yourself, you mustn't disappoint him." And then the door closed.

What? What was that? He lifted the head and laid it on a palm as carefully as he could and braced the elbow so nothing would collapse. Disappoint who?

He did not understand it. All he understood was the pendulum and the Mexican jumping beans and something new—a buzzing. The buzzing ran around inside his head like a zipper in constant use. It opened him up below the brow, on the bridge of the nose, the other brow, above the ear, and around and above the second ear to the eye again.

There was another knock on the door, but this one gentle. "You *are* coming, aren't you, Uncle Ryan?"

"Yes," said Ryan gloomily. You are doomed, he thought. Love swallows you. And he zipped his head tight against the world and got out of bed and leaned on the wall for a minute.

When he came downstairs he found both Asa and Fen in the parlor, looking starched and Sunday-dressed.

"Hurry up with your coffee," said Asa crisply. "Mr. Barnes will be by in a few minutes."

Not today, thought Ryan. It was an entreaty. "What does he want?" He saw that a little vase of ivy sat neatly between Asa's shoes. Ivy off the carriage house. His mind reeled. *Ivy off the carriage house?*

"You've forgotten," said Asa in a flat voice. And she turned to look at Fen like a schoolteacher conducting through museums. You will please to notice the clay feet, there on the floor. Authentic old clay. "You've simply forgotten." Fen wiggled redly in his chair. "It's the first of September. I never thought you'd forget a day like that."

"The first . . . ?" Then he knew. He sat on a chair and the zipper flew around his head. He did not guess Asa kept such a ritual for the dead. And made Fen keep it. He said with his face and his eyes, *What manner of woman are you?*

But he did not say it aloud, so she did not have to answer.

"We always go," she said. She had lowered her voice; since yesterday she had become a mourner and she carried her loss with dignity. "I shall never forget that terrible day."

"But this—what does this prove?" And he stared at Fen. Your mother was not like this. Your mother was not an anniversary. She was alive and had blood in her and when she cried her shoulders shook and the ribs moved in and out. I have held your mother when she cried, Fen Godwin.

"Why," said Asa, "it proves that we have not forgotten."

"To whom? Edward Barnes?"

"There's no good talking the reasons with you. We always go on the first of September. I took for granted you would go with us. He was *your* brother. She was your brother's wife."

Ryan looked down at the vase of lush green ivy leaves that had gone on living when Jessica had not, and he begrudged the life that was in them. "Sorry," he said shortly. "I've got a headache."

Now Fen was on his feet. "But you said . . ." (his face was honestly bewildered), "the other day in the orchard you said . . ."

Hell hell hell. "I know what I said."

And he remembered the stones that would be set on Methodist Hill (he had not seen them since the day they were bought), the twin stones that would say AVERY GODWIN. JESSICA MAPLE GODWIN. He had bought the grave stones himself, from an old man in neighboring Bascom County. The man had been small, bright-eyed, weasel-toothed. He had chewed tobacco, dripping it brownly onto his hands and tools. He had said in a bored tone, "You want this lettering block or script?" But Asa had said of the stones, "You must admit he does good work. Expensive." Ryan had never wanted to see that stone again when she would be under it.

"Aren't you going to go?" Fen persisted.

"All right," he said. And he got out of the parlor toward the kitchen and coffee just as fast as he could. He left Asa sitting in her chair like the Sphinx, not so much inscrutable as self-contained.

Lady Malveena said drily that she saw they had got to him.

"Cup of coffee," he ordered grimly.

She raised an eyebrow and poured it silently. He said, "They do this every year?"

"Every year."

"What does he think about Avery and Jessica? Does he think they were saints or something, after all that?"

Lady Malveena said how should she know what anybody thought inside? "Why don't you ask him?"

"Glump," he muttered to that, not meaning anything. He took a big swallow of coffee. His head was settling down so that all the sensations—while still there—were duller. The pendulum hit with less force, the pyramid was some tons lighter, the broom handle turned in his temples with less ferocity.

"Don't have to go, you know," said Lady Malveena, watching him. "You was out late. I heard you come in."

"How late?"

"You mean in time or temper? Was late enough I heard you swearing at that old tree in the yard what never hurt anybody."

"You can stop being picturesque," he growled. "What time was it?"

"Two thirty."

"What time's it now?"

"Quarter to nine or so."

He almost went back to bed right then, coffee cup and all.

Lady Malveena said, "Miss Jessica won't ever know if you been or not. Or care, probably. You could go back to sleep."

"Quit gloating. I said I'd go."

"He's a nice boy," Lady Malveena said.

Everybody told him that. He could see that, couldn't he? He had never felt more miserable in his life, huddled in this smelly old kitchen with that talkative old woman and this head on his shoulders that was too large and did not fit at all. He felt as though he had shuffled it with someone else's late the night before.

Lady Malveena took the broom and went up the back stairs to do the bedrooms.

He looked into the coffee morosely until the color sickened him and he fixed his eyes elsewhere. This is what happens to me, he complained mentally. A little concession made every hour. And he had a vision of hundreds of people in Stoneville hourly releasing this and that part of their individual selves so that they aged and were in the end empty-handed, having in their fingers now only a few dried shreds of some forgotten stranger.

What a hell of a metaphor that was! he thought, and felt of his head to make sure it was still intact.

But here he was—and what he himself thought and believed was now subject to what the local standards said one "ought" to do, say, be. So he was going to do something today which he hated. Because he "ought" to. For Fen's sake. In memory of the dead. Out of respect.

And he knew he would rather keep in his mind one picture of Jessica standing by a car in a railway station with a white scarf in her hair then make all the pilgrimages there were.

But say all this is true (he thought)—that in this place one sinks down under the sea of "ought"—say that is true, whether good or bad. If that is so, what will become of the young? What will become of all the boys like Fen?

And he answered himself: They will relinquish. Day after day something (that stuff that was *them*) will slip away and become forever lost to them.

But (and he stirred his coffee here, thoughtful), but they won't ever really *know*. That's the essence of the thing—that what they give up becomes irretrievable, not missed, unmourned.

So maybe it does not matter much, he thought desperately. But he was not comforted.

Then Fen came back and stood in the door and all the words fell in. Reasons and reasons, he thought. But why do we really make most of the compromises? Out of love, big or little. So all of it can't be bad.

And he said, "Come in and sit down," and Fen did.

Fen said, "Are you very sleepy?"

"Pretty sleepy."

"I heard you come in."

Lord God, who else? "That was pretty late, wasn't it?"

"I just happened to be awake."

"I see." He drank a little more coffee. "You awake much at that hour?"

"Sometimes," said Fen. "I see the lights on the wall when a car goes by. I look at the inside of my eyelids."

"You what?"

"You know," said Fen. "If you close your eyes tight in the dark you can see the veins in your eyelids. Then in a minute or so you see colors and patterns and things. It moves and does a lot of changing. That's what I do when I can't sleep."

Ryan said he guessed that was as good as anything. It had sheep-counting beat all hollow, he said.

"I'm sorry you don't want to go," said Fen. "I thought you would."

"I know you did," said Ryan. "It's not that exactly. It's like I was trying to say that other time. To me, it seems like something done for other people. Suppose I went away tomorrow—would it help anything at all if you went every day to the room I had stayed in and stood there for a minute? It seems to me . . ."

Fen had jumped up. "Are you going away tomorrow? Are you going to leave?"

"No, no. Not now. Not yet." He was flustered at the interruption.

"Don't go," said Fen. And desperately, "I'd never been to a carnival before."

Ryan was grateful when he heard the front door close and he did not have to say anything particular to that. "Was that the front door?"

"I guess it was," said Fen.

Lady Malveena came down the stairs and said she had heard the door and thought all of them had gone.

"Probably Barnes," said Ryan.

"Okay," said Lady Malveena. "Face on. Smile up."

"That's right, you never liked him."

She grinned. "He's a mighty happy man."

Happy wasn't the word for it. Edward Barnes was the happiest man in the world. He glowed. He laughed richly. He was fond of making talks to the young people in which he said you didn't have to be a sourpuss to do the Lord's Business, no sir.

"Happy man," said Ryan. He could remember people said that being around Edward Barnes was like being dipped in sunshine. Not merely dipped—drowndèd, he thought, giving it the grammar school pronunciation. Absolutely *drowndèd.*

Lady Malveena said in a whisper, "He's gonna come back and speak to me in a minute. He always does that. That's so I'll be sure to know that *he* knows the Lord made everybody."

"I never knew you didn't like Reverend Barnes!" cried Fen in amazement. "I thought you *liked* it when he came all the way back to the kitchen to speak to you." He frowned. "You always tell Aunt Asa how grateful you are to Mr. Barnes for being open-minded."

Lady Malveena grunted. "You getting old enough now to see behind what people says to what they *means*," she said. "Course the Lord did make everybody. I know that. It musta been the Lord, or else somebody else so busy he didn't have his mind put to it."

And at this Ryan grinned, for this was the start of one of Lady Malveena's oldest stories. She had put him to sleep many nights years and years ago by explaining how a man ought to be built to make things go along better. And he remembered that a man ought to have his ears fixed on the ends of his fingers, so he could put them in his pockets out of the cold. A man ought to have his mouth in the top of his head—then he could throw his dinner in his hat and eat it on the way. His eyes ought to be one front and one hind before, so he could see both which-a-ways. His nose ought to be 'tother side up, so it would drain in instead of out.

And he could remember how she would say, "Course, Mister Lord had other things to do than work out all them dee-tails. He had all the un-i-versies to fix. He had every single one of the stars to hang by hand. You've fixed Christmas trees; you know how long it takes to get the lights in just the right places on the tree. Well, look at all he had to fix so none of it would fall down at a bad moment. I mean, you can't have a chunk of the sky come down just because an airplane flies through it. I tell you, Mister Lord had all them things to think about."

But Lady Malveena did not launch into that story now because Reverend Barnes was coming into the kitchen, laughing and smiling to the Glory of God. Asa was behind him, looking proprietary.

Mr. Barnes looked like a very fat robin. (Everybody looks like birds to me lately; what does that signify? thought Ryan.) He was tall but his tummy came out and under in a lovely hemisphere. He had a hook nose and reddish hair and when he laughed his belt and shirt front trembled from here to yonder.

Now he came in (stiff-legged, laughing) with his hand thrust out in front of him. At first Ryan thought it was for balance, to counteract the stomach or something, but then he saw it was in greeting.

Ryan took his hand and Mr. Barnes gave him the kind of hearty handshake that puts pressure on first one finger and then another.

A kind of sincerity by repetition. "Ryan!" he cried, in mingled pleasure and astonishment, and Ryan experienced that familiar irritation he often had with preachers. They always seemed to assume that their position gave them the right to address everyone familiarly while remaining, themselves, inviolate.

"Mr. Barnes," he said, a little coolly. And he reminded himself that he had known, in his day, preachers whom he had liked very much and they were not like this.

"And Lady Malveena, how are you?"

She flashed her teeth. "Just fine," she said. Fen frowned at her.

"I was just telling Asa how much we all hope you're here to stay this time," said Mr. Barnes. "After all, a man who has succeeded in the way you have as an educator is naturally one of Stoneville's favorite sons." He chuckled, although at what Ryan could not imagine.

"That's very true," said Asa cordially, including Ryan in her smile. "That's what I'm always telling him."

Ryan stared at her, astonished. And Lady Malveena said, with so delicate a sarcasm that it was lost on all but himself, "Ryan always was a smart boy."

Fen was still frowning. Evidently he was trying to practice Lady Malveena's admonition that he listen to what people *meant* and he was having a hard time of it. We're starting you off with professionals, boy, thought Ryan.

"I've always been very interested in education myself," Barnes confided. "Probably our most important function, the transmission of values from one generation to the next."

Ryan gritted his teeth at the man's tone, which seemed to him to indicate that a position in the ministry qualified one as an expert in all fields. But he said to himself, This is part of their counseling—Being Interested in Other People's Work. I've got to remember they teach them things like this in seminary.

He said aloud, "That's what I've always thought about education, too." Then he could not resist adding, "And it's very important not to pass on our errors and prejudices, too."

"Quite right." Barnes smiled. "Quite right." And he looked at Asa as if to say: See how we men understand each other?

Fen asked Lady Malveena for a drink of water and she got him one. Mr. Barnes watched all this as if it were the most fascinating thing he had seen all week and Ryan wondered how the mind of the other worked. Is he always seeing parallels? Does he say to himself now, "Blessed are ye that hunger and thirst after righteousness?" And he shook his head to clear it before the buzzing began again. Another cup of coffee would have helped.

"Perhaps if it turns out that this projected college is built we shall have something to bind you to us," said Barnes.

Ryan mused on the choice of words. Blest Be the Tie That Binds. There was a moment when he wondered if now and then the imprisoned realities of people might rebel into the language so that some men spoke glibly of "bonds of matrimony, ties of family, strongholds of faith"; and so betrayed their own imprisonment.

"Do you encourage the college then?"

Mr. Barnes looked inscrutable and wise. "It's very hard to say at this point, isn't it?" (They teach them that at seminary too—The Rhetorical Question.) "It could be a wonderful thing and a blessing for all of us."

"It's not that I question the idea of a college itself being a good project, but I do wonder if it will have any value for this community," said Ryan carefully.

Mr. Barnes positively beamed. "Exactly! Exactly our own concern, isn't it, Asa?"

Asa, inclining her head, slipped the word flatly out between small gray lips. "Exactly." Ryan had seldom heard her so quiet and —when she did speak—so agreeable and he thought, Why in the world don't you marry this man? You probably wouldn't have to sleep with him. He'd probably be very good-natured about that sort of thing. And then, too, you'll both grow older. And older.

Fen came over and stood by him and Ryan felt absurdly that reinforcements had arrived.

"I love this town," Mr. Barnes was saying. "People here have been good to me." (He glanced at Asa warmly, and she flushed.) "And that—if you'll pardon an old-fashioned word—that imparts to me a sense of responsibility." He looked quite modern and apologetic about using the term. "There's a definite element of protectiveness which the ministry assumes. The Shepherd quality, wherein one has to make certain judgments not by one's personal desires, but for the good of the group."

It sounded very decent, very objective. Ryan felt like a small boy who, seeing a cluster of brightly colored balloons, thinks longingly of pins.

Pins are never quite fair. He took one up now and said with an innocent face, "Familiar and perfectly understandable precept you have there. Same principle on which dictatorships are founded."

Barnes was shocked. "Oh no," he cried, "not that at all. The motives are altogether different—power in one case, love in the other."

And Ryan wondered: Have you never seen one masquerading as the other?

Barnes was pleased with the phrase he had thought of. "Dictators fear lest they be overthrown," he explained, spreading his hands patiently. "The church fears lest the soul of man be overthrown."

Into what? thought Ryan. Into freedom, naked and very difficult? He dropped his hand onto Fen's shoulder, very lightly, and kept it there.

Having dismissed this last, Mr. Barnes wrinkled his forehead. "What was I saying?" He and Asa exchanged looks of perfect understanding. They were Insiders. They could afford to be generous—like God, they had the ages on all sides; they had all the time there was. Their souls were secure, packed up and stored away against the judgment morning.

"Oh yes," said Barnes. "A true education undergirds and upholds the truths of all time, even those truths it cannot—on its own level—understand."

So what do I say to that? thought Ryan. Part true, part false. He felt embarrassed and made a little nod to Mr. Barnes and Asa. There I go again, he thought wearily. The second surrender of the day.

It was as though his nod had been some sort of signal all of them had agreed upon, as though they had determined to stand there talking until he gave them some concession. Now they stood up and began to make motions of departure.

"I just hope these educational leaders will have that sense of humility," Mr. Barnes finished vaguely. "I'll take that, Asa." He reached politely for the vase of ivy.

"Fenwick can carry that," said Asa.

"Excellent. You're a quiet young man today, Fenwick." Then he seemed to remember they were, after all, going to visit the twin graves of the boy's parents and he grew quite flustered. He rearranged his facial muscles into a Cheer-Up pattern. "A sad day," he observed in his deepest tones. They came up, vibrating, out of the round stomach. "A very sad day."

His momentary confusion did not last long. There was the front door to be opened for Asa (with another of those kindred spirit smiles) and an arm to take her down the steps, and after that the opening of the door to his sensible black Plymouth. Fen fell back a step or two and walked beside Ryan and that made Ryan happy. He was surprised and wary to find how happy he was just because a little boy had chosen to walk beside him to a car.

"It's funny," said Fen. He had the ivy held nearly to his face and he grimaced at the tickles.

"What's funny?"

"Oh, you know." The boy stumbled a little in the walk from embarrassment. "You and him. You know."

Ryan was not sure he did. "You go like this every year? Every September first?"

"Of course. Ever since I can remember."

Ryan made a vague gesture of objection. "And do you like it, going every year like this?"

Fen stopped dead in the walk and peered at him above the ivy. "I don't know," he said, a little puzzled. "I never thought about liking it or not liking it."

Then they were all climbing into Mr. Barnes' car and settling themselves onto tired springs that sighed and seemed to be trying to get out of the way.

"Everybody in?" said Barnes, glancing around. Shall I close the ark now?

They drove slowly down Walnut, under the trees and by the tall houses and around Gimcrock Circle, which by-passed the business district.

"I thought we'd drive by the church," said Mr. Barnes to Asa, who was sitting with him in the front seat. "Ryan hasn't seen it since we got the new steeple."

"That's right, he hasn't," Asa replied. Neither of them spoke of it directly to Ryan.

The Trinity Baptist Church was red brick, with four white wooden columns, square and freshly painted, and slender windows which rose up into points. It made Ryan think how much of church symbolism was involved in the upward motion and he remembered that he had once heard a sermon preached about it, a good sermon, someplace else.

All of them had to get out of the car and squint in the morning sun at the new steeple. It was new and taller and painted white and had on top (here Ryan stared) a black iron rooster which moved around complacently to let everyone know which way the wind was blowing.

"It's now the tallest steeple in town," Asa was saying proudly.

"Handsome, isn't it?" (This from Mr. Barnes.)

"Very nice," he said.

Mr. Barnes told him how many feet tall it was and where it had been ordered from and the difficulty they had had swinging the thing in place; and Ryan said that was very interesting. All the time he stared at the top of the steeple. Any minute now, he thought, that damn cock's going to crow thrice.

It did not crow and after a while they got back in the car.

Methodist Hill, where Avery and Jessica were buried, was quite a ways out from town. It wasn't a hill any more except in the center, for people had kept on dying and the graves had spread out on all sides; and it wasn't Methodist any longer. The Methodists had finally sold part of the property to the Stoneville Ministerial Association for the use of all denominations. The cost of plots went into upkeep and maintenance of the roads which ran through the area; and there were also regular organized "cemetery cleanings," at which the men went out with rakes and scythes and clippers while the women set up picnic suppers on the broad stone wall at the entrance. Whenever it came dusk and the cleanup job was done, all of the men came up to the wall and consumed vast quantities of ham biscuits and fried chicken and deviled eggs and homemade pies; and the children took their suppers off and spread them laughingly on the flat white gravestones. Sometimes they left there the marks of small greasy fingers for the wind and the rain to wear away.

When they got out of Mr. Barnes' car at the cemetery entrance they met a worried raisin-faced old lady who was just leaving and who now stood at the gate as though she were not quite able to go away. She kept glancing back inside at the rows of mounds and rubbing one small hand on the stone wall. When they came closer they heard her clicking her dentures in great nervousness. She was evidently a fellow member at Trinity Baptist; Barnes said tactfully that Ryan "remembered Miss Castors, didn't he?"

"Of course," said Ryan.

The little lady took her hand off the wall and put it into his briefly. It was as cold as the wall would ever be.

"How are you, Miss Castors?" said Asa and Fen said, "Good morning, ma'am."

Click-click went the agitated dentures. Miss Castors looked very much upset. She looked absolutely helpless. She also looked, thought Ryan, like that type of Southern lady who says she "always left business matters to menfolks," and at the same time has made consistently shrewd investments all her life.

"I just don't know what I'll do," Miss Castors wailed above the persistent activity in her own mouth.

"What's that, Miss Castors?" Barnes was transformed from Acquaintance to Minister. He frowned down upon her sympathetically.

"Papa's grave!" she cried. "It keeps sinking and sinking, you know. Just sinking and sinking."

"That *is* sad," Mr. Barnes agreed.

"Distressing," nodded Asa.

"They must have sold me an inferior plot. You just can't trust anybody. Not even any respect for the dead."

Everybody sighed and looked reproachful.

"Have you spoken to the caretaker?"

"Spoken to him? *Spoken* to him?" Miss Castors closed heavy lids that were thickly veined. "I should hope I *have* spoken to him. I just *live* out here from talking to him about the thing. I'm always telling him I hope somebody takes as much interest in *my* grave when *I'm* gone."

"And what does the caretaker say, Idaline?" asked Asa. Asa was a great one for wanting to get to the point.

"Oh, he's no help at all!" *Click. Click.* The little creature looked as though she might sit down then and there and burst into tears. She tugged at her hair. "He keeps dumping on sand. Just dumping on sand."

"That ought to help," said Asa.

"Some graves take years to settle," added Mr. Barnes in a comforting way.

"I know, but I just hate to keep putting dirt on top," said Miss Castors. "It seems so heavy. Like we're just pushing Papa down, deeper and deeper."

Suddenly Ryan had a picture of old Mr. Castors being pressed firmly and ever more firmly underground, lifting perhaps from his satin cushion a skeletal hand in protest.

"He could never even stand more than a light blanket," wailed Miss Castors.

"It'll settle, Idaline," Asa promised.

"When he was sick we bought him satin comforters. The real light kind. They didn't have electric blankets then. Papa would have *loved* electric blankets."

"I'm sure everything is going to be *all right,*" said Mr. Barnes.

"I hope so." She sighed. "I have an electric blanket myself. Seems sinful, somehow. Do you think so, Reverend Barnes?"

"Not at all, my dear."

"Ah me, it's so hard to know sometimes," she fluttered. "It's good to see all of you. Are you visiting Avery's grave?"

"That's right."

"Dear Avery," said Miss Castors. "I remember he played at Papa's funeral. 'Abide With Me.' Played beautifully, too."

"Thank you, Idaline," said Asa, dropping her head.

Miss Castors gave a last frenzied look inside, as if she might rush back to see if the ground had dropped another quarter inch where Mr. Castors lay.

But she went on, sighing; and the four of them walked into the cemetery, passing the little-lamb headstones (the old stonecutter in Bascom County had told Ryan this was his most popular item; angels had gone out of style;) and the plain tall "Washington Monument" types, and the square ones that had one large surname in the center of a plot. Standing on a hill one could read hundreds of names:

> Baker Remington Shelby Forester Shelton Ransome Hinton Jernigan Simmons Mitchell Walker Snipes Haile Scronce Branch Patterson Alexander Carson Robertson Payne Evans Long Bailey Skinner Ross

A *faithful wife and a good mother,* said one small graying stone. The lady under it had been alive for fifty-one years and dead for twenty-eight.

Infant daughter, said another, over an unnamed stillborn and under the ever-present little lamb.

Asleep in Jesus and *At rest* were favorite beflowered mottoes.

Fen whispered to him loudly, "Does it matter if you walk on graves?"

"Not really, I guess," said Ryan. "But it always makes me uncomfortable."

"I don't want anybody walking on *me,*" said Fen.

One step on top of Mr. Castors, thought Ryan, and I guess he'll go careening into the bowels of earth.

Once Asa said over her shoulder, "Don't bruise that ivy."

"I'm not, Aunt Asa."

A little later she said to Ryan, "This is the Chalmers plot. Laura Chalmers had a heart attack last year."

Ryan stopped and read rather dazedly the recent stone. Why, Laura Chalmers had been in school with him!

At last they came to the twin white stones which Ryan had not seen since they sat in the stonecutter's yard ten years before. They were not as white as they had been then and birds were given to sitting on the edges. While Ryan stared he saw that Asa had begun, very businesslike, to divide the ivy between two vases which were there already. She was scrupulously fair about it (he suspected she was even counting the stems), but the lushest and greenest pieces went for her brother.

Nothing about these stones and what they meant seemed real to Ryan. He read the words on them (it was block lettering; that must have been how he answered the stonecutter when he asked) in surprise, as if these were the names of strangers:

AVERY GODWIN JESSICA MAPLE GODWIN

Asa was digging small holes in the earth to support each vase of ivy. Ryan looked away; it was not real; none of this could ever be real. In a hundred years everyone I know will be underground like this, he thought; but it was not real.

He looked around at the other graves which belonged to families of strangers. He noticed that the grass on almost all of them was sparse and stubby, and had a tendency to yellow and droop over. The dead perhaps, he thought irrelevantly, are not good fertilizer.

Fen was watching him. "This is Mother's," he whispered. Why do people whisper in graveyards? "Over here, Uncle Ryan."

"I know it," Ryan said. He stepped between the pair of stones and stood looking down at the one that said JESSICA MAPLE GODWIN, May 6, 1910—Sept. 1, 1944. He had his back to Avery as always, standing between them, making of it a sign; but none of this was real.

And he thought, determined not to believe in all of this, *Her mouth was sweet.*

Fen said, "She was thirty-four years old."

"I know how old she was." He had not meant to sound so harsh.

Now the ivy was in place, looking too green, too absurd in this field of stones. Asa stood up and looked at both vases and nodded her head as if she were well satisfied.

Mr. Barnes said, so abruptly that everyone jumped, "Might we bow?"

At this all but Ryan dropped heads and eyes instinctively; he was so unprepared that he found himself watching the rest of them.

"Giver and Taker of Life," prayed Mr. Barnes, "we thank Thee for the memory of these two fine Christians who have gone to be with Thee. We ask Thee to continue to sustain their loved ones in this loss. And this boy, oh Father." (He raised his voice; was God deaf? Was the emphasis for God?) "We ask Thy special blessing on this boy that he might be a blessing to the memory of his parents as he follows Thy will. Use him, oh God. Make him subject to Thy will and wholly surrendered to Thee. Amen."

Ryan thought it was a pretty cheap trick on Fen. He thought if he stood there a minute longer he would take up the ivy and toss it high, or go stamp vengefully above poor dead Mr. Castors. So he strode off ahead of the others, but not rapidly enough to miss Asa's whisper to Mr. Barnes.

"I think he's very moved. It's the first time since the accident."

"I understand," hissed Mr. Barnes.

He was almost to the car when Fen caught up with him.

"But what's the matter? What in the world's the matter?"

He slowed. "Nothing's the matter, Fen."

"Why did you rush off, then?" Fen wailed.

"It's all right," said Ryan, just as he had said it in the kitchen the other time. "Everything's all right."

But Fen was miserable. "Nothing's the same any more," he said. "Everything I've always done; it's—it's different since you came."

"I'm sorry, Fen," he said and meant it. It was that way with him, too.

The two of them got into the car and sat down. Asa and Mr. Barnes were walking about among the tombstones like sightseers, like prospective tenants considering real estate.

"Everything's changed," said Fen again, crouched miserably on the back seat.

A sweet mess, Ryan thought. What now? He said weakly, "It's all right, Fen."

"I wish I remembered other things about my mother," said Fen defiantly after a moment.

"Other than this, you mean? So do I." He had never spoken more fervently. "Isn't there some small personal thing you do remember?"

"No," said Fen. "There isn't anything."

"She wore an opal ring," said Ryan, casting about desperately. "She . . . she had a little strange stone she wore hung on a chain about her neck. I gave it to her for Christmas once. She hated poached eggs. She . . . she loved you very much. Her eyes were as brown as yours and the lashes as long."

"Yes sir," said Fen.

"She had a nice walk, proud. In the mornings she listened to the mill whistles. I guess you hear the mill whistles. Her hands were very small." He was tired and his head had begun to ache again.

"I'll remember that," said Fen.

And what good will that do, every September first when you come out here? thought Ryan. "You would have liked her," he said after a minute. "She would have liked you, too."

Then Asa and Mr. Barnes came up and he opened the door and helped her into the car.

"A lovely cemetery," Asa was saying with a little sigh.

"So peaceful," Mr. Barnes agreed.

11.

When they got back to the house on Walnut Street and Mr. Barnes had finally gone (calling jovially over his shoulder that he would see them all on Sunday, wouldn't he? ha ha) Lady Malveena drew Ryan aside and gave him a small white calling card.

"A gentleman," she said. "He left this for you."

"What are you whispering for?"

She spoke in her normal voice. "People with printed cards—I thought you was in trouble. I thought it was the F.B.I. or something."

"What was that about the F.B.I?" said Fen. He was just starting to follow Asa up the stairs.

"Nothing. Of course I'm not in trouble." Ryan looked at the card curiously. The paper was expensive, the engraving well done, and the name was inscribed in firm block letters—JOHNSTON K. PEYTON. He did not know anyone named Peyton. He turned the card over and read the message which had been written there with a stubby pen: *Mr. Godwin. I have something I'd like very much to discuss with you. The hotel lobby. 2. p.m.* JKP.

"Who brought this?"

"That's what brought me to mind of trouble. Thin little fellow, looked scared. What does it say?"

"None of your business what it says. What do you mean, looked scared?"

Lady Malveena frowned, considering. "Looked like a man waiting on his army call. Or behind with his taxes. You know—waiting on something sure and certain to catch up with him." She looked very pleased with herself.

Ryan tapped the card on his thumbnail. "You have such a gift for drama I never know when to listen to you."

Lady Malveena was insulted. "He was tall and thin and had a mustache," she snapped. But even as she delivered the words so crisply she was leaning slowly forward to see what the man had written on the card.

"You're too old to snoop," said Ryan absently.

"Might as well," she said. "That's all the interest old people's got—minding somebody else's business. Listen, if you're in any trouble, you up and say so."

"I see you think of me as a fine and honorable character. I told you I'm not in any trouble."

She said in a threatening voice, "I've got eleven hundred dollars." She made it sound like a weapon. She made it sound as if she might bury him alive under all that money.

But he knew it was an offer and he was touched. "Thank you, Lady Malveena."

She drew up immediately and raised her eyebrows. "Don't be thanking before taking. I'm just telling you what's on the books. I ain't took none of it out, yet."

"Now who's scared to be caught in a kindness?" he teased.

"Listen," she said, "listen, I'd be willing to turn all that money over to you if I thought it might be spent proper."

And Ryan knew what she meant by "proper." She meant to send some boy to school and to start him in college. She meant to buy red bicycles.

He said, "If I'd been born with your determination I'd be on top of the pile by now. I'd own Ford Motor Company at least."

"Who wants it?" said Lady Malveena. "How'd you like the tour this morning? Pick out your plot?"

"There's more than one blasphemer in this family," he said.

She was not concerned. "White people supposed to set examples."

Then the doorknocker interrupted and she opened the door to reveal Ian Travis standing on the porch. Travis had a stack of ledgers underneath one arm. He looked like a man who has had a good night's sleep.

"I don't know how you do it," said Ryan. "Come on in."

Travis came into the hall and put the ledgers down on the table. "Asa wants to see these," he explained. "Always double checks. Such a trusting soul. How do you feel this morning?"

"Don't be so cheerful. I've had a harder day already than you'll ever have."

"Good morning, Mr. Travis," said Lady Malveena a little stiffly. "Just put your hat down there." Lady Malveena did not approve of gentlemen who had to be reminded they were wearing their hats in the house.

Travis took it off and seemed to get two inches shorter. "Doorknockers are damned impressive, did you know that? Always intimidate me. Ringing a bell is like a command, but this is really asking admission."

"If you were able to use that doorknocker and keep your head in one piece you can consider our acquaintance canceled," Ryan said.

"A little hung, are you? That's what cheap liquor will do for you. Not the amount, it's the *quality*."

"I'll remember that," said Ryan. "Come on in and sit down."

They went into the parlor. "I told you to come with me last night," Travis was saying. "No point in winding a spring too tight without some way to let it out again."

"Know Edward Barnes?"

"You've not seen *him* today! I take everything back. You're a sick man."

"I'll live," said Ryan.

Travis shrugged and leaned against one of the chairs which Ryan feared might give in with him. "Such stoicism convinces me you're over the worst of it. What are you doing seeing the Preacher? Repenting of our evening?"

"Went to the cemetery. Keeping trysts. Seeing graves."

"Alas, Poor Yorick," Travis said. Then he sobered abruptly. "Your brother and—"

"Yes," said Ryan before he could finish.

Lady Malveena put her head in from the hall and said there was coffee in the kitchen if anybody wanted to ruin their noontime eating.

It appeared both of them did. "We'll just go on back," Ryan called to her.

"Into the *kitchen*?" At this Lady Malveena came to stand between the two curtains with her hands propped on her hips. "Are you taking Mr. Travis into the kitchen?"

"Sometimes she can't tell me and Fen apart," said Ryan. "The boxing of ears is general and impartial." And he called to Lady Malveena, "Yes, and be damned," and they went through the dining room and the butler's pantry, and Ryan put the coffee on to heat. Lady Malveena said loudly to Mister Lord that times were certainly changing and it was a shame the kitchen-eaters couldn't be turned into the kitchen-workers while they was at it. She said a whole way of life was going down somebody's drainpipe.

"You always bring the books for Asa to go over?"

"First of the month. She likes it. The arithmetic rests her." His voice was more amused than anything else.

"Does she find errors?"

"She finds things done like she would never have done them. Which is an error, of course, by definition." In another minute he added, "Asa is shrewd, you know. She's a good business*man*." The emphasis was on the last syllable very faintly.

Ryan didn't doubt it. They poured coffee and soon had gotten into an argument about the individual and society. They argued about Father Zossima and Raskolnikov and Alyosha, and Travis quoted a lot from a man named Durkheim.

Once Ryan put his hand to the faint ache remaining in his temple and Travis abruptly stopped what he was saying. "How do you really feel?" said Travis. "I mean here," and he touched his own throat.

"Last few days I haven't had much chance to think about it. Probably just as well."

"From your own psychological point of view maybe. But how about time? Aren't you supposed to be making a decision?"

Ryan said other things kept coming up. He said it in a wry voice.

"Other things always keep coming up when you don't want to bear down on a specific thing."

"I warned you I'd already had a hard morning."

"Okay, okay."

After a while Fen came into the kitchen and spoke politely to Mr. Travis. He climbed onto a chair. "Is the F.B.I. coming by this afternoon?" he asked, big-eyed.

"I told you that wasn't the F.B.I. You and Lady Malveena have a great gift for melodrama. Where's Miss Clara?"

"Radio."

"That all she does?" said Travis. "I've only seen her once."

"She goes to church. I think she reads the paper sometimes."

"I went to the carnival," Fen broke in proudly. "Uncle Ryan took me to the carnival."

"If you tell me he's got a heart of gold my last illusion will be shattered. What did you see?"

"We saw everything there was to see. Did you go?"

"Not this time. There's to be another one next month, you know, when they have the county fair."

At this Ryan meant to say firmly *I won't be here then,* but when he looked at Fen's face he found he could not say it after all. There was a small empty place in the conversation. Fen was watching him; Ryan turned the cup up and finished the last of the coffee to shut that look away.

"About that college," Travis said, "there's a sweet irony you'll like."

"Not today," said Ryan. "I wouldn't like any kind of irony today."

"They've picked out the property on which the man wants to build the thing. You'll never guess who owns the most of it."

It was too much. "Godwin Realty," said Ryan flatly.

"Worse than that—Asa herself. Remember the old Walton property?"

"That white elephant?"

"Never was any good for anything. Asa's had it for years. I don't know why she bought it in the first place—it isn't like her to make a poor business decision. Nothing short of the discovery of oil could have given that land any value. Except for this—that it's big and it's in one piece, and the college wants it."

"Too far from town," Ryan objected.

"They'd buy two farms this side of the Walton property as well. Owners of those are willing to sell. But the whole thing hinges on Asa."

"And she won't sell it."

Ian Travis turned his spoon in his coffee with great care. "She might," he said slowly. "Asa loves to see a good blue entry in the books. She'd probably sell it in a flash as long as she felt it wouldn't . . . wouldn't interfere with plans already laid." He turned his cup. "Asa could be persuaded."

"By Edward Barnes maybe," Ryan snapped. "A visitation of angels."

"She might be made to see certain further advantages in it," Travis said carefully, very carefully. "There's the money for one thing—she'll never get half that much for this property any other way. She might see a local college as a way to hold certain," he glanced at Fen, "certain things here longer."

"I'd have no part of that."

"You wouldn't have to have a part in it. It wouldn't have to work out that way—not if you are able to come back next year or the year after or four years after and take things in hand." He emphasized the word "things" very slightly. "And if you're not able to come back then, why nothing will be lost. Everything will work out the way it would have worked out anyway."

"What things?" said Fen. "What everything?"

Ryan was genuinely puzzled at Travis' appeal. "Why in the world do you think I'd use any influence—not that I have any—to get her to sell that property?"

Travis looked impatient. "Well, apart from any personal reasons you might or might not have, I think there's a chance that college might mean something to this whole community. I think lots of people might be able to get hold of books the local library doesn't have now. I think there might be some good music and some good theater and some good dance in town occasionally. You're a college professor. Why are you asking me?"

No time, thought Ryan. No ties. He said, "You really think I owe something particular to this town, don't you? Just because it let me get born in it?" He knew he was exaggerating his resentment out of sheer perversity. They were pushing him too hard—all of them.

Travis made an angry motion. "Hell, only you can answer that. I've got to go."

"No call for you to get excited about it."

But Travis was already on his feet and he looked very much annoyed. "When I was a kid," he said, his voice gone quick and impatient, "I used to play around a little stream ran near the house. I used to squat in that stream for hours and hours on end, taking out rocks and sticks. I used to move rocks to one side just to see the water go through a little faster than it did before." He snorted. "Hell, if you can't understand that much there's no use talking to you."

Everybody's pushing me—Lady Malveena and now Travis. Take hold, lift up, leave your mark. This isn't what I came here for. I wanted a rest, that's all—one small rest to think things out.

(Somewhere in his skull there was a little man shaking his head and clucking his tongue, but Ryan let it pass. He felt like shouting into his own ears: *And you stay out of this!*)

Asa came to the kitchen door and asked if Mr. Travis had brought the books.

"I left them on the hall table," Travis said, and followed her out without another word.

Immediately Ryan knew what he should have said to Travis' analogy. He should have asked Travis how many rocks he was taking out of streams these days? He should have . . .

Then the little man won. Ryan was suddenly ashamed, and he put out a hand for no reason and banged Fen lightly on the back. Fen was so startled he almost fell out of his chair.

Ryan refilled his coffee cup and they were sitting quietly again when Lady Malveena came back into the kitchen and said they looked like two stachoos sitting there.

"Uncle Ryan's thinking," Fen explained.

She was not impressed. "There's others got to do that on the run," she said. "In between cooking and working and having babies."

"Ivory tower," said Ryan to his nephew. "Lady Malveena thinks I've gotten out of touch with life. Academic. Lost the emotional responses." All the time he was thinking that there had been one shabby baseball and a cheap chemistry set.

Lady Malveena was frowning. "I ain't troubled about you *losing* them. I see them all there and in the right places but you always picking fights with them. Mr. Travis make you mad?"

He was angry about that chemistry set. "I've gotten along fine for years without your counsel," he snapped. "Why don't you just do the cooking?" During this time he had only meant to tease, but his voice was too sharp and he saw immediately that Lady Malveena was hurt.

"I'll work on that," she said coldly, and took up his cup that still had coffee in it and poured it out and washed the thing. "You two go on out and let me get some work done."

Ryan knew he should have apologized, but he was too tired. He got up from his chair and went upstairs and did not come down for lunch, not even when they called him. He yelled instead (not kindly), "I'm not hungry! Going to sleep!"

And he lay up there and thought about all the men who had slept with women the night before, in how many beds and how many positions and with what a waste of semen.

Fen put his head in once. "Are you sick?"

"No. Just tired."

And after Fen had gone he wondered if just one night and one small final spasm had come to this—a boy, aged twelve, with eyes too brown and lashes much too long. It seemed a very simple way to arrive at such a highly complex being. There was nothing in that to warn you about throat cancers and red bicycles.

Soon after one o'clock he came downstairs, dressed and a little rested and very much calmer. He stopped briefly at the foot of the stairs when he heard Asa talking to Miss Clara in the parlor. He was surprised when he heard her, for he realized she was talking in her normal tone of voice, which meant Miss Clara could not hear a word.

Asa was saying quietly, "I really wonder if we ought to plant boxwoods on the graves. They looked a little bare to me."

Miss Clara said to herself that she did not understand what had become of the ace of spades.

"Boxwoods are so common somehow. I noticed the Richardsons have set a small azalea on their plot. That'll be lovely in bloom." She sighed. "Of course, I'd have to find what color they've set so we can get a different one. I wonder how expensive azaleas are."

"It has to be here somewhere," said Miss Clara. Ryan heard the sound of a chair pushed back and he had a vision that while Asa was discussing this serious subject, huge Miss Clara might be going about the parlor on all fours, peering under things.

"I suppose we could only get one," Asa went on thoughtfully. "Should we put it directly between the headstones? On the other hand, it'll be so shaded there. The best spot, purely in terms of location, would be right in front of Avery's stone. Do you think people would talk if we did that? Perhaps they would think us neglectful of Jessica. Of course, I never really got to know Jessica very well. She and Ryan had quite a friendship for a while. I never understood that, because Jessica wasn't the bookish sort."

"*There* it is!" cried Miss Clara. The chair scraped back again. "Now I can play the deuce."

At this Ryan smiled where he stood at the foot of the stairs. Miss Clara could play the deuce—that struck him funny.

"I always thought there was something between those two, Clara. Oh, you know, not anything *ugly*. But there was some attraction there, on Ryan's part at least. I don't mean, of course, that anything *came* of it."

Miss Clara said that she thought that was very nice. She said if it never rained again it would be too soon for her.

"But mercy, Fenwick does look like Ryan. And he has that same way of looking at you as if he wanted to see all the way into your head. That boy's a great responsibility to me."

"I think you're absolutely right," said Miss Clara. She said it so mechanically that Ryan wondered how many afternoons she had sat and had held just such conversations with her cousin Asa. There are all kinds of ways of earning your room and board, he thought.

"I meant to go on to Father's grave today," said Asa, "but Mr. Barnes is such a busy man and it's so good of him to go with us at all. I ought to take Fenwick more often, though. You can't impress too much upon a child that sense of responsibility to everyone who has gone before."

And his responsibility to himself? thought Ryan. Don't you think you've soft-pedaled that a good many years?

He walked suddenly into the parlor and Miss Clara said how was he feeling today? Asa looked at him a little warily, he thought.

"All right," he said, medium-loud, but nodding his head at the same time so the message would be conveyed.

"That's good," she said.

"Where's Fen?"

"Outside somewhere," Asa said. "I'm sure I don't know what he does with half his time."

"Well, I'm going uptown. I probably won't be home till time for supper."

"It seems to me you're getting very friendly with Mr. Travis. I can't believe you honestly like the man!" said Asa. She was very curious to know what Lady Malveena had given him that morning in the hall. Her eyes flicked to his breast pocket where the card might be and away again.

"Travis is all right," said Ryan. "Do you think Fen's out back?"

Asa was surprised. "Probably. Why?"

"Well . . . I . . . I just wanted to tell him when I'd be back. Thought I might take him to the picture show tonight." That was a lie; but after he had spoken it, it did not seem such a bad idea.

Asa raised her eyebrows. "Well, for goodness sakes! You never cared for children, Ryan. I've often heard you say so." She gave him a steady look and he almost put a hand to his face so she should not see how like Fen's it was.

"Fen's a nice boy," said Ryan defensively, and then he had to smile because that was exactly what Travis and Lady Malveena had already said to him.

So he looked out the kitchen door into the orchard, but he could not see Fen anywhere in the grass.

"Tell Fen we might go to a movie tonight if he wants to." He said that to Lady Malveena's back, which was armored against him.

She did not turn and her voice was cool. "Come over that again a little more careful," she said.

Ryan surrendered unconditionally. "What I mean is that I'd like to take Fen with me to a movie tonight." When Lady Malveena turned and smiled broadly at him, he forgot whether he had won or lost a battle.

Then she looked concerned. She said, "That thing you're carryin' weighs a lot, don't it?"

He shrugged and turned to go, but Lady Malveena would not be put off.

"Sometimes it drops a little heavier than others, I take it," she said, pressing him to answer.

He grinned. "Sometimes," he admitted.

She tossed her head. "Well don't you think I mind! I used to fix skinned knees and get kicked for my trouble. I've not forgot the times you bit me when we was pulling wobbly teeth."

"All right," he said.

"I mean it. That it *is* all right." Lady Malveena turned her face away and said in a menacing voice, "And don't you forget I got that eleven hundred dollars."

"I won't forget that."

"You're gonna be late if you stand around talking all the time."

It was dim inside the hotel because all the blinds were pulled against the sun and it was—of course—unheard of to burn electricity in Stoneville in the daytime. Ryan blinked when he first came in out of the August brightness and then he saw a figure bob up out of one of the lobby chairs.

Bob was exactly right—the stranger looked very much like an apple and not at all the way Lady Malveena had described the man who left the card.

"Mr. Godwin?" His voice was crisp and a little impatient, and came out of a round bald head set on a round body. He looked as though all the blood in him lay very near the surface.

Ryan nodded. "You're Mr. Peyton?"

"That's right, that's right. Come over so I can see you."

Ryan went over and shook a broad hand which was full of soft fingers.

"Sit down, sit down. I haven't much time." Mr. Peyton took out a notebook and, sitting down himself, spread it onto his lap. "My name is Johnston K. Peyton and I'm a businessman and I plan to build a college here. Maybe you've heard of that."

Ryan said he had heard something about it.

"I used to know your father," Peyton said. "Used to be in and out of Stoneville a lot when I was younger. You don't much look like Flim-Flam Godwin, I must say."

In all of his life, Ryan had never heard his father nicknamed Flim-Flam.

"Your sister looks like him, though," Peyton continued. "I saw her on the street the other day. She looked as though she'd be tougher so I decided to start with you first. Does that insult you?"

"Not particularly," said Ryan. He was a little wary. "Don't count on much from me, though."

The man flicked his right hand out so that the wrist popped. "I don't count on anything till I've got it there. Right there." And he frowned briefly into his empty palm.

Ryan leaned back and took out a cigarette and the man promptly

(which he almost never did) and had taken up a pencil and turned it over and over in his fingers, watching it as though the procedure required great care.

"I have the results of the biopsy." (Fingertips against eraser and then the turn, and fingertips against the point of lead.)

The face was too worried; Ryan focused on those carefully moving hands. "It's bad. How bad?" And for one minute he knew the child in him had never died, had always believed in divine intervention and miraculous last-minute reprieve—and where were they now?

"Tell me, Ryan, haven't you noticed anything until now?"

"Not really. A hoarseness. A feeling of fullness just back of the nose like . . . like a head cold." The child in him despaired. There would be no miracle—he had flunked after all, the principal would expel him, and the boy he had so lightly struck was dead. It was Time again, all of a color, everywhere.

"I wish you'd noticed before. But people never do. Any nosebleeds?"

"Not lately," Ryan said. "Anyway, I've often had those. I had them when I was small. I wouldn't think there was anything unusual in them."

It was a red pencil, with barbershop white stripes like a stick of candy, and when Jim turned it the whole world seemed to be spinning and blurring.

"If we'd only caught it sooner. It's got at least a year's start on us now. Maybe more. I wish you didn't smoke. You'll stop it now, of course."

"All right," said Ryan. And he thought, How long is a year when something is growing in you? Could I have come in 365 days ago and stopped the thing, or 364, and killed it small?

And since that day in Jim's office (two weeks ago? Who believed that lie?) only thirteen days and fourteen nights had gone by him and passed on.

But there was a recompense, perhaps. The shortening of time (or its *apparent* shortening) possibly intensified all the senses: they grew hungry and watchful; they would let nothing pass without taking it in, photographing it meticulously in sight or smell or color, hoarding it away against sparse days. In such a way had these two weeks gone by. It approached the uncanny awareness of small children who—not knowing yet what is rare in the world and what is merely ordinary—dare not overlook a thing.

After his interview with Mr. Peyton (that was a turning point, a hinge somewhere, but he did not know on what) Ryan found himself more restless than before. The two weeks had been two years; he was an old resident bored with his habitation. He began to find it difficult to sit still anywhere, to concentrate except in isolated efforts, or to attend closely to what others were saying. He *supposed* they were saying things; he had retreated down into Ryan Godwin so that sometimes there seemed a veil between him and them and only their lips moved, soundlessly.

And maybe that, too, was kin to the greedy-minded child, too conscious of vastness and multiplicity to concentrate for long on all the separate things his senses brought him. I've got to hurry, thinks the child desperately. I've got to hurry before I grow up.

This was his mood. I've got to hurry (thought Ryan grimly) before I, too—and here he paused—grow up? Perhaps. Give up one thing, known and familiar, for something unknown and not desired.

Saturday passed brightly like the other days, so clear and sharp that all his senses seemed weary from the extra workload. It was as though the storerooms of his eyes and ears were loaded past capacity.

Only one early morning incident disturbed him.

He had seen these same three Negroes pass the house each morning since he came. There was an old man, and a woman presumably his wife, and their daughter; and every morning at seven they went by the house on Walnut Street. They were perpetually quarreling.

By now, thought Ryan, they had forgotten what the quarrel was about. It was a habit with all of them.

The two women would walk along in front, bored and angry, and the old man followed them always some three steps back, grumbling and waving his arms. Now and then the women would stop and the old one would scream a disagreement back at him, or the young one would take issue with something he had said. At this, the old man would take three hasty steps and come to stand right in front of them and fuss. He seemed to be berating them for their laziness, and they hated him for his drinking. Every day they went by the house yelling about it. It gave Ryan an awful feeling that none of this ever stopped, that they went to bed angry, that they yelled at each other around the Christmas tree, that when the old man took the old woman in bed, both their teeth were clenched in bitterness.

As a matter of fact, the first morning he had laughed at them heartily. What a spectacle they made—the tubby furious old man following the two uninterested women, dragging their family quarrel along the public streets! When the old woman had turned and screamed back at her troublesome husband like a fishwife, Ryan had stood at the window and laughed at them. When the old man had accused his daughter of having no respect and she had said she didn't respect a sot in no man's family, Ryan had thought it very funny.

But by the third morning he thought it was time they got over the argument.

"Out sleeping with men till all hours!" the old man yelled that day. "A whore and an evil daughter!"

"You shet your mouth!" The old woman was very fat but she looked as though she would jump up and down in rage at this moment if she could only get her feet off the ground the first time.

"A bitch mothers a bitch!" thundered the old man, catching up to them to stand shaking his fist.

"All the money I make you pours down your throat!" the daughter cried. "You gonna drown from the inside out and you know who ain't gonna care? I ain't gonna care, that's who! Mama ain't gonna care! Nobody ain't gonna care!"

The two women stalked off and left him and he followed them three steps back, quarreling and fuming.

Thus it had gone on every day since Ryan came back to Stoneville, until when he heard them this Saturday he thought he would not be able to endure the thing.

When he heard their voices growing louder as they came toward the house ("You gonna lose your job from all this likker drinking." . . . "You'd never starve. Milly can always make a living on her back.") he leaped out of bed, suddenly furious with all three of them; and rushed across the room to the window with some notion of shouting down to them, "*Stop that! Stop that, do you hear!*"

But he only stood leaning against the windowsill, a little sick, and watched them walk and stop and walk again, arguing, until they disappeared from view—the fat old man going out of sight last of all.

For he did not know exactly what it was he would like to have told the three human beings passing in the street unless it was something trite and foolish, such as *Life is very short.*

And he walked back to the bed again and sat down and stared without seeing anything. But his eyes betrayed him; they were hungry—these days they were so very hungry. In no time at all they were flashing the pictures in: a million roses on the wall, seen to the detail of each painted petal; a cobweb in a corner which floated and floated and rose and fell like a membrane over breathing; the twisted hideous old furniture with all the carving and turning; and on top the marble table at the side of his bed, one Bible. It lay there like a trap Asa had set for him, and he frowned at it.

He said to himself, still frowning at that book, that these three people would go on arguing long after he was gone and there was no need for him to be upset about it.

His mind went leaping off then, building some plausible structure—would it never be still? Why was it building arguments it often did not believe, replying to its own questions?

It went speeding out from him then, turning and selecting; and it came to Ryan that perhaps it was Jesus' very foreboding of death that had lent the strength to his words. Perhaps Jesus had known more surely than the rest of them that All Men Die (not divinely, but just ahead of time, while He was still young) and that knowledge had goaded Him into urgency—into putting down the tools that had for years cut wood into sharp clean doors and strong beams—and had sent Him out into the fields of Galilee to talk to strangers. Perhaps He had said to Himself: "I cannot bear to think of things going on in the same cheap way when I am dead."

So there He had been in Galilee, walking (yet not sadly) under the shadow of that certainty, and going up into the hillsides to tell them all that life was important, that life was not to be shabbily treated.

"Therefore," He had insisted over and over again, "you are all blessèd—the mourners and the poor in spirit, the meek, the men who hunger for God, the merciful, the pure, the makers of peace whether in big or small ways, the persecuted and the homeless . . ."

Yes, and sometimes (Ryan thought) the ugly and willful and narrow, and the mean and spiteful. Because life is not trivial, even for them.

And he grew very angry because only those who were seeing it depart from them too rapidly could know that for a fact. (We hate the old men who are always telling us this.) And as for others, the three-meal-a-day others, there was no use trying to tell them about it. They would have to find it out for themselves.

And suppose Ryan had run all the way downstairs to catch up with the two women and the fat angry man and had told them, right there on Walnut Street in a loud and desperate voice, *Life is very short!* What would they have said?

They would have said, "Yassuh," staring a little.

They might have said, "Sho. Everybody knows that," and thought they spoke the truth.

And later they would have asked each other, wonderingly, "What you think's the matter with that man?"

His mind pounced on the possibility of Conclusion. Perhaps (he thought), they *would* have asked each other that and asked it for once in accord, without quarreling. Maybe that was all one could do—maybe all Jesus had in mind was seeing a lot of people quiet down for one minute and ask each other: "Why do you think He let them do that to Him?"

And then Ryan smiled and drew his mind back, in, contracted. It was like catching a thousand swift tiny thoughts and bundling them into a fish net. I have done this all my life, he thought in self-amusement, constructed and torn down and reconstructed, trying to make . . . what? Trying to make Intelligibility, even out of the small and the irrational.

Late that Saturday when Stoneville was cooling and darkening about them on all sides, Ryan sat with Fen on the broad front porch and watched the sky open out to space. He remembered another night when he had sat on this same porch with Jessica and Asa and Avery, and how he had thought then: *She will never come away with me*; and had planned then and there to break it off. Love is no dry stick to be snapped apart so easily. A lean and living thing, like stems on the weeping willow, and very hard to sever. And he looked at Fen furtively where he sat on the front porch steps, half in shadow.

Fen said, "I thought we could have taken a walk today. I wanted to show you something."

"I'm sorry. I went uptown. Had lunch with Mr. Travis at a place called the Buffalo Grill. You know where that is?"

"Yes sir. Aunt Asa has pointed it out to me."

I'll just bet she has! He got up from the chair and came to sit on the steps where Fen was and watch the sky seem to move back farther and farther into the universe. Everything moves out of the way at night, he thought, to remind us of how vast things really are.

"Do you like Mr. Travis?" said Fen. He sounded a little mournful.

"Matter of fact, I do."

"I don't know him very well," said Fen, stiff and formal.

Ryan glanced sidewise at him in the dark. In a minute he said, "What were you going to show me?"

"Oh," said Fen, very offhand, "Nothing special. I thought we might walk to a place I know of. Feed some squirrels. It was very hot today, wasn't it?"

"Pretty hot," said Ryan cautiously.

"Too hot to take a long walk, I expect," said Fen. Before Ryan could answer he asked quickly, "Is it very far to the stars?"

Ryan let the other pass. "That's just what I was thinking a while ago. Thousands of light years, I expect. Maybe millions."

"What's a light year?"

"Light goes a hundred and eighty-six thousand miles a second. A light year is how far it will travel in a whole year at that speed. It's trillions of miles, I think."

"Trillions," whispered Fen in awe. He seemed to have completely forgotten the walk Ryan had failed to take with him. They sat and stared out for trillions of miles to where the stars were. "Will we really go out there in spaceships and things?"

"We might," said Ryan. "I hope so."

Fen was silent. "I guess God will just have to move back a little more," he said in a minute. "Out of the way."

Ryan cleared his throat. "Could be," he said. He felt that if Asa came upon them while they were talking in such a blasphemous way he would feel very guilty.

"What do you think lives out on the stars?"

"Nothing on the real stars, I guess. Maybe some green things grow on Mars."

"If you dig down, would you go to China?"

"No, I don't think so."

"It's not so that they walk upside down in China, is it?" said Fen. "Badger says they do."

"No. They walk just like we do."

"Badger doesn't know anything," said Fen.

"Badger a friend of yours?"

"Kind of. He's in my grade at school. It's different, talking to you and talking to Aunt Asa."

"How so?"

"If I ask *her* about the stars, she says God made them and there are some things we aren't supposed to know." He paused. "Is it true there are some things we aren't supposed to know?"

"I don't think so," said Ryan. "I hope not."

"Isn't there some way you can tell for sure?"

"You can if you've made up your mind already, one way or the other."

Fen looked puzzled at this, but as if he did not wish to have it all repeated.

"I hit a home run this afternoon," he said in a few minutes.

"Where do you play ball now?"

"Go over to the school lot mostly."

"We used to play in a field near town. They built an office building on it."

"I remember that," said Fen. "I watched them mix that see-ment. There was a man showed me how to lay bricks and scrape off the extra when they were building that."

They sat there quietly, watching the stars blur and brighten like lamps going down and up, and once Ryan put his hand down on his trousers leg and felt for the cigarette burn. It was gone; it was completely vanished—the little Jew tailor had made fabric where none was.

Fen said he wouldn't mind being on the first ship to the moon.

"Maybe you will be," Ryan said. In a few minutes he said abruptly, "Do you want to go to college?"

"Oh, *yes* sir. As soon as I can." Fen made it sound like the equivalent of a lunar voyage any day. As for Ryan, he was a little sorry he had brought the matter up.

On Sunday, all of them went to church, even Miss Clara who could hear nothing of the services and only tried to keep time (very much off beat) when the congregation sang. Asa (thought Ryan) operated under the same principle which insists on the church attendance of infants and very young children—that the very atmosphere of church has a beneficial effect and is not directly related to the understanding of the soul involved.

But seeing Miss Clara counting thoughtfully under her breath Ryan had the happy thought that perhaps she counted the hymns out in her own fashion: one-two-three-four-five-six-seven-eight-nine-ten-jack-queen-king-ace; and this thought so delighted him that he was saved from bad temper.

He had not been inside the church for years. He had not even gone on the day when they carried the two identical coffins in and set them up—at the front, he supposed—for final rites. He had, instead, sat out back on a little carven bench which read *Lord, Make Me an Instrument of Thy Peace,* and this prayer he had read over and over again that day without its calming him much.

So now when he came inside ten years had passed, and he found things greatly changed. There were new pews, he noticed, almost white; so that if it were not for the same narrow stingy windows, the church would have seemed brighter inside. The pulpit was the same (it was traditional and had been in the first church in 1881); it was a mammoth carved box and the preacher stepped up into it. The choir bar had been removed and replaced by a long metal rail on which were deep green velvet hangings, and a green rug was on the floor.

And the organ pipes had been painted very gold. When he had been small, these had always reminded him of large pencils and he had gone mentally walking about on the tips of them, stepping up and up to the top of the tallest one, and down and down again.

"The whole interior was just repainted," Asa hissed in his ear. "How do you like it?"

Ryan started, glanced up and winced. The ceiling was pastel green, like young peas; he even preferred the dingy off-white color it had been before (which the ladies had called eggshell, or cream, or ecru).

The choir got suddenly to its feet behind the green velvet with a great chair-scraping and knee-bending and rattling of programs, and began to sing "Praise God From Whom All Blessings Flow," looking out accusingly into the congregation until everyone there straggled to his feet and began to sing, too. There was another organist, of course, a little woman who seemed too small to pull a single stop out by herself. But she went at it with a great thumping vigor and the golden pencils over her head all but rattled and tumbled down.

During the second verse, Mr. Barnes came in from the anteroom door. At this, Ryan smiled. Mr. Barnes still turned back at the door and shut it quite carefully behind him, as if he had been communing with various heady spirits he did not want turned loose on the Uninitiate. He closed the door quite carefully behind him and made the familiar gesture of testing the latch, for all the world like poor Pandora's box.

Then Mr. Barnes turned and, catching sight of them all for the first time, rewarded the filled church with a radiant smile. After the Doxology he climbed into the pulpit and held a hand, palm out, for prayer.

After the first few sentences, Ryan's mind was off and gone. He peered at the inside of his eyelids and found that one could see, as Fen had promised, the fine network of veins. He rubbed at them and lights flashed and gray cogwheels whirred across and something yellow formed away way off in the blackness, like a sun coming together. He listened to Asa breathing and to a clicking somewhere behind him that he thought was bound and certain to be Miss Castors with her dentures loose. Someone sneezed and a child asked a loud quickly-silenced question. For one minute he wanted very much to do what he had done in this same building as a child; he wanted to put his fingers in his ears and put pressure on and off, so that the sound of Mr. Barnes would come in spurts, incomprehensible, rhythmic.

He thought about praying for recovery but he could not. There was a thing in his throat; he did not really believe it would be lifted out. He pictured himself praying, and the thing suddenly yanked from his flesh, pulled up on invisible cords to hang redly above the congregation like the Holy Spirit's tongues of flame. *That* was a baptism for you!

Then the prayer was over and Ryan lifted his face, smiling, and Asa gave him a warning look. Whatever was in his mind, she disapproved.

From the pulpit Mr. Barnes reminded them of the announcements in the bulletin, welcomed visitors, and read the Scripture. He read well, except that the *g*'s and *d*'s and *t*'s on the ends of words were apt to be explosive in their finality.

He read from the last chapter of Job, the reaffirmation of the greatness of God.

"Therefore," read Mr. Barnes, too loud, "have I uttered that I understood not; things too wonderful for me which I knew not . . ." But the way he read it, loud and in the Billy Graham style which was so fashionable these days, it made the words seem to deal with other people than these, distant and sinful people who moved in pride and lust through worldly apartments in New York City.

The sermon was vaguely against materialism. Against dependence on earthly wisdom as opposed to revelation. Against worldliness. Against setting up the here-and-now as sufficient for man's soul. ("Man shall not live by bread alone.")

The congregation thumbed to various references and Mr. Barnes talked and read, and they read. Once an old man cried from the back "*amen!*" but a few people frowned. They did not encourage that kind of participation any more.

"Lean not unto thine own understanding," charged Mr. Barnes, looking out of his box balefully like a caged lion. "God has chosen the weak things of this world to confound the strong."

He said "*weak*" with that sharply punctuated rise of voice that the radio had made every preacher's property and technique.

It was almost over. Mr. Barnes was summarizing his three points which, so far as Ryan could tell, had heretofore been buried under words. He wondered if all sermons had three points to them—if they had to be constructed a certain way, like Spenserian sonnets.

When it was all done, Mr. Barnes prayed fervently that the U.S. might turn again, like Israel, from its worldly ways; that our President might refrain from sports and games on the Sabbath Day; and that—above all—God's will might be done as it is done in Heaven.

Ryan said to Asa that if they went out the side door they could get to the car quicker, but actually it was so he would not have to take that finger-by-finger handshake another time.

He walked down the side steps and into the waiting, penetrating gaze of Amos McBane.

"A visitor," cried Amos, delighted. "Happy to see you, sir. Delighted to have you with us!"

And before Ryan could remind him of who he was, the old man had gone fumbling through the pages of his Bible, muttering to himself and squinching up his eyebrows.

"Wait a minute. Got something for you. Something to remind you that you came and worshiped with us." He pressed a wrinkled folder into Ryan's hand and vanished, muttering other things under his breath like incantations.

Ryan barely glanced at the *Seven Steps to Salvation* before he dropped it into his pocket.

Part Two

A VIRTUOUS DAY

13.

THOSE NEXT DAYS, things began to settle.

Whether the cause came from within or without Ryan could not have said; but all the rubber bands which had held his limbs together began to ease back merely to a healthy tautness, and the bones which had seemed tight to brittleness within him let go a little at the joints and felt like his own again.

It was as though his body returned to him from some journey. He flexed it and walked it and touched it curiously like a garment he had not worn for some time; and had he not known it was his own wishful thinking, he would have said the malignant masses were gone in the burst of well feeling which came to him now. He would have said that small internal workmen had finally gotten around to those, and had chipped them away and trundled them off in little barrows. This made him smile; it was part of an old old health book he had owned as a child, in which a "Good Health Brigade" of white corpuscles had been pictured as dashing up and down the body on repair calls, in response to a great switchboard built carefully in the skull.

And he thought about Time again, how the past and present were so meshed together in the sum of himself that practically nothing was ever forgotten. It was his past and his present that made up the unit of Ryan Godwin. Time *was* the quantity of life, but it was Is-Time and Was-Time. The Time that might come—what did any of them know about that?

And the Is-Time which came to Ryan now seemed especially precious.

He began to walk alone a great deal, even on days when he knew Fen was desperate to come along. He would go striding off in a determined military fashion, pretending he did not see the boy where he stood hopefully in the yard looking after him, or closing his ears to the sound of feet hurrying up out of the orchard grass.

For, although Ryan liked Fen's company, sometimes it was heavy to him; it weighed on him in the same way the overabundance of sounds and smells and colors tired his senses. And there were whole days when he wanted no more than to get out from under the weight of the look in Lady Malveena's eyes.

She said nothing. She said only, "You look a little better."

"Feel better."

"People up North must cook poor trash," she said, in satisfaction. Yet he would not meet her glance for fear of being buried under it.

At first he took the walks mostly for that, to get away, and he walked aimlessly and glanced up at sounds or bright colors. There was no plan to it. But then something almost physical seemed to shift just behind his eyes and he felt himself walking in *directions*, alertly, as if he were looking for something. He could not, at first, imagine what it was he was always expecting to see around this bend or just across that hill. When finally he understood it the whole thing was so simple he could hardly credit it at all.

He wanted to see the town.

Almost he wanted to come upon it unawares, when it did not know it was being observed and evaluated. (Like, he thought grinning, a *Life* photographer whose chief ambition is to catch a celebrity picking his nose in public.) He wanted to catch Stoneville like that, cussing and picking its nose and plowing its nearby fields, and perhaps doing some unsuspected deed of kindness. He had been away; now he could come at it whole and see—perhaps—past all the varicolored surfaces to the inside, where the veins and organs were, and life moved.

Every day he widened his walking radius from Walnut Street, went down small lanes he had forgotten and others he was sure he had never seen before, looking and looking.

From this Ryan learned something about the shape of the town, perhaps about all towns. They were neither in the form of circles nor squares as they seemed on maps or out of the windows of high swift airliners. Rather they were like amoebas, great changing living globs; so that here a pseudopod of industry went out a long way into the countryside, but here you turned a corner and the farm and forest encroached far in.

Sometimes a walk of only a block or so would take him off hard-surfaced roads entirely and onto the yellow sandy ones, with rain ditches at each side and three-rowed barbwire fences holding cattle in.

Off one such road atop a grassless hill there sat a Negro shack which he remembered with a pang: this was the Dipping Place. Here, in the old days, men from the farms had brought their hounds to be "dipped" against fleas and mange; and boys (like Ryan) had slipped away from school to watch the scrawny Negro woman (she was no bigger than a fice bitch herself) take up a dog by scruff and tail and pitch him into the great wooden tub of foul-smelling stuff that steamed eternally in her yard. The boys had heard the dogs yowl, seen them climb out and run—slicked down and wet and thin, with tails cupped under—wildly about the yard until the wetness dried on them; had seen the old woman turn unconcerned to get her thirty cents apiece. It was said to be foolproof. It was said to be good for dogs after the burning stopped.

She had no rival in all of Stone County for no one else could stand the smell of the stuff she brewed.

And in those days when she saw the boys hanging around the hill, staring, she would wait till the white men had taken their dogs and gone; and then she would come out and throw small sharp rocks at the boys.

They were all secretly afraid she would catch them, like a real witch, and throw them into the vat of Whatever Was to be bubbled and dissolved, and they would flee down the hill breathless from terror.

And the old woman (would he ever forget that sight?) would stand on her hill as if it crowned the universe, with the old tub smoking and seething, and she would laugh and laugh to see the boys run away. There was no humor in that laugh. She hated them; they knew it; they hated her. Never a word passed between her and a single child, but the hatred was immense. There were no exceptions.

Now when Ryan found that hill again the old hatred rose in him like something off a sour stomach. The shack seemed empty; he walked uphill and crossed the yard to where the old slats had sagged off the metal hoops that once held the Dipping Tub together. Standing there, he felt a little sad because she was gone; it seemed to him he could still smell the old flea-killing fluid, that all the rains and years since eternity would not have been able to fade it out. What was it—that hot, sour, salty, Red-Devil-Lye smell that he had never run across again? He smelled it sharply and disagreeably off the wind of Time.

And now the old woman who had run the Dipping Place must be dead and all the adventure gone out of this little hill with its broken tub. He scuffed at the stones in the sand—they were not so sharp and murderous as he remembered. And the shack: he glanced inside and it was nothing but an empty shack with tattered newspapers pasted on the walls to hold the winter out. He had a sudden vision of the bitter old Dipping woman quite dead and every dog in Stone County overrun with fleas. It pleased him—the fancy that even this old Negro woman who had hated them all had been, in her own way, indispensable.

He walked along the part of railroad track that ran on a high hill and remembered the day he had raced beside this track because a train was coming, and he had always heard the steam from trains would suck you underneath the wheels. To this day he remembered that from the steep drop to his right honeysuckle vines had reached out to trip him across the rails.

And in walking about like this, day after day, Ryan found other places he had almost forgotten but wanted to see again, like one old old graveyard where long-dead Southern ladies lay, and at the other end their favorite old slaves who had raised them. He read their names and found them rich and full: Almeta Crabtree. Nonnie Stallings. Tabitha S. Bateman. And the darkies' names: Volsie. Kattie Fee. Mame. Lizzie Fan.

And he tried on his tongue: Johnston K. Peyton. Ryan Godwin. Jessica Godwin. But these were not the same.

One place he rediscovered in his walks came to please him especially and he found himself going back to it. For all of its attachment to the past (once he would have called it "moldering" attachment) which was so typical of the whole town, he liked it better than any of the other places he had been. He did not know why. It was part of that spectrum of Time again—he lost his identity here. He was not only Yesterday's Ryan Godwin and Today's

Ryan Godwin—there were fibers in him that reached into lives long dead he had never known.

When he went through the iron gates into that park he went into a mysticism of which he did not know the name.

The park (it was out of the business part of town) was named The Memorial Park of Stoneville, dedicated—it said on the monument—*to our Confederate Dead who died bravely defending a way of life.*

He would go through the gates and read that line each time (he had often poked fun at that kind of thing; he had demanded to know why that old war was still sitting on all our courthouse lawns?) and then he would take half a dozen steps into that new dimension.

It was cool, it was shaded. It was not so much that Time *stopped* as that it blended here. He did not resent that monument now—that war was over such a short time ago. And wars did not have to be just in order to leave memories or burn fields.

He had often said that the South clung to the past and that because the past was often smaller, that had made them cramped. And there was truth in that. But in the park, where the trees grew and the old grass and the dirt that was so fertile it was black rot lay, the sense of age and time and timelessness was beautiful.

The trees on all sides were gigantic and very old, full of years and forgotten winds and endless accumulation of seasons: Southern red oak, and poplar, and tulip poplar, and sweet gum, and chinaberry.

An old fountain stood near the center of the park with a low stone wall about it that seemed at first glance to be a solid hump of ivy, except here and there where rock showed through. Usually the fountain did not work at all and when it did it ran over the sides. This explained why the ivy was always so lush and green and youthful, and seemed forever narrowing the walled-in circle, reaching out long green fingers toward the water.

Scattered about the park were a few stone benches, appropriately marked.

STONEVILLE HIGH SCHOOL. Class of 1931.
U. D. C. *In Memoriam.* 1925.

AMERICAN LEGION: *To Remind Us Of All Our Dead On All Our Battlefields.* 1946.

Ryan paused at this one and, bending down, touched the words curiously. "*All* our dead, on *all* our battlefields," he repeated. There was something remarkable in that.

The city officials of Stoneville kept the grass trimmed in Memorial Park (a wiry little man ran the clippers around, stepped down, moved stones and sticks, was possessed of infinite patience—was it the atmosphere?) and once a year the Business Women's Club of Stoneville replaced any dead shrubs and azaleas in ordered rows along the sandy paths. There were mimosa trees which bloomed in season and old old crepe myrtle, which they still called "The Flower of a Hundred Days."

There was a bird-feeding station and a squirrel-feeding station where nature lovers left their offerings. The squirrels were tame; if you came upon them unawares they seemed to frown at you before springing away without haste.

Sometimes the grade school children, when they were studying such things, came to the park to find cocoons and discarded birds' eggs, broken now; and to talk about ants and aphids.

There were *no* public bathrooms. It was assumed that if you brought children you would take them carefully to plumbing beforehand, and that Nature would call them genteelly and patiently whenever she did.

On hot summer days, old men would sit and watch the birds swooping in and out the fountain unerringly, flinging up silver drops on all sides. The old men would nod at this as though it affirmed something to them, or give out cautious wheezy laughter so as not to frighten the sparrows away; or sometimes they would argue in violent whispers about what kinds of birds these were. Was not each man an authority? Had they not lived in Stone County every year of their lives?

In summer, too, the dry flies would sing out of the oak trees, calling up rain; and the old men would nod their heads about it and watch the sky.

More than anything, Ryan liked to listen to the old men talk, sitting somewhat apart where he could hear without seeming to listen to them.

"Think it'll rain?"

"It might. Williams hung up a blacksnake yesterday."

"That ought to do it."

"Big kind of snake?"

"More than three foot, old Williams said."
"He's such a liar though."
"That's so. Never pays to give him much heed."
"Comes from a lying family. The Williamses always been big liars in this county."
"Nobody ever took them serious."
"Wasn't no need to."
"Why, them old ones might be still setting outside the Big Gates for all I know, waiting to get took serious!"
This would strike all the old men as riotously funny. They might rock back and forth, watery-eyed, wheezing with laughter and banging one another's knees at the prospect of generations and generations of Williamses locked—as it served them right—outside the Pearly Gates.
And to one side Ryan (almost involuntarily) would himself begin to smile. He would see all the Williamses (stiff Aunt Corah, and Wilfred Jamison, and little Billy Lee) protesting to Saint Peter that this time they were really and truly dead and something ought to be done about it!
In another minute their laughter would have run its course and when they regained their breaths and got the blood out of their faces and back to the old hearts where it belonged, they would go back to talking about the relations of one or more of them.
"What do you hear from your boys? When are they coming back to settle?"
The voice angry, resigned. "I don't know. Say they got good jobs where they are."
"That's too bad."
"Ungrateful. Both of them always been ungrateful."
"Luther's got kids?"
"Got two boys. Awful skinny little boys. Never caught a catfish or been to a thrashing, but Luther thinks they're educated. They told me Lespedeeza was some place in China. And Luther thinks they got the best of everything." (Here the old man would spit into the grass, viciously.) "Little he knows."
"Boys will be ungrateful. Seems to be in the nature of them."
"That's so."
"Conner got kids?"
"Rachel's expecting about February. I tell him he'll get his share. His own blood'll go ungrateful on him, too."

"They won't listen, though. You can't tell them anything."

"That's so. It's a shame, that nobody can tell nobody. Ain't that a shame?"

"Might as well give it up before you start. But you feel you've got to try it."

"Yes," sadly, "that's so."

All the old men would then fall silent on their stone benches around the fountain, depressed by the ingratitude of the young and by the impossibility of transmitting experience. Ryan, on his nearby bench, would stare down unseeing at his own feet, miserable for them.

"Take my boy Sampson. He's in the paratroops. He thinks he's got it nice, spends all his money, lives it up all the time. I tell him he better put some back. I tell him his teeth gonna rot in his head some day and his feet get cold, and he'd better pick out some woman to warm them for him and to make the soup. But what's he say? He says for me to mind my own business. He says he's got it okay in the army. He says he'll worry about that day when he comes to it."

"Don't you tell *me!*" One of the old men looked as though he might leap to his feet from sheer indignation, might balloon up and float along the path for emphasis.

"Daughters is just as bad."

"They're worse. They smile and listen but they just won't mind."

"Don't you tell *me!*"

"Listen, I tell my boy Sampson, I been along that road. I say—Boy, I been right where you at. But you think he believes any of that?"

The answer was bitter. "Sure he don't believe it."

"That boy thinks I been sixty-five since I was born."

"They all think that."

"But tell me this, didn't your Daddy talk to you like that? And did you ever listen to a word he said?"

There was a giggle, half-ashamed, half-proud. "I never did."

After a while (they would grow silent, remembering old lectures and rebellions) one of them would speak out and generalize the conversation again; the others would turn to him happily, thankfully.

"Going to be an early winter. You notice how the birds is going every day?"

An excited nodding of the wrinkled drying heads. "That's so! That's so!"

"I was remarking on that just yesterday."

"Birds know. Birds know such things."

"Something else birds know—they know when it's going to storm. Ever notice how they move off ahead of rainclouds, so that just before the thing hits you can look everywhere and they's not a bird to be seen?"

"Many's the time. Many's the time."

"You wouldn't think they'd have much sense in such a little head."

"Quick, though. Birds is terrible quick small creatures. Maybe they think like that, too, small but quick."

"That's so. Look at a setting hen. Bigger—but there's nothing any dumber than an old slow setting hen."

"I'm thinking that's likely our fault. She's give too much. All she got to do is wait for evening and free corn coming. She just loses track of being smart."

"That's so. You spoil a dog and it's the same way."

"Or a kid either."

"Yes, that's so."

And the burst of high excited chatter about birds and weather would die down, while thoughts turned to Luthers and Conners and Sampsons and Wills and Franks that hadn't turned out as the men had planned.

Until after a while Ryan, embarrassed for them, would ease away, walking softly down the sandy paths between the rows of well-clipped bushes, and stopping curiously again would read aloud the words:

All Our Dead On All Our Battlefields.

So many, he would think, sharing the old men's sadness even though he was not a part of it. So very very many.

14.

EVEN BEFORE he was fully awake, in that intermediate stage when one hears without seeming to hear, or turns in bed and yet feels furiously immobile, Ryan knew it was going to be a good day. He woke to it eagerly and looked around at all the jutting walls as if he expected something remarkable to have happened to them overnight.

He thought: *I live in a deformed room*; but it did not matter.

In another moment he had heard the sound. There was a small persistent scratching just outside his bedroom door. At first he thought it might be some small animal, but he knew there could be no animals in Asa's house, not even one bright-eyed mouse to surprise when switching on a light.

Scritchy-skrack. He thought of beavers working their way through trees.

Creasing his forehead he called after a few minutes, "Fen? Fen, is that you?"

The door came open in a rush and Fen stepped in and closed it behind him. He hung his head slightly but he could not hide his smile. "I didn't mean to wake you up," he lied. "Are you going to be busy today?"

"Not today. What in the world were you doing?"

"The rug in the hall," said Fen, looking a little sheepish. "I was fraying the edges."

Ryan supposed that in some unknown frame of reference this was a perfectly reasonable answer.

It was Sunday and the old colored man and his wife and daughter would not be going by to work; Ryan felt relieved about that. He wondered what they did on Sundays. Maybe they walked angrily to church, wearing their Sunday best.

Fen looked very excited. "I thought . . . I thought we might do something today, Uncle Ryan. I thought we might take a lunch and go to a place I know and everything; it isn't far to walk and Asa's not going to church with a headache so we don't really *have* to." He swallowed, all the breath sucked out of his chest. "That is, if you're really not busy," he finished vaguely.

"No, I'm not busy." Ryan swung his feet to the floor. "Where shall we go?"

"I'll show you when we get there." Fen seemed tremendously relieved that Ryan was going to come, as though all along he had steeled himself for a refusal, not wanting to count on anything too much. Now he went across the room and bounced on the edge of the bed while Ryan searched for slippers.

"Aunt Asa said last night that we could have Miss Satterfield over for dinner one night if you wanted to."

Ryan laughed aloud. "She did, did she? Oh, Lord." He tossed and caught the unopened blades in his hand. "I guess I ought to shave."

"We won't see anybody," Fen offered.

"Okay, I won't." He was still grinning; ask Cornelia Satterfield to dine like a prospective sister-in-law! "What did you do last night? How did Asa get inspired to such generosity?"

"I read a little bit," said Fen. "Aunt Asa didn't do anything much. How old do people get before they shave?"

Ryan turned to look at him thoughtfully. "It depends," he said. "About sixteen, I guess." It occurred to him to wonder what would become of Fen's state of mind as he moved into puberty with only Asa to advise him. He visualized a Where-Do-Babies-Come-From-God-Makes-Them dialogue. What would Asa say if she came in some morning and found Fen's bedsheets wet? He said cautiously, "Are you in a hurry to learn to shave?"

"I think so. I think I'd like to be grown up."

Ryan looked at him frowning.

"If I were grown up I could go away and do everything I ever wanted to do myself. And nobody to bother me," said Fen.

At this, Ryan resisted the impulse to give a scornful "Hah!" He got out a clean shirt and began to slip out of his pajamas. Fen got up off the bed and went to look out the window into the tall oak tree while Ryan dressed, but whether from embarrassment or from fear of embarrassing it was hard to say.

In a minute Ryan said, "Don't let them fool you. You don't ever grow up and away really, you just grow on. After you've come to a certain point nothing changes much except that after a while you stop getting taller. And gradually you forget things," he added, not wanting to leave it too simple. But he didn't want to leave Fen thinking the world's egg cracked open miraculously when one turned twenty-one, either.

"Forget what things?" said Fen, watching him.

Things like raveling hall carpets, Ryan thought with a grin but did not say. That would have brought it too close; as it was he was paying Fen the compliment of an abstract discussion and he did not want to spoil it.

"Oh . . ." he drawled the syllable, giving himself time to think about it, "you forget a multitude of details and the world shrinks accordingly. Gets duller. You forget to notice all the separate parts because all the grown-up world is organized around summaries. Around generalizations and wholes. Just listen to adults talk sometimes. They talk in rules and commandments and explanations and very general ideas." (Except sometimes, he thought, when Time is a cylinder capable of spinning in both directions—forward and back—and all of the senses childlike again.) "For grownups things don't seem so . . ." (He sought for a word. Symbolical? Charged with spirits? How could he explain to Fen that an adult would never hear a particular squeak in a particular tread in a stairway?) "So meaningful," he finished after a while.

"Are people sorry they forget?"

"Well the ones who really forget can't be sorry, because they don't know anything's gone. Some of the others are sorry out of all proportion. They think of it as something precious they had once and then lost. That's one reason some people believe everything was wonderful when they were younger. And it wasn't, of course. It wasn't terrible either. The days went about the same proportions —some good, some bad, some colorless."

He was dressed now. "Ready to go?"

"Lady Malveena said she'd have some breakfast ready for us."

They closed the door to the crooked room behind them and started down the stairs, Fen frowning. They had gotten about halfway down when Fen widened his eyes and threw a startled half-fearful glance across his shoulder at the stairs and Ryan realized they had walked heavily upon them all.

Fen said, "When things have meanings—good luck and all—is that silly? Is that childish?"

Ryan was amused that twelve-year-old Fen should be concerned about childishness but he did not permit himself to smile. "The word 'childish' sounds like something that ought to be punished. Child-like is better, maybe. The ability to think the way a child thinks. Like not forgetting all those details. People who write books try to go back and pick up that way of thinking." He tried to come up with an example and could only find a poor one. "Like a broken flower," he said self-consciously. "It may be very sad to a certain kind of child and pretty unimportant to a certain adult. But the man writing the book wants to make it sad again."

And up in his head the periphery Ryan was considering that unoriginal thought and deciding it wasn't bad as a jumping-off place for something. The periphery Ryan wrote in italics in the air:

> *The author seeks to reawaken the child in each of us, by replacing us in a universe where nothing is either trivial or unwilled, and where the world is peopled with all manner of spirits. In this setting he persuades us to use again the tool of the symbol in interpreting things, not so much intellectually as emotionally; and by this means he forces us again into active participation in events. We become once more as children in a field of grass—we* ARE *the grass and the sun and the passing butterflies at a time; we are the bee and the flower and we are the face of God brooding above it all.*

He had been, all this time, walking through the dining room, and at the end of the writing he stood with one palm outspread on the kitchen table. He was tremendously pleased with himself for a minute; he felt something about the night's sleep had left him remarkably clever and he *would* write that book after all. And then he became aware that Fen and Lady Malveena were laughing at him. With sudden surprise he heard their laughter ringing and re-ringing in the kitchen and their two faces faded into shape before him.

"He's altogether dead," Lady Malveena was saying merrily. "I remember when Jason Wilkes fell out of his box and rolled down the hill and all the mourners had to chase after, but I never seen a corpse walking quite so well."

"Wake up, Uncle Ryan!" Fen crowed.

The laughter of Fen and Lady Malveena filtered in between all the fine words which were still written in suspension; it separated them, flung them this way and that so that they were all gone by the time he had grinned sheepishly and said, "Good morning." It seemed to him he had been thinking vaguely of a writer's ability to stimulate imagination, but beyond that he could not remember anything.

Fen and Lady Malveena thought they had an excellent joke on him.

"You sure was in a trance!" Lady Malveena chuckled, going over to the cupboard now to take down some dishes.

Ryan said, grinning, "Looks like I mightn't be very good company for you, Fen," and Fen looked at him sharply to make sure he was not seeking an excuse. So did Lady Malveena, dropping her smile as if it had been a piece of pasteboard on her mouth. He wanted to say to them: *Don't be so intense!*

But he said only to Lady Malveena, "Your cousin have her baby all right?"

Lady Malveena snorted. "Sure she did. Women been doing it for years."

Fen asked her if she helped the day he was born and Lady Malveena said No, she had been too busy helping his Uncle Ryan at the time. And she shot Ryan a shrewd glance.

"Were you sick that day?" said Fen, surprised.

"Just worried," he said. He frowned at Lady Malveena and she shrugged.

"Okay, just set and eat," she said and she looked as though for two cents she would put her tongue out at him, then and there.

Fen and Ryan ate without too much conversation. They were like people who wanted to be done with it and get the strength and be off to other things. In one corner of the kitchen Lady Malveena packed sandwiches for them to take along.

"Looks like it's going to be one of *them* days," she observed—presumably to the sandwiches. "One of them scattered kind."

"What's scattered?" said Fen.

"People and mealtimes. Miss Asa having headaches and poached eggs, Miss Clara in and out nibbling all day long, and you two carrying lunch away. You ain't ever able to get your energy *pointed* any place." She frowned, looked gloomy. "It'll likely be a telephone and doorbell day to boot, with people wanting to know how come nobody made church this morning."

"You must tell them I've corrupted the household."

"They'll likely think that anyway." She said to Ryan, glaring at him with dark suspicion, "You eat deviled eggs?" and he assured her that he did.

"I'll fix some then—eggs already boiled," she grunted. "There's not much bread."

"Have we got crackers then?" said Fen. "I want to feed some birds."

She grumbled and fussed. "Spoiling them birds. They wild creatures long before you was born. Bothering up their instincts." But the crackers went into the box along with the deviled eggs.

Ryan asked her, "Lady Malveena, is there an N.A.A.C.P. unit in Stoneville?" He had been meaning to ask for several days.

She watched him. "Yeah, we got one. Why?"

"Do you belong?"

She shook her head. "I've got no quarrel with it, though. Sometimes I thinks they yell a little loud. But I'm too old for that. It's not my fight any more."

"What do you mean yell too loud? They have big meetings?"

"No. I didn't mean actual. I mean they so full of this business of striking while the iron is hot they apt to forget they might bend it out of all proportion. They got no patience at all. Maybe you got to be old to have any patience—I don't know. The young folks go."

He felt strange defending the organization to Lady Malveena. "I guess they feel they've had nearly a hundred years of patience," he said.

"You know that church business Mr. Barnes says? That sometimes you don't want to win the argument; you want to win the *man*. Well, Mr. Barnes ain't much but there's some truth in that. What help is it to win this argument and lose the rest?"

"You mean you'd have them stop now? Just when they've got the principle established? You wouldn't have them work to see it put into operation?"

"If nobody agrees with that principle, what's the gain of rushing the rest along?"

But Ryan was genuinely disturbed because Lady Malveena was one of the rare ones; she was one of those who should have had chances to be more than a servant. He would put up with a hundred dolts for the sake of one like her. In fact, as a teacher he had been always putting up with multitudes of dolts to find the few who mattered, he thought now, rather wryly.

And as if she read his mind she said, "But I know how they feel, wanting it hurried. I know a few little kids in Runk's Corners I'd like to rush it for. They ought to have . . . well . . . a few more doors not closed. That's all I want for any of them. If it turns out the stuff between their ears is not so good after all, then I don't want any favors for them."

"Is Bobby Mayhew one?" said Fen. "And Link Sanders?"

She was embarrassed. "Yeah," she said.

And Ryan thought of her talking about Fen and about love and about not meaning to step in that river and go under and downstream one more single time. Some people couldn't help it, maybe. Something inside them was always growing outwards, toward the rest.

Finally they had finished eating and Lady Malveena had packed the lunch to her satisfaction so that nothing would spill or get stale or be mashed. Ryan asked Fen if he had already told Asa they would be gone for lunch.

Fen looked embarrassed. "I was afraid she'd say we ought to go to church instead. I thought Lady Malveena could tell her after we had already gone."

Lady Malveena's interruption was in a threatening tone. "You thought that, did you?"

Fen shifted his appeal to her. "She won't mind, really, especially once it's done. It's ahead of time that she minds."

Ryan was doubtful. "Lady Malveena, you think she'll mind?"

The eyebrows lifted and paused and came back down again, matching her shoulders. "Outward, you mean? You mean is she going to *say* anything? To me?"

He frowned. "No, I mean will she mind?" and Lady Malveena shrugged again.

"Oh she'll *mind*. But not outward."

At this exchange Fen's face seemed to have opened out in distress, the eyes wide, the mouth slack and silently protesting. Seeing him so vulnerable Ryan said quickly, "Well, Asa couldn't mind it as much as I if I missed the trip. Ready to go?"

The mouth lifted, smiled; the eyes crinkled at the edges. "I'll bring the lunch," said Fen.

Under her breath Lady Malveena said happily that for a man who had sure been overeducated he wasn't so dumb sometimes.

Fen and Ryan went out the back door by common consent, closing the screen quietly like conspirators. Lady Malveena watched them through it.

She said, eyes twinkling but the mouth held very straight and serious, "I'll tell Miss Asa that you all aimed to think real holy thoughts."

"And feed the birds," Ryan reminded her. "Tell her to think about what the catechism says on deeds of necessity and mercy. Tell her about not one sparrow falling."

She had to smile. "I'll do that," Lady Malveena said.

Fen and Ryan walked slowly and misused little of their energy by talking. Breathing alone was enough to occupy their mouths and throats, sucking in the already tangy air (an early winter, Ryan thought again) and the smell of wet straw that came to them dimly when they walked in orchard grass where the dew had not yet dried.

At the far end of the orchard a rabbit put his head up out of that grass and gave them one startled look; he sat quite still, trying to be a stone or a clod in the grass, and then he gave it up and went off in broad arcs toward a clump of berry bushes. The way he moved, forever hung between each time he touched the ground. They stood still and watched him out of sight.

"Want me to carry the lunch?" said Ryan.

But Fen shook his head; he was the host. "This way," he said, and led off down through the orchard by a little path along the edge of the arbor. Here, Ryan remembered, there had lived a family of blacksnakes one long terrified summer and even when he had stood by the carriage house in those days the very wind had sounded as if snakes slithered underfoot. He used to dream about those blacksnakes. Even now he was not comfortable; he stared at the thick grass and wondered what generation it would be now—if there were any here.

"Used to have blacksnakes here," he said aloud to Fen.

"Lady Malveena killed one last summer. With a hoe." Fen sounded nonchalant. "They don't really die until sundown, you know, even when they're cut in two."

"That so?"

"Lady Malveena says if you come back before sundown the head can still bite you."

"I used to hear if snapping turtles bit they didn't let go till it thundered."

Fen was very matter-of-fact. "Yes sir, I know about that."

It was passing into autumn; walking like this Ryan realized it more than before. The grass almost squeaked as it flattened under their shoes and Ryan looked behind them where it was coming up again without much springiness.

"The blacksnake—did you hang it up in a tree?" he said, to make conversation.

Fen shook his head. "No sir. We'd had too much rain already. It was early in the summer. Too wet to plant anything."

"Oh."

Suddenly he stopped and bent down. "What's the matter?" said Fen, turning back.

"Well, looky there!" said Ryan softly. He took up a purple flower he had almost crushed underfoot. Fen looked down at it, disappointed.

"What's that? Why, it's just a mollypop!" he said.

And that's what it was—a mollypop—so called because by harvest time the lush vulgar-sweet smelling blooms had gone to pods and these would pop loudly under your feet when you were walking in the furrows.

Ryan was grinning. "I know it," he said. "I just haven't seen one for a long time. I used to call it a pop-molly."

Fen looked the way most children do when adults reminisce about *their* childhoods; he looked as though privately he didn't think that was very bright.

At the end of the orchard they left Godwin property and went behind a row of identical drab back yards with woodsheds and clotheslines and trash buckets. The path behind the houses was almost shiny from travel and seemed to be neutral territory, owned by no one.

"These used to be mill houses," Fen explained, waving his hand like a guide in a foreign land, "but they let the people buy some of them. Now they can even paint them different colors."

Different colors. The great emancipation.

The sight of the mollypop vine which had once been so familiar as to go unnoticed in a boy's day (the way it had gone unnoticed to Fen) had set Ryan to wondering about all the other things he once had known so well—a Satan's Snuffbox, for instance, which was a puffy mound (mushroom?) that gave off brownish dust when you put your foot upon it, and snakeberries, and the pale leaves of rabbit tobacco, and polk berries for war paint and chicken feathers under rubber bands around the head, and chinquapins—the little nuts like chestnuts which came in thorny coats—and long horrid monkey cigars and tents which one improvised with a broom and a hoe and a mop handle and a blanket. One had to be able to make and break camp quickly, since the broom or hoe might be called away into service.

And all of those things reminded him of a game Asa had played when they were small—taking small thin sticks well peeled of bark (or burnt kitchen matches salvaged from the trash) with grapes on one end for heads and morning glory blossoms slipped on the other for gay wide hoop skirts. He remembered the sight of Asa lining up rows and rows of the make-believe ladies in their flowered skirts, and the very thought of it amazed him. What happened to that little girl? he thought.

He followed Fen silently, thinking.

They left the mill houses and went down a reddish bank (he almost fell) onto an unpaved street where other houses were. These were all alike and all the same color, and he supposed the mill had not sold any of them yet. It was Sunday; they passed well-starched people on the way to church and several yardfuls of children and noisy dogs. Some people had pots of geraniums and ferns sitting up and down the steps. Nearby was a small chair factory with unpainted chairs stacked one atop the other, waiting for trucks to come on Monday.

Next to that was an old store building, still covered with peeling old signs about snuff and cold remedies, with one new sign hanging on the door. SALVATION ARMY, it said.

Inside, people were singing and a piano was thumping rather joyfully, Ryan thought. In a minute he caught the words:

> I'm drinking from the fountain which never will run dry,
> I'm feeding on the manna from a bountiful supply
> For I am dwelling in Beulah Land.

"Sometimes Aunt Asa gives them clothes," said Fen, "and I bring them down. One of the men is real nice. He's been to China once. He said if the people there were upside down they sure didn't know about it and I told Badger."

Ryan grunted.

"They had a big meeting down here last summer," Fen said. "They had a microphone I could hear all the way in bed at night."

It must have been an exciting summer. That and a dead blacksnake, too!

They turned off the road into a pine-needled path that led through a small patch of woods and after a while they crawled under a barbed-wire fence into a field of grass.

"There's a couple of cows in here," said Fen. He added generously, "They won't bother you, though."

"Oh," said Ryan, smiling. "I'm glad to hear it." Fen glanced at him sharply.

After a walk across pasture which offered nothing more alarming than unexpected heaps of dung, they crossed two red gullies and went up a honeysuckled hill to the railroad track. Are there always honeysuckle vines at railroad tracks? he wondered.

He stepped up to the rail. "I used to be able to walk this thing." After a few steps he faltered.

Fen was up like a tightrope walker. "Don't look at your feet," he said. "Look a little ways ahead, there where the light hits. It shines exactly that far ahead of you all the way along." He ran a few steps, went forward and back, did a mild dance. Then he looked as though he were afraid he might be embarrassing his uncle and he said, "There's nothing to it but practice."

Ryan walked the ties which were always spaced too long or too short for a good even stride. Sometimes they passed heaps of ties stacked off to one side, waiting until they were needed.

"We walk this nearly to the trestle," Fen explained over one shoulder.

They were going to the river, then. And Ryan did not much want to go there because it was different from the other times, with Jessica. Those times, of course, it had always been dark; they had known the river was there only by the sound of it going by them in the night.

He had not been to the Katsewa River in daylight since (he supposed) very much younger years, school picnics and dates along the banks, or Saturday afternoons when he and the others had worn themselves out swimming against the muddy current.

The river was actually an enemy, had always been an enemy—but slyly. It was so ugly and red-brown that it seemed harmless enough, usually not sufficiently deep for boats of any size, dotted with sandbars and rock and caught (seemingly without protest) at one spot by an efficient-looking dam. It looked like a plain no-nonsense river which, if it would not carry shipping, would at least turn the water wheels of the community in a steady way.

But its current was deceptive; the river had a way of seeming just that plain and placid on the surface while the pull and tug went on in all directions underneath. Countless experienced swimmers had died in the river; fishing trips ended at least once a season in disaster. There was a rescue squad standing by in Stoneville for these emergencies, but it was always arriving too late or putting the victim head-up on an incline or getting the respiration wrong. It was as if the very sight of the river bewitched all of them so they could not function efficiently.

For these reasons, every year so long as Ryan could remember, the City Council had discussed whether this summer they would make it a law—they would declare the river unsafe for bathing and put up signs making it illegal to swim there. But that would have meant patrolling all the stretches of land along its banks (and it twisted and went in and out as though it had all the time in the world—which, as a matter of fact, it did). They would decide that salaries came high this day and time, and even now the city was hard put to have one spotlighted car to check the area at night for couples copulating on the seats of automobiles. And the Boy Scouts had a cottage and a camping ground on the river, and the Kiwanis Club was building a recreation hall. So they never did anything about it, although editorials appeared about it in the *Beacon*. Warnings did not help, they said. They used to quote the old Dwight Moody story about the woman leaving home and calling back, "Now children, don't put beans up your nose!" and coming home again to find, of course, that they had done just that.

The *Beacon* said that as long as the people of Stoneville warned, "Now don't you swim in that treacherous river" everyone would, of course.

But Ryan thought (walking along, stepping from tie to tie) that it was more than money which kept the town from outlawing, once and for all, swimming in the river.

It was, instead, a part of that timeless enmity, the secret trust all of them had that this time they would beat the river after all; this summer they would swim safely all the way across at what had been grimly titled "Dead Man's Point" (some of them did, too; but some of them didn't and the name remained); this time they would show the river that all of them were strong, that all of them had good lungs and firm muscle and a swift clean stroke. . . .

And some of them did. Some of them proved that this was the Day of Man, that the day of the wilderness was past; but some of them failed and the rescue squad came clanging out from town (too late) and applied a fumbling respiration, eying the river in awe.

Ryan had seen one such drowning when he was seventeen. It was a young man, cocky, barrel-chested under wiry hair; he had stood at the point and told his friends he'd make it across in three minutes flat. It was many more minutes than that before they got him out of the water with his chest gone in as though something had pushed it hard, and all the hairs down like wilted grass.

Ryan had stood with the knot of spectators, turning sometimes to look at the river going by and going by, and other times looking at the boy they were working on and the other swimmers standing helplessly around, almost hysterical but not yet. He had heard the river going by (it had been there a thousand years before they came) with a ripple and a blurble that was very like secret laughter; and all of them who were waiting on the bank had turned their heads to look at it in anger. Very well—it had won again; it had an advantage; but there would be other seasons and stronger swimmers, all their eyes declared. When it was finally and for certain hopeless, they carried the body away (people who drown look oddly slick and white and fishlike, as if they have been reclaimed) with their backs hard and straight and angry.

Putting him in the truck to go home, someone said, "He ought to known better."

But Ryan remembered the look on all their faces must have been much like that on Trojan faces as they watched Hector dragged around before Troy by the tendons of his legs.

He said aloud to Fen, who wavered on the rail he was walking, "Is it the Katsewa River? I never can think of the name."

"I don't know the real name. I've always just called it the River."

That was right: one would always call it the River, the Storm, the Sea, the Earth—as solemnly as if one named a pantheon which must be conquered.

Then he grinned at the thought of Stoneville, girded for war, out doing battle with gods with only a leaky respirator.

After a while he and Fen came to the place where the tracks went up on a high bank, and headed for the trestle, although the river could not yet be seen for trees. They left the railroad and stumbled down a red bank that was too steep and made them run, and here a path went off between scrubby pines that thickened to giants and then faded out to low but lush green vines. Beyond that the greenness stopped dead at the edge of a sandy beach as though the growing things had all said secretly, *Let us not go too near.*

They went through those trees and then the vines, which pulled at their legs, and out into the sun.

The feel and sound of sand pressing down under their shoe soles had about it a familiarity that made Ryan want to slip off his shoes and walk up and down on the beach for a long time. It was a small beach; he would have had to go back and forth, back and forth, crossing and over his own tracks in the sand.

Coming out of the last bushes and vines Fen cried, "Over here!" looking very happy and very much alive. He began to run, stumbling a bit in the sand so that the box of lunch which he swung by its string seemed about to fall. Ryan almost ran after him it was so infectious, but he only quickened his steps up the sandy rise. The sun picked out all the brightness in the tiny rocks ahead and the pyrites shone under their feet.

At the top of the slight rise was a group of large rocks. Fen was already sitting on one of them, hugging his knees. They were bulky gray rocks in a semicircle, like sleeping hippos in the sunshine. Ryan sat down on a smaller one across from Fen and looked down and out to where the river moved, seemingly with languor, carrying now and then a box or a piece of wood or a big can. The water was so muddy red that it appeared thick, like syrup; and looking at it, one could not believe in sinking. The two of them sat for a while in silence, resting from the long walk.

It was very quiet. The river seemed to pass with a slight drone and there was no wind. "I've never been here before," said Ryan, casting one long look around, and Fen looked pleased at that.

"It's quiet here," he said. "When you sit down, you can't even see the trestle."

Ryan glanced upriver and it was so; the trestle crossed beyond a thickly wooded bend and could not be seen from where he sat. When he was a boy he had walked that very trestle, fearing for his life.

Fen was the host; he put the box on one of the rocks very carefully. "Are you hungry?"

"Not yet." Ryan lit a cigarette and flicked the dead match away and then, as if he had been reminded, reached down into the sand for a small stone and threw it into the river. The stone sank with a dull plop. Fen got up and found a flat stone and threw it so that it skimmed and skipped the surface of the water, throwing up splashes as it hopped. Even the boys who could not swim it yet—they could throw stones, thought Ryan.

But all the time he sat there in the peaceful sun an edge of his mind remembered he had only to walk downstream a ways and

"I guess so," said Fen. "Maybe it's for next year."

In a few more minutes there were other birds, small and grayish-brown; mostly sparrows, Ryan thought, and perhaps a wren. Small feathered quarrels broke out over the crumbs. The thrush was very belligerent.

"There's a doctor here in town," said Fen, "Doctor Marble. Do you know him?"

The question came from nowhere. "I don't think so. A medical doctor, you mean?"

Fen nodded. "I don't know him either. I've seen him. He gives the typhoid shots at school. He was a pretty well-known man up North so I just thought maybe you knew him."

Ryan had to smile at this. It reminded him of the questions white-haired old ladies had put to sailors on the trains: "Perhaps you know my youngest son—he's in the Navy, too."

"Is he from Stoneville?"

"I don't know. He seems like a good doctor."

That seemed to be an end to that subject. A very fat cardinal flew down onto the sand and stood for a minute making noises before he ate. Some of the sparrows scattered but most of them pretended he was not there until he shouldered them aside. He was very fat, very red, very brilliant against the shining sand.

Fen took up a small rock and began to drop it from one hand to the other. "Why didn't you get married?" he said.

Ryan was startled at this question. He put out his cigarette very slowly against the rock without looking up, to give himself time to think. "I never did have the right woman and the opportunity come along at the same time," he said finally. "Sometimes there was one or the other, but not both."

"Are you sorry?"

He looked across at Fen and it was as if something suddenly tore loose in his stomach; he wanted terribly to reach out and touch him. He said, "Yes. Very sorry."

Fen looked thoughtful and concerned. "It's funny," he said, "that none of us are."

The connection was too much for Ryan. That none of us are sorry? He said, "What?"

"That none of us are married. You or me or Miss Clara or Aunt Asa or Lady Malveena."

Ryan said, curbing his smile, "Perhaps you'll make it yet. Besides, Lady Malveena's been married. Twice."

"She never talks about that."

"Well, she used to talk about it often enough! I never knew her first husband, but her second one was hard on all of us. He was a big good-looking man. His name was Wally Fetterson Kyles and he always had to be known by both names, so that everybody called him Wallifetterson, all run together like that. He used to try to teach me how to pick a guitar. He'd learned it when he went to the penitentiary when he was seventeen. Seemed like a guitar came right into tune just when he picked it up in his hand. At night in the summertime he'd sit on the back porch sopping up Lady Malveena's wine and she'd come out and they'd sing 'Amazing Grace.' It like to drove Asa crazy."

"The hymn? And it nearly drove her crazy?" Fen was frankly unbelieving.

"Well, they speeded it up a little," Ryan admitted. Now that he had mentioned Wallifetterson he could still hear the loud voice drifting up to his bedroom:

> "When we've been there ten thousand years
> Bright shining as the sun
> We'll have more time to sing God's praise
> Than when we first begun! Hay-Boy!"

The "Hay-Boy" had been Wallifetterson's trademark. It came on the end of every song, like an exclamation point.

"Wallifetterson was a real quarrelsome man. He thought the only way to get along was to fight for everything. He was always on the lookout for men and they were always looking for him. There never a wind blew at night but what Wallifetterson yelled at it."

"Yelled at it? What did he say?"

Ryan grinned; he could hear Wallifetterson plain as plain. "He'd say, 'Come on out of there, Black Boy, I already see your eyes!' "

"And was anybody there?"

"As a matter of fact, sometimes there was. Sometimes a bottle would be let fly at him out of the dark and off he'd take. He'd be yanking at his shirt to find his knife and he'd be yelling all the time."

"What in the world did Lady Malveena marry *him* for?"

Ryan was still grinning. He remembered the size of Wallifetterson—a good six foot four—and the shoulders on him that were always banging into doors and shelves. He remembered the hard dark muscles that bound him round and he remembered that he'd come upon him sometimes talking to Lady Malveena very low and quiet with his hand inside the front of her dress.

But none of that would make any sense to Fen—not yet.

"It's always hard to tell why some people marry other people," he said. And he added, "Back in those days—even when Wallifetterson was in some trouble or out hunting somebody down—you'd hear Lady Malveena singing a lot. She used to stop in the middle of stirring things sometimes and laugh out loud."

"What happened to him?"

"Somebody stabbed him finally. There was a fight down in Runk's Corners one night and everybody was drunk. Somebody got him in the throat." They said Wallifetterson was still swearing to get the son of a bitch when the last rush of blood came up and drowned him from the inside out. They said he was saying that poor goddamned nigger was already dead and didn't know it when he got to him. "That poor dead nigger," Wallifetterson said, "whenever I find where he's at." And promptly choked to death.

Signals passed in the air that neither of them knew about and suddenly all the birds rose in a flutter and rush and went off into trees.

Later he did not know if the mention of injury and death had made Fen say it or if he had meant to tell him all along. But suddenly Fen said in a rush that he wanted to grow up and be a doctor. "A real doctor, instead of some preacher or anything. I don't say anything to Aunt Asa because she'd be so sorry."

Ryan said he thought sorry wasn't exactly the word for it.

"Is it wicked for me to want what I want instead of what she's always wanted for me?"

"No," said Ryan. "Why do you want to be a doctor, Fen?"

He turned pink in the cheeks. "That's even worse. It's not . . ." he stammered a little, "not because I want to make everybody well and help people," he said. "I could tell her that. But that isn't the reason, mainly."

"What then?"

Fen said to his own hand, "I know that must be wicked—not to want that mainly."

He sounded so morose that Ryan smiled. "At least it's unexpected, and maybe that always seems a little wicked."

"The truth is, Uncle Ryan, that I'd just like to know. About how things worked." Here Fen looked at him eagerly. "I'd like to be able to look down at my own arm and just know what was going on in it—blood and germs and cells and things. I'd like to know what to do when something went wrong with people so things would go back to working in the right way, all the air coming in and the heart beating and the stomach getting food." He paused for breath. "That's all there is. I'd just like to see that everything went on working." He dropped his head into a stark silence as though he expected fire to fall on him from Heaven any time.

Ryan was also silent for a minute, much more impressed than he would have been by something glib. He said carefully, "That's very honest, Fen. And commendable, it seems to me. I think that's a pretty worthy goal."

Fen was talked out and embarrassed and the river sounded suddenly very loud going by.

"I know, of course, that some people might think it was selfish."

"Aunt Asa would," said Fen miserably. "Aunt Asa says the worst thing in the world is to set up your own will and follow it instead of God's."

He didn't know how to say to Fen to try leaving God out of this particular thing without shaking his whole understanding of what God was. And he didn't want to shake that for him. What became of Fen's belief in God was something for Fen to settle when—and if—it ever came to an issue. He felt like someone trying to take one brick from a wall without bringing down the structure. After a little bit he picked his brick and hoped it was not the vital one. He said as quietly as he could, "God doesn't live on Walnut Street."

"I guess not," Fen said without much conviction. It didn't mean anything to him at all but maybe it would. That was all one could do. For all the twelve years Asa and Edward Barnes had had, that was all they had been able to do. And a great urgency arose in Ryan to *see* what Fen would think about these things when he was fifteen, eighteen, twenty-eight.

Fen said in a grown-up way, "It worries me sometimes."

"I'll bet it does," said Ryan soberly. Things had worried him. The first time he had known about virgins having membranes and had doubted Holy Mary—he could still remember that terror. He could still remember that long season's praying on cold floors at night. And he thought of the old men in Memorial Park in Stoneville saying that nobody could tell anybody anything. He had thought at the time that this was very sad, but now he *knew* how sad it was and the knowledge scalded him for a minute. Again he wanted to reach out and touch Fen the way a mother or a lover might bend down to touch someone in sleep, running a finger down the curve of cheek, cupping a palm about the skull, circling a wrist.

But he held himself tight; he drew up his bones in their sockets to keep from embarrassing them both by such a thing.

"Let's eat," said Fen.

So they opened the box with a great rattling of paper and ate the sandwiches and the deviled eggs, and laughed with more merriment than was necessary at a squirrel who came briefly out of the woods and stared at them in indignation.

Stretched out in the sun they heard the wind and the slow hum of the river slipping by. After a while they made faces and landscapes out of the clouds which passed over them and laughed when one of them seemed Miss Clara, hunched forward intently over solitaire.

Ryan felt better than he had felt in weeks. His mind was by no means free of worry (indeed, he thought ruefully, there seemed to have been other worries added on) but still he felt better and more useful in the world. Before, he had been reminded constantly that he was sick; but now everything about him seemed to testify to his liveness. The sand pressed up and into the flesh of his back and the sun warmed the blood in him and drew it nearer the surface of the skin. His eyes burned slightly from the glare and even the sound of the river (which had been there a thousand years before they came) was not depressing. With the sun warm on his flesh he half believed he could swim the thing if he should choose to try.

And he thought quietly, It's going to be all right. He thought he would write his book, maybe a dozen others. He would go back to Massachusetts and have the operation and it would be a success. And after that he would . . . Here he glanced across at Fen. Yes, he would. What was so unreasonable about that?

He thought that he ought to translate part of his frame of mind into action as quickly as he could. From long years of living with himself, he knew his moods were fickle. He'd start by looking over his notes and making some plans for the Dostoevsky book. He wanted to reread "Notes from the Underground."

Notes—he might even start a journal himself, not for this book but for the other one that he had once thought of writing—about these people and this little Southern town.

I'll do that tomorrow. I'll start tomorrow putting something onto paper if it says nothing but *Now is the time for all* . . .

He stopped, grinned, looked across at Fen. Now *is* the time. Now is all the time there is. That sentence was so screwy he thought he might even go in for involved poetry: My father moved through . . .

Fen, who had been still for a long time, lying on the other rock with his head on his arms and both legs crossed, turned now so that his cheek was flat to the rock. He looked across into Ryan's face.

"You like it here?" he said.

"Very much," said Ryan. And patted him shyly and quickly on the arm.

15.

NOTES FROM RYAN'S JOURNAL

EXCERPTS
September, 1954

THE *Stoneville Beacon* came out today. Mondays and Thursdays, regardless of catastrophe, I've heard the editor say. I always meant to ask him what he thinks a catastrophe would be.

I read it at supper in the usual way, which meant that Asa and I swapped pages back and forth across the table without any conversation except: "did you see where . . ." and "Yes, I saw that." Reading that paper it occurred to me that everyone who wants to write about small Southern towns should bind the issues of some small-town newspaper and read and reread those papers in search of that special flavor, that authenticity. I have read books about the sociological implications of small-town living, but what is the meaning of that? I warrant a front page of the *Beacon* would tell you more about this town faster than a Ford Foundation study.

And I can see why people who have loved some towns grow sad and homesick over clippings. Here they are, expatriates, growing old in New York with daughter Millie and her rather distant (almost *antiseptic*) children, while quietly at home young Warner Brook wins the eighth grade spelling contest; and the Kiwanians lay plans for the annual agricultural fair (at which Miss Hattie's needlework will take the blue ribbon as always); and Mrs. Luther Bradshaw undergoes an appendectomy and Jennie Atwater will sing "How Lovely Are Thy Dwellings" for the Sunday offertory at the Juniper Methodist Church.

Today's issue of the *Beacon*, for instance, contained everything of moment which has occurred or will occur in Stoneville for a space of days; these things are more important in this part of the world than any tariffs or border wars or gigantic medical research. They come, in order, much like this on today's front page and I list them here because all front pages are alike; maybe all towns are alike:

The School Board's Meeting; City Schools to open Wed.
Illness of the postmaster, Wade M. Snipes.
Destruction of a coon and two young ones (via shotgun) by Calvin Branch Vickers, Route 3.
Presbyterian Choir Concert held yesterday at 8 P.M. (included in story is list of soloists and pieces)
Death of Mrs. Victoria Haile, beloved retired schoolteacher.
Call issued for local preacher; the Rev. Ralph Lee Jernigan retiring.
Grass fire in Runk's Corners quickly extinguished.
Safety award made to local men's shop.
Six parking tickets issued yesterday in uptown district.

I thought, reading each item as carefully as if my own name might be there or the names of my cousins (which is the way such items must always be read) that there is something tremendously sentimental about a small-town paper.

Two things are sad:
That a woman with child should die; and

That a man should take satisfaction in sleeping and copulating and finally dying in the same bed in which he was born.

On second thought, that last may not be sad at all. What am I doing home, after all? Why is it when I set pen to paper I begin to generalize and oversimplify as if wisdom had its end with me?

What was it Travis said about continuity? Something about the mere comfort of knowing that I will die and someone else will be born?

I find Fen especially refreshing (how impersonal that sounds!) because he is an intelligent and sensitive boy without being one of those frighteningly sophisticated children one is always encountering nowadays in modern novels. Sometimes when I read about these painfully sensitive young geniuses always skirting the dangerous edge of homosexuality, madness, general destruction, I have to believe that these youngsters seem very genuine to the authors. The authors believe in them. They must have all led very different early lives and it makes me ashamed of mine. Amazingly enough, no enterprising little neighborhood girl revealed to me the mysteries of the female vagina in anybody's garage at the age of five; or if she did I have—in true Freudian fashion—completely forgotten the occasion. One would think that kind of experience would stay with a growing boy for a little while.

But these authors who write of these remarkable childhoods must have led very interesting preschool lives and nothing like mine was. What a dull and colorless childhood I must have had, blundering along through traumatic experiences with all the grace and receptiveness of a herd of elephants. What wasted mangled years! I might have collected a host of more colorful neuroses than these fairly ordinary ones I have managed to accumulate over the past forty-eight years.

Fen will start school on Wednesday of this week. When he talks to me about it now (this year he will study health, which is, he believes, the beginning of a long medical education) I listen very much as if I were the boy's father.

And whatever the physical possibilities of this may be, I know this is the aspect our relationship is assuming. I am still fearful of it. There was—in coming back to Stoneville—the firm resolution that I would not become involved in life here. In fact, it was not even a firm resolution; I had no idea anything in this life could lay claim to anything of mine.

But I know the direction—I know the flow—of the current Lady Malveena means when she talks about going under and downstream one more single time.

I am aware that by taking on a relationship of love I take on also that of responsibility, not only to Fen directly but to all that now concerns or will concern him. Before I am even aware of what has happened, I fear I may in some intangible way be given over to the whole town; it will be important, then, what happens to it. That damn college, for instance. It begins to bother me that I have not done more to encourage it.

This is the way love is—by its very presence it makes important even the things which heretofore you swore were trivial.

I do not want it. For days now I have said to myself that I would not have it. Of all people, I am in no position to assume such a responsibility. But that is the difficulty—this ceases to be something I can take up or not; this is, instead, like Lady Malveena's under-and-downstream, not volitional.

And—let me not deceive myself—having once loved his mother I am perhaps already committed to things I could not have foreseen. And, I suppose, that again is the way love operates. Once it has occurred nothing is ever quite the same again.

Travis and I had a long argument recently over Durkheim of whom, I confess, I had heard very little. It all started because we were discussing suicide. (He was feeling me out on the subject but in a friendly way; all he wanted was to see that I should not cheapen life for the rest of them by blowing my brains out ahead of schedule. Suicide has some personal meaning to him which he did not touch upon.) Durkheim was a sociological determinist, did a study on suicide as being due to a change in the relationship between the individual and society. I couldn't honestly get around the arguments as Travis gave them.

So we talked man and society again for a while and I was pretty full of Dostoevsky and Father Zossima. I fared rather badly in the argument; I have never had an incisive mind. It's all I can do to keep the damn thing made up sometimes.

In our arguments we wind up being the manifestations of Niebuhr's title. We stand "Moral Man" and "Immoral Society" nearly every time.

But I do think that (vague as this sounds) individual blame and individual merit are the keys to social understanding. Apart from some conception such as this, the "crimes of society" seem meaningless. So, too, is "Social Improvement" unless there is somewhere the belief that—even in some indirect fashion, and to a greater or less degree as you will have it—the individual is responsible for what happens to his neighbor.

Reading these last words over again, I had to smile. I have written myself around again to Fen and Stoneville.

I still like the business of the author making his readers "childlike" in many ways. Yet I take that very thought and can go off and build contradictions. I have decided it is not enough to get your reader on the child's level, using symbol and emotion. But I haven't thought much on that, yet.

Travis says I am the perennial adolescent. He believes that for two cents he could make me wonder again and re-examine soberly what I thought about free love.

He asked me yesterday if I didn't think Dostoevsky would have been a great writer had he not believed in Christ, and when I said I did not know he was very much amused.

For the child and for the savage life is very much alike.

It is something that happens to one; it is willed; the world is full of spirits. The dog discusses and the broken tree limb bleeds, and if you hit every picket from here to the corner you can wish for the moon and it will come down for you immediately.

There is in the world punishment and praise, pleasure and pain. There is someone who raises and lowers the suns and turns the rain on and off and moves the crank that makes the calendar go round. There is acceptance or rejection and a kind of practicing for the coming world where there will be School and Work and Money.

As the child grows, after a while there is his own volition. That is the beginning of things. That is the point of choice and freedom and responsibility. That is the place at which one begins, haltingly, to impose some kind of pattern over all this helter-skelter happening.

And what results from this is "meaning," whatever the meaning for the individual may be.

For me, it seems that if there is any "meaning" to a man's life it lies in this—that he has lived his life in such and such a way, that this is the sum of it, this is the boundary with which he has circumscribed his days. There is no other meaning to life than this, that in this manner it was lived and passed and used up and laid down.

The manner in which a man chooses to do this: that is a high and a fine thing because only men can do it and only man can, out of sheer perversity or laziness, choose not to do it. If a dog does not do it that is another thing; it is not in his nature. But if a man does not channel his days in terms of some deed or thought or belief or certain achievement, then he avoids it by choice. He says, in effect, "I refuse to be a man."

But even by choosing negatively he establishes his manhood. The lion does not reject the hunt nor the squirrel the tree, but man can reject.

There seems to me no greater waste than this: that a man—being man—should *elect* to be something less, should fill his belly and sleep long and mate and procreate with only half his energies and capacities; and grow old and die without ever being lost in anything or for anything or by anything.

If there is any "sin" in man this must be it: that he misuses his vision by seeing life small, and by so seeing he makes it small and—even worse than this—he spends it uncomplaining in a little room and never asks himself if he was cramped.

On War

One of the hazards of being a journal keeper is that one desires—sooner or later—to comment on current events or on the state of the world at one particular time.

These world events actually touch journal keepers (as they touch me, personally) very little. International activities in our day and time are a matter of public record; anyone now can find them out. They will be in libraries long after I am dead; I am no Samuel Pepys.

Yet the desire of men who keep diaries is the desire to pinpoint themselves in time and at the same time to be objective, slightly removed from time, like God or historians.

See? say the journal keepers. There is at this point in time a certain war on a certain continent. I know about it. I have recorded certain facts about it here; I am informed. There have been, in the duration of this war, so-many battles and so-many wounded, and so-many ships gone down.

After these facts I can even (here at my desk) draw great sweeping conclusions; I can comment on how foolish the whole war is. I can record here that the warring governments probably have at heart similar ideologies and the same greed for land (which is the same land) and the same kind of blood for young men to spill in all the useless battles, out of similar veins and not widely different-colored flesh past barely different uniforms.

There is something that seems nearly virtuous in knowing these things and setting them down, in being so much removed. How rational one is, and at the same time, how moral! The detached man can afford to be moral; it is not his soul at stake.

And I suspect (a newspaper clipping fostered this whole thing) I suspect it is this very detachment which lends that air of self-righteousness to the photographs of diplomats at truce talks, men debating over a semicolon in the proposed Cease Fire. These are our men of Principle. They know for what their governments stand; they will not relinquish.

And they have some notion they are putting an end to something because as statesmen they will eventually concede here and compromise there. They will finally sign (with honor) the document schoolboys will study in the coming decade. These honorable men will nod crisply to the diplomats of the other country (who are also honorable); each will acknowledge the flag of the other, courteously. Being, of course, gentlemen, they will speak sanctimoniously of the universality of man's desire for peace; they will finally shake hands; the copywriters who make captions for such photographs will call it memorable.

Yet these will not really have put an end to anything at all because they were not—as I am not—involved.

Only the foot soldiers can put an end to war. The men in the trenches everywhere—it is they who make the decisions.

The tired soldier handing a cigarette to a man he has just captured—that is the man who makes peace if anybody can.

For days now, Asa has had an expectant look about her, like a strong warrior awaiting an attack by a weaker one. She has that smug look of the soldier who lies in ambush with all his weapons sharpened.

Yet by today her face took on impatience, and finally she sounded the call to arms herself.

"I hope," she said, waylaying me in the hall, "that you don't plan to argue with me about the college."

"No, I don't," I said.

This was a blow. She had been planning to raise her voice on the next sentence so now she raised it anyway, just to keep to the pattern. "Because I won't sell him the land if I don't want to. You know I won't."

"It's quite all right with me," I said peaceably.

Her banners began to droop. "I know what your education did for you, Ryan Godwin. Now there are others to think about. Fen and the others. I don't mind people studying how to make a living, or how to teach or something like that."

I said only, "It's your land, Asa, to dispose of as you see fit."

"That's right," she argued. "Nothing in the world can make me sell if I don't want to."

"Nothing in the world," I assured her. I left her standing in the hallway, looking a little tired.

On the Great Basic Experiences

With our eternal desire for form, pattern, universality, we always expect to reduce the tremendous human experiences to something that will be comprehensible to all of us. Thus it is that young people wait for the time they will be old enough to be initiated into the great mysterious realm of knowledge they believe the others share. They believe they will mature into knowing those wondrous things: what goes through one's mind on a wedding night, in childbirth, just before dying?

But of course the truth is that no one can really tell, that none of us will have identical reactions to the same major experiences. Because in each case it is the total person reacting; and it took how many years and thoughts and sights and smells to make this whole individual?

Thus it is perfectly right that nobody communicates his final dying thought, and that nowhere is there a detailed and accurate record of what it "feels" like to die.

That is the last and final human privacy; it ought to make us very proud.

Miss Clara came downstairs today to get a Bible; she said she wanted to look up something. Actually, I had not seen her for days. She is like a great bear hibernating through long and endless winters, except that they make her fat instead of thin. She feeds on herself but if anything is depleted it doesn't show from the outside; and nobody knows what the inside is like.

When she asked for a Bible, though, I began to wonder about Miss Clara. Asa has dragged her to church all of these years to sit under sermons she could never hear; and I wondered what kind of religion you could build from that.

So I said to Lady Malveena, "What is God like to Miss Clara?" She was born deaf; when she reads about praising the Most High with timbrels and harp and song, what does that mean to her?

And Lady Malveena said she thought God must be like two great big ears.

When I thought about that I thought how horrible it would be if Miss Clara should suppose the world is rich and varied and marvelous to everyone who hears. Somebody ought to tell her. Somebody ought to tell her it isn't so.

Some Recent Dreams

While I am here, I dream much of Christ. I know this must be partly because Stoneville is associated with "churchiness" in my mind, and when I was a child I found the hills of Galilee nearly as familiar as those of Stone County. There was a time when I knew exactly what occurred on each of the days of Passover Week before the crucifixion, could say all of the second chapter of Luke, knew the sayings of Jesus on the Cross, the Beatitudes, the Ten Commandments, First Corinthians 13, a number of psalms and odd verses, the first and shorter catechisms. Even now, when I say to myself: "What is the chief end of man?" the answer comes like a faulty radio tuned to two stations. One station gives the answer I have come to over years and years, but underneath it my voice parrots still: "Man's Chief End Is to Glorify God and Enjoy Him Forever."

What a child learns is appallingly durable.

And remembered, too, is the long embarrassment I once had not knowing what to do with Christ. It seems to me I have at various times cast him in many roles, trying to make him fit (a seer, a God, a prophet, a king, a Man, a means). It is the same double-radio reception; one does not believe, and yet at the same time one hears the too-familiar roll of John 3:16. Perhaps a psychologist would say I never quite made up my mind, that the conflict still goes on somewhere, is resolved at this level and that, dismissed, and then slips back in some other form. I have been to neo-orthodoxy and to materialism and I have removed this and that belief past ever putting back.

Yet habit and memory remain: If I hear someone saying "He maketh me to lie down in green pastures," I will go and finish the psalm; and even though I can no longer feel as I did about those words, something of that remembered holiness clings. I am no longer reverent, but I recall reverence; it had its values—there were whole reams of colorless experiences it kaleidoscoped for me then.

A *Dream:*

I dreamed of Christ. As usual in my dreams, he looked very different from all the calendars and paintings I have ever seen. In all of my dreams there is usually something strikingly wrong with his face, such as its being a strange and uncommon color. In this one the flaw was a scar which ran raggedly from the corner of his eye to the corner of his mouth. Yet he was beautiful and I knew he was Christ. In dreams, you always know.

He was standing on Golgotha at the foot of his own cross, and he was talking aloud to himself and staring down at the ground which was covered with small stones. I remember at the time I thought in my dream: *He has given up, after all. He is going to make them bread.* But that was not it; this was only something he was saying to himself because there was nobody else to say it to.

And it seemed to me of tremendous importance: a latter-day message from the Nazarene. Was he admitting to fraud, insisting on his position, mourning the means to which his sayings had been put in the world? I wanted terribly to hear the words he was speaking so softly, yet I could not approach him nearer to find out what they were. For some reason, I was not permitted to move a step from where I stood, and that was at the bottom of the hill. Finally I screamed at him, in mingled anger and desperation; "Why don't you speak out?" and he lifted that face with the strange scar down one side and looked at me.

I fell back a step and my foot slid on the stones—I was altogether scalded by that look. It numbed my own eyes, and after that there was a whirring and whirling in which the dream ended.

I have never dreamed of Jessica in my entire life—not when she was living and not when she was dead. What does that mean?

More important, why am I always searching for meanings in everything done and everything omitted? Travis is right; there remains in me a certain adolescence so that I move in a world where everything must be ranked as either blame or justification.

Another Dream

When I came into the tremendous house (it had 7,000 rooms; a sign which blew in the wind against the front door told me that) I thought at first I was all alone. I knew I had to walk through all of these rooms and touch the lintel of each door but I did not know why and I did not particularly care. The size of the task appeared to annoy me more than anything else. After a while I saw that someone else was in the house ahead of me and he was always disappearing down the hall or around some corner. He made no sound, neither footstep nor laughter.

Except for this figure the rooms were empty of any furnishings or objects. There were, however, huge pictures painted on the walls. One was the seven lean cows and the seven fatted cows; and one was the pyramids; one was an old painting I have seen somewhere of a wolf on a snow hill looking down at lighted houses; and one was the ships of Columbus in a rich blue sea.

Everything in that house and on those walls was harmless and yet I began to be afraid. Finally I came out one door into the sun and then I realized it was not the sun but a great wall of fire coming toward me down a long green hill; and I tore up the turf and hid in a pocket in the dirt until the fire had passed over me and gone on.

I was not burned; and when I came out from my pocket of grass I saw that nothing was consumed and I said to myself with great relief: This is a dream.

I had walked on to the top of the hill where I found two Negro men hanging up snakes. When these were dry the two men said they would make money belts for sale. They gave me one and we filled it with oak leaves together and everyone was very courteous and reserved. Whenever the wind blew across us and down the hill the snakeskins would click and clack against each other as if they had been bones, or teeth.

I was starting on with my gift when I heard something calling inside the big house, calling not for me or for anyone, just calling. There was no inflection of fear or pain in the voice I heard; it was only sound; it only existed. I felt I ought to go back inside that house but it had not called for me. The two men did not seem to hear, for the snakeskins chattered and chittered and the wind which moved them was suddenly warmer than breath.

At that I started to run back to the big house before the fire should come again; and the dead snake at my waist grew heavier and heavier as I ran until it was hard to breathe and the scales had clamped on me a little tighter; for I knew who was in that house although I would not say the name even in my own mind. It was a long way down the hill and I could see the house lighting up red in front of me, and I could feel the heat at my back pushing me, pushing me—but not fast enough.

The house went down like an eggshell and nobody screamed inside.

This last was such a nightmare that the disintegration of the house woke me, and I lay a long time in the dark room and could not go back to sleep. I got up and lit a cigarette and saw that it was only three o'clock; and I was as far from sleep as noon. So I had nothing else to do and for the first time in a long while I thought about Jessica herself—all the way from the beginning to the end.

And it seemed to me (as it has always seemed) that there was more virtue in me then than there ever was or will be, because then I was given over in love to something. There are categories for people who prefer thinking in them: and these people would impose the category; they would say, shocked, that this was an adulterous thing.

It was, of course, that too. We never liked that part of it and I, for one, once broke off the thing because it could not help but pick up a little tarnish from the dishonesty. Yet Jessica would not—could not—come away; Lord deliver me from the strange morality of respectable people!

And in the end we accepted the tarnish and contented ourselves with making the core of it as honest as we could. That is all people can do, keep somewhere a pinpoint of honesty at which they know themselves and how they feel.

When I think of Jessica, the thought of Fen comes naturally. Perhaps he is a part of that—the best—and as such comes quite naturally within my responsibility and my jurisdiction. And even if he is not he is an end in himself. It is not really possible to love one person on behalf of some other person; and even if it were possible, it would not be fair.

It cannot be Fen because of Jessica, any more than it was ever Jessica because of . . . well, because of anything. Except herself.

16.

JESSICA

JESSICA MAPLE became the wife of Avery Godwin in the winter of 1936.

For a long time, now, Ryan had been forewarned that things were drifting toward that end. In Asa's occasional duty letters there came the mention of a visitor for dinner in the house on Walnut street, one of Avery's choir members. Miss Maple had moved from Greenway to care for a relative of hers, Mrs. Victoria Seagreaves (here Ryan almost whooped; Victoria Seagreaves was old but far from helpless—she needed protection as much as a shark did or a wounded bear); and Mrs. Seagreaves had brought her, of course, to church.

Miss Maple had, it appeared, no parents and had spent most of her life with relatives. She was very dutiful, Asa said.

Subsequent letters revealed that Miss Maple had finished school at County Lynn High, outside of Greenway, and that she had read a good deal. Asa described her as "attractive"; and when she joined the church and a class and a circle and became a permanent choir member Asa wrote that she had certainly "fallen under Avery's influence."

All of this went almost unnoted by Ryan; he skimmed all of Asa's letters (they were poor fare; they were mental and emotional hardtack) and only at this last did he give a sardonic smile. For himself, he would have preferred to fall under a mowing machine compared to "Avery's influence."

In the early fall of 1936, Asa's letters waxed as close to enthusiasm as she could ever go. Miss Maple had been to dinner again; she was reserved, but charming. Miss Maple was formally received into the church with Baptism last Sunday and she looked quite lovely.

(It was time, Asa began to say at the end of her letters, that both of her brothers married.)

Miss Maple had been asked to serve as one of eight hostesses at the annual Ladies' Bake Sale. She was helping Avery organize his plans for the church cantata.

(It was certainly time, at this stage, for Avery to consider marriage. He had some position in the community and, of course, he would always have his share of the real estate office.)

In time Ryan came to harbor a strong dislike for the unseen Miss Maple going about the streets of Stoneville in such a decorous fashion. He saw her: a thin-lipped, bloodless creature, hair flat to the head, wearing sensible oxfords and rimless spectacles and shapeless suits. The type, he thought, whose idea of amusing children would be to have jolly races in locating scripture references (Bible Drill for Christian Soldiers; or to offer a prize of hard candy for the most perfectly memorized bit of "A Psalm of Life").

Ryan seldom wrote home. What, after all, should he have written them? School was well; it had been cold (it had not been cold); he was very busy. But now and then he did send home a note and in the next one he asked very carefully after Miss Maple's health. With all her good works, he wrote sweetly, she must be careful not to overdo.

But Asa detected no sarcasm.

Miss Maple was fine. She was actually much stronger than she looked. Asa believed Miss Maple was a young person of sterling qualities whose friendship Avery valued.

Nicely put, that, thought Ryan, grinning. And she was healthy, the no-nonsense type, not even with telltale migraine headaches. That was something.

Another Sunday, another letter from home: Miss Maple had a slight cold and was unable to sing with the choir that day; she and Asa had sat together in the congregation. Ryan could picture the two of them bent avidly over a single hymnal, both of them thin and grayish. (Miss Maple by virtue of age, he thought, one shade lighter.) After the song they would sit still and straight as though they had broom handles for spines, not stirring even one black-gloved finger till the service should be through.

And he could picture them around the dinner table at home with rain outside the windows. Avery would say pleasantly that it was fine weather for ducks, wasn't it? and Miss Maple would give a careful laugh.

"Yes, it is . . . Avery," she would say, fumbling a little at the first name.

And Asa at the head of the table would nod and think that it was going very well, very well indeed. What did Avery think? But Ryan knew what he thought—he thought a man ought to have a wife, a good woman—the kind in Proverbs that spun purple and had her children rising up to call her blessed. In time Avery would decide that he loved her in a respectable and limited fashion, heavy with politeness, and he would ask her to become his wife. After that he would be able to call her "my dear" and fetch a shawl for her occasionally and be seen pecking the bloodless cheek, so that everyone would say how really *devoted* Avery was. He would—Goddammit, Ryan thought—never forget their anniversary.

He wrote to Asa with some acidity. "Miss Maple sounds charming. Has she an occupation of some sort? And is she of an age to be an adequate playmate for our Avery?"

He was reprimanded for his levity. He had, after all, no right to pass judgment on someone he had never seen. She was, as Asa had written before, a bit reserved (one was never too sure what she was thinking, sometimes) but she had beautiful manners. If she was shy and sometimes seemed sad, no doubt having no parents could leave that mark on anyone. Asa added that Miss Maple had, indeed, no occupation when she first came to Stoneville other than looking after Victoria's needs; but that she—Asa—had procured for her a small-paying but interesting part-time job reading to shut-ins of the church. Miss Maple read aloud from the *Missionary Journal*, the Bible, and *Pilgrim's Progress*; and the Ladies' Aid paid her a "gratitude gift" each month.

(In the face of this information, Ryan almost went over wholeheartedly to poor Miss Maple's camp. But then he thought: She likes it. She comes away feeling remarkably generous and good. And this saved him.)

Miss Maple, Asa added in her letter, was twenty-six years old.

Eight years difference in age, Ryan thought, and frowned. That was more than he had been prepared for. He wanted to write to Miss Maple and tell her: You don't have to marry *him*. But then he shrugged and put it out of his mind. Miss Maple was of an age. She needed no champion; she was probably like her Aunt Victoria, a fortress of womanhood.

During the early part of fall he forgot about things at home. He had been teaching three summer classes and one extension course and the rush of closing these lapped over into the fever of preschool activity just before the semester opened. That year—the year Avery and Jessica were married—was an election year, and because he was a Democrat he won five dollars from Jim. He had a graduate student who was very good, very brilliant, and that one fact leavened dozens of ordinary teaching days for him. He had a bad bout of intestinal flu which spared him only one thing—the tea in honor of the incoming freshman class. (All of those gloves and those freshly ironed clothes and the shaking of hands and the careful good manners of girls who did not know yet that the sky would not fall if a wrong fork were used—these teas were the worst part of an entire teaching year. He told Jim he wanted to be innoculated with some disease germ every September, but something a little milder next year, please!)

Asa's announcement letter came just before the Thanksgiving recess.

My Dear Ryan:

I am very pleased to be writing you that Avery and Miss Jessica Maple have informed me of their plans to marry before Christmas. Naturally I feel that a match could not have been more opportune or more suitable. Both of them are mature and settled and approach marriage with a full sense of the responsibilities. Miss Maple is without living family now beyond Mrs. Seagreaves—of whom I think I wrote to you—and their interests are altogether compatible.

Naturally, Avery wishes you to serve as his best man for the very simple ceremony. Miss Maple is poorly fixed financially and there will be no attendants or unnecessary fuss. It may be we will hold the service here.

We are hoping that under the circumstances you will find it

possible to spend Thanksgiving here this year so we can make our plans together.

Please reply immediately rather than with your accustomed lack of punctuality.

Yours sincerely,
Asa

He carried the letter out to the car where Jim and Anne Tetley were waiting to take him to their house for dinner.

"Brother's getting married," he said, waving the letter as he got in.

"That's nice," said Anne automatically. Seeing his face she added, "Isn't it?"

He shrugged. "Oh, I suppose so."

"Ryan's maladjusted in his family life," said Jim gravely. "There's some theory among the young ladies on this campus that Ryan was in love with his mother, which is why he had never married and—"

"Go to hell," said Ryan good-naturedly.

They said no more about it. Later, however—because they had asked him to have Thanksgiving dinner at their house, he dropped by the Infirmary to explain to Jim.

"So I'll go home, I guess, and meet the female," he finished, "and I'll wind up agreeing to be Avery's best man, not because he really *wants* me to be his best man, but because he understands brothers always are."

"Dread it?" said Jim.

"Tell the truth, I'm a little curious. Miss Maple's a bit too trite to be real."

Jim said very carefully, "Sometimes I feel that way about all of it. The way you describe your family and that town. So they're Bible-toting people in a little town where everybody knows everybody else's business. I just wonder if that's much different from towns the country over? Midwestern towns? Maybe even New England villages?"

"You may be right," said Ryan—although in his heart he did not believe Stoneville could be duplicated. "I'll send you a post card showing the courthouse. We've got two piles of cannon balls and a Minute Man and a Confederate soldier."

Jim shrugged. "Maybe these two people love each other. Maybe they're getting married because of it."

"*Avery?* Not a chance. I've never been able to make it clear to you what the lack in Avery is. He doesn't feel *anything*. He works hard to be a good citizen and have all the right reactions. He doesn't lose any temper because he hasn't any to lose, but he says carefully: 'That annoyed me,' because he knows annoyance is part of it."

"How can you know what he feels? What if he feels scared to death he won't make it all work? That would be emotion, too."

"I know as much as anybody can ever know about him, from years of proximity and watching. The thing is, Jim, he does the whole business very well. You know these science-fiction stories where the robots get so good you can't tell them from the people?"

"You describe Asa as cold and unemotional, too. Does she feel anything?"

"I don't know. I think she may, but I can't get to it. I think Avery doesn't feel anything at all involuntarily. Now he'll get married, very correctly. He won't be scared at the wedding because—as far as he's concerned—what's there for nervousness? Later on he'll deflower her as systematically as a doctor doing a minor operation. Then he'll roll off her and go to sleep and goddammit, he won't even be out of breath!"

"Then I hope the bride is of like caliber," said Jim drily.

"So do I," said Ryan fervently. "I hope she's not just someone scared she'd be an old maid, who thought that Avery was polite but . . . but, well . . . real," he finished lamely.

"Maybe you could do the deflowering," Jim suggested. "Less systematically."

And they laughed and laughed at that together.

He went home less happily, however. Sitting on the train he felt like a man being abducted by a duty he never cared about, taken away against his will. The trip home was not a good one and the train was full of dull but talkative people. The train was late for about half the stations and always rushed to make up for lost time after one of them, then moved normally after the next one. This made the whole trip jerky and he was achingly aware of each stop they made; each town with its sign about population and elevation was a punctuation mark.

In Greenway, Avery met him in the late afternoon. The train was forty minutes late at that point and Ryan was in a grim mood and prepared for the worst. He stepped down into the station and thought at first none of them had come to get him, and then he saw Avery sitting on an expressman's cart. He looked for all the world like a small toad getting the last of the sun.

Avery got up quickly enough when he saw him.

"There you are, Ryan. It's good to have you home," said Avery. He came across the station, smiling, and took his brother's hand.

"Hello, Avery." He had never understood it but such glib and easy greetings always made him want to be uncivil.

"Did you have a good trip?"

"No."

Avery gave him an indignant look because that type of answer was against the rules, and Avery was a great believer in the rules.

"We'll have to get going," he said a little stiffly. "We're expected for supper."

Ryan lifted the small bag. "This is all I have," he said. "Let's go."

The Buick was very old and it behaved like an old, tired human being. Once it had been still for any length of time it hated to move, groaned and grumbled like an angry old lady who had just got her stockings off. They always had to sit a while and let the motor get well under way.

"Miss Maple is with us for supper," Avery said.

Ryan was genuinely amazed. "You still call her Miss Maple?"

Avery's surprise was no less. "Certainly."

The car started and Avery coasted down the slight incline until he had some confidence in it.

"After you're married, will you call her Mrs. Godwin?"

"Oh no."

Have you kissed her at all, Avery? Has she even some sort of breast you ever wanted to brush your arm against in some church aisle?

"How have you been?" asked Avery politely. It was the proper question after trips of any sort.

Ryan gave it up; he grinned. "Just fine," he said. "And you?"

Avery answered him very seriously. "Very well except for a slight cold. I think everyone has a cold or so during wet weather."

Ryan said soberly that sure enough, he supposed everyone did. "And how is Asa?" he asked very carefully.

Across the car seat Avery visibly relaxed. This was the way he understood people were to talk to each other, and anything else was a violation past his comprehension. He said now with more ease, "She's always very busy, of course. I'm afraid she'll wreck her health, she takes the business so seriously."

"You'll be going into the business yourself, I understand."

"Yes," he said. "After my marriage." After my operation, Ryan thought.

"Lady Malveena?"

"Well," said Avery, "none of us are as young as we once were, of course. She's not as spry. But she certainly was pleased to learn you were coming home for Thanksgiving. I know she'll fix a big dinner."

They did not talk the rest of the drive from Greenway into Stoneville except for new buildings and improvements Avery pointed out to him.

At home he found nothing changed. They drove the Buick up into the drive where it coughed out and appeared to go immediately to sleep. The front lawn was full of oak leaves; Avery remarked that it was hard to hire anybody to rake people's yards any more.

"People aren't like they used to be about doing a good day's work," he said.

Ryan grunted.

"It's a good thing Lady Malveena is such a treasure."

Ryan wasn't sure how Lady Malveena would feel about that classification. They went up the steps and into the hall without knocking (he heard the doorknocker clank behind them in the old way) and put their coats on the old-fashioned stand. Then they stood (Avery stood, that is; and Ryan—not noticing he had stopped—walked on into him) in the hall blankly until Asa called from the parlor, "Avery? Ryan? Is that you?" At this Avery nodded his head in affirmation (which was ridiculous, Ryan thought, since Asa certainly could not see him through the parlor wall) and led the way inside like a boy given a hard permission.

Asa was standing as they entered, for she was small and hated to look up to anybody; and from a nearby chair another woman, confused by Asa's action, half rose, half sat, until she seemed fairly to be suspended in midair. Around them both Ryan was dimly aware of the room looking as it had always looked and he knew that if he now closed his eyes the details would come into focus without thought—the sofa, the chairs, the marble-topped table—everything.

Asa said in an identifying tone, "Ryan," and turned up a cool gray cheek for him to kiss. He kissed her underneath the eye on a hill of bone. Avery had crossed without speaking to a chair near the hearth and had put out his hands over the fire, although it was warm for November.

"And this is Jessica Maple," Asa said, turning to the other woman and drawing her forward with a hand as if she had been a child. "This is our brother, Ryan."

Our brother, Cain, thought Ryan in some amusement; but he took the small hand in his and looked down at her.

Later he thought of Jessica as melancholy and beautiful, but when he saw her in that moment she was only pretty, and the slight tilt at her eye and her cheek was less sad than it was weary. But at that moment, Ryan was startled at finding the woman pretty at all; he stood there perplexed until their two hands warmed from the contact and she drew hers away.

"How do you do?" said Jessica Maple rather shyly.

And he repeated it politely. "How do *you* do?"

Now that this moment was over everyone moved, or let out breaths, and he and Asa and the young woman sat down amid a jumble of dull comments on the weather and Thanksgiving and how his trip had been.

("How was your trip?" said Asa—much as Avery had—and to his amazement he heard himself reply, "Not bad.")

Through all of this hum of nothing, Ryan watched her, adding it all up and trying to check it against the sum he had brought along in his head. Twenty-six, Asa had said; but she looked as though her age fell on both sides of that—the skin and body younger, the eyes and the corner of mouth older and tireder than twenty-six. Her hair was dark brown, he supposed (the light was bad), with hints of chestnut, and that day she was wearing it up in wings at the sides and drawn back in a soft bun low on her neck. The eyes were also brown, not very dark, the amber-brown of old-fashioned bottles in a pharmacy.

He heard Avery say that he thought perhaps they ought to have the Buick looked at again. It hadn't been much on the hills from Greenway. Asa said they would certainly check on that.

"You're looking well, Ryan," Asa said.

He felt generous, good, forgiving. "I'm *feeling* well," he said; and Avery looked as though he thought things were going to be all right, after all. Ryan was perfectly all right, underneath—he just had an odd manner until you got used to him.

But Ryan was not really paying much attention to all of that. He was watching the girl on that stiff chair across the room (suddenly he resented that chair for being so uncomfortable; he looked around for a better and none was there). He watched her, thinking this was not right—to marry Avery Godwin and Jessica Maple. He sat there like a would-be knight errant, searching her face for a sign, for the slightest hint of desperation. And uncomfortably enough she watched him too, an oddly level gaze. (Had Asa called her shy?) The eyes did not waver and the look in them was full of curiosity and candor. It was an open look, like a child's, thought Ryan; and then he stopped, noting again the little weary mouth.

"It's a rare treat, having Ryan home for a holiday." Asa smiled falsely, arranging her face so that everyone could see they were a very close family and the miles were a pain to them.

"I'm afraid I don't get home very often," Ryan said—but not to Asa. He wanted the girl to speak again. He could not remember what her voice had been like when she was holding his hand.

She said obediently, "You're a professor," and he nodded. He felt strangely shy about it. He felt as though if she should ask him what he taught he would not be able to remember any of it.

"There's nothing like an open fire," said Avery. He sat in one corner, quiet but contented, barbecuing his hands. Asa sent him a smile but Jessica did not turn her head.

"I believe Asa says you are originally from Greenway," Ryan said. He caught her voice this time; it was nothing extraordinary, pleasing enough, not harsh.

"Yes," said Jessica. "I grew up there in the home of another aunt. My parents died when I was a child. Now I live with my Aunt Victoria."

"That's Mrs. Seagreaves," Asa interposed. "I believe I wrote you that."

"Yes," said Ryan, still watching the girl. "Yes, you wrote me that."

Avery said, "Don't you think I'm a very lucky man, Ryan?"

There was nothing insincere in his reply. "A very lucky man." He thought he saw her flush slightly but he could not be sure; the parlor was very dim.

"It will surely be your turn next, Ryan." Asa said it for all the world like a jolly old matchmaker who spent most of her days bringing lovers together. If it had not been for Jessica he would already have rebelled against all this foolishness. Even now he had a desire to say to her, very soberly, *Your fiancé and Asa and I have never gotten along very well.*

"I always thought you'd propose to Cornelia Satterfield," said Avery expansively. "Cornelia is a very intelligent woman."

Jessica looked a little surprised and Ryan would have sworn he caught an amused tilt to her lip. "I'm afraid, to tell the truth, that Cornelia Satterfield has always seemed to me to be very dull. And not intelligent at all. She's simply read a lot of things and remembers a smattering of some of them." He was exceedingly annoyed with Avery for having brought Cornelia into the conversation.

"Well, she certainly admires *you*," said Asa.

Conversation lagged for a minute (Ryan would *not* make any answer to that) and finally Asa said irrelevantly, "There'll be early Thanksgiving services in the morning. We'll all go, of course."

"I believe Asa wrote me that you sing in the choir."

Miss Maple nodded her head (yes, there were chestnut highlights; when she moved he could see the firelight flickering on them). She looked down at her hands a bit self-consciously. Ryan looked at her hands, too; they were folded up like something put carefully away; you could not tell anything about them.

Asa said with a rather foolish smile that Avery and Jessica had first met when Mrs. Seagreaves brought her to choir.

"Mrs. Seagreaves sings, too," offered Avery. "Alto. We're doing a special number at worship tomorrow."

That brought to Ryan's mind a sharply vivid picture of Victoria Seagreaves, long-time alto of the choir, a big-bosomed woman of long white beak (through which she sang, with vibrations; and with thin black eyes on each side that seemed always to be just half open, as though in watchfulness. An alligator waiting in the mud must peer out at the world in just that way, he had often thought. And when Ryan thought of Jessica Maple living alone with Victoria Seagreaves (who was a hypochondriac and who—believing she had diabetes—ate, or refused to eat, maddening diets of her own invention) he was silent. He looked across at Jessica and said to her silently: *There are all kinds of ways to get away from something.*

But she only looked back at him with that even level stare and he felt very foolish.

He said into the silence that he remembered Victoria Seagreaves, of course. "I hope her health's improved?"

"Oh no," said Jessica quickly, as though he had said something indecent about her aunt.

"You know Victoria has to eat very carefully." Asa prefaced that remark with two clucks of the tongue. "Jessica is very devoted to her."

"I shouldn't doubt it," Ryan said with a polite smile; and this time Jessica flicked a sharp glance at him, as though she detected something in his tone. Even Asa frowned and suggested that all of them go in to dinner.

While the others settled around the table Ryan went through the butler's pantry and came upon Lady Malveena. She was leaning up against the wall in the kitchen with her eyes closed, and her face was very tired.

He said in a happier tone than he felt, "That's a real expression of greeting on your face!"

She opened her eyes and looked at him without moving from the wall and then she smiled. "Hello, Mr. Ryan," she said. When he came to stand in front of her she put two hands on his shoulders and kept them there tightly.

Then she wiped the sentiment off her face and said sharply that she could feel the shape of his bones with her fingers. "If you'd teach them people to cook their beans with fat, you'd get some cushion on you," she grumbled. "It's all that salt and no greasing that wears you down so thin."

"You look pretty tired," said Ryan.

"Who'd been teaching you not to talk polite? You supposed to answer what I said, not go running off in your own directions." She came away from the wall, dropping her hands and taking something up in them immediately, a cup into which she peered for coffee stain. Her very gaze dared the china to be dingy.

"You've been working too hard on this Thanksgiving business," Ryan said. "The trouble with you is you never got over thinking you could do the same amount of work you did fifty years ago." He was very angry to come upon her unobserved and find her tired; he wanted to tramp into the dining room and ask Asa what she had been doing to Lady Malveena while he was away.

"It always gets me how people that can't cook and clean know so much about it," snapped Lady Malveena. "They know how it ought to be done and how fast and how often. Furthermore, they know how you suppose to feel when you're done with it. Ain't a college education wonderful?" She brushed past him and washed the coffee cup vengefully in the sink.

"Don't be so ill-tempered," said Ryan. "It betrays you."

She was silent and sloshed the water around and around.

"You're getting it on the floor."

"I'm gonna do the mopping, ain't I?"

He said, "What do you think of Miss Maple?"

Lady Malveena said firmly that Miss Maple was *all right*.

"She come around right often?"

"Pretty often," said Lady Malveena. Her mouth was too tight; he knew from this she was afraid she would let something out of it she had no business saying.

He put out a probe. "She doesn't seem much like Avery."

Lady Malveena said firmly again that Miss Jessica Maple was *all right*. She stacked the cup in a drainer with others and looked up at him. "You'd better get back so I can get the meal on," she said —but softly.

"All right."

But he did not go. He stood there looking at her.

She was nervous; she went over and looked in the oven at some bread that was doing very well without her.

"You're not sick or anything?"

She shook her head. "I'm truly just a little tired. And don't go turning that over and inside-out looking for anything."

"Okay." This time he got as far as the door that went through the butler's pantry and back into the dining room where the others were.

She said, "You remember Wallifetterson, don't you? You remember when he lived here?"

Ryan said yes, he remembered that and what about it?

"Nothing," said Lady Malveena.

"I'll talk to you later. Tonight some time."

"All right," she said. Her face was turned away from him.

"Unless you're too tired. Rather get some sleep?"

"You're getting foolish with your years," she said shortly. He went back into the dining room, smiling.

Jessica's face was turned toward the door when he came through it but she looked away quickly at a spot on the wall. He came over and sat down at his place. Asa was saying that Lady Malveena had practically raised them all and they were very grateful to her; and he started to say gratitude didn't have a damn thing to do with it. But Lady Malveena herself came in just then with steaming dishes and he didn't want her to find them talking about her as if she were a piece of livestock.

Asa said he would be interested to know that their cousin Clara was coming to live with them next winter. Clara was the deaf old maid of the family who had, for years, lived with two other cousins in the mountains. Henry and Zelda were rich and had been glad to take her, but now they were getting on in years and they wanted to see her established somewhere else. "They'll contribute to her keep, of course," said Asa.

"Of course," said Ryan.

Avery said the food certainly looked good. "There's nobody can cook like Lady Malveena," he said. He gave them all a smile that was just the proper width and size.

Jessica said she couldn't cook very well; and Asa said she was sure she would learn.

Everyone seemed to be waiting, presumably for someone to mention the coming marriage; and Ryan supposed that as the visitor he was supposed to ask polite questions. He ought to find out when it would be, and where. He ought to tease them about where they were going on their honeymoon.

But all of that stuck in his throat and he looked around the room instead with as much interest as if he had never seen it. He examined the pale striped paper, the sideboard with its eternal silver service from which tea was never poured, the china cabinet to one side. He wondered how many meals Jessica would eat at this table surrounded by this old wallpaper. He was exceedingly depressed.

Asa said, "Ryan, will you ask grace?"

He had seldom been more startled in his life; he shot her a quick look of amazement and then lowered his head before her warning frown. So this was the version of Godwin family life they were giving Miss Maple! He said shortly to his knees, "We thank Thee for Thy love and care. Amen." Then the four of them lifted their heads and he was struck by the fact that everybody—whether four or four hundred—made the same kind of rustle of movement just after prayer.

Avery said that now that they knew each other, Ryan must tell Jessica something about what life was like in a college town.

"Like everywhere else," said Ryan.

"Ryan is too modest," Avery said.

The table was loaded—candied yams, a roast chicken, biscuits and cranberry sauce and snap beans. They began to pass dishes, making a clatter.

"I always thought a college town would be very exciting, with something new happening every minute," said Jessica. And she smiled.

He liked that. "So did I," he admitted. "And that's partially true."

"Well, he must like it since we've never been able to persuade him to move back home," said Asa.

"This town? No thank you."

Asa was angry with him. Ryan could feel it like a pervading sense of heat from the end of the table. He was not quite playing the game. He was not behaving like the Returned Brother full of gentle romantic jokes and genial good wishes to the lovers. But she was going to be stubborn about it. She kept giving him opportunities to step into character.

"Ryan is the intellectual member of the family," she said now (apologetically, Ryan thought, as though he had been the leprous one), and she flashed her eyes at him sharply. He had never seen Asa working so hard for anything. She wants this girl for Avery, he thought. I don't know why; I doubt that Asa knows herself. But she has been picked, chosen, elected. He glanced at the girl and shrugged. But she didn't have to come unless she wanted to. It was none of his affair.

Leaning forward he said pleasantly, "And do *you* read, Miss Maple?"

Jessica Maple flushed and was not able to check the irritated frown that sprang up in her brows. Ryan felt it was her first genuine response of the evening and he was pleased.

"A little," said Jessica coolly. "Not to your taste, I'd imagine." Remembering that Asa had written him of her reading for Ladies' Aid shut-ins, Ryan resisted the impulse to say he fervently hoped not.

"Jessica goes to our library a good deal," said Avery. He was proud of this; women were supposed to read novels as well as do embroidery.

"I believe Asa also wrote me that you do reading for shut-ins. Very generous of you."

Now she was very angry. "Not at all," she said. And he had a sudden delighted hope that she might put her tongue out at him, then and there.

But she did not. Almost she did, but not quite; and he did not know then that this was part of a long long pattern. But he was saddened because she did not quite let go her anger and spill it out at him. He felt tired; he was behaving, he thought, like a petulant child forced to be polite to elders he did not like but determined to come off better in the end. "I'm afraid that sounded rude," he apologized. "I hope it's just that the trip was long and tiring."

Their faces softened, forgiving him. "Not at all," said Jessica, although she looked at him once rather shrewdly, he thought.

But Asa and Avery were won. That was more like it! their faces said.

He went on, doing it right now that he had gotten started. "I hope you're going to be a very happy Godwin, Jessica." More than the rest of us, he thought sourly; but something relaxed in him at the sight of her smile. It *was* a nice smile, he thought. And it was genuine; everything tight deserted the edges of her eyes and mouth and just behind the pupils it seemed as though lights were turned up slowly. She was beautiful. He saw it then.

"I hope so, too," said Jessica, looking at him rather gratefully. He thought she said it with too much fervor and with just a shade of wistfulness; and then he told himself to stop it—he was always reading in too much when he met people for the first time. But he looked at her closely and their eyes held for an instant across the full table.

Then both of them looked at their plates as if the sincerity on each side had been embarrassing. Asa beamed at them. "We thought about a pre-Christmas wedding," she said, now that the subject had come up properly. "Around the twentieth. Will you be able to come then?"

Ryan nodded. The holiday began at Wellman on the seventeenth.

Avery said suddenly, startling them all, "I don't know who they'll get to play the organ if we have it in the church. I can't imagine who they'll get." They turned and stared at him and then realized he, too, was talking about the wedding. Ryan longed to reach under the table with a secret spear and prod Avery in the groin. *Don't you see her? Don't you see this girl at all? Wake Up!*

Asa said comfortingly that she was sure they would find someone. "Or we can get someone from Atlanta. They have lots of musicians in Atlanta."

Ryan went on frowning at Avery's worried face. Then he raised his eyes and looked squarely across the table at Jessica. Is this what you want? he said silently.

But she did not answer him, not even silently.

He went back to eating and he saw Jessica and Avery Godwin living lives of incredible decorum. He saw them with their anchors always down in perpetually quiet seas. He saw them going up and down these stairs and in and out these doors forever and ever, Amen.

There would be early bedtimes ("early to bed and early to rise," Avery would say cheerfully); and early risings and hot breakfasts, because everybody ought to eat a hot breakfast. There would be one or two carefully reared children, for of such is the Kingdom of Heaven. He saw it neutral and colorless and tame; and he longed desperately to have again the Jessica Maple he had been led to expect, the one with the mousy hair and the thick ankles who wore no lipstick and had rimless spectacles.

He was miserable. He did not trust himself to speak.

They lingered over coffee. Ryan smoked gloomily and prodded himself to anger by giving himself a mental lecture. Sweet are the uses of adversity. Sail on, O Ship of State. Mighty Casey has struck out. God Bless Us Every One. A Stitch in Time Saves Nine. He had a feeling that if he said all of this aloud Avery would nod his head solemnly, agreeing with every syllable.

At the end of the table, Asa was very restless. She stirred and restirred her coffee until he thought he could not stand it if she lifted the spoon another time.

Jessica Maple sat silently with one finger linked through the handle of her cup; sometimes she took it out and looked thoughtfully at the ridge it had made in her flesh and put it back again, like the Dutchboy holding in the dikes. That was maddening, too.

As for Avery, he could not have done with the meal; even now he kept worrying the bones on his plate, picking up this one and that to nibble off the last small shred of meat. The Way to a Man's Heart Is Through His Stomach. Them Bones Them Bones Them Dry Bones. . . .

The faint sounds Lady Malveena made in the kitchen were unnaturally loud in the dining-room silence; water dripping from a faucet came to them like the beating of a giant heart.

Jessica's voice was loud in the stillness. "I would think it would be an interesting life. Being a college professor."

Ryan said sadly that he guessed it was. It had never seemed to him less appealing.

"What do you teach?"

"Literature. Criticism, sometimes."

"I wanted to go to college," said Jessica thoughtfully.

He wanted to say: Why didn't you, then? Or, Why don't you go now? But he said nothing at all, and in this empty space Asa's spoon went clinking around in her coffee cup again and Avery took up another bone. A Woman's Place Is in the Home.

He said, surprising even himself, "Do you like Stoneville? Like living here?"

He saw immediately that he had confused her by his sudden change of topic. She was wary, as if for possible traps. "Like it? What do you mean, like it?"

I mean do you want to go on living here all your life in this house with the oak trees outside forever. But he did not say that, of course.

Asa spoke before he could say anything. "Ryan means only that he doesn't like it. Never has. He's always thought that everybody else ought to dislike it too and go away somewhere."

And leave it, Ryan thought in some satisfaction. Leave it to the spiders.

"I've only lived in Greenway," said Miss Maple. "I don't have much to compare Stoneville with. It's . . ." (She finished it defiantly.) "It's a nice quiet little town."

And is that want you want? He asked that question with his face only; and her face said with the same defiance: Yes. Yes, it is.

Why? said his face; and hers, hardening a trifle, said: That's none of your business.

"Why did you leave Stoneville? What is it you dislike about it?" This question she asked him aloud, as though the other had never been.

"When I first went away, I didn't even know. I just wanted to make sure there weren't other places where people had more freedom to be themselves."

"And are there?" said Jessica, softly. She sounded as if she really wanted to know.

"I think so. After you get used to it, you can probably be yourself anywhere. Even in Stoneville."

"Could you, now?"

He said shortly that he'd just as soon not try. He'd gotten used to living other places where people let him alone with his books and his thoughts and his ideas. Where they weren't always climbing up into his mind to make sure it was operating in the accepted fashion.

"You're not very specific," Jessica said.

He glanced at her. She was sharper than she cared to show. "I think it's narrow and nosy. I think too many people here are focused on the great hereafter, and not enough of them bother to make now seem very exciting or worth while. I don't like the way people generally are afraid of new things just because they are new. And it's a smug community. It's so sure that there is only one way to think, act, live. I guess I like that least of all."

"Those are pretty general things," said Jessica. "I could say that perhaps you're just talking about human nature."

He liked this girl. "I suppose I am just talking about human nature. But don't you think there are certain communities in which other aspects of human nature are brought to the surface more often, to help balance some of these?"

She said, "Perhaps there are."

After a while they went back into the parlor and sat around the fire and made small talk about people in the town and what they were doing. Mr. Garris was editorializing about the wanton destruction of the old maple trees alongside Wynberry Street. Miss Delmare had died and Cornelia Satterfield was full-fledged librarian now. Asa looked at Ryan as if he ought to turn on a telltale blush at that information, but he could not manage that—not even to play the game.

The real estate office was doing well. Asa was thinking of taking in some other partners as well as Avery. There was too much work for her to handle. A textile man from South Carolina had bought the old vacant lot where the boys used to play ball and was planning to build an office building as an investment. Asa thought it a shrewd idea.

During all of this, Jessica added little to the recital of town news. She sat quietly on her chair, doing none of the things a bride-to-be ought to be doing, looking at Avery seldom, not turning the small ring to catch the light, not dreaming into the fire.

Ryan wanted to ask her if there were no other men in Stoneville besides his brother Avery; and then he realized with a shock that there could not be many who were not already married. There had always been a curious gap in the generations so that for five years on either side of him there were few people (he remembered how small his graduating class had been); and then there were the barely twenty-year-olds and the balding, graying just-beginning-to-fatten couples.

But, my God! he thought; there are other towns, other people, other lives than these; *nobody keeps you here!* Yet he had visions of the women he had known when he lived in Stoneville, this or that slowly aging spinster who behaved as though Stoneville were an island, as though if you went too many miles north or south or east or west you would be lost in the void. Southern ladies did not go out to seek their fortunes alone, and especially Southern ladies who had lived all their lives with various aunts. Life might appear to them to be incorporated within the Stoneville city limits so that here—seen from the square and the Palmer Building—the horizon seemed to end just on this hill or behind this roof; here it *did* end; here the world stopped short; the sky came down like a curtain; the days and seasons had their boundaries.

But this girl? Ryan wondered. And he wanted to walk across the room and take her chin in his hand and looking down at her ask gravely, Did you think that?

And if she had, why he would . . . he did not know what he would do. Perhaps he would just go on standing there, on and on, her small chin cupped in his hand, asking sadly: That was what you thought? Who told you that?

Asa said sharply, "I don't believe you're listening to me."

He turned his head to look at her. "I'm sorry," he said. "No, I wasn't."

Asa could afford to be generous because the evening had gone better than she had hoped. "It wasn't important. Just more gossip," she said.

They talked on aimlessly about other things (there were plans to paint the church; Avery had been made church treasurer; Lady Malveena had been out of sorts lately and Asa thought perhaps she did not feel well).

Finally Asa said that since Thanksgiving services were at seven (Ryan winced) they had better all get some sleep, thus giving him to understand that Miss Maple would stay the night. Arrangements were explained: Ryan would be in with Avery; Miss Maple was being put in the upper front bedroom, the one which as a child he had called the crooked room because of the jutting walls.

He put his head into the kitchen but Lady Malveena said for him to go on upstairs. "I'll talk to you later," she said. "The time's not ready yet." She always sounded as though the time were something special she had baking in the oven.

Ryan and Avery and Jessica and Asa went upstairs and separated in the hall with something akin to embarrassment. Ryan thought approaching bedtimes always had this effect on strangers or people not completely natural with one another. They were all too much aware that in a few minutes each would be doing undignified things like loosening stays and brushing teeth and looking ungainly in nightshirts and underwear. The vision embarrassed them all, and they were doubly embarrassed at having even thought of it.

As they approached the assigned doors they paused like children awaiting a parent's final word at bedtime; finally said fumblingly, "Good night."

"Good night, Miss Maple. I'm glad you'll still be with us tomorrow."

"Good night. I'm glad to have met you at last."

"Ryan, did you get your bag?"

"I have it."

"It's going to be cold in the morning."

"Just so it doesn't rain."

They went into their rooms and gratefully closed the doors.

Asa's tap against his door next morning was explosive and Ryan awoke into a cold gray room and could not remember where he was. Then he heard the knocking on another door down the hall and he peered across at the other bed and discovered his brother sleeping there. Avery slept curled around himself, like an embryo or a type of slug. There was not much light in the room; it was barely dawn and all of them were going out into the sharp air to church. That put him in an irritable humor and he would have put his head back under the covers, but Avery had uncurled and gotten freshly to his feet. Avery looked rested. "There's nothing like early morning air," said Avery briskly. There's nothing like a dish of hot cyanide. There's nothing to compare with the experience of being in a sinking ship at sea. Ryan closed his eyes for one last minute of privacy.

"Don't go back to sleep," said Avery.

"I'm not."

Soon he heard slippers in the hall and he thought of Miss Maple (where were the sensible oxfords and the thick ankles?) and he didn't want to get up. On the other hand, the thought of not seeing her also made him frown.

"You can use my shaving mirror. The bathroom," Avery blushed slightly, "the bathroom will be in use."

And all Ryan could think about that was whether or not blushes were involuntary or whether Avery had taught himself to do that, very carefully, down a procession of years and mirrors.

"Good morning," said Lady Malveena with a smile when they came into the kitchen.

"You look like you had a good night's sleep."

She admitted that she had. "Good Morning, Miss Jessica."

"Hello, Lady Malveena. Hello, Ryan." She crossed the kitchen and stood with her back to the stove. "I'm cold."

"It's a terrible day to get up in," Ryan said.

Avery came in and spoke very politely all around. "How are you, Jessica?"

"Chilly," she said.

Lady Malveena said that Asa had already had some coffee and had gone back upstairs.

Coffee was all they would have before leaving because there would be Thanksgiving breakfast at the church, and Ryan felt a little better after his second cup. Avery and Jessica and he had sat in silence after the first good mornings with the steam coming up on their lips and going warmly into their noses. It made Ryan think how sleep set men off in separate compartments; they were truly alone at night and it took some time in the morning for them to make contact again.

Asa came downstairs before they were through and did everything but tap her foot impatiently. She always bustled about as though the savoring and slow enjoyment of anything—even coffee—bordered on the sinful; now she prodded them loose from their cups. "I hate to be late for anything," said Asa. But since Ryan did not know of a single time in Asa's life when she had been late, he could not imagine that she really knew how she would feel about it.

"Coffee should never be hurried," he grumbled.

But the rest of them were already moving out of the kitchen—Avery had his mind on matters about the choir; he wanted to make sure the books had already been placed in the chairs.

Lady Malveena grinned at him. "You better run to catch up," she said.

"Looks like it." Ryan turned up the last swallow, which he did not like to do, and put the cup down. "I'll see you in a little while."

"You behave yourself," she said.

He was wide awake by the time they were standing on the porch while Avery persuaded the Buick to stir and come around to the front of the house. There was mist and dampness but the air was wonderfully sharp; the sky, lighter in one half, was still gray with the last dissolving night. Every breath he took seemed freshly washed.

Jessica was standing at his side and he was aware of some of the dampness misting in her hair. This morning the hair was very dark and the eyes, too, seemed darker. He remembered when he was small he had believed all eyes darkened overnight from the closed lids and the long rest away from light of any kind.

He said to her sheepishly (she seemed so very far away), "Whenever I do manage to get up early, I always tell myself I ought to do it all the time."

She smiled but did not say anything. Nor did she turn her head. He saw then that she, too, was looking out at the sky and breathing deeply as though she sucked all of it in and out again—the clouds and the mist and the sharp wet taste of the air.

"I like winter better," she said in a few minutes.

"Not so insipid," he agreed. "Not as much blue sky and white fluff." It was a message he sent her under words. Insipid, he telegraphed. Flat, stale, and unprofitable. Stolid and humdrum.

But even as he spoke a wind went through the tall oak tree and showered the walk with leaves; and Jessica listened to the wind instead of to him.

Asa said that wind was enough to cut you to the bone. They heard the Buick protesting and spitting in the driveway.

Jessica said, "It must be wonderful in New England. I've always thought the air would be sweet in New England."

"Yes," said Ryan in some surprise, "I suppose it is."

The long black car snuffled and wheezed down the drive and stopped like a faithful old dog and waited at the curb. It had a further look of a dog about it—it looked as though any minute it might drop onto its haunches and refuse to move an inch.

"Why in the world don't you get a new car, Asa?" Ryan knew she could well afford it.

"This one is more than adequate. You don't get quality goods like you did when this car was built." She led the way down the steps and through the leaves, some of which were lightly dusted with frost. Ryan, although he was not the type usually, found himself taking Jessica's elbow politely down the steps. "Thank you," said Jessica. The two of them walked ankle deep in the dead leaves to get to the car, but Asa picked her way carefully on top of them all, not dirtying her shoes.

"I thought we'd freeze before you got here," Asa said, climbing in. Jessica sat beside Avery and there was nothing for Ryan to do but get into the back. Here, at least, he could watch her without seeming to do so. He peered ahead as though he were staring out the windshield onto the street.

Thus, in the corner of his eye, he could see the rich dark hair and the small ears and a nice line where the neck met the shoulder. As they drove along Asa pointed out the lot where the textile manufacturer planned eventually to erect an office building and pointed out a house which the Barcrofts had recently sold at a handsome profit. To all of this he nodded; and he watched the dappled light which came through the trees and into the car window and fell in specks against Jessica's hair.

Avery said he hoped the sexton had remembered to close up all the windows so the organ would be dry. "Soaks up damp like a sponge," he said.

"Will you be in the choir this morning, Miss Maple?"

She nodded so that all the lights flickered briefly onto her profile and back into the hair again. Then Ryan thought with something akin to panic: *I'm going to love her*; and he sat back suddenly against the seat and turned his head to look out at the passing houses as though he were angry with them. He had the oddest feeling that Jessica had understood him as surely as if he had spoken the words aloud, that she had stiffened slightly, that a muscle in her face had moved and had been quickly stilled. *I'm going to love her. I do not love her yet—not quite—but I will. Perhaps by tomorrow I will already love her.* He set his jaw fiercely at all the white houses and the winter lawns and at the light coming speckled down between the trees.

"You're awfully quiet," Asa said.

"He's not awake yet," said Avery pleasantly. But Jessica did not say a word, not a word.

At the church everyone greeted him. Everyone said they were glad to see him home again—the ladies who had taught him in the primary classes and given him gold stars for memory work, and Mr. Barnes who was jovial and familiar. Ryan was slightly embarrassed before Jessica, as if he were being cut down to size, as if all these pleasant people were reminding him that he was—after all—only a little boy singing "Jesus Loves Me" with all the other little boys. He shook many hands and asked about absent sons and daughters. He said Yes, he was still teaching up North. He said Yes, he liked it pretty well.

People asked Jessica about the wedding and she told them it would be before Christmas. He thought she looked paler than she had in the sun in the automobile.

Someone whose name he did not remember told Ryan the Godwins were mighty lucky to get a sweet girl like Miss Maple.

Avery was shaking hands everywhere. Avery said the frost was certainly on the pumpkin this morning, wasn't it?

People said, "Are you going to have a big Thanksgiving dinner?"

"We sure are," said Avery, smiling. "How about you?"

They went upstairs into the fellowship room and sat around long white tables. Up and down the tablecloths, children were tugged and prodded into silence. Mr. Barnes stood up and welcomed everybody and gave a brief talk on "Counting Your Blessings." After that the ladies brought out thick white plates full of hominy grits with gravy and thick white cups of hot chocolate with sugary doughnuts in the saucers.

The Godwins sat together—Asa first, and then Ryan, and Jessica was seated between him and Avery. Any time during the meal he knew he could have touched her, brushed her shoulder, moved an elbow slightly out; and the effort not to do any of these made him stiff and unnatural so that he ate with precision like a soldier, like—he thought wryly—one of Gideon's brave three hundred.

When the meal was over, the treasurer of the church stood up and reminded them that friendship offerings would be taken to defray the cost of the food and to support the denominational orphanage. He added that offerings for the orphanage were taken on two special days during the year—Thanksgiving Day and Mother's Day. Someone passed a pie pan up and down each table and every coin that went into it rang like a cymbal. All of the children wanted to put the pennies in, one penny at a time, making a terrible clatter.

Before they adjourned to the church auditorium there was an informal period of witnessing. During this time several members stood up and testified how good God had been to them this year.

Mrs. Potter got to her feet (she did this every year and she had heart dropsy; all of them were nervous to see her there out of her bed) and told them she was most grateful for peace. She said that never a night passed that she did not feel drawn up under the wings of the Lord. And she meant that, too; her faith had kept her serene through much pain and loss; and dignity had settled on her face like a delicate overlay. Ryan had always thought sick old Mrs. Potter one of the most handsome human beings he knew. She was in strife with nothing and no one; she floated in the fluid of God's love like a foetus which does not yet know hunger.

"He has kept my wife with me," said Amos McBane—who stood up after Mrs. Potter had been helped back to her chair. And the plump woman with him who was brown as a berry sighed, "Amen."

"And food and house and clothes, Amen."

"Amen," said his wife. "Amen," breathed a few of the others.

"The Giver of all Good Gifts," said Amos. "Opened the windows of Heaven. Closer than hands and feet."

"Amen," said the others.

After a prayer they went down the stairs and out into the cold air and over the walk on which frost hung at the edges, and into the main building. It was chilly; the old furnace had never worked too well. Jessica and Avery slipped away into the little door behind the pulpit and Asa asked if he wouldn't like to sit up front where he could hear better.

Ryan said he supposed he would.

He sat half turned around and watched some of the others filing in. He saw Miss Carter who had taught him in high school; she fluttered a gloved hand at him. He had always liked Miss Carter. She had read the Lucy poems in a voice that trembled with emotion and "Annabel Lee" had almost made her cry, class after class and year after year.

He saw Tom Baker, one of the County Commissioners. He saw Mr. Nelson, who owned a plywood plant and was said to be one of the richest men in town. The young girls who sat together in the front row were about fifteen, he guessed—very dressed, very lipsticked, very tickled over enormous jokes he could only guess about. In a little while the sexton walked up and down each aisle and looked down the registers angrily, as if he found them uncooperative.

After a while Avery came out and flourished his arms (as though loosening them in the sockets) and everybody quieted to a murmur. He settled at the organ and played a dressed-up arrangement of "Come Ye Thankful People Come" which roared out of the bass pipes like a caged lion; and then the choir filed out and into their box carrying lighted candles. As they came they sang very martially, "All is safely gathered in, ere the winter storm begin . . ." They stood in three rows of dark garments with the round blobs of flame jumping and weaving, and on Jessica's pale face was a yellow pool of light. Ryan looked at her so hard that finally he could no longer see the others at all; she was abstracted from the rest of them and there was nothing but darkness all around her golden cheeks and forehead where the candle shone.

They sang, softer, "We gather together to ask the Lord's blessing . . ." while the congregation bowed heads; and then everyone sat down for Mr. Barnes' message. He had come out of his own study, carefully closing the door behind him, when they first came in; and after the song he prayed briefly. Then he began to speak on "The Greatest Gift of All."

Ryan could not blame his inattention on Mr. Barnes but rather on the face of Jessica, dim now the candles had been put out. He sat and watched the shadows play upon that face as he had formerly watched the light. Now the eye socket was darkest, and now a gray line made the cheek hollow, and now a whole side of her face was eclipsed and dark, like a moon. Once she put her hymnal down into her lap and the very movement startled him. Most of the time she sat as still as a statue in some eternal twilight garden.

The sun was bright and coming through the thin windows as best it could when they finally stood to sing "Praise God From Whom All Blessings Flow," groping behind them for their coats during the final lines, slipping the books back into the racks, glancing secretly at watches. Mr. Barnes blessed them with outstretched arms and they went out into the sunlight. It was a pale sun in a cold day; but the mist was gone. The grayish sky had bleached out in the hour or so they had been inside. Avery was playing something very loud and military. "Postlude," it had said on the program. The white sky had the effect of snowfields; up and down the front steps people stood talking and squinting.

Asa said, "We could wait in the car if you'd rather. They'll have to get their robes off."

Ryan said he would just as soon wait where they were unless Asa was cold.

They shook more hands and smiled and Ryan was introduced to several people whom he did not know. Reverend Barnes was shaking hands here and there; he asked after sick children, businesses, absent families. When he came to stand by the Godwins he, too, squinted off into the sky for a minute and he looked so intense that Ryan thought he might be expecting Gabriel to come out of it.

"A fine message," Asa said. And she shot Ryan an acid look because he had gone against protocol by not stating the compliment first.

"Thank you, Asa," said Edward Barnes. "It *is* something we need to remember. Our indebtedness." Ryan could not think of a good reply to this so he cleared his throat as though only an obstruction prevented him from agreement.

"We all know how fortunate Avery is to have found a wonderful woman like Miss Maple," said Mr. Barnes, addressing him directly.

Ryan said she certainly was a wonderful young woman.

"I know they'll be very happy," said Mr. Barnes. He was not married himself; Ryan had always felt that in some secret way, Asa burned for Edward Barnes. He could not imagine what she thought about him in her own mind (his bottom was bulbous) but he thought the vision must be well etched and pure, whatever it was.

The Johnsons came by with four of their seven children. Ryan had always liked the Johnsons, too. Mr. and Mrs. Johnson obviously *liked* each other, liked being married, liked having children. Something of the honesty of blood and bone was in them. They stopped to speak.

"You stop that," Mrs. Johnson said in an undertone to her son Freddie. Freddie was picking his nose and hiding the results under the stair rail.

When they went off down the stairs Mr. Barnes said they certainly were a happy family. "Christian marriage is at the heart of the church," he was saying when Avery and Jessica came from around the side of the church. At the sight of them Mr. Barnes fairly chortled with playfulness. "We've just been discussing you two," he crowed and—rewarded by the red which came to Jessica's cheeks—"We two bachelors here were just envying Avery."

"I certainly am a lucky man," said Avery. He put a hand onto Jessica's shoulder.

As for Jessica, she looked at Ryan once and then looked away quickly and he felt absurdly that he had betrayed her. Then he was angry at himself for presuming so much; she had no way of knowing his real reactions nor he hers. For all Ryan knew, she found him highly objectionable compared with his brother. He grew morose and jammed his hands into his pockets like a boy.

"You're going to go on living here after you're married, I hope," said Mr. Barnes.

"Oh yes," said Avery. "We'll stay on with Asa."

"That house is too large for one woman," Asa said.

And Ryan said silently to Jessica that she would still be living in other people's houses as she always had; but she did not even glance at him. She moved toward Avery very slightly and she gave Mr. Barnes a careful smile.

"You've all been very good to me," she said sincerely.

"We *like* you!" Mr. Barnes objected. Asa looked very happy.

Ryan frowned up at that snowy sky and thought bitterly that if Gabriel planned on coming any time soon he could do worse than drop out of it just that minute. But that did not happen, of course; and after a few more remarks they got into the car and coaxed it home and ate a tremendous meal that Lady Malveena had fixed.

Ryan supposed it was a tremendous meal, with everything prepared as wonderfully as always. For him, it might as well have been gall and wormwood, served in ashes.

The other two days of his holiday passed just like that sharp Thanksgiving Day. Jessica was around the Godwin house a good deal; he spent his time self-consciously watching her or self-consciously not watching her. He raged, he joyed, he despaired.

He said to Lady Malveena that he just didn't think she was suited for Avery.

"You turn that around and you might be on to something," Lady Malveena snapped. She was as short-tempered as he was. He knew now what she had meant about Wallifetterson, who had been a bum and yet had made her blood flow better, had made her warm in the times and places it counted most.

He told himself he was *not* an unbiased observer. He repeated Jim's words: Maybe these two people love each other. Maybe they're getting married because of it. He said that over and over but he could not believe in it at all.

Saturday he knew that something must be done; he had this day and one more and in a month she would marry his brother.

He had to come right out with it and ask her. Then if she told him everything was all right he would never say another word. So he grew feverish with the sheer effort to see her alone and then—when there *was* one moment or another in which they stood together in a hallway waiting for the others, he would remember how little he knew her after all; he would imagine how shocked she would be if he spoke. And so in her presence he took to lashing out desperately at inanimate objects; he rattled umbrellas and stamped his feet and flapped his coat when he hung it up or took it down or put it on. And by this he intended she should know his helplessness, that one time she should have caught at the umbrella or smoothed out the coat for him and said only, "Let me help you."

Then he would have kissed her where she stood.

But all this time Jessica, in turn, was as still as stone when they were together, as though the merest lifting of a finger would let down avalanches.

Once he blurted at her, like a boy, "Why are you marrying Avery?" And she took that for some criticism and hurried away without answering.

And another time, feeling really desperate, he went to Avery himself. He made a long speech about love. Avery was completely bewildered.

"But of course I love her," Avery said mildly. "She's a very fine young woman."

"Dammit, I know she's a fine young woman!" Ryan groaned.

"I hope to be a good husband to her."

"No no no no no," said Ryan impatiently. He paced up and down the rug. "You two are not at all alike. You're very different from Jessica."

"Variety is the spice of life," said Avery. He added a small laugh to that but he looked at Ryan uneasily. It seemed to him Ryan had been prodding at him all his life.

"You don't . . . you don't . . . Avery, this will never work out!"

Avery grew slightly stiff. "I expect to make certain adjustments, of course," he said gravely.

"Listen, people ought to get married because they can't help it," said Ryan. "They ought to need each other so badly and so deeply nothing else will do! They ought to need to spend whole lives together. . . ."

Avery was bewildered. "I believe in the permanence of marriage," he protested. "Surely you don't think I'm just . . . just, well, dallying with Jessica."

Ryan didn't think Avery would understand dallying if it were pointed out to him.

"Why, I'm devoted to Jessica!" Avery said. "Do you think for one moment I'd ask her to become my wife if—"

"Hell, no, I don't think that!" shouted Ryan.

"Then what in the world is the matter with you?" Avery considered this very seriously and then came up with it. Obviously Ryan, himself, was uneasy about his own future and whether he would ever find a wonderful girl like Jessica with whom to build a home. Avery said gently that he was sure Ryan just hadn't met the right girl yet.

If his brother had not been so heavy Ryan would have lifted him off the floor and shaken him in mid-air.

So when he was sure nothing could be done on that level with Avery he went to Asa—who had engineered this whole thing capably—and he made his face as firm as he could.

"Jessica must not marry Avery," he told her decidedly; and when those words were out the rest of it fled away and he could only say it again, earnestly, "She must not marry him, Asa."

Asa was unruffled. "And why not? I introduced them myself. Avery is of an age and he needs a wife. She's very suitable and—I must say—very charming."

"Not for Avery. Jessica must not marry Avery."

An eyebrow went up, but not hurriedly, in Asa's face. "I'd like to know why not! It's all arranged."

He was completely thwarted. He felt like a child when its wants are such that adults pretend not to understand. He wanted to say to her, "But that was before I sat behind her in a car and saw the sun on her hair!" He took a deep breath and said instead, as calmly as he could, "She's too alive for him. She's genuine and honest and outgoing. I think all of you have taken advantage of her loneliness and her gratitude."

"What in the world are you talking about?" said Asa mildly.

He tried it once more. "She's never had a home. What kind of future does she seem to have—living with Victoria Seagreaves all her life—"

"Victoria Seagreaves is a fine Christian woman."

"All of her life," he persisted, "and nothing in the world belonging to her. She doesn't know anything exists outside this town."

"Oh my, this town again!"

"This town and these people, and within that Avery is about the best there is at this point. But he isn't good enough. Do you hear, Asa?"

She would not quarrel with him for she had Jessica already; who else was there to win? She said, "Don't you think Jessica has the right to decide who is good enough for her, Ryan?"

"Asa . . ." he tried again.

"Well, don't you? Have you asked Jessica about this? Did she send you to see me? Does she wish to be relieved of her obligations to Avery?"

"No. But Asa . . . Asa, do something *good*. Do something *good* for once."

"Sometimes I find you very strange," said Asa calmly.

Later he never knew why the words should have been so hard for him, why he could not have said, with calmness and possession, "I love you, Jessica" and "I love her, Avery"; and to Asa, "But *I* love her, Asa." He had said these words before of other women; he had spilled them out on a dozen occasions as though they were raisins—sweet-tasting but short-lived—but now the matter was real and earnest, and saying it was like extracting bone.

So on that last Sunday he was home Ryan walked through the house angrily, scuffing the carpets and brushing but never quite overturning the marble-topped tables; and he went savagely up and down the stairs as though he hoped they might fall in with him and put an end to everything.

Then it was time to go back and nothing said; and now he lied to himself. He was sure that all of them knew it, really, that he had accomplished it with his silence and his rage; and they had only been pretending not to see. It was, perhaps, a form of teasing. So all that last day home he deluded himself; he waited for the others to admit it, to give up, even to say they had been only teasing and that they wished him well.

He watched Jessica closely. When he heard her laughing in the kitchen with Lady Malveena he thought it a good sign; when she looked at him he read promises in her face.

And it was not until the very last moments at the train station in Greenway that he knew how foolish he had been, and now there was nothing left to him but a second.

He used it as best he could. When the time came for him to give Jessica an awkward brotherly kiss, he slipped it into the little hollow at her eye and nose; and by this he meant she should foresee all the still-ungiven kisses for all the secret places. She was not married yet; he would write her a long letter from the train—but in the meantime he left this small sign behind him. When he kissed her she seemed stiff and frightened and did not step into his arms. He caught her shoulders with his hands and once it seemed to him she moved her head a trifle, as though to rub it on his mouth and make it linger.

But when he looked at her after he had dropped his hands he could not tell; and Asa was putting forward her own cool face and Avery was smiling possessively. Ryan put the expected kiss on Asa's chin like a man stamping a letter, his mind on other things.

He thought her eyes unusually bright and he hoped against hope for tears. "Jessica," he said once and then, floundering, grabbed at his luggage.

She said, "Good-by, Ryan," very sadly.

Avery said for him to have a good trip and Asa said she hoped from now on he would write home once in a while.

Then he was on the train and the three figures at the station were no taller than his little finger, and then the nail; and then they were altogether gone. He sat with his bag in his lap thinking of her without moving for more than twenty miles, so that when he was asked for his ticket he was so startled he lifted his arm, almost in defense.

After that he was beginning to be calm again. He was no schoolboy. Life had not ended just because he had let certain opportunities go by the first time they came. He would write to her. In this way he would steal the private moment they had not quite had.

And that would pose the question squarely: she could tear his letter up and throw it away; or she could show it to Avery in anger (he had nothing to lose there); or she could write him back as he firmly believed she would—and then all the umbrellas and marble-topped tables in all the houses on Walnut Street would make no difference.

And all the way home to Wellman he heard her name sung on the rails: Jess-i-ca, Jessica, Jess-i-ca, Jessica; and he thought of her shoulders under his hands and the curve of nose where he had hidden his most unbrotherly kiss until a next time, and he was relieved. She *had* understood. It was not possible that she could have missed his meaning.

It was good to go to sleep with her name in his ears.

He was back at Wellman late on Monday, and Wednesday morning the letter came.

When he first saw it—small and neat and white—in his mailbox in the college post office he hated to reach inside, for he was sure that everything was wrong. It was as though when he took that letter out and held it in his hand the world lurched a little on its axis, ever so slightly, so that everything on all sides of him shifted out of joint.

Somebody said, "Hello, Mr. Godwin." Ryan nodded vaguely into the kerchiefed crowd. Somebody else jostled him and he gave way slightly.

It was raining that Wednesday (the way it always did on mass assembly days; it was a campus joke; they even wrote it as an established fact in the handbook for incoming freshmen) and the post office was crowded. The whole bored lot of professors and students was glad to be finally out of the hot auditorium which had smelled of rubber and wet dogs. Now they milled about him where he stood holding the letter. All he could think about was that he hadn't had time to write his own letter yet and this one had no business coming. He began to edge by yellow slickers and umbrella points without knowing they were there. He was that sure that this small letter had upturned the world.

Somebody wailed, "But he isn't *coming!*"

Somebody else said, "I thought at least he'd send me a little money. He *knows* I hardly have enough to . . ."

Somebody else said, "Bad news?" and he attributed that to the rest of the crowd until Dr. Boolin, who taught ancient history, began to wave a picture post card in his face. "I say, you've not had bad news, have you?" said Dr. Boolin.

"I don't know," said Ryan, focusing him in. "I think so."

"Now, that's too bad. Anything I can do?"

"No. No, thank you." He got around a group of girls who were listening to something read aloud (*And after that her mother went to see his mother and her mother said* . . .) and he headed for the door. Still he did not tear the letter and open it and see what was inside. It was too soon for a message telling him how good it was to have had him home. It was too quick a letter to have anything to do with the plans for Christmas. It was air-mail; it had come from Stoneville on Tuesday morning.

He found his face in a tremendous mass of red hair that seemed to be coming off one student's head in all directions. He was half afraid the girl would think he was nuzzling her. "Excuse me," he said. She did not even turn around. She was saying to her roommate, "They haven't come to my section yet. I'm sure I'll hear from him today. He's never stayed mad this long *before!*"

"Good morning, Mr. Godwin," said someone else. He stretched his mouth properly in that general direction. "About my paper on *Paradise Lost*," said someone earnestly and he told her to come around to his office that afternoon.

Then he went outside into a fine rain. The drops were so small that they did not seem to be coming down; gravity was too much for them. Instead, they hung in the air and went about horizontally.

"Hi, Ryan!" It was Mary August, also History. She was younger than most of the faculty (Radcliffe, 1932) and every freshman class for the past three years had tried to foster a romance between the two of them. Ryan thought her very disagreeable.

"Hello, Mary."

He began to walk across the campus, past Langley Building and the Home Ec house; and as he walked he watched incuriously the steady lifting and placing of his feet on the intricate checkerboard of the brick walk; and he thought of all the balanced patterns formed by all these bricks, and the way human feet trod on and overlapped and ignored the patterns, day after day. He was glad to be such a human being.

But all of this was a pretense; this was a way of acting as though he did not feel that letter written in Asa's spidery hand, burning in his pocket.

He kept up his usual habits on the homeward walk. He frowned at the new library building (the only thing to commend it was size; it had the look of an unbelievable mausoleum filled with generations of corpses) and grinned when he came alongside the School of Music. From many rooms many pianos were playing many different things; voices were singing in a variety of keys; other instruments could be heard from other practice rooms. It made a stunning cacophony.

He lived on Dorset Street in an apartment house. It was made of stucco and had the look of prisons built by people trying to be humane. When he came upstairs he saw that Barney had left a note on his door (Barney lived across the hall and taught Psychology: Basic Principles) and the note said, *Please let Sybil in.* Ryan went into his own apartment and, sighing, opened the window and whistled; and in a few minutes the Siamese came up the silver maple tree outside and sprang lightly in. She sat on the windowsill, brooding.

"Go home," said Ryan. He was still postponing the moment. The cat pawed at the curtains without much interest and ignored him. Sybil was very much aware of her position in the world of cats.

He dropped his notebook onto a chair and took the letter out of his pocket and then sat absently on top of the notebook, turning the envelope in his hands. "Go home," he said to the cat again. "You make me nervous." Sybil cleared the radiator and came down like a feather and yawned. Then she came over to where he sat with the full intent of clawing his trousers. Ryan fingered her ears aimlessly and told her she was a bitch among kittens, whatever that might mean.

After a while there was nothing to do but tear back the flap and unfold the sheets and spread them in a palm and read.

The five dreaded words (he could almost see them through the envelope; he had almost read them through the very wall of the post office) those five words leaped out at him and he sat staring at them before he went back and read the rest of it. AVERY AND JESSICA ARE MARRIED, said the five words. They were down in the middle of the first paragraph but they sprang up and out and assailed his eye, and Ryan knew there had not been one second when he had not known what was inside.

DEAR RYAN:

Well, after all our plans, you'll never guess what the two of them have done. Avery and Jessica are married. I hardly know the details myself except that after you left Jessica grew depressed and finally they decided to marry right away. I'm half afraid she realized you had certain objections to the wedding and that these upset her.

Also I believe Jessica dreaded a church wedding at Christmas time lest there be too much fuss and feathers. She is, as I am sure you noticed, rather shy about such things. She told me over and over again that all she wanted was a *simple* life, and I told her in this day and time that was certainly admirable.

At any rate, Reverend Barnes officiated at a very simple home ceremony this morning (Tuesday) and I have turned over two rooms to them for their apartment. They decided against a wedding trip at this time. Once the decision was made, Jessica was very insistent about what was to be done—married immediately, she said, and married in the same house in which she would live all of her life, and Reverend Barnes and no wedding trip. And she asked me to write you immediately and tell you for her. She said I was to be sure to tell you they were married in this very house.

Avery will take over a small interest in the Realty office. He will not devote his full time to this since—as you know—he has never been too suited to business, and his many church duties are pressing.

Although the wedding has come and gone, we will still look for you to spend Christmas with us. I believe Jessica enjoys having a sense of "family" and will be looking forward to seeing you, although she asked me to tell you that you were in no way obligated to come now that the wedding was off if you had had other plans.

Still, we *do* hope to see you. Jessica and Avery join me in affection,

ASA

And Ryan thought, sitting bitterly in his chair, She *did* know. She knew, and she took what was safe and near at hand. Sybil came up in his lap and lay down across the letter. "Go home!" he said, irritably this time, and stood up and spilled her onto the floor. I hate cats, he thought grimly. He went into the kitchenette and opened the apartment refrigerator and then closed it again without taking anything out. My fault, he thought miserably. Why didn't I say something? She could only have known that something was there, and not how important it was. Maybe it looked to her like an attraction that was no more than jeopardy, not very deep, not lasting. He put his hand in a fist against the porcelain. Why didn't I come out with how the whole thing was?

After a while he opened the refrigerator door again and took out the milk and poured some into a coffee can for Sybil. She condescended to taste the stuff and, when it appeared he was no longer watching, lapped it up with gusto.

Ryan could not have been less interested in Sybil at the moment. Damn crazy business! He hardly knew the girl! And he stamped back into the other room and took up the notebook off the chair and wondered what it was. Then he recalled he had put it there himself, and he laid it down again irritably and remembered that he still had on his raincoat which was dripping on the floor. He swore softly.

When he took it off he hung it up as if lives were in the balance, as if every wrinkle must be out and the hanger flush against the seam. He was still frowning at it when Barney came into the apartment without knocking.

"Got the cat?" said Barney. He was thin and hook-nosed and nearsighted. He seemed always to be peering into people's faces as if he could not quite believe his eyes. It was very disconcerting when you met him for the first time. You felt he had spotted some subtle deformity which had somehow escaped you all these years.

Ryan had never cared for Barney. Barney knew everything there was to know in the world. "She's in the kitchen," said Ryan shortly. "Eating."

"Saves me the trouble," Barney said. He sat on the couch without asking if Ryan was busy or if he wanted company. Barney took for granted no one could ask for a greater blessing than his presence. Barney said, "How'd the classes go?"

"All right."

"It's always dull after a holiday," Barney said. "Mine were half asleep."

"You managed to interest them, though. Didn't you?"

Barney nodded. "I always hit 'em with something juicy when

they've been away. Homosexuality today. Woke them up a little. That's the way you do literature, too, if you want to keep their interest. Today, for instance, you should have read them some hot piece of fiction."

Ryan was familiar with Barney's views on teaching literature. You sandwiched Shakespeare in between Henry Miller, James Jones. Ryan was, in fact, familiar with Barney's views on everything. He picked up his notebook and thumbed through a page or so with what he intended to be great absorption.

"Lots of work to do?"

"Lots of it," he said firmly.

Barney said that if he organized his work he wouldn't have to bring any of it home. The students were supposed to be bringing theirs home—that's what their daddies were paying for. Ryan said be that as it may, he still had lots of work to do tonight.

"Here, kitty kitty," said Barney, and went on sitting there. Sybil did not come, of course. She had a mind of her own.

"I really have to get to work," said Ryan shortly.

Barney was magnanimous. "Sure. Don't let me bother you." Sybil came to the door and examined the two of them without much admiration and went to sit over the radiator where the windowsill was warm. "How are you, Sybil?" Barney said in a conversational tone. She washed one foot. After a few minutes Barney asked Ryan if he was going home for Christmas.

"Doubt it." He had no wish to see Jessica as Avery's wife.

"I never go home myself," said Barney. "My mother's old. All she talks about is her spine hurting and how I used to be a lovable little boy."

Ryan doubted the last, but he believed in the aching spine.

"You can't, you know," said Barney in a clipped way. "Really go home, I mean."

"Goddammit, cut it out. Every time you think you're being profound you start talking in that British accent." Barney was from Kansas and the sun set on Kansas regularly, about once a day.

Barney whistled. "Boy, are you touchy! Hard day, huh?"

"Lousy."

"What's the trouble?"

Barney was a goddamn leech; he loved to be set on other people's wounds. Ryan said, "Dandruff. Dysentery. Rain. Germany. High prices."

But the so-called psychologist in Barney had risen to the surface like something in a tepid pool. He said, with what he thought was just the necessary man-to-man brusqueness, "Want to talk about it?"

"No," said Ryan.

That attitude violated sacred canons so far as Barney was concerned. He managed to look surprised and worried, and he gave Ryan one of those squinting looks that was supposed to rake into his soul. "That's bad for you, you know," he said. "The worst thing people can do with difficulties is to keep them bottled up inside."

The poor man's counselor.

"Things only get worse when you aren't able to talk about them to somebody." Barney leaned forward and looked understanding with all the energy that was in him.

It was then that Ryan found himself thinking angrily: I am from the South, where the individual still works at retaining his sense of privacy in spite of his gossipy town. Where the aristocrats close up all the old empty rooms but will not sell the house!

And that sharp thought amazed him—that he should have laid hold of some value out of that way of life and defended it. I must remember that, he thought; but he did not, of course.

He spoke to Barney as if he had been a child. "I have a headache. That makes me short-tempered. Body-mind. Psychosomatic around and around the circle. Now will you take your cat and go home?"

But Barney did not go until he had given him a long explanation about why one particular headache remedy was far superior to another and added the further free advice that all of this correcting papers at night probably resulted in eyestrain. That was what one had superior pupils for, to help take some of the routine off.

Ryan thanked him drily for his assistance.

Sybil wanted to stay because she had found a break in the baseboard, and she suspected it of mice. She had lain down at the edge of the rug for a long siege and only the tip of her tail jerked occasionally to show she was awake. Barney wound up carrying her home against her will; and she climbed up on his shoulders in protest and bit his neck lightly. Ryan almost gave her another can of milk for that.

When Barney and the cat had finally gone to their own apartment across the hall, Ryan sat down at his desk and took out his pen and filled it, and stared at the point and made some experimental squiggles; and then laid it down on the desk as though it were too heavy to hold up a minute longer.

He no longer knew what it was he had meant to write when he finally got rid of Barney. An acknowledgment of the news to Asa? A note for Jessica? (I congratulate you; you have passed beyond hazard.) A card to go with a wedding gift? (Enclosed please find a shawl, dark gray, which Avery can bring you on cool evenings for the next fifty years.)

He sat there a long time with the pen and paper lying on his desk and he wrote invisibly over and over: *Jessica, Jessica, could you not have waited?*

It was unreasonable and illogical and he was not sixteen. That was the gist of the angry lecture Ryan began to give himself daily, nightly, hourly.

For after that day when the letter came from Asa he was absolutely committed, and the absurdity of it made him furious. He seemed to have lost all chance of putting her out of his mind; her name hung always in the air like an unspoken question. Sometimes he would start up from sleep as though he had heard her walking in his room.

(Barney said if his headaches were bothering him enough to make him *that* ill-tempered, he certainly ought to see a doctor.)

He sent Asa a very short note:

> I certainly wish them well in every way. Please give them my best.

Jim Tetley saw him in the post office; he stood with his jaw set staring at the slot through which he had just dropped his letter.

"Mailing time bombs is illegal, you know," said Jim.

"Huh? What?"

"Anne and I haven't seen you lately. We thought maybe you'd come over for bridge tonight."

"I will," said Ryan with the air of a man making momentous decisions. "I'll bring Mary August."

Jim's eyebrows went up at this but he said nothing. So Ryan went and he took Mary August, and she was every bit as disagreeable as she had been the time before.

Jessica's face—the memory of it—had blurred in his mind until he could only remember the brown eyes and a little bend at the corner of one lip that made her face seem tired; and once in a while he could see again the dappled light as it had lain across her hair in an automobile on a Thanksgiving Day that must have been in some other century.

He thought nothing had ever been so adolescent.

But after a week of it he marched himself to his desk and tugged at his pen until it was firmly in his hand and he wrote, in rather defiant letters, *I will be home for Christmas. Arriving 6 p.m., December 18. Don't bother to meet me, I'll rent a car.* He sent it off to Asa immediately, walking in the sharp air to the corner mailbox where he banged the handle as though it had done him some injury.

And an hour later he had put down the phone from wiring roses (one dozen, very red) to Jessica in the tall old house on Walnut Street with no word inside except his name. It was December 11, 1936, and it had just begun to snow in Wellman, Massachusetts. By the next morning, the world was stacked full of it.

Jim said, "I thought you didn't like that town."

"I'm getting mellow," Ryan said.

Barney told him he thought he might go home and see his mother after all. Would he keep the cat?

"No, I'm going home myself."

"I dread to go, of course. I don't like my mother, never have. She always wanted to devour me. Goldfish actually eat their young, you know. I have an idea her sexual relationship with my father must have been very unsatisfactory."

Ryan told Barney he was the damnedest damn bastard he ever knew, but since Barney thought he was kidding it didn't make any difference.

Sybil wound up in the wind and snow where, it turned out, she lived bountifully on birds that were too cold to fly.

When he came into Greenway a week later and rented the Ford that was always kept on reserve in Elk's Garage he was very tired. He didn't feel like coping with Harry Elk, who very seldom rented the car and was never sure what he ought to charge for it. Bertha Elk said finally she thought five dollars was fine and they would pick it up on Monday. She also told Ryan that she thought he was looking peakèd.

He agreed with the whole thing, even the free medical advice.

He felt too tired to drive the thing home when he finally had it and had paid the five dollars. It was not from effort but rather from a dread of getting to that house, going up those steps, and finding Jessica happy. Or finding her unhappy. Which would be worse or better?

There was a light rain so he drove very slowly from Greenway to Stoneville. He told himself this was only being careful.

But time and distance are only so long and no longer and when it was dark he drove up to the curb in front of the house, turned off the ignition, rolled the windows up, checked the brakes at least three times. Only then did he look up and see the old house and it was suddenly beautiful because *she* was inside; and when he thought of that he could not get out of the car and up the walk soon enough.

He hid his disappointment when it was Avery who answered his knock.

"Ryan!" The two of them shook hands like brothers.

Although it hurt his throat he said, "How's the bridegroom?"

"Fine, fine," said Avery. "Everybody ought to get married. Come in. This all you brought? One bag?"

"The life of a teacher is a frugal one," said Ryan, lifting it into the hall and then, because he could not stand it any longer, "Where's Jessica?"

"Said she wanted some air. Walked around the block," said Avery. "I thought she'd be back by the time you got here."

Ryan was very pleased. Perhaps she, too, had dreaded that first minute of seeing him. Perhaps it confirmed things.

Asa said, "Ryan, is that you?"

"Of course it's me." He kissed her when she came through the curtains that hung in the dining-room doorway.

"This horrible rain!" said Asa vaguely. He could already hear the fire crackling. "It's been raining for two days. Come in the parlor and get warm."

"In a minute. I want to see Lady Malveena about getting something to eat. You've already eaten?"

She said they had. "Jessica should be back very soon." To Avery she added, "I really don't think Jessica ought to be out walking at night. And in a cold rain like this!" Avery said he was sure she had wrapped up well.

He went back to the kitchen. Lady Malveena had heard him come in; she was already setting things out of the oven onto the kitchen table. She rested a hand on his arm. "It's good you're home," she said.

He found it amazingly good himself. "I'm hungry."

"It's coming," she said. "Let me heat the gravy. Cold potatoes is an insult to the stomach."

He agreed that they were. "How have you been?"

"Tollable."

"And how are things?"

"All right," she said. "You better put some salt on them potatoes. Mister Avery don't eat salt these days so everybody got to suffer."

He raised his eyebrows, salted the potatoes and accepted hot rich gravy.

"Miss Asa were right pleased about things going ahead."

He could not keep the word out of his mouth. "And Jessica?"

"I've not heard her complaining."

But Ryan thought she said it a little grimly and he hoped with all his heart that Jessica was miserable.

Then Jessica herself came in at the back, hurrying; he heard her coming through the back yard and up the two steps and all of a rush to the door. "Has he come?" she cried and saw him, and stood very still.

He was on his feet. "Jessica," he said and swallowed. Lady Malveena made a great noise of opening her stove, which she stared into suspiciously.

Then Jessica put out both her hands in front of her, like some gracious lady. "Hello, Ryan. How good you look!"

He took a step toward her and covered her hands, meaning to speak only an ordinary greeting and heard himself instead ask roughly, "Why didn't you wait? Why didn't you wait at least until I could write you?"

She said, "Oh, my goodness." He thought it was probably the least appropriate answer in the world. Lady Malveena said in a muffled voice (she had her head halfway in the oven) that they didn't make stoves this day and time like they used to.

Jessica took her hands away and stared down at them. "I don't know," she said in another minute. He saw again the little dip in her chin which made her mouth seem lax and tired, and he thought that her eyes had grown older for the two weeks that had passed. "Where are the others?"

"In the parlor. By the fire." He could not control his bitterness. "Asa always builds a fire in the hearth when it rains. She does it every winter. She'll do it for the next three dozen winters."

"What does that matter?" Jessica said, putting out her chin. But she *was* tired. He was ashamed.

"It doesn't," he said. He made his voice gentle. "I wish you'd waited."

"I was afraid," she said simply.

That didn't matter either, now. She had not waited and he had —there was no logic to it.

Lady Malveena was terribly embarrassed and she could not look into the oven forever. "I'll fix another cup," she chirped, emerging now, carefully not looking at either of them. "The coffee's hot. You'll have a cup, won't you, Miss Jessica? It's cold out."

Jessica sat down. "Yes," she said. "It's very cold." She propped up one hand and put her head into it as though it had long been too heavy for her. Ryan sat down across from her. She said, "I didn't know . . . I wasn't sure."

Lady Malveena turned on the water for no reason except to keep herself from hearing. In the kitchen it seemed absurdly loud.

Jessica looked up at him, still holding her head in the palm of her hand. "Why should I think that you . . . well. You know."

"Having been such a damned idiot, I shouldn't have come back at all," said Ryan angrily. "I ought to have known better than to come." And all the time he spoke Jessica was shaking her brown head No no no, without ever taking it out of her hand.

They said some very silly things. Jessica said that they didn't even know each other. Ryan said he had fallen in love with her the moment he saw her. Jessica said they had to be sensible.

Lady Malveena turned off the water and slipped the cup of coffee almost surreptitiously on the table. She began to edge out of the kitchen, muttering something about closing one of her windows against the cold night air. She never, of course, opened her windows from one summer to the next; on the first of September every year she nailed them tight. The two of them never knew when she left.

"I half thought I'd dreamed all of it. You never said anything. Not really."

He jumped and sloshed his coffee and burned his hand. "Dreamed all of it?"

She said simply that there had never been any man like him in her experience. "Why should I think you . . . Did you hurt yourself?"

"No, no." He was impatient. He was absurdly angry, like a man with all his armies massed and no one to set them on. "This can all be undone. And it will be." His voice was harsh; this time he was going to take whatever action was required. "We'll make this whole thing right. You and Avery . . ." He saw then by her face that she was shocked and he stopped without finishing.

"Oh, no!" said Jessica; and he thought, *Damn this town.* Damn this queer respectability! He was just about to damn it in words when Avery came in from the dining room, smiling.

"Oh, there you are!" he said to Jessica. "I was just getting anxious. It's very cold and wet outside." (*I brought your gray shawl, dear.*) "It's good to have Ryan home."

Jessica said with an averted face that it certainly was; and Ryan gulped his coffee, furious, burning his tongue.

"I'm glad we're all present and accounted for," said Avery. He smiled at his wife again. "Where did you go?"

"Nowhere. Just walking."

Let her alone! screamed Ryan silently.

"Tomorrow we'll have to go Christmas shopping," Avery continued. "What do you think we ought to get for Ryan?"

Jessica lifted her eyes and looked across the table into Ryan's and then away, and up to Avery's face. The smile was not large but it was courteous. "Something nice," she said firmly. "Something very nice for my new brother." She looked back at him again, her brown eyes very wide and blank.

That was the way it was going to be. That was how she would have it.

Avery was jovial. "What would you like to have, Ryan?"

Your wife. Would you give me your wife for Christmas, please?

He said, "I never know how to answer questions like that."

"Christmas is wonderful," said Avery to both of them. "It's a shame we can't behave as if it were Christmas all the time."

"Yes," said Jessica.

"I guess we'll just have to make your gift a surprise then," said Avery.

Ryan could not help himself. He watched her while he said, "I've already had one surprise in your unexpected wedding. I don't know how many of them I can take."

He heard her breath break slightly against her teeth. She said she thought she would go in and see what Asa was doing. In another minute she added, "I think I'll get warm by that fire." And she gave Ryan a level look.

Well, maybe she was right. Maybe it would be able to warm her deeper than he believed.

"You'll have exams soon after you get back, won't you?" asked Avery when she had gone.

"Yes. About two weeks."

Avery banged him on the shoulder. "Then you'll have to take things easy while you're here. They say those things are harder on teachers than students. You just rest up while you're home."

Ryan said he guessed he would do that.

There was never any other two weeks that lasted the length of those.

It was like the picture shows he had built as a child in grammar school, made of a cutaway box with a crank which rolled past the clumsy crayon-scenes drawn on the back of old wallpaper. That was how those fourteen December days went past, jerkily and by fits and starts, looking just as unreal as those grade school movies, looking as though some careful six-year-old had drawn in the precise round yellow sun and then only colored the top half of the sky and given the whole thing away.

Because he was so much aware of the hypocrisies it seemed to Ryan all the Godwins passed each other like the stiff stick-men in such drawings. They smiled falsely, put out lifeless hands, sat in chairs as though every bone were an agony. The shoulders and elbows of all of them were built to painful right angles.

Even Asa knew that something was wrong. She came to decide that Ryan and Jessica did not like each other and that this was all connected with Ryan's thought that Avery and she should never have married.

"You ought to try to be a little nicer to Jessica," she would say. "I think you make her feel strange."

Or she would scold, "You and Jessica have hardly said a word to each other all day. Why don't you get to know each other?" She thought they ought to talk together, perhaps go some place together in the car.

Often she said to Ryan, "I've never known you to be so unfair with anyone before!" He fell to giving Asa looks that might have made a lesser woman stone.

Avery, of course, was not aware of any tension. He would say to the two of them in bland conviction, "I'm certainly glad you get along so well." Even Asa was irritated with him. He went about the house smiling, dropping a few maxims, nodding his head. Every day he rode dutifully to the real estate office with Asa where he fingered paper clips and made small talk with clients. Avery could not *sell* anything; he had no enthusiasm to impart. He served the function of a glorified receptionist; he sat talking to people about the virtues of owning a home ("Every man needs a little corner of the world he can call his own . . .") and after a while Asa came out and turned this into something more specific.

As for Lady Malveena, through all of this she dusted and cleaned rather feverishly; the house had never been scrubbed so hard or so often. She walked in and out of the rooms muttering, and began to save her nail parings in a butter dish against an evil day. She was especially gentle with Jessica, but she wasted no sympathy on Ryan. "What's done is done," she snapped, "and what ain't done is already too late for."

"You're a great help," growled Ryan. He was not very even-tempered those days.

"Some cakes just bakes soggy in the middle," said Lady Malveena with a sniff. "Time to stop *that's* in the making. I never riz one afterwards to this day."

"I ought to leave."

"*Sure!*" She was very belligerent. "Just tuck your tail right under!"

Ryan said that inconsistency was a female prerogative; and Lady Malveena said she never heard him talk that way except when he was already out-argued.

Thus it was left for Ryan and Jessica to pass self-consciously in the great old house, to stand aside politely in hallways, to sit across from each other at luncheon when the others were uptown. Jessica was very still and she never looked into his face.

This part of it lasted for three cold days and nights.

And late on the third night both of them came downstairs for a book to read; each groped through the darkened library toward the light switch, not knowing the other was there. When their hands touched on the fixture Jessica let out a sharp little cry and jerked her hand away. At this, Ryan had meant to say politely "It's only me," but before he could even form the words in his mouth his hands were already out, catching her, drawing her in, and then there was nothing to be said. It was no longer necessary. He felt her stiffen once before her mouth went loose (could this be the same mouth that had always seemed so small and tired?) and then she came forward against him and caught him on the back with all her fingers.

She made some sound from her mouth into his, but it was not a word. It did not matter.

They were thus locked warm in the dark of old Flambert Godwin's library and every part of her was sweet to him; he flexed his knee and slipped it between her two and she came in closer than ever. He thought briefly how a man and a woman filled up all the space in each other, took up the slack, slipped into the hollows; and then he thought of nothing at all but Jessica and the feel of her and the depths of her mouth.

He said her name very softly but she said nothing, nothing at all; and when he took his mouth away to speak she was impatient. She kissed him again.

He began to love her with his hand, cautiously at first so as not to startle, and then going lightly down her back and cupping her hip and once very quickly inside her thigh. At this he felt her stiffen toward him in the stomach and then heard her say, "Oh Lord"; and he slid his hand between her legs and stroked her, very easy.

She put her head onto his shoulder and turned her face in his neck and he could not tell from the sounds if she was crying or only breathing hard. He tried to kiss her at the eyes to tell.

But in another minute she had pulled free and leaned back silently against the wall. He heard her breath coming and going as though her chest were too small to hold it all, and in the dark she put out one small hand and touched his temple and ran her finger on his ear.

It was more than he could stand; he reached for her again but this time she was gone to one side and behind him, and out the door into the hall. He heard her feet on the stairs, running.

He said to himself, *She is my brother's wife*; but he did not at that moment believe it. He did not believe anything except that he had held her and touched her only a minute before. That much was real. If beyond these walls the whole world had gone to crumbles, he would not that moment have cared.

All the next day Jessica went crimson at the very sight of him. Talking, she would run out of breath in the middle of words and sentences; she talked too rapidly so that her tongue was always fumbling along a syllable behind.

But as for Ryan, he had never felt so strong or so male. He told himself (with a certain satisfaction) that today he must let her alone; he must not hurry her. He must let her achieve again her own balance. Overnight he had grown sure, because he remembered there had been nothing of her withheld the night before.

Now, in fact, he could even smile. Her embarrassment and confusion made him feel very tender. Whenever he came near her that day he wanted to catch her sleeve and say to her gravely, "It will be all right, Jessica. You'll see."

And whenever she stammered or would not face him or meet his eyes, he had to turn his head to hide the pleasure on his face.

With Avery he felt a little strange; with Asa, defiant. Only before Lady Malveena did he experience some of the embarrassment Jessica felt. When he came into Lady Malveena's kitchen he was sure she knew that something had been subtly altered. He was in dread lest she might question him about it.

At dinner that evening, Avery said he was going to the church to practice a few things for Sunday.

"I'll go with you," Jessica said quickly.

Avery protested that the church was too cold for her to sit in it and wait for him. "Why don't you drive me over and come back for me later? Maybe you'd like to take the car a while."

Asa wanted some of the tension reconciled. "Why don't you and Ryan drive around and look at the Christmas decorations? Some of them are very nice." The room was full of silence.

Ryan was considerate; he did not even look at her. He turned his knife carefully in his hand, studying the pattern of the silver. "Would you like that, Jessica?" he said, trying to seem unconcerned.

It was she who lifted her head to look at him. "Very much," she said steadily, watching him. He found he could not return that gaze for very long.

"Fine then." He was grateful for the careful tiny flowers on the knife handle. He traced them with a nail. "When did you want to go, Avery?"

"Right after supper." The matter was agreed upon.

When they walked out to the car together, they kept more than an arm's length between them. Ryan had a sudden feeling that the whole world was full of eyes, that the very leaves were blinking at them. He opened the door and she got in the middle of the front seat, between the two brothers.

"Pick me up about nine, nine thirty." Avery was saying.

"All right."

They drove through the main part of town. A great Christmas tree stood in the center of the square where the Palmer Building faced the *Beacon* Office which, in turn, faced the Stoneville Hotel. There was nothing on the fourth corner, that building having been destroyed by fire some years ago. People used the empty lot to park in, especially at night because it was near the picture show.

Avery got out at the church and Ryan came around and got into the car under the wheel.

"About nine o'clock?" said Ryan.

"Make it ten or after," said Avery. He was looking at the sky. "I think it might snow. It would be nice to have snow for Christmas."

"Temperature's about right," Ryan agreed.

"Manger scene's nice, isn't it?" said Avery. "I helped fix it myself." He indicated a well-lighted Nativity on the church lawn, and Ryan said it was very nice.

After Avery had tried the church door and gotten it open he waved toward the car, and Ryan and Jessica drove away.

"Well?" said Ryan.

But she was working hard to be his sister-in-law and no more. "Well, what?" she said. He shrugged.

They drove back through town, past the bright Christmas Tree and alongside the silver wreaths which ringed all the traffic lights. There was a papier-maché reproduction of the wise men, and the star on the roof of Stoneville's major department store, and "We Three Kings" was amplified from it, very loud. Every other verse there was a monstrous clanging of recorded chimes.

"One thing about the Christmas spirit in 1936," said Ryan, "if you're going to have it, you might as well have it full volume. Anything less is probably un-American." He was trying to put her at her ease. He glanced across but she was looking out the car window fixedly, and he thought that if she kept her head held so stiffly very long she would get a crick in her neck.

Her voice was cool. "Are you talking about the commercialization of Christmas?"

"Lord, no! I leave that to Avery. I'm sure he talks about it often enough."

She said only, "Yes, he does."

They drove past the Court House where the pyramids of old cannon balls were standing and saw there was a spotlight on the War Dead Memorial and the holly tree which stood behind it, and that a small paper Santa Claus was standing brightly under that holly tree. The shadow from the statue of the Minute Man fell blackly across the lawn, and the very tip of his flintlock shaded the face of Santa Claus.

In silence they drove, out by Memorial Park—which looked like a dark jungle in the night—and around Gateswood Drive, where Mayor Carmichael and Lemuel Garris and most of the County Commissioners lived. All of these had blue multipointed stars hanging at the entrances of their large houses.

"Conservative," Ryan pointed out. He was glad to see her smile a little.

Other houses in that neighborhood had hills of blue electric candles at the windows, and a few enterprising wives who read the *Ladies' Home Journal* had spatterpainted snow scenes on their picture windows.

"I think we ought to put up a tree," said Jessica wistfully.

He would have shaken stars down for her if he could, real ones. "Sure," he said. "A big one."

"Do you usually have a tree?"

He considered. "Not since my father died. He used to have one because it was expected. Asa felt they dropped too many needles on the carpet."

"Will she mind if I ask for one this year?"

He looked at her closely. "What does that matter?"

Her jaw was firm. "I want everything to go smoothly." I want to be a good wife. I want the world safe and understandable.

"Did your Aunt Victoria have a tree?"

"No."

"How about the other aunts—the ones you grew up with?"

She said, "They were all very much older." Then she said, "Look there!" and on the windows of some apartment someone had written things in soapflakes. *Peace on Earth, Good will to men!* said the soapflakes. A snowman made of Duz and Rinso and Bon Ami sat underneath.

They came back through town and saw a little boy whose face was growing violet from cold, standing at a shopwindow where the eternal electric train went around and around forever. Both of them smiled at that.

"I'd like to have a little boy someday," said Jessica.

But not Avery's. Ryan could not help but protest inside himself. Not Avery's little boy, Jessica. He glanced across at her again to see if she had heard his thought, but she was a pale and indistinct figure. He could not see what was on her face. She had on a dark suit and a white blouse which seemed to shine when the coat parted. Under that she was very soft—he knew that from last night. When he thought of that he found it difficult to look back at the road again.

As she relaxed, she began to ask him questions. She wanted to know what all the Godwins had been like as children. She wanted to know what they had done, where they had played, if they had been happy. He was as honest as he could be without putting himself in the position of criticizing her husband.

But one thing he could not prevent himself from doing. He found himself—while never directly saying a word against Avery—always pointing out the differences between Avery and himself. He painted the contrast in bold black strokes. He was not proud of it, but he could not help himself.

Then he sensed that she was growing quieter and quieter, and he stopped talking.

After a minute he said, "I apologize for that, Jessica."

"Why should you?" In another minute she added, "I knew what I was doing."

Neither of them could think of anything to say after that. They rode in silence, and if the whole town had been jammed with Christmas trees—if, even, they had been growing in the streets—Jessica and Ryan would not have noticed.

"What time is it?" she said.

He looked at the Western Union clock as they went by. Western Union was closed, of course; it admitted of no emergencies except between nine A.M. and one P.M. He said, "It's about nine thirty."

"Let's go on to the church."

"All right."

They parked the car in front of the Trinity Baptist Church and sat for a minute listening to the sound of Avery at the organ. It was "Hark the Herald Angels Sing," and Avery was playing it with vigor, like a drinking song in an operetta.

Ryan and Jessica walked across the lawn to the manger scene which had a real stable made of pine slabs (*courtesy Bryan's Lumberyard* said a discreet sign) and Jessica stepped beyond the lights to see what was in the manger.

She came back looking very disappointed. "I thought at least they'd have a baby doll," she said.

"What's there?"

"Nothing. Straw around a stick of wood. That's all."

The organ went into "Good King Wenceslaus." Avery was rolling the bass chords upward with a marvelous thumpthump effect. It ought to have gone with a marching division at the very least.

Ryan and Jessica walked behind the stable and it was much darker there than they had realized. He thought she looked distressed at this, but he could not tell. His eyes had not adjusted from the spotlight on the scene. He thought, At least I can touch her hand.

But she had moved on ahead of him, very quickly, and had stopped in front of a small stone bench which sat before dark bulbous shrubbery.

"Remember this bench?" she said. She leaned forward in the dark and began to trace lettering with a finger.

"No," said Ryan. He put his hand out to touch the lettering himself but her hand was too near and he took hold of it instead. She did not draw it away.

Then she began to recite what was written on the bench. "Lord, make me an instrument of thy peace . . ." She kept her face turned down, away from his, as if she were reading in all that darkness. It was the prayer of St. Francis of Assisi; she turned the words on her tongue as though each of them was too valuable to let go and Ryan was touched and at the same time a bit embarrassed.

But when she had finished she did not comment on whether it was beautiful or reverent; she said only that it had once seemed dreadful to her that people should sit upon prayers carved into benches in this way.

It was very easy. He had her hand in his and when he drew her forward she came very quietly into his arms and hid her face beside his collar. Nothing was said. They simply stood very close for a minute.

After a while she whispered, "This is terrible."

"No," he said. He turned up her face to see into her eyes, but she kept them closed. He kissed her in the hollow of each one, the way he had kissed her clumsily at the railway station, and then on the lips, very slowly, opening them up beneath his own. There was a moment of timelessness, so unhurried they were, so still it was in the shadow where they stood behind a scene two thousand years old.

This was different from the kiss in the library at home. It was not because Avery was near (Avery? Who was he?) nor was it because of the dark church rising into stars behind them; this was a promise they were making. Ryan was trying to tell her: This is more than flesh. Their very restraint was a vow between them.

"Jessica." He turned her face up again after the kiss and this time she looked at him. "I've always loved you," he said. She tightened her arms and stood on tiptoe high enough to kiss him underneath the ear. He ran his hand up to the nape of her neck and spread his fingers on her head, underneath the wealth of hair. She was wearing it loose; he liked the feel of it falling about his hand.

She rubbed her face on his and as her mouth came by she kissed him. Then she said, muffled into his other cheek, "We shouldn't, Ryan. I shouldn't." But it was not for him or for her that she said it; it was to someone unconcerned, the dead Saint Francis or the porcelain Mary watching over her straw and her stick of wood.

Ryan kissed her for an answer, less gently this time, and she put her hands on his neck and moved them in patterns against the prickles of his hair. When he turned his mouth slightly to one side she said his name over several times. He kissed her in the ear. Then she leaned back in his arms as in a swing.

"It sounds like bad movie dialogue but I *have* been an awful fool," she said.

"I thought you were never going to admit that much," he said. "Now we have some place to start from."

"I've never felt so helpless." Then some of her strength seemed to sag and she put her face into the front of his coat. "What will become of us?" she said.

He took her shoulders, made her sit down beside him on top of the carven prayer.

"That's just what we have to talk about. Jessica, you must see that we have to do something about all of this. Make some plans to change it." She had already begun to shake her head and he raised his voice a little. "I didn't say I thought it was simple or comfortable, but it has to be done. Surely you can see that."

She said, shaking her head, "I couldn't, I couldn't. Ryan, I simply couldn't." And then, with a child's fierce simplicity, "I'd rather die."

He wanted to shake her. "You want to add one error on top of the first, is that it?" He had been holding her hand but now he dropped it. "What else do you think you can do, Jessica? Do you want to be Mrs. Avery Godwin that badly? Is it that important to you to go on singing in the choir with all the other matrons? And as for me, you kiss me during vacations in dark corners. Is that all you want?" He was angry; he grew childish himself. "You want to go on sleeping in his bed, not for love but for respectability?"

She was upset. "Hush," she said, and leaning forward sought his mouth. "Oh Ryan, hush!" But this time he turned his face away from hers.

"What else then, Jessica? Slip down the hall to me? Is that better? Is that easier, safer?"

She was on her feet. "I can't talk about it now."

"We've got to talk about it!" He caught her arm. "That's what happened before—I didn't say anything. And you wouldn't wait. Now you don't want to wait again; you want to run away. What does that solve, what does it prove?"

She said, "Let go of me." Her voice was very sharp.

"You're going to press me into the same pattern you chose for yourself. Is that it, Jessica? Pretending and pretending and pretending! On stage twenty-four hours a day! The only time you can be yourself is when you're in the bathroom with the door locked. Is that it? Can you do it, Jessica?"

She shook free from his hand with a rage which astonished him. "I've done worse things!" she snapped. "How many old women do you think I've lived with? How much of my life do you think I've been nothing but a glorified servant, running up and down stairs for all of them? Do you think I liked that? Do you think I wanted to be polite all that time?" Her voice lost some of its sharpness. "Besides, it would have been all right without you. In time I could have believed what everyone said—a good marriage, a good secure position." There was a note of sadness pressed too far, worn too long. "And I could have loved him! Do you hear me, Ryan Godwin? In time I could have loved him—I could have loved him off the top of my mind. I could have called him 'Dear' and it would not have sounded strange at all!" She was beginning to cry; when he reached for her she thrashed her arms to knock his back. "I could have clucked about him. Tended his colds. Minded the children. I would have been safe, Ryan! All of my life I would have been absolutely safe; nothing could have touched me!"

He reached for her again but this time she ran toward the car, striking the edge of the mock stable so that the flimsy structure wobbled and the pine slab roof lurched a little. When he came after her he was suddenly aware of the organ. He had not heard it for a while but now the air seemed to be full of "Silent Night, Holy Night" played high in the treble, very penetrating.

She was already in the car with the door left open, and she had her face in one hand. She shook her head. "Don't touch me, Ryan. Please don't touch me. Leave me alone."

"Jessica, I'm sorry."

"Will you please and forever leave me alone." Her voice was very flat.

"I love you."

Nothing. She kept her hand over her face.

"Do you want me to go tell Avery we're here?"

The voice was still absolutely flat. "Yes, you'd better."

He wanted to touch her. "Jessica . . ."

She looked up at him furiously. "Yes. Yes yes yes. Go tell Avery we're here. Please go get him!"

"All *right*." He slammed the door.

On the way home, Avery did not notice how silent the other two were. He told them the B flat was sticking again. He asked Ryan if he thought "Good King Wenceslaus" was not quite sacred enough for the sanctuary and Ryan said he thought it was as sacred as all hell.

"My goodness," said Avery mildly. "How were the decorations, Jessica?"

Jessica said they were fine, just fine.

At the Godwin house she was out and up the walk before he was able to make a move to walk in with her, so he told Avery he would put the car away.

Avery got out. "There's a hole in the drive on the left," he said. "Don't hit it too hard."

If it had been a thousand feet deep Ryan would gladly have gone into it headforemost. He drove the Buick into the drive (it was a small hole really; he hardly felt it; and turned off the motor and sat in the dark and choked the steering wheel. Then he had a cigarette before he went inside.

It was beginning to snow. The flakes were still few and small and far between; he watched them land and vanish on the windshield in front of him—cold, delicate, quickly destroyed.

When he walked to the house (where the lights had already gone out in the room that was Avery's and Jessica's) he held his palm out once into a little flurry, and every flake was like a pinprick on his hand, leaving a tiny pain.

Christmas, 1936: It came whitely.

In a Southern town like Stoneville, good snows were still rare enough to be altogether remarkable, especially to the children. These were out all day long, shrieking and running, and their sliding places left the sidewalks too slick for grownups to walk upon. There were some sleds and every hill in town was precious. One very good hill was roped off from traffic by the Stoneville police department, and at night children and their parents came over and built a big bonfire at the top and went careening wildly down. Between rides the fathers would warm their hands at the bonfires and admit sheepishly to each other that they were not as young as they once were. All of them said this in mild surprise, as if they had doubted it would ever be true of them.

Ryan went over one night and stood around the bonfire and had a nip of corn whiskey and talked to some of the men he remembered. He went down the hill once with four younger boys on top of him. They were so heavy all he wanted to do was concentrate on getting air in and out of his lungs all the way to the bottom. When he got off he felt his whole body could be no more than an inch thick.

Avery and Jessica did not go sledding of course. Avery did not go because he had never seen what pleasure there was in that (or in baseball, or in books, or in any form of expending oneself; and Jessica did not go because she was Avery's wife.

Asa loathed the snow. It was damp; it clogged her nasal passages by its very presence. It was, after all, only a colder form of rain and she had always hated rain.

The snow seemed especially appropriate to Ryan that year. It had taken too many drab ordinary things and made them appear beautiful, but underneath they were still the same. Outside the windows of the house, Walnut Street and its lawns and trees were iced over like a succulent cake so that the world seemed full of peace and beauty; and inside the Godwin house, he and Jessica had spread the surface of their lives with falsity. All the time he knew how thin the coating really was and what sharp twigs and dead brown leaves lay underneath. So the very beauty of that December landscape set his teeth on edge. It was like living in a perpetual Christmas card—he did not believe in it.

Whenever he was outdoors he found himself scuffing his foot in the snow down to the dirt and the leaves beneath, looking, he supposed, for something *real*.

They put up a Christmas tree in spite of Asa's grumblings. Avery said he didn't see what there was to get so excited about. But Ryan put it up almost in rage: he bought the biggest one he could find; he carried it into the house with his hands full of pricks; and he himself went uptown and came home with enough decorations for four or five trees. Jessica did most of the decorating. The coolness of the others made her nervous, but when it was done she could not help herself; her eyes shone. "It's magnificent!" she said. "Thank you, Ryan."

He was triumphant. He almost swaggered from her pleasure.

On Christmas Eve, Lady Malveena brought out a small jar of wine which she swore was nearly ten years old ("No ma'am, I didn't snitch none of them grapes last year!") and Asa tolerated while Ryan had a tremendous amount of it and Avery and Jessica had a tiny glass. Avery said it made him feel like he was taking communion. And Ryan wondered: If you ever got Jessica drunk, what would she be like?

Lady Malveena was miserable the whole holiday season. She seemed to have penetrated into the heart of their peril; she went through the rooms heavily and would not even look at the Christmas tree, as though it were obscene.

But she knew it pleased Jessica. And when Jessica was near, she praised it.

Ryan sensed her feelings. He wanted to tell her: Don't you see there will be no explosions? There will be only years and years of outward sweet decorum?

On Christmas morning they breakfasted late in a steamy kitchen. Ryan was already uncomfortable, wishing he was back in bed.

Across the table Asa sat like an aristocrat who had, nonetheless, a warm heart. "Your first Christmas with us, Jessica," she said. Jessica swallowed as though the coffee in her throat had suddenly gone hard.

Avery smiled. "The first of many."

Lady Malveena said loudly that she thought the snow on the ground was right pretty.

"Ryan must think so!" Asa said. "I haven't seen you out in the snow so much since you were a little boy. I think you're coming into your second childhood."

"Probably am."

Lady Malveena confided to her breastbone that they could use some childhoods around this place.

He didn't mean to say it then, but he did. "I don't think I'll get home for Christmas next year," and then he was sorry for having said it. It was too sharp a weapon to draw out on a Christmas morning, even a morning in which he was unhappy and irritated. And when Jessica jerked her head and looked at him with her face grown suddenly sharp and tight, he felt worse. He wanted to say: Don't look like that, Jessica! Everyone will know!

For by now he found himself accepting her own wish to be left secure. He had begun to guard and undergird her position.

She had turned her head to look at him too intently.

"Or maybe I'll get home after all." He tried to make it light. "I'll wait till I've seen this year's presents."

Jessica managed a shaky smile.

And behind them all during breakfast Lady Malveena plodded from stove to sink and back again, like one taking a long and unrewarding journey. "You gonna sit in here all day?" she said finally.

Avery was the first one on his feet. "Of course not! It's Christmas!"

And here we go, marching to Jerusalem, marching through the dining room, carrying our heavy merriment. We hanged our harps upon the willows. Ryan followed the rest of them.

Finally they stood around the tree. They looked like children at an outing where no one is supposed to spill the jam or wet his pants.

But Avery was trying hard. "A real old-fashioned Christmas!" He beamed. And when he put a hand on Jessica's arm, Ryan had all he could do to keep from taking it off, gently but firmly.

"That tree is wonderful," Jessica said. He knew she wished he had not come; without him standing there she would have been able to smile at Avery; she could have nodded and appeared to enjoy herself. Now she was too conscious of his words about pretending; none of these things would ever seem natural when she did them under his gaze.

"Well, let's open them!" Avery said.

Asa suggested that Ryan hand them out, and for one minute Jessica looked at him very carefully. "Yes, you do that, Ryan." You be the Santa Claus. Come on in, the water's fine.

He stooped at the tree, glad to have something to do.

Picking up the first box and glancing at the tag (it was for his sister) he knew still another time how empty is anything given with less than love and he was ashamed of what he had bought for Asa and Avery. He was ashamed for not loving them; he had a fear that he might suddenly turn from the tree and say apologetically, "I wish we might have loved each other, even a little." The fear was so strong in him that for a moment he was half afraid he might actually have said it, the way one is afraid he may have let his guard slip for a moment and laughed aloud in church.

He said, not looking up, "For Asa." He handed out the red box toward the sofa where she sat. "For Jessica," "For Avery," "For Lady Malveena," and so on. He stacked his own to one side, not really wanting to open them.

Avery went back to stand in the kitchen door and call Lady Malveena and in a minute she came in, wiping her hands on a dish towel and looking uneasy. There issued some embarrassed silence, broken by the tearing of paper and popping of string.

Then Asa said, "Why Ryan! How beautiful!" And she held aloft the soft shawl that was cool blue and had come from Nassau. He nodded, hating the thing, not able to look at her. She put it around her shoulders. "You can think of me in rainy weather!"

There was a wallet for Avery from his sister and a pipe and pouch from Ryan and a dressing gown from Jessica. (Ryan hated that, the thought of those two together and Avery wearing a new green dressing gown.)

And Asa had his shawl and a china music box from Avery and Jessica which was rather pretty and played "Juanita" in a faintly mournful fashion.

Ryan had shirts and ties from Asa (she believed firmly that no bachelor remembered these things, and that everything he owned was frayed and buttonless); and a really fine set of books from Avery and Jessica, a collection of the Russian novelists bound in soft leather. These pleased him; he ran his fingers up and down the spines.

"I'll like these," he said smiling, glad to have come to some sincerity at last. He looked at Jessica when he said it (she had chosen them; he was sure of that) and he was glad to see the little mouth smile and the dark eyes lighten and crinkle at the corners. He was moved because his pleasure gave her so much pleasure in turn; and he was also sad because their fulfillments were as small as this—a look exchanged across a Christmas room.

He went on looking at her face—the lashes were long and the brows delicate and lighter than her hair. When she was pleased, he noticed, she had a habit of smiling to herself and bending her head and running one hand awkwardly around her neck. It was an oddly boyish gesture that made him smile.

She had not yet opened his gift. She had already unwrapped a pair of blue bedroom slippers from Avery (the casualness of this intimacy outraged Ryan, and for the first time he thought that all married people were brazen) and a set of brushes and combs from Asa. These Ryan recognized; once they had belonged to his mother and had been kept packed in a satin box. Now they had been cleaned and polished, and the faintly yellow edges were lovely.

She looked up at him and saw that he was looking at her and smiling and her face stiffened. All her natural pleasure in the combs

was furious with Jessica (narrow-minded, priggish—she will never risk anything); and then he was suffused with tenderness. The curve of her brow could do it, a movement of her hand.

He could walk into a room so angry with her that there was no room for love and when she turned to look at him all of it went to nothing.

When he was out of the house he was more objective, and his behavior amused him. He had always believed that the women who came closest to being important to him were the Loved-Not-Wisely-But-Too-Well variety; and who had ever thought there would be a small-town careful Jessica, who did not believe in divorce?

He did not make it till New Year's. That *would* have been an irony. He preferred to go into 1937 without the sight of Jessica and Avery working crossword puzzles. That was something they had taken to doing in the evenings and it set his teeth on edge.

On the 29th of December he found her in the upstairs hall and he said (he had to tell *her*, first), "I'm going back tomorrow."

Her hand jumped to her face but she did not say anything.

He put out his own hand (How clumsy the body is at the few times it might serve you with some grace! he thought) and put it down again. "I have to go, Jessica."

She nodded her head, but the fingers kept a little cage across her mouth.

The silence angered him. Had he hoped she would protest? Did he have any wild idea she would come away with him? He said, more harshly, "I won't be back until summer and maybe not by then."

She repeated his words wonderingly. "Not until summer," and suddenly leaned forward and put her forehead on his chest and her hands up on his shoulders. He had not expected it; he was off-balance. Rocking suddenly, he found his hands again and put them at her waist and, with a groan, he wrapped her close. "Jessica, Jessica." He said it into her hair and the very name was despairing.

She raised her head and the hairline, sure enough, came to his chin. "I have to say . . ." Here she swallowed so the sentence was awkward and broken. "I have to say—I love you, Ryan." And then her voice splintered on his name and she put her head back against him and cried as a child cries, wailing, knowing deep down there is no help for it. Nothing can be undone.

He was numb with his feelings; he kissed her hair and temples.

Someone will hear, he thought, and then thought, *Let them hear!* He nearly broke her in his arms. And the very misery of her crying convinced him—it was true; there is nothing to be done against the world; it is too strong. They ground their faces together, hungry for comfort.

Knowing she would not, he said, "Jessica, come with me. You need never see this place again. You need never see any of these people."

Her crying slowed. She almost smiled at him and laid a finger at the edge of his mouth. "How silly you are," she said tenderly, after the way of women. He thought of Hecuba watching the city burn. He put his hands about the strong bones of her face. Between his hands and those bones they would hold her face forever just the way it was, the eyes set just so, the mouth almost smiling, the cheeks full with a tear or so streaked down.

"It isn't silly," he said softly, holding her face against time. "It's the other business that's silly. The business of trying to act as if none of this ever happened. Trying to act like nothing else is going to happen."

"What's going to happen?" She was almost ready to tease him.

"We're going to make love, you and I—one time or another, one place or another. Come with me now, tomorrow, when I go." He pulled her in; he would make her go with kisses.

But the teasing faded; this time she only leaned against him like one tired and her hand slipped down his neck and lay flat against his chest. She said, half sleepily, "I hear your heart."

"Do you?" He was a little sharp at the change of subject.

But Jessica had closed her eyes listening to it. She moved her hand slowly across his ribs until she found the spot where the beat was strong and sure; then she looked up at him wonderingly. "It is this that keeps you alive," she said.

He kissed her before she had closed her mouth on the final word.

Every muscle in her stilled. "Did I hear somebody?"

"Only Lady Malveena," he said. "She's downstairs."

"I'm always hearing somebody. Even when no one is there."

"That's the way things are going to be, Jessica. It would be so much simpler if . . ."

She put two fingers to his mouth. "Do you like Wellman?"

He said, muffled in her hair, "Not any more."

Her voice still had that sleepy quality and she seemed to be talking to herself. "It's very far. Not until summer. Very far and very long."

"I can't stay here."

"Why can't you?"

"I have to teach," he said, but that was not the real reason.

"In the summertimes what do you do, Ryan?"

"Sometimes I teach then, too. That's what I did last summer. Sometimes I don't do anything. Travel around. Sometimes I work at other things. Teachers don't make much money, you know."

"Do you . . ." she swallowed, "do you see women?"

He was delighted; he chortled foolishly. "Dozens!" he boasted, and then it was no longer funny; he went hollow with loss. "Come with me, dear," he said. He kissed her neck. "Please come."

Jessica looked at him so gravely he thought for one moment she might then and there put her hand in his and go down those stairs and out the front door forever. But then she looked down again. "You're tall," she said awkwardly. "When I turn my neck up too long, I can't swallow."

There is nothing in the world like the practicality of the feminine mind! he raged.

"When you come back," she was saying, "you'll be ashamed of all this." She watched him shyly. "You won't want me any more."

He thought of all the beautiful exaggerations. Deathless. Endless. Forever. But he said only, "I'll always want you," and then, "I've always wanted you." It gave her claim to all his past and future; that was a gift he made her.

But back to practicality again—he wanted to add, "Come to me tonight; at least do that." He looked at her face, not sure if it was the time. She raised her finger tips first to his mouth which she rubbed, shaping each lip, and then brought his head down and kissed him. The inside of her mouth was warm; there was no end to it.

"I love you. Jessica, please come."

But she, like someone grown old and wistful whispered, "Ryan, you know I never can."

He watched her face. "Can you for one night?"

She drew back. "This night, you mean?"

He nodded.

"Ryan, I . . . I couldn't . . . why, I just got married!"

In spite of himself he laughed. "Will it be so different next month or next year? Will that mean you're truer to him?"

"Don't talk like that."

She was a child. "You don't ever want me to say anything you don't want to hear, do you, Jessica?"

Her eyes were full of candor. "Does anyone ever want that?"

"Maybe not."

She caught his shoulders tightly in her fingers. "You haven't stopped loving me?"

"In the last five minutes? No."

"Don't stop." She put her head down again and rested against him. "I know I'm a coward. But please don't stop."

"How could I do that?" He put his face in her hair and found it very soft and warm.

"Will you write me? When you're back at Wellman, will you send me letters?"

"To this house?"

"You could send them General Delivery." She looked suddenly frightened. "Ryan, summer is so very far away."

He warned her. "Stoneville is very small. It won't be long before people will know you get mail at the post office. Someone will comment on it."

She shook her head defiantly. "I don't care," she said.

And he hated her because her daring came in such small containers. He smiled at her; she was very young. "Oh, Jessica," he said.

"What's funny?"

"This town. What it does to people."

"I think you mean me."

He loved her and he lied. "No, I mean the gossips."

"I'll always wear this stone." She had taken the silver chain with his Christmas gift and dangled it in her hand. "I . . . I even wear it at night."

That was a concession for you! Not with me you wouldn't! The damn thing probably scratches. Do you think I'm sixteen, that it pleases me to believe your soul is mine though your body belongs to someone else? Poor foolish Jessica, and I should have the luck to love you!

He said that was good. "I don't like having to remember you

always in this house," he said. "I hate seeing you in this hallway always full of shadows, or going up these steps. Every suppertime I'll have to picture you eating endlessly in that old dining room, making conversation." He saw the days stretching ahead forever, grayer than shawls on docile shoulders.

Her breath caught a little. "Come sooner, Ryan. Come for Easter."

"I will," he promised. "I will, Jessica." And when I come you will be slightly less a child than now. You will be four months and forty years older by April, and maybe in bed one night we'll break that silly silver chain and drop the stone off, down into empty shoes.

But he loved her; sex was not all of it. And now he put his hands on both her breasts, very gently, and he kissed her long and slow until her breath in his mouth warmed and speeded and she came forward thrusting her nipples at his fingers.

For that he would wait until April unless she should decide, after all . . .

Downstairs the door banged and she was gone from him instantly and three steps away. "What was that?"

He smiled. "Your conscience, from the looks of you."

In another second she patted her hair. "I'd better go down. Look all right? Are you coming?"

He looked down ruefully. "I think it will take me several more minutes to be presentable in public."

Her laugh was light but warm and the thought of what she might be like in April ached in him. "Ryan, I love you!" she said, and swooped by like a flicking bird and kissed him sweetly before she went down the stairs.

And so he returned to Wellman the end of December and took Miss August to a New Year's party at which he got very drunk and made a pass at her; and as a result had his face slapped so that his head rung like a pair of cymbals.

He said to Jim, "Miss August, naked and panting, was never worth a swat like that! And to have gotten it for nothing!"

"The trouble with you," said Jim, "is that your taste is bad."

"Indiscriminate," said his wife Anne, twinkling.

He only grinned at that, and told them nothing.

Winter at Wellman that year seemed slower than most of them.

The lectures were duller, the concerts badly attended, the weather wet and drab. Even the campus poets grew bored with the effort to keep their souls long-fingered in the damp. Frequent colds made the faculty ill-tempered, and the whole staff was finally split into quarrelsome factions over some action President Simms had taken. Once the lines were drawn, battles could be fought on anything: soon it was an action he had failed to take, and after that it was a controversy about hanging paintings of nudes in the Art Gallery when the trustees were coming to visit. Biology and English were not on speaking terms (they fought out the old business of material and spirit, science and humanities) and the young assistant in Classics returned her diamond to the Chemistry lab assistant because as winter wore on it was apparent their ideas would never be compatible.

It seemed to Ryan that semester that all his students were—at best—ordinary, and at worst they were faintly feeble-minded. He had a few he would gladly have set to basket weaving all of their days.

Life was dull. It walked yawning out of one day into the next.

Time began to divide itself in terms of Jessica's mail. Her letters were (he wrote her once, rhapsodically) like street lamps in a dark town: they stood tall; they were all that was visible above detail; he walked from one to the next.

He was in and out of the college post office every bit as often as homesick freshmen or girls who were going steady with soldiers overseas.

Sometimes her letters were long and rambling and he liked these, because they let him inside of her head a little. Up to now, he had been given no chance to *know* her. Now all of the details were important: what foods she liked; what colors; what she thought about; how things seemed to her and in what ways she really reacted to that town and those people.

She did not have much to do in the house on Walnut Street because Lady Malveena took care of the housework, and sometimes he suspected she wrote him partially out of boredom. On gray afternoons she would go to the library and write him there. (*Cornelia Satterfield is going from shelf to shelf, cooing like a dove. Her hairnet is drooping. She wears the big open kind, like something to catch whales in. Sometimes she smiles across the room at me and I smile and she nods and I nod. If she knew what I am doing!*)

But many of the letters were not letters at all; they were things she had dashed in haste on lady's notepaper. That made him uncomfortable. He saw her finishing the sentence just as Asa bent over her shoulder or Avery reached out to borrow her fountain pen. Often they were no more than a line or a phrase with the date and her signature: *It's raining and I love you*; or again, *Lady Malveena says that when you were a little boy and had nose bleeds you would run outside and put the back of your head against the gutter pipe to stop it. She said you were too independent to let anybody help you.*

Once she wrote, with a soberness she seldom used:

> Ryan, I know sometimes you think I treat this like a game. I act as if you are some kind of icing on this cake, or I am a schoolgirl with two boy friends between which I cannot decide. And this is not true, except that I keep acting that way. Because this is easier and sometimes I believe if I really thought about it and let myself admit the seriousness of everything, I would not know what to do. I am afraid of many things and I am sorry about that, because you have made me wonder that if I were perhaps even slightly different, strange and wonderful things might have happened to me. But nobody can change what they are after so long a time of being it. Not even you can change that. Better we should keep it like a silly game or else I might be too sad, and then the bargain would be for nothing at all—and the life I have here would always be shutting me in on all sides.

In return for her letters, short though many of them were, he wrote her volumes, long typed things which were too bulky so that he had to Scotch-tape the envelopes. He told her how he felt and what he thought, and what had happened or failed to happen, what he had read, done, remembered, forgotten, misunderstood. And, of course, he wrote her the usual things. He said that the world was up-ended with his love for her, that he thought of her constantly, that last night he had dreamed of her and she was beautiful.

At Easter he was in bed with bronchial flu and could not go

home. She sent him a book; she and Lady Malveena made candy and mailed it to him. And he lay in bed and kicked at Sybil every time she tried to get hidden in his blankets, and stared at the bitter rain that looked as if it might go by forever outside the house where he lived. He had never wanted to go home so badly.

Her letters began to change, very slightly.

She began to write that she wanted to see him. She began to remember in her letters that he had kissed her in the dark. *It is terrible,* she wrote, *but I remember the feel of your face in the library that night much better than I remember how it looks, although I have seen you dozens of times in good light and although I thought I knew perfectly how you looked the day you went away.*

Or she would say: *I know how tall you are. When I stand in front of you I can put the point of my chin in the little hollow just under your Adam's Apple. . . .*

In the spring, when he was up and out again and the rain had, after all, gone away, the absence was very much harder.

He had not thought of it before but now he knew that spring is always the hardest time for lovers. It is too fecund and too fruitful; buds are bursting everywhere like a million wombs. When he was rid of the flu he found the world had abruptly gone to blossom and bees and sprouting leaves, and his hunger for Jessica grew as primitive as seasons.

At one time he had enjoyed evenings at Jim's house, but now the sight of Anne moving in the kitchen irritated him. If she should come out and touch her husband casually, that irritated him even more. Thus—he would think savagely—Jessica and Avery live. If he wants to run his hand all the way down her spine and under he can do it, every night!

The year moved into May—drowsy weeks when he and the students passed each class in mutual toleration—and then toward final exams when there was an undeclared enmity between them.

By exam time, everyone was cross and tired and out of patience. There is nothing (Ryan told himself this year after year, semester after semester), *there is nothing* in the world equivalent to the refined torture of reviewing a term's work before an exam. Teachers grow exasperated because they make the very discovery they had been fearing daily: that nothing much remains in all these minds of all the words they have said in class. And the students are out of all patience before the thing is done because what they want is not this nonsense but to know *specifically* what questions they will be asked; and this they are not told. Teacher and student eye each other over desks as over ramparts. All right, goddammit, Ryan thought (he thought this every year), since you can't remember anything I ever said, I'll ask you questions on nothing you've ever heard! He never did this, of course, but that did not matter; there were scores of students to swear it happened each semester.

Barney, of course, used a psychology text that sent along a suggested exam for teachers. "What do you think you can teach these people in undergraduate school?" he would demand.

"At the very smallest, correlation," said Ryan wearily.

Barney snorted at this. "Have you taken a good look at these girls? This is the bridge-club set. It's all they're going to be able to do to remember what's trump, one rubber at a time."

"Okay, Barney. Okay." Barney knew all there was to know about education, of course. He had already made that clear to Ryan on numerous occasions.

When the final tests were done and the grading over and the scores posted on appropriate bulletin boards, it was as though everyone for miles around let out a great long breath. They were over into the first green edge of summer and in a few more weeks he would go home to where she was. He began to whistle, to step briskly; he grinned to himself at things no more amusing than a squirrel running, stiff-tailed, for cover, or a tree in bloom or a group of girls directing perspiring daddies loading trunks in cars.

Jessica wrote that the japonica was blooming and the buttercups were out in a yellow line against the orchard fence, and none of it was any good because he was not there to see.

Neither of them mentioned Avery in their letters, as though by not speaking of him they took him out of existence. And rarely did she write about Asa or the others; it was as though she said, in effect, *These have nothing to do with us.* When he had asked her, she would not come away with him to Wellman—and yet, by her words and lack of words, she took herself out of Stoneville every time she wrote. It was a small escape; it was a tiny fleeing but perhaps it was all they had; perhaps it was all they would ever have.

When he left in June, Jim Tetley went with him to the railroad station. They had parked the car and come to stand in the sun outside the depot, and Jim said it was damn hot.

Ryan agreed that it was pretty hot for June.

"How long's it been since you went home for the summer?"

It would have been sensible to wait inside for the train to come, but he had been impatient. Now he looked down the tracks to where they came together and dropped off. "Too long," he said absently.

"Someday they're going to plant trees in railroad stations. Get rid of all this concrete and make the thing a damn park."

"Hummn?"

"You'll have to walk through wet lilacs to get on board. That ought to suit your frame of mind."

"*Lilacs!* Did I hear you say something about lilacs?"

Jim laughed aloud.

"What in the hell are you laughing about?"

"I'm enjoying the sun in my eyes. Tickles my retina," said Jim, grinning.

"You want to go inside and wait?"

Jim shook his head. "I'd rather enjoy the experiment—whether or not constant gazing and staring on your part will be able to yank the engine in view. That would be telekinesis on a grand scale."

Ryan shrugged. He felt he was already a hundred miles away, going south.

"Must have been a good Christmas," said Jim. "You'll have to overlook us doctors. We can't get out of the habit of diagnosing all kinds of things."

"That so?" said Ryan. He felt good-natured, but Jessica was nobody's business, nobody's at all.

"Pretty?"

He tried to seem offhand about it. "I think so."

Jim's face was a little more serious. "And available?"

"If there's anything more relative than that, I don't know what," said Ryan. "Some things are available in different ways."

"I thought not," said Jim, ignoring all of that. "You wouldn't have been here all winter playing footsie with Mary August."

Ryan lowered his voice to a whisper. "It's a matter of heredity. Girl's got her sex organs in her toes. A little strange till you get used to it, but—"

"If Mary August has any sex organs I should be very much surprised," said Jim.

"I always admire the medical objectivity. I bet you only see women as something to put a finger up, looking for polyps."

"Lots of women I could recognize more by their bottoms than their faces," Jim admitted.

"I'll tell Anne that," said Ryan. He searched the track again. "What time is it?"

"Still early. I told you we were early. I guess she won't be coming back with you when the summer's over."

Ryan thought for a moment of all the beautiful wild impossibilities, staring off at the point where tracks met sky, not turning his head. Then he said (he knew how it would be), "No."

"Okay," said Jim, and looked down the track, too. "Maybe two stares are better than one," he explained. "A Diesel's pretty heavy."

Ryan said he hadn't tried one lately. "I wish Anne had come."

"She wouldn't have let you alone either, if that's what you mean. There's nothing sharper than one woman on the trail of another, and Anne's been trying to get something out of you all winter about what this girl was like."

"Has she?" Ryan was genuinely surprised. He had not said a word about Jessica all the time he had been back; he didn't know the Tetleys had anything to wonder about.

"It's all right. Have your secrets."

"They grow upside down in you, like carrots, and poison the soil. That's what Barney would say. All problems and secrets ought to be rooted out."

"Oh, *Barney*." They stood for a while, not talking.

Then Jim said, "Anne was just saying . . . well, she was saying she hoped it didn't matter too much to you. That she wouldn't . . . that this girl couldn't come back with you."

Matter? Ryan turned the word over and thought about it. It didn't matter as much as he had once thought. He found he could only express the feeling negatively, by thinking that there were people in the world who had no one to love. That was how it was. That was what you held to.

"Tell Anne not to worry," he said. The train showed, very small, and began to come to the station at tremendous speed.

"All right," said Jim. "I'll tell her."

Later, when he was on the train, he thought of Jim and Anne Tetley with a special warmth—because they had been good friends to him a long time. And he thought about the permeating quality of love and how it managed to enrich dozens of smaller ones. He was happy; the train itself was friendly because of where it was taking him; he punched his seat with something like affection. Even when he was drowsy there was a feeling of excitement in him and he thought of Asa and Avery, and that he was going home like a bridegroom, "rejoicing as a strong man to run a race"; and he thought of Jessica. He had never understood until now how other people felt on that one subject, but now—thinking of Jessica—he knew what it meant to be "going home."

Ryan had not expected it, so that the sight of Jessica herself leaning against the old Buick shading her eyes to see the train was like a gift to him. For a minute while they were slowing down, he stood up at the window and simply stared out at her, in disbelief that she should really be there. She had on a tailored white dress and some thin scarf slipped through her hair, and she had not seen him yet.

She was propped against the front of the car in a forward arch watching for him (like a moon, curved in the shape of a white quarter moon) and her bottom lip was held tightly in her teeth.

The train was still moving; when Ryan looked down he saw that he was holding onto the back of one seat very tightly, and the lady who was sitting there said he was going to fall if he didn't sit down till the train stopped. "Do you want to get hurt?" she snapped.

"Not this time," said Ryan underneath his breath, but it was not to her.

He began to weave down the car. He was suddenly conscious of a surface hunger up all his limbs for the very feel of her pulled next to him. Before the train had stopped he was off it, staggering a bit from his jump; and at the car Jessica straightened and saw him and then suddenly (wonderfully) began to run. He thought, defiantly, *Let the world know!* and took a step and caught her in midstride.

For the first minute he could not feel anything—her very existence was enough to sear him. But after a while he was aware of the touch and shape of her, the softness of her hair and her breasts, the edge of one hipbone in his flesh. He realized that for some time now she had been saying his name over and over again at his ear. He held her back a little then to see. He took her face between his hands and saw that her eyes were amber and full of sun. He said, "Where have you been?" and kissed her full on the mouth.

Then they looked at each other again.

He said, "I lo—" but she stopped him with her hand.

"Hush, hush!" she said. "I want to say it first. I love you. Ryan, I love you!" And he caught her tight.

It was she who said finally (she had begun to hiccup and to cry very gently, almost from relief), "I don't know what they'll think . . ."

He was too happy. "I know exactly what they'll think! And let the whole town think it!" Then, suddenly remembering, "My God! Is Asa with you?" Even then they did not speak of Avery.

"I ought to say she is just to see if it would make any difference! No one came but me. I only meant the others—all these strangers."

He was warmed throughout. He boasted, "Today there are no strangers!" And that was true. And that moment he believed only in benevolence—for a million miles on either side it was a kindly world.

Together they collected his bags and they were very silly. They giggled at nothing; they were patronizing of every other passenger in the Greenway station because he or she did not feel as they did. When Ryan opened the door of the Buick for her, she put her hand upon his hand and squeezed. "Are you really here?" she asked.

He borrowed the jargon of his college students. "You'd better believe it!" he said; and they leaned weakly into the old car and laughed together like fools.

That laughter stopped as quickly as it had come. One minute they had been roaring helplessly together and the next they were stark and cold and silent up against the car, looking at each other. It was late afternoon; there was one minute when the downgoing sun seemed to drop two sudden shadows on their faces and they stopped laughing and stared.

Ryan said then soberly, "Go call them, Jessica."

When she began to shake her head, it jostled all her brown hair and the little white scarf flicked into her mouth. "I . . . Ryan, I can't."

He had already closed his ears. He went on, making his voice absolutely sure and inescapable. "You're to say that I wasn't on this train. You're waiting for the nine o'clock one."

Her head was still going east-west, no-no, but not so far. "They're waiting for us. They won't believe . . ."

He said that the telephone was just inside the station door and he watched her. "I'll wait right here. Until you come back," he said.

"Ryan . . ." Then she said, "All right."

She turned and walked quickly away from the car toward the station. She looked very tall in the grayness, like a too-young soldier starting out from home. She was maybe one quarter of the distance when she turned and ran back and kissed him, and let her hand linger a moment on his face. She whispered, "I love you," and turned and went off again, into the station this time. In the early evening the white dress seemed to shine, making her look unreal. He lit a cigarette and watched the door of the station, and after a while he counted the first stars visible in the still light sky, less than a dozen of them, looking very faint and far away. When she came back again she was hurrying, out-of-breath; she looked as though she felt guilty and a little strange.

But she said only, "There you are. I was afraid you'd be gone." She smiled.

"Was it all right?"

She was impatient. "Yes. Let's don't talk about that. Don't talk about *them*." She kissed him too quickly and too hard.

He held her for a minute and then he whispered in her ear, "Slow down. Don't try so hard."

He could feel her stiffening. She said, "I want to please you. I want so terribly much to please you."

He kissed her eyelids. "You please me," he said.

"Do I?" She searched his face. "In spite of how I am? In spite of everything."

"Oh, Jessica." But all he could think about to reassure her was how he had felt waiting in the Wellman railway station, and he said it aloud now, embarrassed. "There are people in the world who have no one to love," he said.

She took up one of his hands and rubbed it on her face. "Thank you, darling."

When he turned his hand it covered half her face and his finger tips reached over her ear and into the brown hair. "Let's go," he said, holding her face so in his hand.

"Let's do."

Jessica slid across and under the wheel; when he lifted his eyebrows at that she said simply, "I know a place." He got in and closed the door and looked at her wonderingly.

"If you knew a place to go to . . ." He started that sentence over again, "If you'd already thought of a place, why . . . why were you so reluctant to telephone?"

"Women are like that," Jessica said. She looked very crisp and distant and efficient turning the steering wheel and watching the traffic light. Ryan said as much. He liked the way she smiled.

"I never saw you smile enough," he said.

"Perhaps you will . . . now."

They were coming to the outskirts of Greenway and onto the highway where there was not so much light.

"Shall I talk?" she asked and Ryan said whatever she felt like.

"Give me a cigarette." He lit two and gave her one. After a while she said, more to the highway than to him, "Lady Malveena knows."

"Does she?" He was not sure if Jessica meant she had confided in Lady Malveena or not.

"I can tell she knows. She always has, I suppose. Do you think they have some sixth sense that we don't?"

In the darkness he smiled. "You mean Lady Malveena or the race in general?"

"Ouch," she said. "The race in general, I guess."

"In general I suspect they may be just a bit less complicated."

"Children are like that. Seem to see right to the heart of things sometimes."

"Which is only convenient part of the time," Ryan said. "Sometimes the things which matter are the very subtleties."

"I suppose so." Her laugh was a little nervous. "That's not what I planned to talk about."

He was trying to let the talk go easy, like water downhill. "What did you plan to talk about?"

"You and me."

"What were you going to say?"

She shrugged. "All of it was wrong," she said.

He moved across the seat next to her; he touched her thigh. At first she almost winced and he took his hand away and put it down more gently and left it there. Suddenly she smiled and turned her head to glance at him, half shy, half bold.

"That makes me ache," she said.

He said he hoped it did; he meant it to.

She dropped one hand from the wheel onto his hand and began to run her finger lightly over the hairs on his wrist. He kept his hand where it was on her leg. Then she said with an embarrassed giggle, "How can men drive and make love at the same time?"

"Singleness of purpose," Ryan said.

She was teasing him. "The driving, you mean?"

"No. Not the driving," Ryan said. He moved his hand in and up a trifle. "Stop this damn car."

"Maybe I'd better. I can see us in a wreck before you even arrive on the proper train."

She pulled into a side road and stopped and turned to him and he caught her so hard that he knew he really meant to hurt her, perhaps to frighten her a little. He had some idea of making her understand the size of this thing through sheer intensity; and he let her be surprised and wriggle and push her hands against him ineffectually. He felt quite strong; much as he loved her he liked the feeling that she could do nothing against him.

"Ryan," she was saying; and he kissed her on the neck and inside her dress at the shoulder until she shivered slightly and began to relax a little in his arms. When she said his name another time the tone was altogether different. Her arms went around and onto his back. Everything, even the air in the car was hot, moist, sweet; he nuzzled in her neck until she began to arch her back slightly toward him and then he touched her knee and her leg and put his hand all the way under clothes until he felt her flesh grow wet to his touch.

She broke away from him then, stiff in the elbows, suddenly angry. "All right!" she said sharply. "Are you satisfied? Is that what you wanted to know?"

Ryan felt so pleased that he admitted secretly it was exactly what he had wanted to know; but aloud he only said her name as gently as he could.

On all sides she was shaking free of his hands and his clothes and his touch, the way a dog shakes free of rain. "You might take your own advice!" she snapped. "Slow down. Don't try so hard!"

He was too pleased because of the very presence of her desire to mind that she was sharp. "Why are women always so careful?" he said. "What is it they are afraid to give away?"

"Women have more at stake," she said shortly. She was starting the car.

He could not help it; he reached across and pinched her impudently on one breast. "Yes ma'am," he said, teasing. "Why don't you let me drive a while?"

"Was that a double-edged question?" She looked beautiful and furious in the dimness.

"You mean something about male superiority?" He shook his head. "Single edges guaranteed. I just thought I'd give you a chance to make love to me while *I'm* driving."

Jessica got out of the car and slammed the door and came around and got in on his side. "I hate you when you're cocky," she said angrily.

He leaned across and kissed her on the nose.

"Stop that," she said.

After a little while he asked her why she thought women had more at stake. "Why is it they turn lovemaking into such a bargain?"

She was silent. Then she said thoughtfully, "They know it isn't endless."

"Don't men?"

"Not in the same way. You can make love and finish it in fifteen minutes, but men don't seem to think past that. A woman never quite gets the other twenty-three hours and forty-five minutes out of her head."

Ryan said he thought that sounded pretty damn practical and he hated the thought of being clocked in bed like a racehorse.

"Skip it," she said. "You don't know what I mean." And she smiled, a little tolerantly he thought.

But at least she was past her anger. They drove perhaps another hundred yards before she slid across and under the hollow of his right arm and leaned her head on his shoulder. He put his chin against her forehead.

"Thought you were through with all this," he said. "Remember those other twenty-three hours."

"I reserve the right to make statements about women and not live up to them myself."

"Then that's all right," he said.

"Have you missed me at all since Christmas?"

He wondered if it was for the other twenty-three hours that women required such perpetual reassurance. "Silly question. I love you, remember? Where are we going?"

"On through Stoneville. Go out Third Creek Road and turn off on the one that runs by the river. I'll show you."

It was already dark. The early half dozen stars he had counted in Greenway were lost among thousands. It was warm; they rode with the windows down between singing banks of crickets and frogs and dark. She sat very near so that he was acutely conscious of her very breath, and the swelling and ebbing of her side against his side was a terrible tenderness.

Abruptly Jessica said, "I wish I didn't love you."

He was hurt. "Why not? Is it so bad?"

She plucked at a button on his shirt. "Nothing is safe any more, not for me," she said. "I'm so . . ." she stumbled for the words, "so altogether in your hands. Everything you say tears me. I can't," here she turned up her head, kissed him lightly on the chin, "I can't be casual at all."

Ryan said he certainly hoped not.

"And it's not only with you . . . it's with everything."

Ryan said what was with everything.

"Everything changes. I'm even not the same with myself because I'm pulled to one way and another. I'm guilty and happy and funny-feeling. And with everyone I know . . ." She swallowed. "It's like singing in a big choir and suddenly finding you're completely out of key. Even when you sing the same song and the rest of the choir hasn't noticed it yet, *you* know you're different."

He tightened his arm on her shoulders. "Do you want so terribly to sing like the rest of the chorus? Is that how you see the world?"

"Yes. Yes, I suppose it is."

He didn't know what to say to that. He thought again of what she had already said, and he thought that it wasn't that women minded giving themselves—that they could do easily enough. What they hated was the thought of giving themselves for nothing.

"Doesn't it help that I love you?"

She shrugged. "If you didn't love me I could have kept it a secret all my life and not even you would have known about it."

He said seriously, "You really hate to let go of yourself, don't you, Jessica? I can feel you holding on in all directions to everything secret and private in you."

"I never thought it would be this way. I didn't know how strong this would be until you got off that train this afternoon. And now

I feel all . . ." she spread one hand out in her lap, helplessly, "all gone out of myself."

"Nothing is irrevocable. You can take back any time you like."

She shook her head. "That isn't true. It isn't the same."

He slowed the car, trying to see past what she was saying to what she meant. "We can go on home to Walnut Street if you'd rather. We can walk in and see the others and drop the whole thing."

Jessica said impatiently that the male mind was like a pile of stones.

"Well, isn't that what you meant? Don't you mean that some last wall of defense goes down if you make love to me?"

"Oh hell," said Jessica.

She had, for all practical purposes, taken the words right out of his mouth.

They drove in silence for a little longer and then Jessica said they were spoiling it all with talk, and she'd never meant to talk so much and please please please—couldn't they not talk any more?

Ryan said that was all right with him. And he kissed her in the corner of her mouth. They drove through Stoneville and out along the spur tracks on Third Creek Road, where all the mill houses were, and then cut off to the right before they came to the bridge which crossed the railroad. This second road ran parallel to the river, which they could not see in the dark. But they could hear it, going by and going by.

After a while Jessica had him pull off into a little clearing and they locked the car and stumbled in the sudden dark.

"Where are you, Jessica?"

Out of the darkness she took hold of his hand and he could see her white outline. "I'm here," she said. "I'm always here." They began to walk down a thin path which was barely visible, and he was strongly aware of the sound of water. In the dark the river hummed. There was some breeze, and it went through the trees above their heads rather impatiently.

Her whisper seemed very loud. "I hate snakes!" she said. They stepped more carefully in the underbrush. June, he thought; snakes would be out by now.

Then they were on a cleared beach, pale and flat, where a small house stood, and when he looked at the house and at Jessica she nodded her head. Her hair was silver from moon.

"No one will come," said Jessica. "It isn't open yet."

He had a sudden conviction that he was not awake. Everything looked too strange—the light-colored sand, the very white dress, the silver hair, the dark water, lighter sky. Everything was black, white, gray, beige, neutral—strange. He had a feeling that if he should put a hand on Jessica now she would grow very still, even whiter, like Lot's wife going into salt on the plains before Sodom.

Then it passed. The world returned; it was a June night full of stars and he loved the woman he was with. They took hands, crossed to the house and to the window Jessica indicated at the back. "You'll have to help me in," she said.

"Isn't it—"

She shook her head, impatient. "I broke the lock on Tuesday."

At that he almost cried, incredulous, "*You what?*" But he swallowed it. He would never understand the feminine mind; better men than he had died trying.

She stood on tiptoe and kissed him. "Do you mind that I'm so shameless?"

"No," he said. He kissed her again. Then he pulled the screen loose and raised the window (it rasped, absurdly loud above the sound of the river going by and going by) and lifted Jessica up and through. She held out her hand to him from inside, but he shook his head and came up backwards, pulling himself to a sitting position on the sill. Then they were inside and he lowered the window in case anyone should come.

The room in which they stood was incredibly dark after the pale sand and the stars outside. It might have been no room at all, only a space without ending. He could not even see her white dress in the blackness.

"Jessica? Jessica?"

She came into his arms. After a few minutes she said, "This is the living room. There's a kitchenette. And a hall and a bath." She swallowed. "And the bedroom, to the left. There's a small bed."

He said, not caring much, "What place is this?" He had picked her up in his arms; he wanted to carry her in and put her down gently. He wanted to move very slowly until some of her great care and tension eased and she could be Jessica with no one to see her.

She said, muffled in his chest, "It's the Boy Scout hut. For the camp counselor."

Ryan could not help it; it was so unexpected and the irony hit him so strongly that he began almost with hysteria to laugh. She wavered in his arms from his laughter and seemed about to fall. "The Boy Scout hut!" he repeated, weak from his laughter and not able to hold it back.

When he felt her growing stiff and heavy to hold he stilled his laughing as quickly as he could, but it was too late. She turned her head away from him and began helplessly to cry.

He stood her on her feet; he caught at her quickly. "Darling, I'm sorry. I'm sorry, Jessica . . . it was just for a minute . . . Jessica, don't cry. It's all right. Everything's all right."

But now she would not come. She broke away from him, crying and gasping, and he could not find her in the dark. He went about groping, calling her name, trying to reassure her. He said it was all right, he was sorry, he hadn't meant it the way it sounded—but always she was just out of his reach. He ran into a door jamb and he said "Goddamn it all to hell!" with fervor and then went back to calling her again. "Jessica?" But she was always somewhere just ahead of and beyond him, and he could hear her crying.

When finally he caught hold of her they were already in the bedroom and some of the reflected light from the beach showed the flat bed and Jessica near it. He took her gently and went on saying all the things he had been saying. After a while he lay beside her on the bed and held her in his arms and let her get the crying over at whatever speed and quantity it took. Now and then he tried to say something comforting, but mostly he just held her. He didn't know what else to do.

She grew a little quieter. As the crying subsided the other sounds came in, and he thought for one moment the whole room was full of crickets. "Hear the crickets?" he said, feeling absurd.

She nodded her head in his neck so that his Adam's apple cringed.

Once she said brokenly, "How terrible this is! We have so little time and I've gone all to pieces!"

"I love you," he said.

She put her arms around him. "Say that again."

"I love you."

She grew quiet except for sniffles. She slipped off her shoes and dropped them onto the floor.

"Feel better?"

She turned her mouth and kissed him.

He had meant after this to love her gently and slowly. He had intended to persuade and coax and capture. But he found she was all over her crying as suddenly as he had gotten over his first unfortunate laughter, and when next he kissed her she put her hand upon him. Then she rolled away and up and out of reach.

He was frustrated; he sat up and tried to find her in the dark, half afraid she was going to evade him again.

But when she came back she was naked and tearless, and they kissed until mouth and tongue were hot and raw and he did not remember any plans to be gentle. The silver chain he had meant to break was not there—only the rib cage was there and the delicate bone in the center and the breasts soft on each side.

She said into his ear, nibbling the lobe, "I want you to love me so I forget there is anything else anywhere."

So he did; and for a little while in a borrowed room both of them forgot.

All of those summer days that year were like beads strung too tightly on a string. Any time now, the pressure on one or the other of them would be too great, and the whole season would spring apart and scatter. Ryan told himself it had not been a good idea to come home, not for the entire three months. Had he been different, had Jessica been different, the tension would have eased by the middle of June; they could have savored what they had.

But some beliefs are old—old as infancy—and they were troubled back in the roots for what they did.

During the day, he and Jessica were alone in the house except for Lady Malveena—who never said a word; but even then they felt forced to play the game of in-laws and no more. Jessica put it well when she said, "It's one thing for Lady Malveena to *know*, but for us to *know* that she knows—that would shame her."

The cold practicality of things was a constant bother to both of them; there was so little they could do in warmth and spontaneity. When a touch or a caress had to be carefully timed and calculated, something was gone. They felt like actors in a particularly awkward play.

It seemed to Ryan that the two of them were perpetually and nervously clutching and letting go, coming together and then separating hurriedly when a door slammed, putting a hand out to each other and having to let it fall without touching.

All of this made Ryan nervous and jumpy. He felt his every movement was made beneath eyes. He was reminded of what he had said to Jessica not too long ago: *The only time you can be yourself is when you're in the bathroom with the door locked.* He had not been too far wrong.

As for Jessica, she found she could not hold anything in her hands. Pots, vases, hairbrushes—everything she lifted seemed to slip from her grasp and clatter to the floor. They made a joke of it but actually they were apprehensive. It seemed to them that by these small signs they must give themselves away; everyone must know, every act be suspicious.

Once, after a day in which everything she touched had gone downward with a bang, Jessica said with a nervous laugh, "Do you suppose this means I know deep down I can't hold on to you?"

Ryan thought of Barney. "No," he said. "Because you have. You do."

"Not really." She was very depressed; she sat on one of the parlor chairs and put her face in her hands.

Such moments were the worst. If he put his arms around her, Asa might walk in. If he bent and kissed her, the postman going down the walk would see them through the glass. He put his hand on her shoulder and squeezed (I hate having to count the risk, number the chances) and spoke her name. "Can't I make you see that I love you, Jessica? I've never been able to make you see that this is more than a pastime for holidays."

She said sadly that love was not enough to hold people together.

He was exasperated with her. "What then?" he said.

She had still not lifted her face, and now she shrugged her shoulders and spoke through the fingers. "Shared experiences. Troubles. A relationship of responsibility."

"Marriage, you mean." He thought, *Damn the postman!* and he put his arm around her. "I always wanted to marry you, Jessica. This was never what I had in mind."

Then she looked at him, defensive. "I know it! Are you blaming me? Are you always blaming me?"

He felt very tired. "No."

She said, "What I like least is that outwardly we have no position, you and I. No position at all. I never thought that mattered if the center was sound, but it matters terribly." She sighed. "If you should be dying off in Wellman, Massachusetts, I would not be called. Whenever I need you I find I must go on needing until we can work it in."

He reminded her that it did not have to be this way. "We can still go away. There are divorces. You could marry me."

She shook her head.

"Why are you so afraid, Jessica? Why would that be so difficult?"

She went on shaking her head and hardly seemed to be listening to him. "In a little while you won't even love me any more."

He kissed her angrily as a denial of that.

But she was not won. "It's like trying to put a rock on toothpicks. Building something good and honest on a foundation made out of lies and deceit."

It was such an old argument; it would never be solved while she felt the way she did. He said rather bitterly that things didn't have to be that way.

"Oh, Ryan." She sounded quite put out with him.

He lost all patience with her. "If you loved me enough—really enough, Jessica—you couldn't come away fast enough to suit either of us. You'd come tonight. You'd quit *talking* about honesty and try to make this thing honest by breaking off absolutely clean, starting again. That's all it really is, Jessica, that you don't love me enough to let it put some of your respectable ideas aside. You'd rather live in all this falseness, which isn't respectable at all!"

"Perhaps you're right." She, too, was tired and when he saw that her eyes were wide and hurt, he was sorry. He kissed her on the lids.

"It doesn't matter," he said. "I love you enough for both of us."

"Both of us," she said dully. "Both of us and all of them."

It was hard to find reasons to be together in the evenings, even with the co-operation they had. Avery and Asa were glad to see the two of them were learning to like each other and Avery, of course, would never be jealous on his own. Someone would have to suggest it to him. Still, they were careful; they wanted all their reasons to sound bona fide.

Once in a while they left together to go to see a movie, but more frequently she left on an errand or a meeting and he borrowed the car to "get some air," and met her. It was always an hour or so stolen and guarded. Asa liked to know when people would be home; there were time limits.

When he came back he would often sit in the car and smoke a

while before he could bring himself to go inside the house. He hated the idea of facing the others as though everything was as it seemed, smiling and talking to them about unimportant things. Asa and Avery seemed to accept everything he said at face value and that, too, made him uncomfortable. That made him feel that perhaps there was really no believing anybody. Lying was too simple; living a lie might be a tremendous personal strain but outwardly one seemed all right, one functioned in all the acceptable ways. It isn't desperation that gets us all, he would think, but that good old business of leading lives of *quiet* desperation, held down, pushed under.

And in spite of himself he was half disgusted to find that deceit was—in many ways—so simple. He was not sure he liked himself as well as before, now that he knew how glibly a lie could come to the tongue and fall out, sounding plausible and true. Here was a thing so large it touched all aspects of his life; and after all, it was so easily hidden from view. To all intents and purposes it did not exist at all. That gave him an ominous feeling about everyone he met—all of them might be unreal; they might all be, steadily and skillfully, playing some careful role, even as Jessica and he. Sometimes he had visions of man stripped bare, past all his pretense, down to liar, murderer, Lesbian, thief, addict, hater without cause.

Perhaps this was what he and his fellow man had, after all, evolved to—such a complexity of thought that each of them could exist on many levels as totally different and yet believable people. He could live a lie within a lie within a lie, and often manage to keep all of them straight and separate and neatly circumscribed. If this was true, it was perhaps no wonder that the new disease of man was mental illness. Perhaps the real wonder was that millions of well-barbered businessmen maintained happy homes and office love affairs, gambling debts and Sunday school classes and political intrigues simultaneously and did not crack at all.

Then Ryan would shrug. He was making more of it than necessary. As usual, he was using his specific experience to generalize on the whole race of man.

But so do we all, he would think. What else can we do?

By the first of July, he and Jessica had begun to quarrel.

The separate quarrels were never important. They were nothing and yet taken together they added up to everything. Both Ryan and Jessica were snappy and sharp from strain and when it grew hotter and the rooms in the old house baked them daily, the strain began to tell. There were sudden flare-ups (quickly stilled) and sharp outbursts of inexplainable tears on Jessica's part (swiftly dried) and sudden angry words (taken abjectly back by both of them).

"We're going to destroy everything!" Jessica would say. "It won't be the others doing it. It's you and me. What in the world is the matter with us?"

How could he answer her? All of the years and the days that had gone to make each of them up was the matter with them; what they had always been was now in conflict with what they were.

"We're not very good liars," he said. That was all he knew to say.

The days were hot and long, and they saw each other alone too seldom. As a result, Ryan and Jessica found themselves dwelling constantly in the world of Double Meaning. The remark one made at dinner where the others were must be always held up alongside what it secretly conveyed. They had to hide their love in commonplace conversation and pass it along in code, under politeness, behind trivialities. Because of this, whenever they *were* alone they found themselves still searching each other's words for more than was actually said, and then they would be hurt or angry at some secret message they believed was there.

Everything was too exaggerated between them. When Jessica brushed her hand against his back in passing it was a way of imparting love. The merest lifting of a brow might mean, "Can we get away tonight?" It might mean, "Do you love me?"

And after all of that it was no wonder that the simplest smallest frown was like a terrible accusation, and a shake of the head could be received as the end and the death of love.

In July he did something he had never done before in all of their friendship. He wrote Jim Tetley a letter.

I have what I wanted and it is not enough, he wrote. *I suppose that is the whole history of the race of man.*

Jim and Anne were spending that summer at a university marine biology station where Jim was the medic. He spent his days watching over the sniffles of young scientists in a bored fashion while Anne, as he put it, "grows brown enough to shock your Southern sensibilities." He also wrote Ryan that the place was quiet, that it had its advantages including one blonde who was worth a bachelor's note, that Anne was anxious about him. *Why don't you come up for a week or so and let the kinks work out?* he finished. *Here you need do nothing but sun and find shells and swim.* We *won't even talk about anything controversial.*

But Ryan could not leave her. It was that simple, so he never answered Jim's letter. The situation here with Jessica was not enough for him, but such as it was he could not put it down and go away.

The town itself bored him more with each sunny day. He had come to hate that brash sun and what he mentally referred to as those goddamn blue skies every day. The little things that took the Godwins in and out of the house—committees, clubs, business deals that seemed to him infinitesimal in size, church suppers, a rare bridge game—these things were not for him. He sat in the kitchen (except when Lady Malveena was cooking and moisture hung hotly everywhere) and on the back steps, looking for shade and breeze.

He sometimes asked himself if he could have liked this town had he been somehow involved in it. If he worked here, within these city limits, from eight to five every day, and paid taxes that built these streets and sewers, and was in the phone book and the local Elks—would all of it have looked different to him and more desirable? Had he any right to blame the town because there was nothing for him to do when he was there?

When it was not too hot, he took walks. (Once he had told Jim. "In Stoneville I'm like an Alpine climber; I walk about as though *somewhere* there must be a peak to try.") And everyone he met said the same thing. They said they were glad to see him home. They said this was the hottest summer they had ever seen, and they had seen some hot ones! They said a rain would cool things off.

He spent some time in the Stoneville library. His old card was still in the file. Cornelia reinstated him happily, saying he had always been one of her best customers. She gave him a coy look as she said it.

Ryan had to smile at all the things he remembered about that library in which he had spent so many hours. There was the adult library, which was all shelved behind the circulation desk. Only the one gate led into that, right by the librarian's desk, so that no teenager could slip by and read passages of *Ulysses* or *Tobacco Road.* There was one Reference and Special Room, where the Britannicas and six magazines and four newspapers were, along with History, Geography, the Garden Club Corner, the Stephen Foster Memorial Collection, and some Poetry.

It always surprised Ryan to find that the library was very small, because when he had been a high school student it had seemed so large a place with such an endless number of books.

Now the library had two purposes, one for reading, one for meeting Jessica. Sometimes they walked to the library together. What could be more innocent than that the two members of a family who liked to read should walk together to check out books, and possibly discuss their choices on the way home?

Yet when they were there together, Ryan had the oddest feeling Cornelia Satterfield *knew*. He had always been slightly uncomfortable about what was commonly called Woman's Intuition. He did feel that certain women in situations which were personally important to them managed to think less with mind than with corpuscles. It was as though their very flesh was attuned to all the thousand revealing things by which another's flesh gives him away.

Because he felt this way, he was careful not to look at Cornelia whenever he came into the library with Jessica at his side. He felt strange and guilty when he first came in the door and would begin fixedly to look at certain books on certain shelves. He was convinced that across the room Cornelia had fixed him with a stern and knowing gaze, and if he once looked up at her he would be impaled upon it forever.

For Ryan and Jessica the small brown library rooms were a place to talk. They would sit in the shadow of all the encyclopedias and Jessica would put her head in her hand so that the brown hair fell down almost to the tabletop. And they talked.

Their talk went out and around in all directions—it touched many things; but always it was attached to a point of origin. In this way their conversations, like spokes in a wheel, radiated out from love, returned to love, fed and went out again.

In time as well there was a fixed point from which they took their departures. Jessica led him back along long corridors to her childhood, back to lost scared years without parent or love or safety, and Ryan told her all of his other days; and they came back finally to the present and each other. It was a little axis which they had, but the world turned on it and turned well.

He was always to see her as he saw her at such times, head in hand and long hair falling, the other hand spread out on the table making some gesture. She loved to talk with her hands. She was forever drawing shapes and strange animals upon the air.

If Cornelia was out of sight and no one else was there he would sometimes take that hand and press it to his face briefly.

"All right, go on," he would say.

Jessica would smile dreamily. "Where was I?"

By such long talking afternoons they built some structure around the inner thing. They built it back on two lines into time, and coming along back gave it a shape to where their two lives had intersected. They built towers of their ideas and their arguments. There were long warm buildings made of the things they liked.

And always the central thing was there—like a cornerstone or a keystone in a precarious arch—and they knew that if that one thing should go the whole house would come down. Worse than that, it would dissolve, vanish; not even a wreck would stand to show where Ryan and Jessica once had been.

Always in late afternoons when they had talked long and well, they were as weary as laborers. Now that the words were all nailed in, the two of them went slack. They would walk home in absolute silence. If it was already dark they would walk slowly along shaded walks, holding hands between the headlights. Jessica always said laughingly that this made her feel like a prisoner sneaking along the outer wall who had to duck when the regular searchlight went by.

Sometimes in that darkness she would be stepping off the walk, touching tree trunks, turning her head to study the shape of his face when they passed a streetlight. She would say, "I want to remember how you looked at certain times and in certain places."

Or she would say, "When you are gone again, I'll want this evening back. This very evening." (She said this about many; all of them were good.) "I'll think of all I might have said to you and didn't say."

They sometimes behaved like children, walking with their heads turned back on their shoulders so they could see the stars and the tangled limbs of trees. "Walk like this and catch raindrops in your mouth when you were small?" Ryan would ask.

She was delighted. "Of course. Did you?"

"Everybody does," he said.

Often she sang, hummed really, something high and nasal. He never heard a familiar tune and he never heard her sing the same one twice. He thought they must be things she made up just as they walked, not particularly conscious of doing so. Her tunes had the quality of chants about them—thin, twanging, faintly sad.

They went once more and made love in the hut by the Katsewa River, but it was not the same. They would always remember that he had laughed and she had been hurt in those rooms. For the first time Ryan realized how hard it was simply to find a place for making love.

He would tease her. "I never knew flat surfaces were so hard to come by."

But she did not like that kind of teasing. It seemed to make her consciously label herself a Woman of Easy Virtue, and her laughter was almost always forced.

Once when Victoria Seagreaves was in the hospital for one of her frequent checkups, they drove to that house and parked the Buick at the curb. But when he saw Jessica shiver he caught both of her hands in his and kissed her on the temple.

"Let's don't," he said. "Not here."

And when she nodded her head he saw that she was fighting back tears.

Finally he rented a little furnished house out on the county line. He rented it by mail, saying that he was a businessman and this was only for week-end rests, and that his name was Horace Simpson. He didn't think anyone would believe that this was true but all he hoped was that no one would bother to spy on him. So for part of July and August, they had a place to go.

Whenever he and Jessica came into that shabby house, a certain domesticity fell over them. Jessica would make coffee or fry eggs; they would sit on the floor in the living room, laughing and arguing and teasing. The setting was *theirs*. Within these walls at least they had certain rights and privileges. It was an ugly little house, but they never noticed that.

Because they had more a sense of privacy, some of the other strain began to ebb slightly. They were not so much tuned for the sound of other people's footsteps coming near. And in love they began to achieve a certain skill. Their need was still urgent, hurried; they were just learning to prolong pleasures. But now each could give more and gain more. Afterwards Ryan would remember the low sound of her moaning in his neck, but at the time he never heard it. Always it was afterwards that the world—which for a little time had broken off on all sides—returned to compass them again; and they heard frogs and crickets outside and saw patterns on the bedroom wall when cars went by.

He tried to explain that image to her once. "Up to now," he was saying, "that kind of image always seemed to me a great extravagance. Hemingway used something like it—"

She interrupted. "You mean Maria! Maria and Robert Jordan. And Maria tells that gypsy woman—what's her name—that the world moved!"

"Pilar." He was lying with her hair partly in his face, partly tickling his neck and shoulder.

When she shook her head the hair brushed him. "I always knew it could be like that."

"How could you know a thing like that?" He was teasing her. He bit her on the shoulder where her collarbone ended.

"I just knew it. Deep. In the stomach. In the bones."

That puzzled him. "And knowing that you could still . . . you could still marry him?"

"Yes." She turned to look at him, put her hand in the small of his back so that their stomachs were pulled together close. "I didn't mean I knew it could be that way for me. I just knew that it could be that way. For some people."

He turned on his back. "You're funny," he said.

Suddenly she rolled atop of him and lay spread as on a crucifix. She was very warm and her limbs were slight. Her voice was soft and dreamy. "Now when you move your arm it will move mine, and when you breathe it presses my own ribs. I am . . ." she kissed his throat, "I am all mingled in you."

When she said that his love went sharp and painful. It was like all the clichés he had ever heard—like a knife and a fire—and it did not seem he would ever make it known. There was too much of it. What could one say that Jessica had not already said with her "mingling"? One could only touch, hold, kiss. The flesh is used to being dumb.

She was laid on him limb to limb so that he had only to turn to love her. This time it was more in desperation than in tenderness and both of them ached with it.

And this time when the crickets and frogs and moving lights came back it was a long time before either of them saw those things. They had been so far away they had almost forgotten what these were.

The worst thing was, as Jessica sometimes said, that they could do so little for each other. They could give no gifts and could perform only the most innocuous of services, and these perfunctorily—as though each were half annoyed.

On that part of it, Ryan agreed. What of the many times when he wanted merely to lay his hand upon her openly, the moments when he saw her mouth tired and tense and could not kiss it? Always there had to be care and precaution; even when he smiled at her it could not be too warmly; when he met her eyes it must not be too long.

If he saw something he would like to buy for her, he could not. He was reduced to an occasional handful of flowers with a slightly smaller bouquet for Asa, to mask any specialness.

There were moments on end when he wished only to run a finger at her hairline and had to discipline his hand quickly in a pocket.

He began to hate the orchard which he had heretofore enjoyed. During the day when only the two of them were left in the house, they sometimes went to the orchard to talk. They would avoid Lady Malveena's eyes when they came through her kitchen and down the back steps, although she never said a word, not a word. But even when they were out there in the grass and no one could hear, they were still not quite at ease. They did not quite dare to touch, too much aware of the world stacked neatly in white painted houses on all sides.

All of these things accumulated in his head to worry him.

There are, Ryan would think, at least two kinds of love and God knew how many others. But of these two, one was at its best in an affair, like the sweet stolen water of Solomon and the bread which is more pleasant for being eaten in secret. The other kind—his and Jessica's—was the type whose need had called forth the whole institution of marriage. It wanted talk and quietness and time. It fed on small deeds. It sought for an intimacy so deep that it might even grow irritating without ever being, at the same time, dispensable.

It all sounded dull when he described it so. It sounded like a hopeless pipe-and-slippers thing but it was not, not any more than most of the other things he did often and well were really dull. They were the framework which held his life together. On these planes he built out in all directions; and when he departed from them too much the whole structure faltered and went bad.

There came an August night in which the four of them were sitting on the front porch facing Walnut Street. Asa had thought it might be cooler there because the big oak had shut much of the sun away all day. If it was any cooler there Ryan could not tell it.

Avery and Asa were talking of some real estate arrangement which he found too dull to listen to, and he and Jessica for some time now had said nothing. He did not know what she thought about on such evenings, and when he tried to imagine how she passed the long winter and would pass the ones to come, he was appalled. He did not know how much pretending one human being could do.

And sitting there in the growing dark, drowsy after the long day and not listening to the talk around him, Ryan felt a long and sudden sadness. He thought (although he had known it before, although he had always known it) *Things will always be this way.* When he thought of that with such sudden clarity, all the vigor in him sagged and went down and he felt hot and sweaty and ineffectual.

He could picture the four of them a dozen summers hence (or two dozen, for that matter), grown older and plumper, talking of real estate late on another summer evening. Asa—grown sixtyish and seventyish—would be saying that it was cooler on the porch. Jessica, her hair grayer and vaguer, would be sitting to one side, not talking. There was no chance of any of these things changing. He and Jessica were as much committed to each other as people ever can be; but nothing was changed, or would be. When all of them were old, were—in fact—bored, there would always be Avery and Asa rocking gently in these chairs. There would be Walnut Street, looking identical, and these same trees and stars and problems to the end of time.

Thinking these things, he looked across at Jessica once. She was leaning back in the green rocker with her eyes closed, and in the pale light her cheeks seemed ashen and unwell. And he heard Asa's confident voice coming from a great distance: "But in ten years, Avery, the town will move that way and you'll find that will be very valuable property."

So Ryan leaned forward out of his chair suddenly and wound his hands on the banister (which am I holding up, he wondered briefly, the house or myself?) and he said rather loudly without looking up at anyone, "I have to leave tomorrow." It was the hardest thing he had ever said anywhere and he gripped the wood until his finger tips were numb and felt as if none of them were his.

Asa said sharply, "What in the world brought that on?" and Avery, puzzled, said, "But I thought school didn't begin till after the first of September."

But Jessica never said a word. She only sat like a piece of marble waiting in a chair.

He wished there was a breeze. He wished Jessica had said something, anything at all. "I have to go."

"Most ridiculous thing I ever heard! You're not even packed, I know you're not! Lady Malveena hasn't even ironed all your shirts from yesterday. Why do you suddenly announce—"

His hands crushed the wood. "It's time for me to go, Asa. Nothing remarkable about it."

Then Jessica stirred slightly, but it was only to clear her throat as though something oppressive had risen there. When Asa heard that sound she turned. "Can't you persuade him, Jessica? You seem to have more influence with Ryan than the rest of us."

Jessica's voice, when it came, was low and very careful. "I suppose he knows when he has to go."

At that Ryan put his hands back on the arms of the chair where they lay for a while without much feeling in them. For one insane moment he had half dreamed she might have said, "I'm going with him," making her decision as suddenly and surely as he had made his. What foolish thought was that? Whoever heard such an impossibility?

He felt tight all over, like Gulliver strung in Lilliput.

"You'll be back Thanksgiving," Avery said.

"No. Not this year."

"Ryan, you're the most provoking . . . Have we offended you, for goodness sakes?"

At this he had to laugh; for a moment he felt almost kindly. "No, Asa."

Jessica's voice was very measured. "When *will* you be back?" And then, hesitatingly, "Ryan?"

He ached at the way she said his name. Be careful, Jessica! You'll give it all away! He could not look up because he knew her eyes were on him. "That's hard to tell," he said.

Meantime he was thinking: Let her come now. Without me looking up or reaching out, let her get up from that chair and walk over here and say she wants to come along. He made that petition desperately but without any hope. It was the way a child asks God to alter the unchangeable, to make it snow in June, to make the dead dog in the gutter live again.

She did not move. Asa said, "I don't know what's got into him."

"Ryan," said Jessica, husky-voiced, and this time he did look up at her. "I do wish you wouldn't go. What . . . what will we do without you?"

He felt his face harden. He said, half amazed that he was able to say such a thing to her, "You'll probably do just what you did before I came."

Over the usual protests of Asa and Avery he heard her breath catch and hold and then flee out of her, rushing. How could the other two have missed that interchange of words? He saw Jessica stand and walk across the porch and look down into the dark shrubbery as one seeing into a terrible abyss. And right there, he thought angrily, is always the real chasm. It always lies at the edge of the porch, in that corner of the room where the light does not quite reach, in a pool of dark at the end of three shallow stairs.

She did not say anything. He could have touched her by extending his right arm and he did not extend it. So he would go and she would stay—that was how it would be, how it had always been. And when he remembered that only in June he had said to her, as though it were sufficient, "There are people in the world who have no one to love," he wanted to laugh aloud. What a mockery that was! The lucky lucky unloved and unloving, he thought now angrily, for they are not vulnerable.

Automatically he answered a question from Asa. "I thought I'd catch it in Greenway. Or does the local train still go twice a day?"

"It never makes connections. Jessica can drive you over," Avery said.

From somewhere fathoms deep Jessica said yes, she could do that at least.

"All right." He had not wanted that. He felt tired, hotter. There was nothing in the world you could break simply because it had to be broken. Everything had to be torn and prodded and worried and prolonged.

"It's going to be hot for your trip," said Asa.

"Be cooler at home," he said.

In a few more minutes Jessica said, as though she were surprised, "And tomorrow it's going to be fair and sunny. And a little warmer."

"What's that?" said Avery. When he leaned forward the rocker, which was very old, creaked loudly.

Jessica turned from the shrubbery where she had been staring for so long, and moonlight fell on her small bewildered face. She looked at Avery and at Asa, but not at him. "I heard it on the radio. Fair and sunny, it said, and four degrees warmer than today." Then she turned again—mouth moving slightly—and went through the front door and left them alone on the porch. From where he sat Ryan could hear her stumbling slightly in the dark hall, could hear her hand brushing the wall which was guiding her to the stairs, and he longed to get up and go in to her.

But he sat very still in the chair and he heard the creak in Avery's rocker, almost obscene in its sharpness. He heard her bump her shoe against the bottom step and then start slowly up as though it were a long way to the top of those stairs, as though it might take her all the way till morning to reach the upstairs hall.

They set out for Greenway next day as silent as strangers. Ryan said nothing because he was waiting for her. As for him, he was worn out with the summer; he had said all there was the night before. But she had protests hidden in her; he could tell by the firmness of her jaw that it was clamped down hard on many unspoken words.

They drove through town without speaking and only when they had gone out Third Creek Road and across the Katsewa did she speak at all.

"Why didn't you tell me before the others?" The voice was beautiful in its control.

He said truthfully that he hadn't known it himself. "I just decided it while I was sitting there."

The control slipped a little and he could hear the anger. "How can you decide a thing like this on the spur of the moment? As if it were of no consequence." She glanced at him crossly and then corrected that last to what she really meant. "As if *I* were of no consequence."

The day was already warm; he was already tired. He loved her but it did not at that moment seem worth mentioning. He said without great emphasis, "Why do you try to put things in my mouth that you know in advance aren't true?"

"What else can I think?"

He was a little snappy. "You might try thinking what your reason tells you. You might remember various things we've said and done together and decide whether all of them were lies."

There was silence. A fly buzzed in the car and Ryan thought that if it once lit on the windshield he would kill the damn thing if he had to put his fist through the glass.

"I knew this was all going to happen some day." Her voice was still clipped and angry but even as she spoke, misery crept in and softened it. She cocked her head into her own shoulder slightly and said again in the now blurred voice, "I always knew that."

He shifted on the seat. It sounded as if that fly had got shut up between his temples. "Jessica," he said patiently, "I didn't know myself until last night when . . ."

She was not listening. "And suppose I'd gone with you. Suppose the first time you asked me, I had gone away. Would all of this have happened then, too? Everything over in one evening and nowhere to go but back to Stoneville?"

Ryan groaned. He told her he had never heard such rationalizing in all his life.

"Well, how would I know? How do I know this wouldn't have . . ."

He was really angry with her now. "Wouldn't you like to think that though, Miss Stoneville Matron of 1937! What a nice justification, leaving you very much intact. Now that you think about it, Jessica, that was probably the only reason you didn't come away when I asked, wasn't it? You could probably tell right away that nothing would last for long. Isn't that it?"

She ignored his sarcasm as if it had been dust on some object she wanted; she merely took up the words he had said and blew the scorn away. "No," she said, giving him one long look out of those eyes which really *did* seem to darken overnight. "No, Ryan, that wasn't the reason, of course. I'm a coward. As Avery would say—I wanted to have my cake and eat it too. A bird in the hand is worth two in the bush, isn't it? Isn't that always and forever true?" (If her voice broke a little she got it quickly under control again.) "I've never wanted to run any risks or take any chances. I can't seem to learn. I don't quite dare to . . . to put myself in peril."

He leaned forward because she was facing the road and he wanted to see her face. "Jessica?"

She glanced at him and her face looked ashamed but not changing. Quickly she looked away and said in a formal polite way, "There's a later train. A few hours. I checked on it early this morning. Will you love me once before . . ."

Now he spoke her name again and slipped his hand across the seat and along the crease where her leg and body met. "I was going to ask *you,*" he said. "You should have let me ask *you.*"

She dropped one hand from the wheel on his. "Human beings are very inconsistent. So brazen in some things and so . . ." She caught his hand in hers, slipped it in and down so that it cupped her like something warm and familiar. She sighed, moved her hips a little. "I love you, Ryan," she said, watching the road.

"I know."

"If you could drive," she said, "I could put my head in your lap and nobody would be able to see inside the car."

"All right," he said. When they stopped he held her shoulders so they were very face-to-face. "I love you, too, Jessica. Will you remember that? Can you keep that in mind, hold on to that?"

"I don't know," she said.

When he let go of her shoulders she said in some confusion, "Nobody ever knows."

They switched seats and she curled up and lay with her head in his lap and her eyes closed. He drove with one hand curled on her throat, the fingers exploring the soft lobes of her ears and the slight dip of her temple. Once it occurred to him that this was symbolic of their whole relationship: a driver manipulating a car with his face proper and polite, and all the time caressing the face of a woman in his lap.

Not a woman. *The* woman. Jessica. He said, glancing down at her, "I *do* love you, Jessica."

She did not open her eyes, but she moved her head slightly against his hand. "Sometimes that doesn't seem to help much, does it?"

Her lower jaw seemed to be trembling slightly; he quieted it with a finger. "Sometimes not," he admitted softly.

They went back to the rented house which now would go unpaid and re-rented and Horace Simpson gone forever. They did not usually come in daylight; he thought of someone seeing the Buick parked there and then he stopped thinking it. In another hour he would be going away and when would they meet again? They went inside and locked the door.

He was holding her hand. She turned against him suddenly and put her face flat against him and stood there—very still. Ryan did not know she was crying until he felt the damp through his shirt.

Then he tried to get his hand at her chin. "Jessica? Darling." But she turned her head away from his fingers, first right and left and then down hard so that her forehead was in his shirt and her chin tucked safely under.

He did all he could do to get in to her. He fumbled at kissing her hair and the edge of her cheek and neck and touching her with his hands, but it was like walking around and around a little house where all the windows were locked against him.

Then he just kept his arms about her and tried to talk. "Jessica, Jessica. It's not that I really want to go. But what is there left to do? There isn't any more for us than what we have already; and ever so often it's going to hit one or the other or both of us that it isn't enough. And we'll quarrel and part and come back and make do again. And all the time it *won't* be enough, not really, not for either of us."

She seemed to be listening although she never stirred.

"It's not just that *you* don't have courage. Look at me! I've been a prize specimen all the way through, haven't I? You can't come, but I can't seem to go in any definite final way. I'll be back. It looks as though I'll always be back."

She said finally, "You make things sound so on-and-on. So tiring. Like the world turning and turning for a billion years and nothing anybody can do about it."

He shrugged. It was how he felt.

Now she was angry. "So it's not enough, Ryan. Not even this—evenings at this house, walks and talks and making love." She was flushed, pretty, unreasonable. He half expected to hear her say in a dramatic voice: *I have violated my marriage bed for you and you can stand there and tell me that isn't enough! Men are beasts!* And although she did not quite say this, she did proceed in exactly that vein for some little time. He would have smiled if she had not been so very serious and angry.

Then suddenly she broke off in mid-word and her face was startled. "Oh Lord!" she cried. "What time is it?" And then, before he could even answer her, "Not time for this! Oh Ryan, don't go. Don't go!" She threw her arms about his neck as though she would hold him back by force and she kissed him as if she would thus take him into her own body and hold him there.

Their lovemaking was very violent. It was as if in this way Jessica was giving a last wordless argument why he should not go. And he was convinced; lying in bed beside her afterwards he thought in amazement, But what more is there than this after all?

But the little demon did not quite sleep. Later, curled all about her, drowsy, he could not help but wonder that she could give so much and still . . . and yet. . . . There was no need going over that ground, not even inside his own skull. He kissed her nape instead. "Sleep?"

"Ummm. Not quite."

Her breasts were in his two hands, soft and used.

"Too many nights between this one and when I see you next," he murmured. "How many of them will I want you just like this. . . ."

She was half trying to be light, halfway still feeling that first resentment. "Purely as a bed companion, you mean, Mr. Godwin? But that isn't enough, remember? You yourself said that it wasn't enough."

He put one hand down her rib cage and over her stomach and, as always, he felt her suck it in slightly to make it seem flatter to his touch. That always amused him. In all of our lovemaking, he thought ruefully, I never once got her so altogether gone that she forgot to suck that tummy in.

"You know I didn't mean that," he was saying. "Why are you always playing this game of being angry with me for something both of us know I didn't say?"

She backed into him closer. "I'm sorry," she said.

He nuzzled her back. "If not Christmas, in the spring," he said.

She turned over, lay up against him on her side. "That's so long!" she whispered, taking his face in her hands. She slipped one leg between his legs and kissed him, lingering.

Suddenly and sharply (and for the first and only time) Ryan thought of their mortality. He thought of all the lovers there must have been who had lain just like this on many nights and who finally had died since time began. And that he and Jessica would also die, and nothing any richer for all this love and all these kisses.

But it was only a flash-by thought and he let it go as quickly as it would. It was no time for such things. Not with Jessica in his arms and the train too near that would take him away from Stoneville and toward the colder season.

Christmas of 1937 he did not come, nor yet again the following spring. Now he had been away almost a year; even with the letters which went back and forth he was more objective than he had been once.

At Christmas he wrote and promised he would come Easter. He wrote to Asa, saying that he had been sick with flu and did not want to make the trip for Christmas, but that he would see them in the spring; and both those things were lies.

To Jessica—not wanting her to worry over an illness that was not real—he wrote privately:

JESSICA, MY DEAREST:

By now you have heard the news from Asa that I will not be home for Christmas and you have heard the reason that I gave her. It is not true, so do not be concerned about it. The truth is that I simply cannot—will not—come. I think this may upset you more than the thought of my being sick, but there has never been any room for lying between us until now, and I will not start it.

I have thought this business through as many times as there are days since I saw you the end of August, and in the end all of it comes to nothing. There is no consummation for us except what we have already had, and that is adequate only when we are able to isolate it out of the rest of our lives. And the trouble is that it won't stay isolated like that. It isn't trivial enough to be placed and held in such a small compartment.

You must know, Jessica, that I do not really believe love to be deathless and endless. I would have to be eighteen again before I could credit that. Nor do I believe that love—a living thing—can thrive for long on memories and letters.

You then, dear, who have always set such store by safety's sake, should be glad of this opportunity to gain it back again. If I am right, in a little time—a year or so—we will be able to meet with nothing stronger than acute embarrassment at remembering. And people seldom die of embarrassment. You will thus achieve what you wanted originally, Jessica: the ability to call him "Dear," and sew up his pockets dutifully and have a careful son or so. If it will please you, you may remember me as a gay seducer from the Yankee world, and that will give you something secret to smile about long winter evenings sometime when you are older. Women should have such things.

I have left you now three times. The first was ridiculous, because I somehow could not say what I felt in such a situation.

This is nothing but your own kind of fear in my terms. Why do we care so much what people think? Maybe a small-town upbringing makes us that way in spite of all we can do. The second time I left, in August, was because I was out of all patience with making love smaller, quieter, tamer, uglier than it was. I left then, as you know, in weariness and impatience; and that leaving does not count for much.

But this third time, Jessica, this is a decision made over time in thought and—yes, do not frown—in love. It is not the only possible decision we might have made, but by your choices and mine up to now we have managed to forego the others. We are stuck with it. When you have thrown away every coat but one, there is no need complaining that it feels a little snug.

I have just read this letter over up to this point (which I never meant to do; I set to writing it firmly and with purpose and I promised I would not reread) and what an irritating lot it is! It sounds very smug and conceited. I had meant to anger you so you would have something to start off with for protective coloring—but not this much. These words all have a certain heed-your-elder-brother twang about them, and I know already that while you read there are two angry creases above your nose between your two brows. I know that frown. Even at this distance I half feel I could smooth it with a thumb, so familiar it is!

(And so you see: all the starch is going out of me! I will not be able to maintain the mood in which I started. It drains away when your face—even your frowning face—comes into mind.)

But Jessica (Jessica, my darling) it is not possible for me to make it clear to you in what a feeling of loss I have decided these things. Down on paper like this it looks diagrammed and neat and as if it were easily arrived at. There is no way of writing in all the ten thousand times I have come to decisions at the other pole.

And of course you know how when doing something difficult one almost always leaves oneself a loophole— Even while I am writing these lines I can hear myself arguing deep inside: *She hasn't read this yet.* You can still tear it up, Ryan Godwin, and go on to Stoneville and she will never know these things. Just as if you mail it she will never know how close it came to being the other way.

But at this moment I am engaged in playing the simultaneous game of pretending I do not hear myself and that that loophole is not there. This is already a definite, decided, altogether settled thing, I tell myself.

I am sailing May 29, 1938—this spring, Jessica—for England and Europe.

And that makes me smile a little, Jessica; it gives me a vision of brokenhearted young men taking the Grand Tour, of sad-eyed girls with reticules and big skirts being sent abroad with dour aunts for the purpose of "getting over" all the rakes there ever were. What will you think of me, having to go half a world away in all time-honored tradition to forget you? Does it enhance in your own eyes the difficulties I anticipate?

The supposed purpose of this tour is to study. It is very cheap and is conducted by a professor and peopled by teachers and old ladies. I am not really going to study, of course. What do I care for Corinthian and Doric columns as such? And I do not even own a camera! But when I write to you from Europe, I will make much of my letters read like travelogues, so that you may read them aloud around the fire that Asa will build every time it rains. This will keep you respectable. They will be glad you have been able to bring me out of my shell a little.

And Jessica, Jessica, I will think of you. How much I do not know, but probably no less than I have since summer and that is too much. The thought of you has weighted all the others down.

I have said already that I do not believe love will persevere forever, but deep-down I cannot help but wonder, half-hopefully, *what if it should?* I feel like a dying man who has fought all his life any belief in immortality, and yet secretly fears that after all he may wake up over yonder, bodiless, in some more lovely world for all his protests! Jessica, I do think this will pass—but what, my darling, if it should not? What if, apart from all the psychologists might say about desire and motivation and remembering what one chooses, love should, on its own, *persist,* not because we force it to. Not because we feed and maintain it for conscious or subconscious reasons but simply because that is—after all—the nature of love. What if man, having evolved far enough to be capable of love, should find himself more in its possession than the other way around?

Jessica, if, after all, you and I should find that to be true, we would have had a part in one of the great discoveries of man.

Not that we would know or care. The only important human discoveries seem to be made by just one person at a time, and never easy to communicate or pass down or catch in words. Which is perhaps why every generation has a fresh chance.

For all of that, Jessica, this is what I have decided. We will see what comes of it.

The high resolve with which I started this letter is all gone. I cannot close (I had meant to, but it is not possible) except in love and loneliness and longing to see you, and no small doubts that this may be just another flight, just another foolishness. Certainly it is no less miserable than either of the other two.

I love you, Jessica.

RYAN

JUNE 15, 1938

RYAN, MY DEAREST:

Until your first letter came today with the strange stamps, it was not possible for me to think of you as really gone. And gone so far! Wellman was different, because we had talked about it together and I knew about the brick walks and the library building you think is so ugly and about Barney and the cat. You had sent a picture card or so, and Wellman was a *place* to see you in.

But Plymouth, England? I have read and read your letter and still that is nothing but a word. During the whole trip I will perhaps see you suspended in space except for big words—names of cities and rivers in capital letters. This is a geography-book trip for me, across a colored map. It may be there are streets and old women and little girls in all these weird places, too, but I—for one—have trouble believing it.

Now, while I am writing you (it is upstairs; there is no one in the house but Lady Malveena and me) I look out of the window into Walnut Street. June has made it very green, very quiet. I look up from your letter and this letter and I tell myself as firmly as I can, "There will always be an England." But it is a lie. There will never be an England for me except as a word you have written and a name in the newspapers.

I went back and read part of your letter again—low cliffs, you said, that seemed golden; and how a barge came to the ship carrying "little bureaucrats" and newsboys (I like that—"little bureaucrats") and that all the compartments on the train into Paddington Station were crowded and hot. All of that seems very far away.

But what I can see from this window—these trees, and the house across the street and Miss Gelene's up the way, the oaks and the orchard and four times a day the train going by between here and Greenway—that is real to me. And not much else, I'm afraid. We will never be able to alter this—that I think Stoneville is small, and you think it is cramped. Perhaps, as Avery would say, 'tis all in the eye of the beholder?

Now that you are abroad I know you will do just what your letter said. When I think of how I spend my days in comparison to all you see and do, I know surely that you will forget me and that we will have nothing to say to each other after this trip is over. What do I know about Paris? I cannot even give anything a French pronunciation.

This morning when I woke up, I heard the first whistles from the cotton mill. (You said once they sounded like hungry wolves, but I never thought of that—not until you said it.) The first whistle warns the women in the kitchen to get the oatmeal hot and the coffee perked, and fifteen minutes later the shift starts and everybody hurries. It gives me a funny feeling to hear those whistles in the morning and know that people are hurrying and running about because of them, and here I lie quietly in bed, listening to things that do not call me. Lots of mornings, though, I do not hear them at all; because I have waked up with the whistles blowing almost all of my life. Did they wake you when you were home? I never thought to ask.

Lady Malveena fixed me breakfast. She never mentions you to me nor do I mention you to her. That seems strange, because we two love you; and each of us knows.

You know, of course, that I have very little to do with my time. During the day Lady Malveena does most of the work and when I help her I feel like a child being permitted to bake cookies in spite of the fact that flour will soon be all over everything. I belong to a number of young married groups, clubs and things. I go to the library, shop, read. On Saturdays I run the mimeograph machine that puts out our church programs. Sometimes I sew.

This morning I went to a Coca-Cola for Dora Pharr, who is getting married next week, and Avery and I had lunch together at the hotel. Then I took the car to have it checked and the oil changed and left it. I went to a movie which was very bad. Coming home, I remember that I set my watch by the clock in Western Union, and while I was doing that I thought of you. I thought that you must have seen the Tower of London by now. Somehow that made me very sad—to think that I will be losing you, after all, to things no warmer than buildings in other places. I wanted to put my face on the glass of the Western Union door where it was cold, purely because you had a tower and I had only this electric clock in Stoneville. When Mr. Ashley saw me standing there, I hurried off.

But that clock, Ryan—it keeps good time. Will it never be enough for you that it keeps good time?

Tonight Asa and I will go together to our circle meeting at Milly Roberts' house. It has been very hot today. Milly will serve a congealed salad with cottage cheese (I like cottage cheese but I remember that you say it has no taste) and when someone asks her about it she will bring out the page torn from a new magazine in which that very salad is all explained beneath a color photograph. Everyone will say that hers looks even lovelier than the picture and Milly will smile and say she *does* think it turned out pretty well. She will use her good silver (French Provincial—I know all the silver patterns in town) and her hobnail crystal plates with little green napkins on them. No one will smoke, of course. Adelaide Poston will lead the business session and Rachel Greer will mention the love gifts which the treasury has not received. She will manage to look both stern and simpering at the same time—a difficult feat, but she will do it. She has been doing it for years. Mary Lee Pfeifer will have a portfolio full of liquor advertisements. She brings these every meeting to show how young people are being seduced by full-color ads. A vote will be taken and we will agree not to subscribe to any of those magazines which carried these ads, all of which Mary Lee will have listed.

Oh, Ryan, I almost have to laugh—seeing your face as you read this. How dull this must sound to you! I can hear you saying, "Why in the world do you bother with that kind of thing!"

And I tell you, Ryan (you will never understand this), such days as today are a comfort to me. To know this life so well that it fits about me comfortably, even to know these people and these things well enough to anticipate that they will be very dull—I take a certain pleasure in that. It was what I wanted, remember?

And as for you, Ryan Godwin—you are the only unexpected thing in all of that quiet "comfortableness" I am speaking of. The very *fact* of you breaks in upon the quiet circle. You are the thing I never meant to want or need, much less to have.

And yet I do want and need you. And yet I do love you.

This is again that old old dilemma. This is what prompted that horrible letter you wrote (have you noticed my discipline, that I have not mentioned it till now?) to me before you left. Always I wanted to be safe and I was safe; and now everything wobbles because of you and may fall. So, Ryan, I do take a risk because of you—but it is never a tall risk and you hate that.

You will be reading this without any patience. I know how you are frowning about now (you see, my darling, I know *your* frown too; you bring your brows out like shelves). But Ryan, what else can I do? I do not know how to take this risk except to a certain point and then everything in me stops deadstill and cannot move. Even now I am amazed that I (me! *Jessica!*) should ever have done what I have done thus far. It is not enough, of course. I know. I have read your letter how many times?

What a mess this is! I always end up writing about myself. Not solving anything.

Only one more personal pronoun, and it is important only because of the *you* involved. I love you. Love you. Love you.

JESSICA

309 WALNUT STREET
JUNE 20, 1938

RYAN, DARLING:

By now I had hoped there would be a second letter from you. The first one which came last week from Plymouth and London was duly read aloud after supper and even Lady Malveena listened without saying anything—although I thought she watched me carefully. It was as if she thought I might do something as unexpected as go up in flames before her eyes. But I will not, will I, Ryan? I will stay here and grow old and cozy by this hearth and smile about you —as you said—on winter evenings. Strange that your letter hurts still. Perhaps it will always hurt. Back in the intellectual sticks we have a saying that the truth always hurts. (And now I am ashamed of having written that. You see how defensive I am? Forgive me.)

I have two messages from the family. Asa wants to know if you can still get Brussels lace; and Avery says you had better come away and home while the coming is good. He does not really believe there will be a war, but he says for me to tell you that a local skirmish is as good to get killed in as anything.

I hope there will be nothing at all, not even a border clash or a village uprising to amount to anything. Hitler seems even more unreal to me than Plymouth and the cliffs. And he looks so absurd in all his photographs and makes such a racket in his speeches. It is hard to believe that a man who would grow so ridiculous a mustache could be a threat to anyone. He looks as if the most he could do would be defy his wife at a shaving mirror.

It is new to me to discover that, after all, I am completely selfish. I am afraid I am very unconcerned about the Germans, and whoever it is in Czechoslovakia that Hitler thinks ought to be somewhere else. All I can think about is you and me, and what would happen if you were to die. That must be at least one of the big differences between men and women. (We were always talking, you remember, about the male mind and the female mind.) Men are able to think generally, in all the words politicians use in speeches such as Democracy and Man. But women live on specifics—this man, this house, this child.

So that as for Hitler, I would gladly give him all of Europe just to have you home again.

JESSICA

JUNE 29, 1938
LATE EVENING

DEAR RYAN:

Only one thing in your report disappointed me. I had always thought the heather bloomed in spring and summer. But Scotland sounds wonderful even if you have missed the heather season, and I would like to see it. I keep a Heathcliff fixation, after all these years. I used to write a long story about a little girl who lived on the moor and wanted to learn to play the violin. I used to write it in nickel notebooks, the yellow ones, and I tied them together with strings! Isn't that funny—I hadn't thought of that in years!

Your descriptions are always good and I liked the thought of the tidiness of all those hedges and stone fences. But then you say also much of the land is rugged and there are black crags. Perhaps that kind of country makes us all build careful fences and plant our hedges evenly?

Did you ever play in the stone quarry which is on the other side of Greenway, toward the mountains? When I was small, I thought that the wildest most beautiful place in the world. The aunt with whom I lived at that time, on a farm, thought it wisest not to venture far from home in all your life, so I did not get to see it much and the wonder didn't wear off. I remember the big hill—the one they've cut nearly half away to take the rock—has muscadines and moss and lots of scrawny trees which can't get roots down far enough to amount to anything. The hill is nearly all rock, and it has cracked and bulged in an ugly shape all over it. After a rain, water stands in these cracks and holes and all manner of small flowers spring up overnight and die. Most of them are lavender in color and very delicate. When I think of the Scotland you wrote about in your letter, it seems to me much like the old quarry, except vaster and more lovely.

During the day now, Lady Malveena and I are cleaning out the attic, which is very hot and dirty work. Do you have any idea how many of your possessions are still there? Lots of old books and an arrowhead collection and some U.S. stamps and some benches you built once. Lady Malveena is very embarrassed during all of this. She tells me all the time that I really do not need to help, as though I were a widow cleaning out my dead husband's things. The truth is that I am not much help to her anyway. I keep putting my hand onto things you held once, and mooning in all the dust and cobwebs. I do not know enough of what you were like when you were small, or how things were then in this house. I was so lonely when I was a little girl that I am always looking for the child in other people. I always wonder how things were for them.

Asa has had a summer cold but for the most part all of us are well. Avery has joined the Kiwanis Club and for initiation he had to beg on the street corner to get treasury funds. Asa and he are buying some important property uptown for an out-of-town buyer and they are very pleased with themselves. Avery has begun to talk of a new car, but Asa will never have it.

I miss you, dear.

Do you remember (or did you ever?) how when you were little you would pick and choose very carefully the last thought that would be in your head just as you fell asleep? As though it were something you could drop in a slot to make your dreams sweet and to wake you up happy?

Ryan, you are that thought—but you are always there.

When you leave Edinburgh, you say you will be going to France for your longest stay. How long is longest? Will you be back before fall? And if you are back before school starts again, will you come here?

Ryan, please do.

JESSICA

July 4
And in a Very American Frame of Mind

DEAREST RYAN:

After I got your letter I went to the library as you said and took out *Mein Kampf*, at which Cornelia looked a bit dismayed and said she had a lovely novel she thought I would like very much better.

I must say that it was such a long book that the prospect of reading it all, from front to back, was too much for me. I *did* read enough of it to understand what you mean when you say it is not enough to dismiss Hitler as a ridiculous man. I know how you have always hated oversimplifications.

So here's to America! To freedom!

And that reminds me that we rode down Walker Avenue today just to see if old Mr. Cates had his American flag hung out, and because of the occasion he had *two* of them. I saw him sitting on his front porch, but for once he did not run out and wave his umbrella and yell at Avery about going to the county home. He spat right out in the yard, over the banister, and I could almost hear it hit and splat, there was so much force behind it! I thought of how you would have smiled at that! Do you know he won't come to church at all now? For a long time after he quit playing the piano, Asa says, he would come and sit up front behind Avery and sing one half tone down, to throw the choir and organ off. But now he doesn't even come. Mr. Barnes said the other day that he was just sitting at home with that flag hung out, basking in his sinfulness like a snake in the sun. That tickled me. . . .

Tonight we went to the picture show, even Asa. Now (I am writing on the dining-room table) they are playing the radio very loud in the parlor and talking about something in the *Beacon*. Avery wants to hear what Mr. Murrow has to say about the news.

Lady Malveena just came in and said to tell you hello and not to eat too many fancy foreign foods with too many peppers in them. I think she has it mixed up with Mexico.

Today I played bridge with a whole group of women at the Woman's Club to benefit the charity drive. I am very bad at bridge. By now I must have a dozen candy dishes for low score, and if you and I ever run away together we shall eat always from candy dishes.

While we played, Cassie and Sue at my table were talking about their husbands. As a matter of fact, women at these things always talk about their husbands. The talk is tolerant, of course; everybody sounds as if husbands are poorly trained house pets which are, however, not without value. Something like hamsters, or goldfish.

They were talking about marriage in general and after a while they began to talk about triangles and "other women" and adultery. I was nodding, sorting my cards, not listening much. And all of a sudden I thought: *That's me! I am an adulteress!* Ryan, I was never more startled in my life!

Sue was saying she could not understand how any woman could have an affair, how she could live with herself, go on being a wife at the same time. I wanted to tell her it is much easier than one would think. But most of all, Ryan, I wanted terribly just to do *something* to shake her sureness. I wanted to tell her that she did not *know* if she might have an affair sometime or not. How easy it is to be virtuous if one is never tempted! Sue says she never saw a man she could seriously consider in that way. And since she has had no opportunity and no desire, how can she know? What if a new man moves to town and is thrown with her and every time she sees him things begin moving in her stomach and she has to hold her arm rigid all the time to keep from touching him?

I was very angry and played abominable bridge from then on.

And sitting there slapping my cards to the table (the wrong cards, trumps thrown away and things) I decided that only a handful of people know whether they are really *good* or not, and those are the people who sometime have wanted very much not to be good. The rest of the people are not good—they are just neutral. They are just waiting to find out.

Or am I just rationalizing? Am I trying to make my own actions more acceptable? Does one ever *know* when he is thinking honestly or not?

This afternoon Aunt Victoria was by. She said she thought I looked a little sickly and ought to take blackstrap molasses and eat yeast cakes. She always says I look sickly—hopefully, I think. It would please her to think the blood is just thin and weak in our whole family. She also asked if we had heard from you. Everybody asks about you now that you are in Europe and the *Beacon* mentioned it in the last issue. You are a celebrity.

Ryan, I hate my Aunt Victoria. I have always hated her. Growing up in her house was terrible, and I hated her when I was very small; and I felt doomed because I was able to feel that much hatred. I knew I would go to hell for it, sure enough. In her house I felt like all those bloodless-looking plants trying to grow up under stones, and I used to tell myself that any kind of living was better than her kind.

I wish I had known my parents. Or even I wish I had some surety that things might have been better and happier if I *had* known them! I do not even know that. Perhaps we would not have liked each other. My father was a barber and my mother used to have a house and yard in which she grew hollyhocks and black-eyed Susans and purple iris. That's all I know about my parents. That's everything I ever knew.

What a rambling letter and how dull! I wish I could see you.

Do you know that thinking of you is a luxury? I permit myself the luxury of thinking your name. Sometimes I go to bed very early so I will have the dark to myself, and I can think of you and the shape of your face and how we felt against each other in other nights than these.

But sometimes you come unbidden. I have never told you this before and I do not intend to mention it again, for I shut this part of my life off separate. But Ryan, when *he* touches me I think of you. That is the worst thing. To do one thing and think another . . . nothing is worse than that. This is the most dishonest I have ever felt. It is the only time I feel like that word, like an "adulteress."

It seems to me that if you were here, Ryan, you would have something sensible to say to all this raft of things and I certainly wish you were. Here, I mean.

I love you. Do you ever remember that?

JESSICA

JULY 18, 1938

MY DARLING;

I have been listening to the radio and reading (a rainy day, good for such things; Asa is lying down) and trying to pretend I would not sit down immediately to answer your letter. Now I feel I have performed real acts of discipline; it is fully an hour since your letter came.

Cornelia Satterfield asked me to remind you that Eddie Cantor and Sonja Henie and all manner of famous people are also in Europe this summer. I think she believes this will make them friends of yours and that you will probably run into each other in cafés and things. She also says the King of England will be in France the same time as you. Mr. Garris is hoping that when you get back you will write some articles for the *Beacon*. I promised him I would mention it.

I saw the movie *Blockade* this week, with Henry Fonda and Madeleine Carroll. It was about the Spanish War. I take it that tourists probably cannot go to Spain these days? Knowing where you are and all that you must be doing, I am reminded of the multitude of things we never did together. I can dance; did you know that? We never danced. We haven't been swimming together or held hands in the movies except once. We never once had dinner by candlelight, and I thought that went with every romantic love affair.

I wish you were here.

JESSICA

AUGUST 10

DEAREST:

Two letters from you! I feel better than at any time since you have gone. And the news that you will be back in the States before September 4! I know when you wrote that sentence, you never thought it capable of transforming the world! But I tell you, all of Stone County is more beautiful because of it!

Lady Malveena has a tomcat which she calls Falanges. She says he won't stay long; he has too full a life to lead. He is very unaffectionate and self-sufficient and Lady Malveena likes him very much. She says he makes her feel like the *en*-tire animal kingdom ain't gone to pot.

I know your plans are not complete about whether to try Budapest or not, so I will not write again until I hear from you about an address.

If—as you say—you will be home by the fourth, then surely you will come to Stoneville. Even for a day? For a night? Just writing that down makes me ache to see you. I am beginning to learn that one human being can miss another to the point of hunger. I had not known before now that the mere thought of you could affect me so strongly in a physical way. When I dwell for long on the size and shape and remembrance of you there begins a slow opening and closing deep in my stomach, and after a while I cross my legs very tightly. I cannot say it more accurately than this—that both body and spirit can grow lonesome.

And now I am a little amazed at myself for writing such things! I will stop before I have shocked you completely.

Ryan—darling darling—come as soon as you can!

JESSICA

But when Ryan came back there was not enough time before school started and he did not get to Stoneville until November, 1938. It was two years since the day he had first seen her. He was tired and winter was coming early; he rode toward home in a blaze of red trees that were already going into brown.

Since his return from Europe two months before, Ryan had worked harder than he ever had before. He was carrying an extra teaching load; he wrote articles and made talks to student groups; he took to going to faculty meetings and clubs, about which he had never bothered until now. All that fall he had behaved as though each day were a box of a certain size into which he would put everything he could until the whole capacity was taken, leaving no time for Jessica.

Jim said where in the world did he get the idea he had to cast a lovely light, for God's sake?

"You doctors!"

Jim shrugged. "You don't *have* to get any sleep or have any extra time of your own. It's not compulsory."

Sometimes the method almost worked. The same thing had happened occasionally in Europe, when new sights and sounds had sometimes for whole hours made him disremember her name. But he learned one thing. He could think "nothing" or he could "not think of Jessica"; it was not the same thing. The second had her name involved, and that made all the difference.

She had mailed him with one of her letters a bad photograph of her made with a Brownie. Asa and Avery had taken it on a Sunday afternoon and it showed her standing in front of the ivy which grew over the carriage house, with the sun shining on her hair.

When the photo came, Ryan put it carefully in a desk drawer under papers and envelopes. He wanted to remember her face in his own mind rather than memorize a photograph, so he avoided taking it out of the drawer and looking at it. However, he kept his things (at first he was sure it was accidental) so that only the corner of the photograph was always visible underneath the clutter; and in sorting things he would touch that deckle edge without taking the picture out. He felt oddly comforted, just knowing it was there.

The visit home that November, 1938, was like the other times except quieter.

When first he saw her, standing near the car alongside Asa and Avery, he felt as though everything in him had shifted, not with a wrench or a jerk, but simply that everything of which he was made had moved—the heart slightly up, the lungs in, the stomach downward. He had expected it and yet he was surprised. He thought to himself in some amazement, Am I always going to love her, then?

And the answer was: Probably.

When he came up to them, he could not tell whether she was anxious. She stood very quietly while Ryan spoke to his brother and his sister. When he came to her, she looked up at him with a careful smile. "Hello, Ryan." Only last week she had written saying that she loved him and that it no longer mattered whether he loved or not. *Nothing can change me,* she had written. *It's a relief to know at last the size of it.*

So when she spoke to him she looked up quietly, not asking him anything. He bent and merely put his face against hers for an instant. Then he said, "It's very good to see you, Jessica. It's good to be home."

Her smile went over into a reality. Avery said, "Be it ever so humble, isn't that so, Ryan? Even after Europe?"

But Ryan had not taken his eyes away from hers. "Even after Europe," he agreed.

That was really the beginning of all that each of them became because of the other.

From that moment on they accepted the way things were because it was better than nothing; it was all they had. They were resigned to holidays and visits, but these visits were like the sum of time. The letters they wrote were as if nothing at all happened in the months between Christmas and Easter, between Easter and summer, between summer and Thanksgiving. That world was separate and the door to Stoneville closed.

Jessica's existence on Walnut Street was shut away, and his life in Wellman closed off—these things they kept to the far east and west of each other. It was as if they lived on separate sides of a very large house, from which they could sometimes come into one room by opposite doors and be together for a while before going out again.

In time, a certain calmness came. Whatever happened in those other rooms in those other wings did not touch this central one. Or if it did touch it, they elected to pretend that it did not.

And out of this there grew a certain paradox. Once Jessica wrote to him about that:

> Darling, let me tell you the strangest thing of all. It seems to me that for years I have wanted whatever it is that answers one's uneasiness. Some stable center, some hollow of quietness. In a word, what you would probably call Security.
>
> And now I tell you a riddle: that, in this unlawful and unrecognized love for you, which is made without vows or sureties and even without enough rewards and satisfactions, still I find an answer and a homecoming. There does not appear to be any security for anyone except the security of being understood.
>
> If I were stronger (or even, Ryan, smarter) I would be able to throw all of the rest over just to hold on to this. But what would I do in your life, which I do not understand, really? And how you would hate it in a town that I might like!
>
> But at the very least I have now the outer trappings without

having paid too high a price, and at the same time I have been able to find the inner quietness. Is it not good that you should —after all—be the one to give me that?

He could not quite feel that way, and yet he had passed through that first strong feeling of Not-Enough. Now it was enough after all to know that she was *there*, that things were better just because she was.

Now that they had this frame of mind between them, separation was not so difficult. Time—which so long for them had been erratic, stopping and starting and coming in sudden bright bits—went back to steadiness and flow. When they came together after long absences they were not so much aware of having been apart. That which they had between them, while it was not marriage, had a quality of permanence about it. What was a month or so out of lifetimes?

And Europe bubbled like a pot too much boiled; the Nazis signed a treaty with the Soviets; Hitler invaded Poland and the nations went to war; and these things flowed in time like objects in the Nile, and Ryan and Jessica loved each other.

This is not to say that they had an emotional island. It is not to say that they could (or really wanted to) step back and away completely from all the turbulence. Even Stoneville—which usually was merely "disturbed" by things so huge and far away—was shaken by these events. Dunkerque was one of those human explosions which got through to everyone; it took John Doe by his handpainted tie and shook him rather violently. It staggered the imagination, like Thermopylae.

And the siege of Britain was another event of like magnitude. There were people in the world who felt proud to be a part of the race of man, merely because of unknown and undistinguished Britons—Londoners who, with their buckets and sandbags and air raid helmets seemed to be heroes of some understandable stuff. The little men in America grasped something of that. Men who might never rush up a hilltop unarmed under heavy fire—they could still see the stubbornness with which grocerymen and shoe clerks and librarians were running nightly about the roofs of London putting out incendiary bombs, or digging out bodies from wreckage and rubble and ruin. These were the men who would never capture dozens singlehanded, but who were capable of cleaning up blood and dust and still were able to go on selling those shoes and lending those books, and feeding cereal to their children at breakfast time.

Workers at arms factories in Coventry saw their stores and houses lost—and went on making arms. Plymouth (where Ryan had so recently been) was badly hit. Seven raids over Liverpool could not close that port.

Later, of course, this war was to seem as ordinary as others. These first events of war, however; these were the Glory Days. This was Churchill (". . . on the landing grounds . . . in the fields and in the streets; we shall fight in the hills; we shall never surrender.") and the V-for-Victory sign, around-the-clock R.A.F., a woman in a newsreel rescued after being buried for eighteen hours, Spitfires and Hurricanes and Wrens, people in subway tunnels overnight.

And time passed in holidays, summer and Thanksgiving and Christmas and Easter—the way time had once passed in seasons: spring and summer and winter and fall. It was winter of 1941, and he had bought a record player and some records for her Christmas present. There was a Sunday on which 183 planes left their carriers to fly over a Pacific outpost almost no one had ever heard about, and flew back leaving 2,403 dead Americans behind and some thousand other wounded.

When Ryan came to Stoneville for Christmas in 1941 he was startled to see that little sleepy town so up in arms. It seemed to him that the mere *fact* of the existing globe had been thrust in upon them. People stood on the streets and stopped with their feet propped on the running boards of parked cars to shake their heads angrily, and mumbled in barber chairs about it. Ryan was reminded of the way some families close ranks when any outsider attacks them.

It was a sober and a quiet Christmas. They listened to the radio, went to church, bought presents, wrapped presents, opened presents. On the new record player they played Gershwin, Sibelius, Wagner. Ryan and Jessica were together and apart in all the old ways, although the little house was gone. They rode out by there, saw a pickup truck parked in the drive.

"I hate the wintertime," Jessica said. "No matter where we make love, some part of me is cold! If it's not my bottom, it's my feet."

"How romantic!" said Ryan, laughing.

Evenings at home they turned from station to station, seeking news on world events. Ryan and Avery talked about the possibility of army service.

That year it did not snow; it only turned bitter gray cold and every leaf in town seemed dead and fallen. Ryan did not get to stay the full vacation; there was an English Teachers' meeting in Baltimore on December 28 and he was Wellman's delegate. Back at school he found the girls restless and excitable. They had boy friends volunteering for marine service, or brothers, and upset mamas calling them up long distance every night. When Ryan lectured on Milton he could see the pity in their eyes. They seemed to be saying, *Mr. Godwin, don't you know there's a* WAR *on?*

He was at home at Easter and in June he had the letter from Jessica that she was pregnant.

That was too much to believe at such a distance. He called the family long distance that night, made the usual talk; but when finally he had Jessica on the line he did not know what he had intended to say.

He fumbled around the question he really wanted to ask and said instead, "Jessica, are you happy?"

"Not yet," she said. "I'm not anything yet."

"How do you feel?"

Across the singing wire for miles he heard her laugh. "Just the way I did before."

He did not know if the others were standing with her in the hall or if they had gone back into the parlor to stand in front of the fire. He wanted to keep it so all of Jessica's answers would be harmless just in case.

But he had to ask the one question. "Jessica, is it mine?"

There was a little silence. "I don't know." On the word "know" her voice stumbled ever so slightly, as if it had hit a kink of some kind. "It's very strange, not knowing."

"Well, what do you think?" He was agonized. Deep down he had believed women would have intuitions about such things. If they were going to have intuitions about *anything* it ought to be on such a subject.

"I don't know."

So it was an accident either way; it shouldn't have happened at all and it had, and she could not be sure.

All of this was terrible, talking and not being able to see or touch. If Ryan could only have seen her face, he was certain he would have been reassured. As it was he felt oddly lost and shut away. He pressed her. "Do you hope it is, Jessica?"

He thought her voice sounded older and more introspective. "I don't think so," she said. One month of expectant motherhood could not have quieted her this much; he did not believe it.

"Why not?"

"Because that would be just too much," she said firmly.

"Well, I hope it's mine." He hoped so fervently; and he wanted her to know that. "I hope it's mine and not his. I don't want you to have his."

"But I'm going to."

"What do you mean, you're going to?"

"I mean it doesn't matter which because that's what it is."

He wondered wildly if Asa and Avery were listening in the hall and if they thought she had lost her mind.

It was a very unsatisfactory conversation. When he had hung up the telephone and paced the apartment, he went out into the hall and kicked Barney's cat when she tried to nip him on the knee. He thought about going to see Jim and Anne and thought better of it. He wondered if there were blood tests and if Jessica would submit to them secretly. Then he knew how crazy all his thinking was.

He finally walked uptown to a movie he hadn't the slightest desire to see.

Between that time and February, 1943, when Fen was born, Jessica did not write him much. At first her letters were as frequent as before. She wrote that she would walk uptown and spy on herself as she passed in plate glass windows, sucking her stomach in. She did not believe that there could be a baby in it, drawing life, making ready.

She wrote him that being pregnant was like being in love; one felt no one could miss it. The very eyes would glow and the walk and tone of voice be different from before. Strangers passing in the streets would *know* and smile.

And after she wrote him:

> Ryan, if this should really be your child, I do not intend that either of us should really know it or admit it. I have made it Avery's child out of will and intent if not of flesh; and his child it shall be. That is all there is to say about it. Some hypocrisies are too monstrous for me, and I do not intend to

spend the next years watching my son or daughter play and thinking of the resemblance to his father—and by "father" meaning someone quite different from the man they know. He *is* the father. By my choosing I make him so.

So that is all, and let us not speak of it because I do not intend to vary from that course.

And through this Ryan knew all over again the waste of having certain privileges without any attendant responsibility to make roots and foundations. What could he have said to her about it? After that letter she never again mentioned the possibility that this baby might be his. He was already the child's uncle; he had no choice.

And it seemed to him that the name of Avery crept into her letters more and more after that because Avery was the Father-of-Her-Child. That fatherhood was a gift she had made him unbeknownst to him and had insisted that he have. The facts were irrelevant.

Ryan accepted that. There was nothing else for him to do.

In February—because he *had* to, he actually had to—Ryan asked for two weeks off and went home to be there when the baby came. Jessica hated him for that. That day when Ryan came up the walk she stood in the door and stared at him with more anger than he knew she could have in her. "What are you doing here! Why did you think I wanted you to come?"

"I wanted to see you." He was hurt. He had thought it a sign of the permanence and depth of love that he would not leave her alone through such a thing.

"*See* me! Hah!" she snapped. She went upstairs with the grace of a giant frog.

He found her very unreasonable. She was large and awkward and furious. The week he was there before the baby was born, she would not talk to him. She would not be touched. Sometimes she did not come down at all during the day.

Once she asked him bitterly if he had only come to shame her, to see her big and ugly and horrible.

He was astounded. "No! No, of course not. I wanted to help."

"Help? What in the world could you do?"

He did not know. "I only thought—"

"I have never hated anybody like I hate you now," she said through her teeth, viciously.

Ryan told himself shakily that she was far advanced in pregnancy and women were not quite stable at such times.

Sometimes when the others could not hear she would look at Ryan with utter contempt and expel the one bitter syllable "Oh!" He had never heard so furious a single sound. It wilted and shrunk him. He grew timid as a bank clerk.

The child was always between them, huge and active. When a bump appeared on her stomach from some tiny fist within, he could not help but stare. And when he stared she turned her back on him as if she did not trust herself to speak for rage.

Asa herself was amazed to see him home. "This is certainly not like you, Ryan Godwin!"

He told her as lightly as he could that he had never become an uncle before and he wanted to see it through. But that was not enough for Asa. She watched him as though he were a sum she was constantly adding and checking in her head.

And for the first time Ryan thought: Asa suspects. That made him very nervous.

Still, there was no danger in it so long as he could keep Asa from doubting Jessica. She could not touch him; and the worst she must be allowed to think was that Ryan was smitten at a distance by his sister-in-law and that Jessica had not noticed. So he moved and talked as circumspectly as he could, for *her* sake.

Avery had become, of course, a caricature of the expectant father. He was an exaggeration of all he thought was expected of him. He had already bought cigars. He asked Jessica too solicitously and too often how she felt until even Jessica showed her annoyance. These days she wore a look of anger which seemed to say plainly that she was completely alone in the world. No one could help her. Alone she had carried this baby all these months and alone she would give it birth, and probably in pain. She would have looked like some tragic figure in a play had she not also appeared so ill-tempered about the whole thing.

Now, of course, Ryan and Jessica had no alliance against the world and he was altogether miserable. Now she was Avery's wife all day long and all night long. There was not even any secret communing with the eyes. It was Avery who brought a pillow to her and received her smile. It was Avery's hand which was permitted to rest upon her to feel the child turn over.

Every night Ryan sat on the back doorstep until very late and smoked and smoked and told himself that coming home this time had been the craziest thing he had ever done. There was no necessity to put himself in a position where he had nothing to gain. There was no advantage if he invested so much self in a situation where he had no place, where she did not want him to be.

Lady Malveena was always raising her window (it was warm; she had not nailed it down against the cold) to yell at him late at night, "Why don't you go to bed?"

"What's the matter, me puffing so loud on this cigarette keeping you awake?"

"Smoking never changed anything," she would say.

Sometimes Ryan would walk around and lean his elbows on the sill of her window. She slept in an old red flannel shirt which was too hot for the weather and always smelled of perspiration.

"Listen, Lady Malveena," he would say, "is she going to be all right?"

"Thousands been all right ahead of her."

"I don't care about those thousands. Is she healthy? Is it going to be easy?"

"It's never easy."

He would blow out smoke in a cloud; he would tell her she was certainly a big help. "I thought there would be something I could do . . ." he would finish, miserably.

Her voice would be suddenly and unexpectedly gentle. "Dying is always the worst on the widows."

"What? What was that?"

"Being left and out. Always worse than going your same self."

"You're so damn profound you scare me!"

To this Lady Malveena would say that she had better be sleeping than hearing blasphemy, and would close the window almost on his sleeves.

The day finally came and Dr. Harris parked his car at the curb and came in the door smiling. Why do they smile? Ryan thought. And why are undertakers so damn pleasant? He went off in the kitchen and sat with his hands clasped on the back of his neck and his head down.

"Has he gone upstairs?"

Lady Malveena said sure he'd gone upstairs; wasn't nobody else having babies in this house.

"What was he smiling for?"

"He just always does, that's all. It doesn't mean anything."

If it didn't mean anything, why did he do it? And Ryan thought, If she makes any noise I think I'll run all the way up those stairs. He stiffened to hold his body in the chair.

After a while Lady Malveena got out the drawer of silverware and a cloth and polish and put it before him without comment. He polished grimly.

As the day wore on, he heard her. It was never screaming; it was not very loud but he heard it. He thought he would have heard the mattress creaking when she turned in bed.

Early in the day he heard only a tired sigh, an occasional little moan that sounded as if she might be merely taking the measure of pain, tasting it in her mouth. Later it was less screaming than it was a strange wrenched sound. It was violent, forced out of her from down deep.

When this part began, Lady Malveena bent over him once and said, "Now don't you mind that. It's nothing but the pushing. Nobody can push that hard without making a lot of noise."

"All right," he said. He was holding the cloth so tightly that his hands were white.

Lady Malveena patted his shoulder, brought him the silver service with its complex trimming of tiny curlicues. She gave him a box of toothpicks to slip under the cloth and outline the miniature roses and the tiny tiny ferns.

Ryan was more meticulous than clocks.

Around five o'clock the baby was finally born. (Five o'clock, thought Ryan, quitting time. A good day's work.) When he heard the new sound from upstairs he let go of the polishing cloth and saw that his hands were shaking.

In a little while Dr. Harris called down for hot water and Lady Malveena took it up. When she came back she said it was a boy.

"Miss Jessica's just fine," she said. "You hear me? She had that baby just right."

Just *right?* He was sure it had been in profoundest agony.

Dr. Harris came down and had a cup of coffee. "A nice fat boy," said Dr. Harris. "Fine coffee, Lady Malveena."

Lady Malveena thanked him.

"Avery's with her now. Proud as can be."

"I bet he is," said Ryan, a little bitterly. He could not go up.

He loved her and for all he knew that baby was his son, and here he was with servants and idiotically smiling doctors. He said, "Is Jessica all right?"

"She's fine. Went at it like she'd had babies all her life."

"It's in the blood," said Lady Malveena hastily. She gave Ryan an anxious look. "You want some coffee, Mister Ryan?"

"No, I do not," he said decidedly.

When the doctor had finished his coffee and gone away (still smiling; would he have smiled had the baby come two-headed or with three feet?) Ryan took up the silver teapot he had been polishing and walked across the room and dropped it into the garbage can. Lady Malveena watched him, but she said nothing about it. She had the look of someone watching a child do foolishness which one will undo when that child is out of sight.

He walked out of that kitchen and off the porch into the back yard. He leaned up against the ivy on the carriage house (let a snake bite me! he challenged) and he smoked a cigarette and ground his leg against the stub of a rosebush until his trousers tore slightly, and he felt the skin smarting from his ankle to his knee. Then he thought, *That* was foolish. What did that prove?

It was very much later that night before he was allowed to see her. First she must sleep and the baby had to settle down and sleep. When at last he went in, the others stood in the doorway, smiling in ownership.

He stumbled on the rug. He could not look at her. He looked at the baby but it didn't even look like a baby yet. It looked just like what it was—a piece of flesh newly torn out.

When he sat down on the side of the bed, Jessica reached out and took his hand and when he looked he saw her eyes were standing deep in tears. "Jessica," he said. "Oh, Jessica."

But she only watched with those eyes grown tremendously large and dark in the paleness of her face. She looked toward the bedroom door and when she saw that the tall footboard of the bed hid her face from the others, she took up his hand and moved it to her mouth and bit it savagely, over and over. There were whitened dents where she put her teeth along his knuckles and over the back of his hand.

Ryan went on sitting on the bed, not moving, not speaking. He did not know what she meant by that and yet he understood; and all the time she bit his one hand as hard as she could bite, he took the other and rubbed a small and gentle circle on the corner of her shoulder.

It was just before Fen's second birthday that Avery and Jessica were killed.

In those two years, Ryan had been home often. He had seen the boy walk and cut teeth and throw temper tantrums. He had seen Jessica giving him baths. He had seen Avery smiling paternally, smoking a pipe (he had taken more often to a pipe, now that he was a father) and Ryan had loved Jessica more than ever. They had done many things together in those two years, written many letters, shared much laughter and many thoughts. Ryan had thought: Nothing will ever hold me as she holds me.

He had asked her, "Why were you so strange before Fen was born?"

"I was pregnant!" said Jessica in surprise. She sounded as though that should explain everything.

"But why didn't you want me here?"

She shuddered. "I looked so terrible."

Ryan gave up trying to understand that. It did not really matter, not since they were closer than before.

Ryan was in Wellman, getting ready for a new school year, when Jessica was killed. He had written her only a few days before (to General Delivery, as usual), and he thought with pleasure that in several more days her letter would come to him in answer. How could he ever have thought that? Should something not have warned him?

The day was August 31, 1944. Nobody knew what happened; no one would ever know. They all said afterwards that it had been an ordinary day in Stoneville—Fen had fallen down the back steps, skinning one leg; Lady Malveena had baked a lemon pie. Jessica appeared to be in a good humor (my letter—she had just gotten my letter) and Avery was expansive because he was trying out a '41 Ford and thinking of buying it.

Supper, perhaps, was a little quieter than usual. A light cool rain had fallen about an hour before, leaving Asa disgruntled and suspicious of life. Fen had grown tired and cross; he ate in the kitchen listening to Lady Malveena talk. She remembered she had talked a great deal "trying to cheer him up." Avery was very quiet at supper;

he went about his eating in a businesslike manner and did not talk. Miss Jessica (Lady Malveena said) looked as if she had her mind set someplace else and paid no attention to Avery's silence. An ordinary supper—no one was uneasy.

(But Ryan always wondered—did something happen? Why was Avery so still? Why was he not telling Asa into-each-life-some-rain-must-fall? Had Avery come upon some small suspicion? Did an envelope bearing a Wellman postmark fall out of Jessica's things? It was foolish to ask such things but Ryan wondered, all the same.)

When supper was done that night, Avery suggested a drive to Greenway to visit Mrs. Seagreaves. "We don't see your aunt enough," he said. "Besides, I want to talk with her."

("It must have been about buying that Ford," said Lady Malveena—but what if it were not? What if it had been about Jessica herself?)

Neither of them arrived in Greenway to talk with Victoria Seagreaves about anything. When they left, the roads were wet but not dangerous. It was dim but it was not dark; they had their headlights on, of course.

The accident was as simple as this: It was only that Avery and Jessica drove up a slight hill in their borrowed car and another car was already there on their side of the road, coming fast. Avery turned and the other driver turned (Could either have acted faster? Who was to say?) and the two cars hit hard on the side. The first went over quickly and rolled away, but the Ford rocked and recovered and went headlong down the bank into a tree.

The impact of the other car was on Jessica's side; when they hit the tree she was thrown out onto the wet grass. Avery was driven forward into steering wheel and shattered glass, and bits of the dashboard twisted themselves into his flesh. But Jessica, broken, lay outside in the wet and the dark.

Both of them were still alive when the crowd gathered, when the ambulance men carried them carefully into the Greenway County Hospital, still alive on the tables being mended.

Asa telephoned. Ryan was lucky to get a plane immediately. He sat in that plane numbly all the way and stared down at a hundred trivial towns over which they passed. The roar of the motors was almost comforting because it helped to deaden him against the stark fear which rose and rose in him and would not be put down.

He and Asa were at the county hospital, waiting, all of that next day and the next night. They talked very little. Ryan would think of the little boy crying at home with Lady Malveena and he could not believe that Jessica would die. He and Asa sat and walked; they drank from the fountain more water than they wanted or needed; they read newspapers over and over. Now and then a nurse would come in and speak to them. She kept trying to get Asa to lie down but Asa said she was all right.

"How are *they?*" Asa would say. In those moments she had looked very tiny and very vulnerable.

The nurse was distressed and would not look in Asa's face. "We'll know very soon," the nurse said.

In the end Ryan did not even get to see her. He did not get to speak one word or hear a word or put his hand upon her. He was never sure that Jessica had even known he was on the other side of walls, waiting.

Avery died very soon, the next day. He had been too mangled in the steering wheel; it had gone into his lungs and stomach and there was not enough flesh to go on throbbing and living over all that metal and plastic and paint.

Jessica lasted into the night of September 1. They said she was never conscious except for a flash here and there. She never asked for Ryan. Careful little Jessica—had she wanted him near, thought of Fen and Asa and keeping things safe and simple, and lain there alone and silent? Or had she thought of anything, even him? Had there been nothing but black and scarlet pain?

Ryan was never to know.

Nor was he to know whether she had looked up that night and had seen those headlights coming and thought for one wild second: Was this what all my care and effort were for? Is this all it comes to, after all?

He never knew if she had been wearing that silly orange stone when the car hit, or if it had later been buried with her. Had she fingered it once or twice in the hospital?

When Dr. Harris (the same doctor as before, and this time he did not smile) came into the waiting room with that last message and stood there, Asa cried out in one wail and then was silent. She did not make another sound but her mouth shrunk up and dried in her face.

"I'm very sorry," Dr. Harris said. He had to say something.

Ryan saw the slightness of Asa's body tremble and she began to cry real tears and he put his arm about her. Still there was no way for them really to close together. He was holding her; she was leaning on him; that was all.

As for Ryan, all he could think was Hellhellhellhell—because there was nothing to do except realize; there was nothing to accomplish but acceptance; there was nothing to keep except all the things that were over; and finally he said aloud, "Oh hell, Asa. Hell hell hell."

And suspicion welled up in him that Avery had known . . . had known *something.* Avery had been trying to see what was proper for him to do. Perhaps when he drove the Ford over that hill and saw that car already so near he had turned the wheel one second too slow; and into his mind the thought had flashed: *Accidents will happen in the best of families.*

"Hell," said Ryan. He helped his sister into a chair.

He grew cold; he grew lost and lonely in the vast spaces of himself. There were no edges to him; there were no limits he could come to and peer over.

When over that distance came finally the funeral plans, and he saw they were all behaving as though death were ordinary and natural, something to be dealt with routinely and thus understood—he exploded into bitterness.

He said, "I will come to no funeral."

Asa could still be shocked. He saw with distant surprise that she could still react in customary ways to customary things. How could this be true with the world ended? She said, "Of course you will come. Avery was your brother."

Ryan remembered a day he had said to himself: *There are things these people can do which I can never do*. And he eyed his sister, at first in amazement and then with growing bitterness.

"I will never do it," he said firmly.

And so they quarreled. At such a time they quarreled about duty and obligation and about what people would think. The very bones in him drew back a little from such a spectacle.

They quarreled, and he would not give in and Asa said he was unnatural and strange. "Even small Fenwick will go," she said and he was too sick to answer.

When it was all finally done—the service and the burial which he did not attend, could *never* have attended; and the quarrel cold between them; and some carven woman lying in a long black box;

and a scared little boy eating cookies he did not want—when all of that was finally over, Ryan went away from Stoneville with the taste of death in his mouth.

And he did not come again for ten long years, when the taste was that of his own cancer and he thought: *I will go back, and see if anything is there.*

17.

Notes From Ryan's Journal
September, 1954

This morning I woke at about three o'clock and could not go back to sleep and I sat in the dark and smoked, thinking. For the first time, I thought today of Jessica wholly—from the day we met on up through the day on which she died ten years ago. I was surprised to find it took me under an hour to go through a second time all the peace and misery and love and loss we had in those years, even though I held it slowly. The mind is very strange. There were some things I wanted to savor again and could not catch at all. But there were other times when the mind had caught hold of something and not let go one item—one color, one sound, one reaction.

Still I was surprised to find that ten years later there is so little left except the knowledge of love. Maybe that is not so little. Maybe that is big enough to write books about.

In the end, I think it all came to this: that I loved her as well as any of us can love each other; that we came together as much, perhaps, as we could. Not only because of our circumstance but because of the very humanness which shuts always so much of us in, so much of others out.

I realized this morning, at the end of all that thinking, that much of the sense of loss is gone. It is true that no time since then have I been able to invest so much self in any other thing—in love or work or future—but then there was no such investment till the time of Jessica, either, and there were thirty years before that.

And one learns; one grows older. One cannot maintain intensity or wonder for very long; the organism itself is set up against it.

But the other thing one learns is that love is *more* than perpetual wonder. It is also perpetual familiarity, and even now her name causes the warmth to rise in me. Something we once did together in love and joy can return to me so large that I am swollen with it.

The other result of today's thinking had to do, of course, with Fen. It made him seem realer and more made of flesh, for I could remember when she was heavy from carrying him. I could remember the day he was born in this house; his connection with her is emphasized and sharpened and outlined all over again.

And it gives me the feeling (I can sometimes remember her so well!) that something remains within my very hand and fingers which recalls the shape of her chin; and that if sometime I took his chin and held it in that hand it would be—obscurely—a homecoming, and a joining of two things large and incomprehensible.

Part Three

IN THE END BY COMPASSION

18.

Now THAT it was September, Fen had started in school again.

In the afternoons Ryan would meet him in front of the school, and each day his anticipation was stronger. He would stand waiting on the corner across the street (smiling, because he had gone to the same school, stood on this same corner when he was no taller than now his whole leg was) and shift from one foot to the other, impatiently.

As he stood, willing that final bell to ring, he would play again the same waiting games he had played in these same places as a boy. In such ways he came to know a second time the number of pickets in the fence across the street (there were thirty-two; it seemed to him now he had always remembered that) and how to recognize Fords and Hudsons and Buicks by their grillwork; he explored again with his eye the pattern of cracks which spread out across the asphalt roadway toward the school. These he considered as solemnly as if they had been lines in his own palm which might have special meaning—how one line broke into another, the growing and multiplication of fine networks. It was infinite, this mere branching of cracks on a little shaded street.

Finally the bell would sound and Fen would come out of the building with the others, yelling at someone, running, looking for him. The sight of Fen with his head up and his face expectant made Ryan want to hurry toward him. He would wave his hand. He would ask himself as he always had, *Can this be my son?*

But it did not really matter. That would have been to look on Fen as a mere detail in an experience now gone away, while to love him for himself was something different.

He liked the way Fen smiled at the sight of him and waved, and came across the street without looking back. Ryan would say "How're things?" and clear his throat—embarrassed—and Fen would say in a belittling fashion that things were okay. They would go off together, taking long ways home.

Ryan *did* love him and he was very stern with himself about it. He almost disapproved. I am clinging, that's all, he would tell himself, because Fen is young and has everything to come; and I do not know how much I may have or not. In this way I'm trying to participate in what is his, to borrow out of his future.

And it might be true, some of it or all of it; but this he did not, deep down, believe. He believed only that he liked Fen as he was and that was the sum of it, devoid of complexes and secret thoughts, and this pleased him. He would say to himself: *A few things in this world are wonderfully simple.*

"Did you walk home from school this way when you lived here? Down this street?"

"Every fall."

Fen would walk to the right of the cement, scuffing his feet in leaves and smiling to himself; but whether at the thought of leaves or fall, or a younger Ryan in other leaves and other falls one could not have said.

One afternoon Fen came out from school slower than usual, walking with his head down, thinking. He had once told Ryan that he watched his feet when he thought because they came and went and he did not have to consider them, whereas when he thought with his head turned up there were always cars and people and things to see and make a clutter.

So when Fen came out of the school, head down, Ryan was properly solemn, and more so when Fen said quietly, "Hello."

"Hello."

They walked down the street and a boy came by and pushed at Fen and they told each other they were Dirtynoses. Fen took off the other boy's cap and threw it in the street and they laughed at that loudly. The school bus went by and everybody waved out of it and yelled.

Fen smiled and waved back but when the bus was gone he took the smile away completely. He eyed his shoetops. "I've been thinking," he said.

Ryan made a grunt that he intended to be an encouragement.

Suddenly Fen looked despairing; he said, "It doesn't matter. Let's walk through town."

They turned left at that corner and Ryan asked him what didn't matter.

"You'd never do it."

"Well, I might. If I knew."

Fen scratched gently behind his ear with a forefinger. "I was just thinking why don't you stay here even without the college? You could teach high school. Teach English maybe, and things wouldn't cost you much—living at home and all." He finished up defiantly and his eyes were already angry when he looked at Ryan. "I bet you'd like it better than some old girls' school!"

It was very involved. Ryan said cautiously that he might, at that.

Fen was impatient. "Of course you would. And the way I've got it figured, we could help each other."

Ryan gave another grunt, also encouraging.

"You could teach me, Uncle Ryan. Books and lots of things so I could get smart enough to win a scholarship some day to be a doctor with, and I, well I could do . . . things to help you write your book. You know. Get books from the library for you. I could . . . I could take your suits to the cleaners. You know."

Ryan was very grave. "Yes, I know." He was thinking suddenly how he had wanted Jessica to leave Stoneville and she would not; and now Fen wanted him to stay, and he could not. And he thought, Things go on and on and on.

He shot a cautious look at Fen, but there was only the top of his head to see and a few brown hairs raised up like grass blades.

For a minute he started to tell Fen he was sick, that he would be going away to doctors; but he could hear that turning into some Holy Grail while he told it, some charge to Fen as a future doctor to go forth nobly and seek out cures for things. He thought that if he could smooth down those few hairs he would feel better about everything, and he put his hand in his pocket for safety's sake. I can't tell him yet. Not now.

He said aloud, "I'll think about it."

Fen kicked at a rock. "I know what that means. That's what people say when they mean they're going to say *No* tomorrow."

But tomorrow came and went and Ryan said nothing, nothing at all.

Once the two of them did talk of cancer, but as something which did not affect them. Fen had read some pamphlet in the school library and he was excited about it. It was an account of the use of cobalt rays in treating various cancer forms. Fen said dreamily, "Think of doing that."

"Is that what you'd like to do? Find new ways of treating old diseases?" Watch that Holy Grail, thought Ryan cautiously.

"Maybe. Just to—you know—beat them."

And Ryan thought even of the river outside Stoneville, and about swimming across it just to know that one *could*, and that the river was no master just because it was older and without volition; and he thought he understood a little.

At night Fen studied and Ryan read, or wrote, and on Saturday nights they went to the uptown movie and sat through the new serial chapter and the cartoons and the Three Stooges and movies about the Dead End Kids. Sometimes they also saw Hugh Herbert and Edgar Kennedy, or a feature about Lash LaRue.

Fen had a friend named Badger (so titled by his father for heartfelt reasons); and sometimes on Saturdays Badger went along. The two boys ate popcorn and whistled loudly when the cavalry came over the hill or the rustler dropped off the cliff into the river.

Ryan thought Badger was a thoroughly unpleasant boy. He was Fen's age, handsome, almost pretty; but he had an eternal runny nose and an eternally missing handkerchief. During each movie he snuffed the fullness of his nose loudly and gave great gulping swallows. That made Ryan close his eyes for an agonized moment and finally hand his popcorn over to Fen.

"What's the matter?"

"I'm not as hungry as I thought I was."

The colors in the trees went darker and finally into brown, and October was passing. The time went by so simply and so calmly that Ryan hardly knew; and whenever he thought of it he would say to himself, There have never been such undistinguished days.

Or again he would wonder if this was the end result of happiness, that it took away the sense of time. For he *was* happy, and obscurely that was Fen's doing, although he hardly understood how it had come about.

And sometimes he would wake at night in the crooked room in Asa's tall old house and know with finality that he could not leave Fen behind whatever happened.

"You look different," said Ian Travis once when he met him on the street.

"How so?"

Travis squinted. "Gone over to the enemy?"

"Only a small enemy," Ryan said.

Travis grinned at that. "He's a nice boy. Don't let him down."

The mere possibility that he could ever disappoint Fen made him angry (at Travis? at himself?) and he said, "What do you mean, let him down?"

"Nothing," said Travis affably. "Don't struggle so much. Makes the web stickier." And he went off down the street looking happy and malicious.

That web widened at the edges. Ryan began again to play gin rummy with Miss Clara. At first she was horrified; she stammered, flushed, misread her cards, but soon she played with him as if she had been a grim professional all her life. She threw down a card like a general sending out his best regiment, and she would peer up at Ryan to see what he would do next about that!

When these games first started, he lost them carefully to encourage her, but whenever she began really to play the game he would not humiliate her by playing less than his best. And after a while Miss Clara was winning in spite of all he could do; and on such a victorious evening she stalked up the stairs proudly, looking not left nor right nor down.

They began playing for money when Asa was out ("Just for interest," said Ryan vaguely) and soon Miss Clara had accumulated enough winnings to have her hair fixed uptown. They dyed it pale lavender at Stella's Beauty Shoppe. Asa was struck dumb with the splendor of it, but Miss Clara was pleased and a little vain.

"Where did you get the money?" Asa said.

"Can't hear you." She patted the colored fluff with a tender hand.

"I SAID WHERE DID YOU GET THE MONEY!"

"You'll have to speak up," said Miss Clara mildly, and left the room in a manner that was rather grand.

Thereafter when the knocker sounded at the front door, Miss Clara would smooth her brows with a forefinger and wet her lips and touch once—almost reverently—the mass of purple hair. Ryan thought privately and fondly that she looked something like a retired madam from an expensive house.

Lady Malveena was pleased with Ryan during this time, partly because of Fen and partly because of Miss Clara and the purple hair which she much admired.

"Makes you believe she's got thinking going on underneath all that, don't it?" Lady Malveena would venture proudly.

She let her pleasure go out into the rooms and envelop him. Ryan could feel it simply by being within the same house she was in. Once she told him that for a diseducated man he did right well in needed things. And the meals she set before him were not to be compared with any others. Once she left a jar of wine among the bedsheets and there were always flowers in his room.

But for all of that, somewhere within him was a little weary point, like a source or a wellspring weakening; and he tired easily and grew to hate the fifteen steps that led at night upstairs to sleep.

Fen said with satisfaction, "You go slow upstairs."

Ryan was sleepy. He said without curiosity, "What does that mean?"

"You know there's one that makes a noise when you step on it wrong. Sort of—you know—like bad luck or something. You know which one?"

"Which one is that?" He hid a yawn. He thought wistfully of elevators.

"The fourth one—that one there—*look out!*"

At this urgency Ryan stopped; the two of them pressed on the stair tread carefully for the silent spot to the left of center.

"Will I have good dreams now?" asked Ryan when they had walked on it without sound.

"I guess so. Maybe none at all."

That would be nice. Maybe none at all, he thought. For lately he had begun to see again the parlor when it had been banked with flowers on a pair of coffins. He remembered how Miss Clara had smelled those flowers. She had only come to live on Walnut Street that summer of 1941; she had not known Avery or Jessica well enough to be grieved. Ryan had not known Miss Clara well enough to be angry. But now he had dreams; and in them was Miss Clara standing by those terrible gray coffins, smelling the flowers like Ferdinand the Bull.

After his talk with Fen, Ryan could no longer go up and down those stairs in that house without thinking of the Fourth Step, and that maybe if he walked on it just right each time he would get well, and he and Fen would go away together and he would write a dozen books.

But sometimes he stepped just right and sometimes he did not; and he was ashamed for noticing.

The early November air was sharp in the lungs. Or in the throat, thought Ryan, depending on how your mind worked. He was on the front lawn with Fen, pitching a baseball back and forth.

"This is a summer sport," he complained once, trying not to puff.

Fen looked at him out of narrowed eyes. "Will you be here in the summer?"

"Here it comes!" cried Ryan quickly, and threw the ball over the boy's head so that he had to chase it into the next yard. Ryan was glad when Asa came out of the house and stood for a minute watching them.

"You'll get a Charley horse," Asa observed from the porch. There was an omnipotent tone in her voice and she ran her eyes over him as if she were deciding where to locate the thing.

"Probably," Ryan grunted.

"I'm going uptown a while."

That made him look at her. It was not like Asa to explain her movements. Should he give her the satisfaction of inquiring? The ball came roaring towards him so he did not have to decide. He heaved it back. Damn thing was getting heavier.

"I have an appointment with Mr. Peyton," Asa said in another minute.

Ryan grinned. "That so?"

"Well, aren't you even curious as to what I'm going to tell him?"

"I know what you're going to tell him. You're going to say you want to think it over. Try to get him to up the price."

She gave him a look of frank dislike. "Don't let me interrupt your ball game," she said stiffly. She came down the steps. "But I'll thank you not to throw until I'm past."

"Hold up!" called Ryan. It was too late and the ball whizzed by Asa's head as she came down the walk. It narrowly missed taking off her sensible black hat.

"FENWICK!" Asa said in a loud accusing voice.

He hung his head. "I'm sorry, Aunt Asa."

Asa's look plainly showed that she thought all of this was Ryan's fault and that he wasn't fooling her for *one* minute about his curiosity over Johnston K. Peyton. Ryan had a feeling that if a passing car should now throw mud upon her skirt she would come back and hit him on the head with a black umbrella.

"I'm getting hungry," Ryan said.

"Here it comes!" called Fen. The ball came over like a bullet.

He said, a little weaker, "Let's stop and get a snack."

Fen made a gesture of impatience. "It's almost lunch."

Ryan was firm. "Seventh inning," he said.

Lady Malveena herself scurried through the house ahead of them when they came in, and Ryan knew she had been watching from a front window. He walked through the dining room very slowly, curbing his breath to something under a pant. He did not like the way she was smiling when he reached the kitchen.

"Piece of cake?" she said.

"Umph," said Ryan. He was too winded to answer. She cut two pieces and put them onto the kitchen table and he handed one to Fen and sat down. It never paid to rush a good piece of chocolate cake.

"Nice of you to let the boy take a rest now and then," said Lady Malveena. One eyebrow was up slightly, but at least she had kept the corners of her mouth from turning. "Boy like that can't be expected to keep up with his elders."

Fen looked indignant. "Cake's good," said Ryan shortly.

"Where did Miss Asa go?"

"Uptown. Going to see a man about a college."

"Listen, Uncle Ryan, don't they ever take anything but girls at your old college up North?"

"Not so far."

"Suppose somebody was real smart. Studied hard and everything. Would they take him then even if he was a boy?"

Ryan said vaguely that a place could always be found for smart people and Lady Malveena (who had been holding her tongue with an obvious effort) snuffled and said if he didn't know better than that he'd better go back to college his own same self.

"Well, almost always," Ryan said.

"What you think Miss Asa's gonna tell that man?" Lady Malveena put her hip on the kitchen table and half sat, regarding him curiously.

"Nothing. Precincts aren't all in. The man hasn't come down yet out of Sinai."

"She'll sell. I take notice when it's a matter of clear money, Miss Asa and the Lord ain't often in disagreement. Or else, if they is, He don't raise His voice loud enough to make her know it."

"This Peyton's a businessman, in a hurry. Asa's dickering is small-time to a man like that. He won't cajole and I'm not sure he'll be willing to wait." (Didn't cajole *me,* Ryan thought, and then was surprised at himself for thinking it. Did I mind that?)

"You're through with your cake," Fen observed matter-of-factly. He sounded as if he doubted Ryan would notice it if someone did not call the fact to his attention.

"So I am."

Lady Malveena grinned and got up off the table. "Nothing like exercise to work up a good appetite," she said. For one moment Avery was in that kitchen, rubbing his hands together and smiling pleasantly on them all: *Nothing like cold water on a hot day. Nothing ventured, nothing gained. Nothing but the blood of Jesus.*

"Okay, Fen. I'm coming."

Fen had stopped at his frown. "We don't have to pitch ball if you don't want to."

"I want to," Ryan said.

"Sometimes I like you pretty good," Lady Malveena whispered.

When Asa came in for lunch, she did not look pleased. She looked as if nothing had gone right: as though Mr. Peyton had kept her waiting, had answered her brusquely, and had left before she finished talking.

She said sharply, "It's cold out." The wind had turned the tip of her nose pink, and it stood out in her face like a lone flower in a slate hillside.

Ryan and the hidden man in his skull were having an argument.

> *Asa's mad and I am glad and I know what . . .*
> *But you're not glad, said the little man.*

Well if I'm not, why not?
Why not indeed? Try the nose in your face.

Except, of course, it was not Ryan's face which was important. He looked across the table at Fen, who was eating quietly, not counting the mouthfuls or numbering the bites this time. Fen felt his gaze and looked up and smiled.

It was in that moment (because Fen was eating slowly for a change?) that Ryan decided he would see Mr. Peyton again. He would say: You must not mind my sister.

"How did it go?" he said abruptly to Asa.

"I didn't give him a final decision." The sentence slid tersely out of her lips and he knew that she was angry.

He tried to sound unconcerned. "Going to see him again?"

"He's very impatient."

"Uncle Ryan says they might take boys at *his* college if they studied hard," said Fen.

Asa stopped with her fork high and closed her mouth on air. She turned and looked at her brother thoughtfully, taking his size. "Really?" she said.

"That would be wonderful," said Fen. His voice was fast and nervous. "Wouldn't that be wonderful, Aunt Asa?"

"That remains to be seen," said Asa. She took the bite of food off her fork and chewed as if it had been dry grass.

"Lots of time for that," said Ryan. "But Asa will keep it in mind, won't you?"

She arched one brow. "Very much so," she said.

That night when Fen was in bed (and asleep? Or peering curiously at the insides of his eyelids?) Asa sat down in the parlor and straightened her back and eyed Ryan warily. "You mustn't put notions in the boy's head. He's at the age when he takes everything seriously."

Now it was he who measured his sister with a look. "What would be wrong with Fen coming to stay with me by then? That's college territory. I'm in commuting distance of several of the finest."

"Out of the question," Asa snapped.

"Whose question? Yours? Asa, what is it you want?"

She turned her face from him slightly and he saw that her face was full of bone. "I've raised the boy. I've cared for him. I've done everything for years." She turned back to him angrily. "Who are you to come in now?"

"I'm sorry about that." He was completely sincere; what were a baseball and a chemistry set spread over a dozen years?

She gave him no chance to finish whatever else he had meant to say.

"Avery dead, Father dead. As for you . . ." She looked at him once and looked away. "We've never been close. But this boy has a future. Have you noticed how much he resembles Father?"

Ryan said there was no resemblance whatsoever.

Little *you* know, said Asa with her eyes. "He has Father's intelligence and Avery's spiritual qualities. With the right help . . ." She paused. "If Fen has someone who understands him, he can make something of himself."

And suddenly Ryan saw her in ten or twelve more years—not Mrs. Edward Barnes and yet keeping a manse, retired and contented. He saw Fen grown tall and pale and busy; he saw him dreading the rainy seasons for Aunt Asa's sake; he pictured Fen in the evenings bringing the gray shawls Ryan once had thought would lie forever on *her* shoulders.

He made his voice absolutely sure. "Fen will lead his own life," he said. "Not the one you pick out for him. And not the one I pick out for him."

She said, "I've given him twelve years—"

"Ten years," he corrected. "His mother lived for two."

"All right, ten years. You want me to have nothing for it. You want Fen to have nothing for it."

"It's not a matter of hurting you," he began; but she looked so outraged that he did not finish.

"Why can't you let things alone!" she cried. "You never could let anything alone!"

Ryan thought for a minute that the hardness of bone lapsed in her for an instant and she looked very tired.

He made a promise to all the ugly furniture in Asa's parlor. "I'll be back for him," he said.

Asa turned and went out of the room and up the stairs without another word.

The next morning Travis came out to the house to tell Ryan that the college plans were definitely off. Peyton had talked with Asa; he was a busy man; he had other contacts.

"Now they're going to declare a special holiday in Stoneville,"

Travis finished, "so everyone can kick everyone else around the block. Asa is mad and the merchants are mad."

"I'm a little disappointed myself." Seeing Travis' look of surprise he added, "You were right. About the college."

Travis kept his voice casual. "What made you change your mind?"

A little boy. A woman dead ten years. Some old men talking in a park. Ryan said, "It isn't enough to criticize."

"Unless you're seventeen," Travis agreed. "Let's go hunting next week."

"Fine. That is, if we take Fen along."

"You think I just wanted you? Bring Lady Wats-her-name if you like. I've got an idea she's a devilish good shot."

"What's Peyton going to do now?"

"Hooked in with some Baptists up around Asheville. Everybody hopped; I think he's going to break ground for them in a few weeks."

Advertising. A name in someone's mouth. And generations of Baptists shall rise up to call thee blessed, Johnston Peyton.

"Maybe," said Ryan thoughtfully, "maybe it's a good thing, Travis. Perhaps a handful of people in Stoneville will start thinking and talking about their own college. Maybe the merchants will contribute funds, and the local churches, and the townspeople. Maybe Asa will even donate the land."

"I doubt it," Travis said. He looked a little surprised. "But it's a good idea."

"It's a damn good idea." Maybe when he came back for Fen he'd put some work into it himself. Maybe he'd offer to teach for a year or so for nothing—if they wanted him. He said to Travis, "Keep that idea in mind."

Travis looked puzzled but he nodded his head. "Comes the revolution," he said, grinning wickedly. "Stoneville emancipated. Academic freedom rampant. A scholar in every garage. Main Street lined with ivory towers."

"Poets in garrets," Ryan agreed. "Waiting lines at the libraries."

"Lights burning late over treatises. Laboratories bubbling. Sweeping intellect!"

Here Ryan shook his head. "Curiosity," he corrected. He tipped a mental hat to Avery; a man must crawl before he can walk, eh Avery? Big oaks from little acorns grow.

"If all goes well, when will you be back? I guess you'll spend most of the winter recuperating."

Ryan nodded. "But I should be back in the spring. In May. Maybe in April if I'm lucky."

"Spring and rebirth?" Travis grinned. "That's going to look trite as hell in your biography!"

So after that there was only Fen to think about because the college was gone; there was nothing he could do through that any more, and although Ryan was regretful he was also a little bit relieved. He was not accustomed to acting in general ways—for him it would always be one human being at a time. It had been Jessica and now it was Fen; and when he thought about it, it seemed too simple and unquestioned an exchange but that was how it was. He put the college thoughts out of his mind till another time.

He and Fen were always together now.

They must have walked Stoneville over, just as a reason to be together. And the puzzle fell in place—all the parts that went to make up one small ordinary town came up and were examined and put in their proper positions.

There was Pop's—a corner grocery where an old man catered to the grammar school trade. It was musty and dark and brown; there were wax objects full of cherry juice and there were jawbreakers and candy cigarettes and Crackerjack that had prizes inside. They bought Fen's notebook paper at Pop's and saved the coupons toward a bicycle. And over this dim young kingdom the old grocer ruled with terrible ill-temper, and suspected all customers as thieves, and never let you leave before he double checked to see you had not underpaid your bill.

There was the ice plant, where you could eat "snow" and walk around watching the blocks cut into squares and rectangles, and where you could stand and see the water tumbling down and down and down in a wooden tower, catching the light like a thousand fish.

There was a small stable where a man boarded horses for the town's doctors and lawyers and its only banker. For a while Fen and Ryan were in love with a horse they called Red, and they carried apples and sugar many afternoons but were never permitted to ride.

There were the cotton mills where people could still go and walk through and watch and see the million white spindles turning, or stare down into the surging vats of dye. The dye smelled hot and terrible; Fen said, "I wouldn't like to work in there."

There was the County Fair and the Carnival attached, and row upon row of pickled beets and prize-winning cakes and quilts and embroidery. They signed up at the merchants' display for stoves and beds and radios and won nothing; and they rode on a Ferris wheel that had St. Vitus's dance and made a great creaking sound every time it lifted them up. It was the second time that Fen had ever seen a carnival.

There was also the train, one of the last steam engines left for miles around. It was called the Junebug and it only ran to Greenway and back again two times a day; and the engineer still blew his whistle when he saw children by the track and waved at them. He had a big hand in a striped glove and the train was slow enough so that they could see dirt and oil on the fingers and laid in streaks on the palm.

There was church, too. Ryan went and came home and said nothing about it, either good or bad.

For upon Ryan had settled by now a quiet independence. He analyzed it, probed at it, was not sure of what the thing was made. But in the end it came to this: that he doubted God more profoundly than he ever had before, and that he could say to himself now without much agitation: When I die, that will be the end of it.

And he was not overmuch concerned about that because of Fen, and he thought of Diotima, and how men mingle their mortality in a coming generation and thus can find it in themselves to pass out of existence without wailing.

They saw an abandoned gin on the edge of town which was thought to be haunted. (A man, it was said, had been crushed in a bale one time, and at night he walked all through the neighborhood, crying like a baby.)

And they saw Molly Moll, the old blind woman who only came to town on Saturdays and walked up and down scraping a bow on a fiddle and singing "The Letter Edged in Black."

They walked in the residential areas, and when they found a new house being built they walked up the slanted boards inside, and made echoes in the skeleton rooms and tried to think what kind of people would live here when the house was done.

They talked to Powell Aimsley, who half-soled shoes at the local Boot Shop; and Powell told them nobody wanted good shoes any more; people bought flimsy ones and threw them away when they got thin. And they fondled Powell's dog, a sad old hound which lay in the corner along with all the unclaimed shoes and never chewed on one. The dog was bitter-eyed; he had to lie inside all day and listen to Powell Aimsley worrying, because nobody else would be bothered hearing it; so the hound was tired and prematurely old and had stretched ears.

They went to the opening of the new supermarket and got free balloons and small sample bottles of Everywoman's Pepper Relish.

Together they saw the high school football games, with the pretty cheerleaders and the small band puffing out Sousa.

And when a medium-famous cowboy star came to town for a one-night stand, they paid a dollar each to go on Saturday to listen to him play a silver-colored guitar and poke fun at a fat man who was his "podnuh."

It was a long sweet autumn and it faded into a quiet winter. Asa made fire in the hearth in the parlor and Fen was always slipping around to throw pine cones in, because they made such a splutter of burning.

Travis came out to the house (Ryan called and invited him) and then came out again and many times. They would wait out of courtesy until both Asa and Fen had gone upstairs to bed, and then they would turn the furnace down and build the wood in the fireplace up, and drink bourbon and argue.

They played checkers superbly; they played terrible chess and won and lost by great accidents because neither would concentrate.

They talked integration of the races in the Southern schools, and the hopes of the United Nations, and the Notre Dame football team. They talked Sparta and Athens, and Jesse Garris and Jesus Christ. They fought Republican and Democrat; they dragged in Emerson and Tom Paine and child psychology. They argued McCarthy and conformity and whether Rhine had found anything in ESP and what were the mutual responsibilities of one man and the world in which he lived. They talked of the historical age they would most like to have known (Travis was Renaissance Italy; Ryan, Periclean Athens) and what would become of Oppenheimer and the British monarchy and the future of science fiction. They argued about what was spirit and matter, and ethics and self-interest, and what was wrong with the way men and women loved and used and misused each other. They talked about communication and how much or how little there was, and where it belonged in literature and art. They talked about Stoneville and about a society outgrowing its gods as the Greeks had outdistanced their Pantheon and about crime and punishment and the penal system. They talked about Fen and about the 1954 new car models, and the obscenity of advertising, and TV antennae, and Brahm's *Song of Destiny* and Josh White or Leadbelly or Susan Reed singing folk ballads. They talked about the Bible and the Hindu wheel of life and time, and the sinking of the Titanic and the Scopes trial and the trial of Sacco and Vanzetti, and about Clarence Darrow and Learned Hand and Justice Frankfurter and Oliver Wendell Holmes. They remembered the Depression and the day Franklin Roosevelt died, and Hiroshima, and Patton striking a soldier and Truman calling MacArthur home, and Jean Harlow and Greta Garbo and Rudolph Valentino, and the Big Apple and the Charleston. They talked communism and Dixieland Jazz and Gauguin's Tahitian women and Rainer Maria Rilke's poems; as well as the difficulties inherent in the proper use of shoelaces, Congress, good steak, electric appliances, education, tobacco, rifles, laxatives, fishing rods, recapped tires, health insurance, philosophy, chewing gum, chromium, eyeglasses, taxes and prerogative.

They talked as men have always talked, of everything and nothing, until the wood had slumped redly in the hearth and the coals were fading fast and the bourbon gone low in the bottle and two chessmen under the sofa out of reach.

And later Ryan, stretching out as the sheets warmed in his bed in the crooked room, would think, If there were nothing more than this, I would be satisfied.

And sometimes, just before falling asleep, he would think of Johnston Peyton dozing off in some other hotel room in some other town; and he would wonder if the old man slept soundly there, or if he was shuffled about by dreams.

19.

In mid-November, the letters from Jim began to come.

They said at first only:

> I do not want to push you, Ryan, and I would not if this were actually some intellectual problem to be reasoned with.

But it is not that; it is a medical necessity that you enter a hospital very soon. I do not know what you really thought to find at home, but as your doctor as well as your friend I must write now and tell you that if you have not found it yet, it is just too bad. You have had all the time that is available for such things. Now the physical need intrudes and I must hear from you when you will be back; and that time must not be very far away. It will be surgery as we said, and arrangements must be made for you at Johns Hopkins. Write me immediately, Ryan, and make it Air Mail.

Ryan started a letter to him and tore it up, and wrote another and lost it between home and the post office; and wrote a third and managed to have it always in the pocket of whatever coat was hanging home in the closet. He would stand outside the school waiting for Fen in the afternoons and he would suddenly remember the letter for Jim and search his pockets, but it was never there.

He grew defensive. He said to himself, It's not Jim's business, really.

There were two other short and urgent notes, and in another week a second letter. It was as if Jim had decided he must be explicit and detailed if he expected to be listened to. This time he wrote:

The fact that I have not heard from you at all since you left Wellman in August makes me very anxious for you. I know you to be a sensible man, yet I have seen illness (not so much that as the *awareness* of illness) jolt the thinking out of all character, and it worries me not to know how you are.

I cannot, Ryan, impress on you too much the importance of time.

And that troubles me, because I know from years of talking with you that you have no real sense of time. I know that you have always delayed many important things, and that you evaluate everything in intensity rather than time consumed. These are great advantages if you are able to live in experiences rather than in days, but this is no such case now. This is no time for you to savor all your reactions to the possibility of being severely ill, perhaps critically so. Nor is this a time when you can add up your life on some leisurely balance sheet, as though you would go to the hospital or not in terms of whatever that sum might be.

I do not know why you are delaying. I never knew really why you made the decision to go home for a while first. I doubt that you knew or know yourself. You are not a cowardly man—I do not believe it is the treatment itself or the possible result that can be making you go so slowly.

I think it is this, Ryan Godwin—that cancer is such a serious word in today's vocabulary, and because of that you are confronted with the conscious possibility of death; and you have thus grown curious as to whether or not your death would be of any consequence. To know that, you must first know whether your life has been of any consequence, and your return to Stoneville seems to me part of the asking of that long and old question.

Whether you have completed your answer yet or not, you must now bring back whatever you have found thus far and let us get on with the business of making you well. The fact that I am working against time and decay to keep you here—is that not part of your answer, too?

I have made your appointment for observation on November 31, and if all goes well the actual surgery can be done by Christmas.

I will not write to you again.

I expect you in my office November 30, and we will go down to Baltimore together. Anne joins me in love,

JIM

This last time Ryan answered, not the long letter he had thought he would write, no lengthy explanations. He wrote:

I will be there. I am feeling well; do not worry about me. There is no one Answer, but it appears there are a lot of little ones, one day at a time. When I am back, I want to talk to you about my nephew Fen, who wants to be a doctor and who will be a good one.

RYAN

But now he *did* have a sense of time, because there were only two weeks between now and the day he must leave Stoneville for Massachusetts. He wrote his note to Jim at a table in the post office, with one of the scratchy pens that had to be dipped and dipped into the inkwell; and while he was writing it Fen and Ian Travis were waiting outside in Travis' car. The three of them were going hunting, not so much to shoot—as Travis said—but rather to walk through the woods being careful and primitive.

Ryan scratched the words, considered the sentence again about Fen (it was so short; but what else was there to say?) and put his name onto the end of it half angrily. When he wrote it down he wished suddenly that the word to write had been John or Tom and that the hand setting it there were bigger or smaller, and hooked onto a different body and person.

He bought a stamp from Mr. Snipes and dropped the letter into the brass slot that always had fingerprints all over it; and went out to the car frowning.

Travis glanced at him curiously.

But Fen said, showing nothing but impatience that Ryan had been so long, "What are we going to hunt for anyway?"

"Rabbits or squirrels if we see any," Travis said. "We won't, probably. You need to start hunting early in the day. Catch them when they're coming out, hungry. You feel up to this, Ryan?"

"Of course I feel up to it."

"There's not but one gun," said Fen in a disappointed voice.

"Can't kill but one animal at a time," said Travis shortly.

"Where are we going?"

"I thought we might go out on some of the land Asa owns. Save us asking everybody for permission."

"That'll be fine," Ryan said. And to himself he thought they might be walking over the very places Peyton could have put dormitories and quadrangles and what difference did it make anyway?

But it did make a difference; otherwise he would not have thought of it.

Travis glanced at him a second time before he put the car in gear and drove off down Third Creek Road and out along the highway toward Greenway. It was a still day; whenever a tree bent anywhere one remembered that the landscape after all was actual and not a painted scene.

Fen asked if he would have a chance to shoot any, and Travis said they would see about that when the time came.

Fen said, "I couldn't shoot, really. I've never been hunting before."

Travis said drily, "Quiet is of the essence."

"Oh, I know that. I'll be very quiet. What does essence mean?"

"Damned if I know."

21.

Fen was half singing, half muttering. They were coming home again from school together. The air swirling in the trees above them was very brisk and cold.

Fen sang, "Two lumps of kindness in a cup of tea," over and over until Ryan finally heard the words above the monotony and the moving leaves.

"What are you singing?" He had to raise his voice above the wind.

"Nothing. Just some words. They don't really have to go together or mean anything. They just have to come out the right size."

"You're no doctor, you're a modern poet," Ryan snorted.

At this Fen was suspicious; poets were bearded people who moralized in rhyme out of school readers. They exhorted students to "Build thee more stately mansions, O my soul"; and they said that "Life was real, Life was earnest," and that a thing of beauty was a joy forever.

"You know any more sentences like that?" said Ryan hastily, seeing his frown.

It appeared that Fen knew a great many of them. They were useful, he explained, in walking so as to assure you got two full steps into each square of cement walk and never hit a line. They also went with the whack of wheel going round on bicycles (flat country), with gate-swinging and hitting picket fences; in fact, hitting any object with any other object.

The thing to do, Fen said, was to start out with a certain rhythm in mind, and if you once failed to hit something with your stick on just the proper beat which the rhythm dictated, you were doomed to some inevitable ruin. Sometimes you had to run very fast between trees and posts to stay on count; sometimes you crept along snail-like so as not to come alongside too soon. It was a contest against space and position.

Some other sentences which Fen used in the game were:

If you should drop your deviled egg you'll have to eat the table leg; and: Charity, charity, fever and lice; the monkey swallowed the three blind mice.

There were also the multiplication tables, the pledge to the flag, the verse of "My Country 'Tis of Thee," and (here Fen looked apprehensive and lowered his voice against the wind) The Lord's Prayer and part of the Beatitudes.

It was a cold and windy day. They were red of cheek when they came inside the house on Walnut Street and stood warming themselves at the open fire. Ryan watched Fen as they spread their hands toward the flames. Good-sized hands, he thought. Soon will be big as mine. Getting tall.

Then Asa put her head at the door and spoke to them while she was putting on her gloves. "Wind still bad?"

"Yes ma'am," said Fen politely. As for Ryan, he thought the very fact that he was now doing everything but taking the coals up in his hand was sufficient expression on the subject.

He and Fen had come by now to such a closeness that when someone alien, such as Asa, came on them unexpectedly it was a plunge into ice water. It was a long and sharp descent. They were both startled; mentally they leaped apart like embarrassed lovers.

Asa, sniffing a little at the meager response, drew on her gloves and turned away. Then she came back and looked in again. "You shouldn't keep him out in the wind so long," she said to Ryan accusingly.

He said nothing, but Fen made a face into the fire.

By now the two of them sensed but never spoke aloud that both of them were allied for all time—Ryan for Fen's future, and Fen, blindly, for whatever his uncle wanted.

Fen said, "You'll give me a hand with that arithmetic tonight?"

"Ummm," said Ryan.

I've got to tell him sometime, he was thinking. He glanced up and saw fleetingly the boy's profile with the firelight along the rim of his brow and nose and chin and he turned his head away quickly. But not now. They heard the front door close as Asa went out into the windy day.

And thus—in times like these—Ryan discovered again how it had been with Jessica, how love creates a microcosm from which the rest are shut away, and by their very exclusion made smaller and

Still the secrecy bothered Ryan a little.

It went against all the tradition that relatives are the first to be informed about such things. In this very tradition men had built waiting rooms in all hospitals; not merely that the few who loved a man should come (these would have stood out in the rain) but so that everyone who had mere *position* could be accommodated amidst ashtrays and magazines.

Ryan had decided he would write to Asa just before surgery. For the rest of it—getting through it, getting over it, getting well—these were his own problems.

There were a number of things he wanted to do in Wellman before he went down to Baltimore. He had to make a will for Fen; there were promises he wanted to extract from Jim about his nephew's future. This meant that he had to leave some days ahead of time so his leaving seemed abrupt to the rest of them.

Asa was annoyed. "I haven't seen you in weeks," she said. "You and the boy are always off tramping somewhere. What's all the rush?"

"Business matters," he lied briefly.

Asa turned the corners of her mouth down and made a shrug. "I don't know why people don't tell me things."

The simplest reason of all: you want to *know*, but for your own knowledge, not from concern. He thought that but he did not speak, for he had passed beyond baiting his sister. Asa did not matter to him now; he moved within a certain knowledge she did not yet possess, and that was the knowledge of his own danger. It was so personal a secret—no wonder the martyrs seem deified for whole moments ahead of time, he thought. For that one flash out of all time they are able actually to *realize* the possibility of annihilation; it becomes as personal as their own familiar kneecaps, breastbone, navel. They have never realized it before; they cannot impart it now.

All one can do at such a point, he thought, is to wish not to be too badly remembered.

Not that Ryan really believed any more that he would die. He did not believe that, but he believed in the possibility. Perhaps that was all the mind was ever capable of accommodating.

During the last days in the house on Walnut Street Fen was as still as a shadow, and he was never far away. Ryan was always turning his head to discover the boy, silent and stricken of face, watching.

Once—only once—Fen had said with his voice at the very rim of tears, "Uncle Ryan, let me go with you, please," and Ryan had thought again of waiting rooms and the few who would always stand outdoors.

But he said only, "Next time I come you will go away with me. I promise you that. I have never made any promise I mean to keep as strongly as I mean this one." He kept his voice very confident, very sure.

"You won't forget."

"I will *never* forget it."

Even when he shaved, his eye would catch the reflection of Fen peeping at the bathroom door; in the mornings before he was up he would hear Fen going up and down the hall, up and down, waiting. When he ate, Fen could do little eating himself for watching Ryan's plate.

Sometimes Fen would burst into scolding like a wife. "You must eat more!" he would say, creasing his small brow. "It will make you strong."

It is you makes me strong, little monkey. But aloud Ryan would say only, "Yes, Dr. Godwin."

"Do you open one window at night?"

"Every night."

Fen would move away, looking irritable and professional.

"And water," he'd throw sternly across one shoulder. "Six or eight glasses of water a day."

"Certainly will." Something would tug him sharply in the ribs.

On the Saturday before he was to leave for Wellman on Monday, Ryan and Fen went to their usual weekly movie for the last time; and when Badger came down the aisle and started to sit with them in the old way Fen whispered fiercely, "Go away."

"Go *away?*"

"Get out of here."

Badger went up the aisle again, stone-faced and wounded.

When Ryan turned to protest at this, Fen stared straight ahead at the screen with his mouth held in small and said angrily, "Next week I'll sit with him. That's all. I'll sit with him next Saturday."

"All right," said Ryan meekly.